SEVEN STARS

By the same author:

The Bloody Red Baron
Jago
The Night Mayor
Bad Dreams
Life's Lottery
Dracula Cha Cha Cha
Anno Dracula
The Quorum
The Original Dr Shade
Famous Monsters
Orgy of the Blood Parasites (as Jack Yeovil)

SEVEN STARS

Kim Newman

POCKET
B O O K S

LONDON · SYDNEY · NEW YORK · TOKYO · SINGAPORE · TORONTO

First published in Great Britain by Pocket Books, 2000
An imprint of Simon & Schuster UK Ltd
A Viacom company

The following stories have been published previously: 'Angel Down,
Sussex' (*Interzone*, 1999), 'The End of the Pier Show' (*Dark of the
Night*, 1997), 'You Don't Have to be Mad . . .' (*White of the Moon*,
1999), 'Where the Bodies are Buried 3: Black and White and Red All
Over' (*Dark Terrors*, 1995), 'Where the Bodies are Buried 2020' (*Dark
Terrors 2*, 1996), 'Seven Stars' (*Dark Detectives*, 1999)

1 3 5 7 9 10 8 6 4 2

Simon & Schuster Ltd
Africa House
64–78 Kingsway
London WC2B 6AH

Simon & Schuster Australia
Sydney

A CIP catalogue record for this book is available
from the British Library

ISBN 0-671-77338-0

Typeset in Sabon by SX Composing DTP, Rayleigh, Essex
Printed and bound in Great Britain by Cox & Wyman Ltd, Reading, Berks.

For Rodney Jones

ACKNOWLEDGEMENTS

Thanks to Stephen Jones, David Pringle, Anna Kiernan, Helen Simpson and Peter Coleborn.

CONTENTS

FOREWORD

Kim Newman is simply amazing. There is really no other way to describe him. For the twenty or so years that we have known each other, he has never failed to impress me – with his fervent opinions, erudite knowledge, remarkable generosity, writing skills and, most importantly of all, his open and honest friendship.

As our careers have flourished side-by-side, he has always been there whenever I have needed him – with a helpful piece of obscure information, a copy of an impossibly rare video, or just the short story I need to round-out yet another anthology.

I guess I first became aware of Kim during the late 1970s at various science fiction and fantasy conventions, or at screenings of old horror movies organized by London's Gothique Film Society. To be honest, he was not all that difficult to miss. If my memory serves me correctly, in those early days he carried a cane and wore a cape as complements to his *faux* Edwardian style of dress. And although those two accessories are (thankfully) long gone, Kim has retained his somewhat eccentric attire, thus neatly providing himself with a distinctive persona as both a writer and a broadcaster.

However, although I can no longer remember the exact circumstances of our original meeting, it was probably over a drink somewhere (invariably his a dry white wine, mine a pint of beer), mutually complaining about the Gothique's butt-numbing seats and myopic projectionist, or else discussing at length an overlooked sequence or obscure actor in some half-forgotten movie which would merely perplex anybody else listening to the conversation.

We both know a lot about movies. However, I am more than happy to concede that Kim knows much more than I do – and he proved it some years ago on stage at a Horror Writers of America weekend in Providence, Rhode Island, when we were the remaining two finalists in a trivia contest which he won by correctly remembering the name of the street-wise singing parasite in Frank Henenlotter's 1987 movie *Brain Damage*. For the record, it was 'Elmer' (and don't pretend *you* knew that).

Already gaining a reputation as an insightful critic and reviewer, it was not long before Kim began turning his talents to fiction as well. One of his earliest sales was the short story 'The Terminus' to *Fantasy Tales* 15 (1985), the award-winning small press magazine I produced and edited with David A. Sutton. It was to be a prophetic appearance.

When I created the movie magazine *Shock Xpress* the same year, Kim's interview with director Abel Ferrara graced the front cover of the first issue, and he remained a regular contributor during the title's four-year existence as a periodical and the two subsequent softcover volumes edited by Stefan Jaworzyn.

It seemed a natural progression when we agreed to co-edit the Bram Stoker Award-winning *Horror: 100 Best Books* (1988), which still has the distinction of being our most enduring in-print title (despite having to threaten to sue the original publisher to regain the rights), and the inclusion of 'The Terminus' in my first anthology, *The Best Horror from Fantasy Tales* (1988), merely served to cement our working relationship.

Since then – as this present volume so ably illustrates (with one notable exception) – we have continued to work together on numerous projects.

FOREWORD

When, in the early 1990s, Dave Sutton and I took over the editing of the venerable anthology series *The Pan Book of Horror Stories* (which was pointlessly retitled *Dark Voices* at the insistence of the publisher), Kim contributed the highly original story 'Week Woman' (recently adapted for the second season of Showtime's *The Hunger* on TV). He quickly followed it up with the novella, 'Where the Bodies Are Buried', a clever spoof on video nasties, Hollywood horror franchises and the career of our old friend Clive Barker. When it came to the next volume, Kim could not resist continuing the story of creator Allan Keyes and his baroque bogeyman Rob Hackwill in the aptly titled 'Where the Bodies Are Buried II: Sequel Hook'. Both of these Hackwill tales were later reprinted in Kim's second collection, *Famous Monsters* (1995).

When the anthology series changed publisher and title (to *Dark Terrors*) in the mid-1990s, Kim was ready with 'Where the Bodies Are Buried 3: Black and White and Red All Over', which expanded the original mythos with a timely exploration of the reaction by a hypocritical media to horror fiction and films. Even more outlandish was his fourth and final story in the series, 'Where the Bodies Are Buried 2020', published in *Dark Terrors* 2. This near-future tale of virtual reality and urban anarchy not only provided a satisfying coda to the series, but also neatly integrated the whole Rob Hackwill saga into the author's growing *gestalt*. In 2000, all four Hackwill novellas were collected into a single volume issued by The Alchemy Press and my own and Dave Sutton's Airgedlámh Publications.

Without doubt, Kim is one of the most accommodating writers I have ever worked with. He is also one of the quickest and most professional. I usually only have to give him a brief outline of the book I am working on before I receive back from him a first draft, apparently hammered out on the computer in a white-heat of creative exuberance, that would put most author's finished work to shame.

Once I have read the manuscript, I may suggest a minor

change or an addition here and there. Usually Kim will incorporate or even expand upon these suggestions, and the polished draft will be back in my hands in no time at all. Unlike many other writers (most of whom probably need more guidance than he ever will), I believe that Kim genuinely welcomes the process of collaboration with an editor. This has never been more evident to me than when we began discussing my anthology *Dark Detectives: Adventures of the Supernatural Sleuths* (1999).

After I had explained to Kim that the book would be themed along a loosely assembled chronology, we came up with the concept (probably over more glasses of wine and beer) that it would be fun to have one serial-like case which would be investigated across the centuries by many of the characters he had created in his earlier novels and stories. These episodes would then be interspersed amongst the contributions from other writers to the book.

The only problem was that he did not have a psychic investigator for the period covering the 1970s. Of course that was no problem for Kim, who simply went back to his very first efforts at fiction while still a schoolboy and revived the character of ostentatious amnesiac Richard Jeperson, along with his striking associate Vanessa and ex-police constable Fred Regent. Inspired by such TV characters as Jason King, The Avengers, Jon Pertwee's Doctor Who and the novels of Peter Saxon and Frank Lauria, Jeperson made his official début with the novella 'The End of the Pier Show' in my 1997 anthology *Dark of the Night: New Tales of Horror and the Supernatural*. A bizarre romp involving Jeperson and his sidekicks in time displacement and mutant Nazis, it led to a further adventure, 'You Don't Have to Be Mad. . .', in *White of the Moon: New Tales of Madness and Dread* (1999). This time the dapper detective and his companions found themselves investigating dastardly experiments in mind-control. With two further volumes due in the anthology series, it is a sure bet that Richard Jeperson will be returning in the future.

Meanwhile, even I was unprepared for the epic novel-length mystery 'Seven Stars', the multi-part story cycle which Kim constructed around Bram Stoker's *The Jewel of Seven Stars* for *Dark Detectives*. Stretching from the Plagues of Ancient Egypt through to the mid-twenty-first century, it ingeniously intermingled numerous characters and themes from his other work. In the end, 'Seven Stars' accounted for almost half of an already bulky anthology, and reintroduced subtle variations on some of Kim's best-known and most memorable heroes and villains, including Charles Beauregard, an agent for the mysterious Diogenes Club; occult investigators Edwin Winthrop and Catriona Kaye; the Chandleresque Gumshoe of 1940s Los Angeles; the flamboyant Richard Jeperson; private investigator Sally Rhodes; techno detective Jerome Rhodes; comic strip vigilante Dr Shade; the undead Geneviève Dieudonné; the diabolical Derek Leech; plus many others, who I will leave you the pleasure of discovering for yourself.

This is fiction in the grand pulp tradition, given an added edge by the author's sly humour and intimate knowledge of history and popular culture.

Although I have been responsible in one way or another for commissioning most of the fiction in this book, the exception I mentioned earlier is 'Angel Down, Sussex'. It involves another case for investigators of the inexplicable Edwin Winthrop and Catriona Kaye, who this time are dispatched by the Diogenes Club to discover the truth behind the reappearance of a child fifty years after she was first taken away by a 'fiery wheel' in the sky. Along the way, the 1920s equivalent of Mulder and Scully become involved with some familiar concepts, as well as encountering a famous pair of gentlemen from the period.

As with many of Kim's stories, the conclusion is not totally unexpected, but the enjoyment invariably comes from getting there. It is the narrative which is important, and he is an author who is always in control of his material.

When I asked Kim for a story for my anthology *The Mammoth Book of Vampires* (1992), he came up with a major novella that was as audacious as it was entertaining. It was exactly what I needed as a powerful conclusion to the volume. However, when I mentioned that I didn't particularly care for the original title and suggested 'Red Reign' as a replacement, the always-affable Kim quietly acquiesced. The book eventually became something of a best-seller, an achievement which in no small way was due to Kim's memorable contribution. But when the time came to expand the novella into a novel, Kim decided to reinstate his original title. *Anno Dracula* (1992) was a commercial and critical success around the world. To date it has been translated into numerous languages and spawned two sequels, *The Bloody Red Baron* (1995) and *Dracula Cha Cha Cha* (1998), with more to follow. Perhaps to hammer the point home just a little more, Kim also dedicated the book to me.

It is an honour which I am enormously proud of . . . and I have also never changed one of his titles since.

Along with his outstanding fiction contributions to my many anthologies, for the past decade we have also collaborated on the 'Necrology' section in my annual *Best New Horror* selection (we both share a macabre fascination with the way many famous people end their lives), and more recently he has been an indispensable advisor and collaborator on my series of monster movie guides.

As you have probably already gathered from the above, I am a little biased. I admit it. Kim is one of the most talented and inventive authors currently working in the field of fantastic literature, and this new collection contains some of his finest work to date.

But of course I would say that, wouldn't I? After all, I originally published most of the stories included herein. So why not discover just how good he is for yourself. Turn the page and prepare to be dazzled by one of Britain's most witty and clever stylists as he takes you on a series of journeys – journeys through often tantalizingly familiar worlds populated by characters drawn from both history and fiction. As he skilfully blurs the borders between fact and fantasy to create a hybrid universe which is unmistakably and uniquely his own, prepare to be amazed by the amazing Kim Newman.

Stephen Jones
London, June 1999

1: Too Late in the Year, Surely, for Wasps

The Reverend Mr Bartholomew Haskins, rector of Angel Down, paused by the open gate of Angel Field. His boots sank a little into the frost-crusted mud. Icewater trickled in his veins. He was momentarily unable to move. From somewhere close by came the unmistakable, horrid buzz of a cloud of insects.

It was too late in the year, surely, for wasps. But his ears were attuned to such sounds. Since childhood, he'd been struck with a horror of insects. Jane, his sister, had died in infancy of an allergic reaction to wasp stings. It was thought likely that he might share her acute sensitivity to their venom, but the reason for his persistent fear – as for so much else in his life – was that it was his stick, poked into a pulpy nest, which had stirred the insects to fury. As a boy, he had prayed to Jane for forgiveness as often as he prayed to Our Lord. As a man, he laboured still under the burden of a guilt beyond assuaging.

'Bart,' prompted Sam Farrar, the farmer, 'what is it?'

'Nothing,' he lied.

At the far end of Angel Field was a copse, four elms growing so close together by a shallow pond their roots and branches were knotted. A flock of sheep were kept here. As Sam hauled his gate shut behind them, Haskins noticed the sheep forming a clump, as if eager to gather around their owner. There were

8

white humps in the rest of the field, nearer the copse. They didn't move. Wasps did swarm over them.

Hideous, dreadful creatures.

Haskins forced himself to venture into Angel Field, following the farmer. He kept his arms stiffly by his side and walked straight-legged, wary of exciting a stray monster into sudden, furious hostility.

'Never seen anything like this, Bart,' said Sam. 'In fifty year on the land.'

The farmer waded through his flock and knelt by one of the humps, waving the wasps away with a casual, ungloved hand. The scene swam before Haskins's eyes. A filthy insect crawled on Sam's hand and Haskins's stomach knotted with panic.

He overcame his dread with a supreme effort and joined his friend. The hump was a dead sheep. Sam picked up the animal's woolly head and turned its face to the sunlight.

The animal had been savagely mutilated. Its skull was exposed on one side. The upper lip, cheek and one side of the nose were torn away as if by shrapnel.

'I think it's been done with acid.'

'Should you be touching it, then?'

'Good point.'

Sam dropped the beast's head. The seams in his face deepened as he frowned.

'The others are the same. Strange swirls etched into their hides. Look.'

There were rune-like patches on the dead sheep. They might have been left by a weapon or branding iron. The skin and flesh was stripped off or eaten away.

'My Dad'd never keep beasts in Angel Field. Not after the trouble with my Aunt Rose. That was in '72, afore I was born. You know that story, of course. Was kept from me for a long time. This is where it happened.'

The wasps had come back. Haskins couldn't think.

'Always been something off about Angel Field. Were standing stones here once, like at Stonehenge but smaller. After

Rose, Grandad had 'em all pulled down and smashed to bits. There was a fuss and a protest, but it's Farrar land. Nothing busybodies from up London could do about it.'

Grassy depressions, in a circle, showed where the stones had stood for thousands of years. The dead sheep were within the area that had once been bounded by the ring.

It seemed to Haskins that the insects were all inside the circle too, gathering. Not just wasps, but flies, bees, hornets, ants, beetles. Wings sawed the air, so swiftly they blurred. Mouth-parts stitched, stingers dripped, feelers whipped, legs scissored. A chitinous cacophony.

Bartholomew Haskins was terrified, and ashamed of his fear. Soon, Sam would notice. But at the moment, the farmer was too puzzled and annoyed by what had befallen his sheep.

'I tell you, Bart, I don't know whether to call the vet or the constable.'

'This isn't natural,' Haskins said. 'Someone did this.'

'Hard to picture, Bart. But I think you're right.'

Sam stood up and looked away, at his surviving sheep. None bore any unusual mark, or seemed ailing. But they were spooked. It was in their infrequent bleating. If even the sheep felt it, there must be something here.

Haskins looked about, gauging the positions of the missing stones. The dead sheep were arranged in a smaller circle within the larger, spaced nearly evenly. And at the centre was another bundle, humped differently.

'What's this, Sam?'

The farmer came over.

'Not one of mine,' he said.

The bundle was under a hide of some sort. Insects clung to it like a ghastly shroud. They moved, as if the thing were alive. Haskins struggled to keep his gorge down.

The hide undulated and a great cloud of wasps rose into the air in a spiral. Haskins swallowed a scream.

'It's moving.'

The hide flipped back at the edge and a small hand groped out.

'Good God,' Sam swore.

Haskins knelt down and tore away the hide. It proved to be a tartan blanket, crusted with mud and glittering with shed bug scales.

Large, shining eyes caught the sun like a cat's. The creature gave out a keening shriek that scraped nerves. There was something of the insect in the screech, and something human. For a moment, Haskins thought he was hearing Jane again, in her dying agony.

The creature was a muddy child. A little girl, of perhaps eight. She was curled up like a buried mummy, and brown all over, clothes as much as her face and limbs. Her feet were bare, and her hair was drawn back with a silvery ribbon.

She blinked in the light, still screeching.

Haskins patted the girl, trying to soothe her. She hissed at him, showing bright, sharp, white teeth. He didn't recognize her, but there was something familiar in her face, in the set of her eyes and the shape of her mouth.

She hesitated, like a snake about to strike, then clung to him, sharp fingers latched on to his coat, face pressed to his chest. Her screech was muffled, but continued.

Haskins looked over the girl's shoulder at Sam Farrar. He was bewildered and agoggle. In his face, Haskins saw an echo of the girl's features, even her astonished expression.

It couldn't be . . .

. . . but it was. Missing for over fifty years and returned exactly as she had been when taken.

This was Rose Farrar.

2: Beyond the Veil

'There is one who would speak with you, Catriona Kaye,' intoned Mademoiselle Astarte. 'One who has passed beyond the veil, one who cares for you very much.'

Catriona nodded curtly. The medium's lacquered fingers bit

11

deeply into her hand. She could smell peppermint on the woman's breath, and gin.

Mademoiselle Astarte wore a black dress, shimmering with beaded fringes. A tiara of peacock feathers gave her the look of an Aztec priestess. A rope of pearls hung flat against her chest and dangled to her navel. As table-rappers went, she was the bee's roller-skates.

She shook her head slightly, eyes shut in concentration. Catriona's hand really hurt now.

'A soldier,' the medium breathed.

The Great War had been done with for seven years. It was a fair bet that anyone of Catriona's age – she was a century baby, born 1900 – consulting a woman in Mademoiselle Astarte's profession would be interested in a soldier. Almost everyone had lost a soldier – a sweetheart, a brother, even a father.

She nodded, noncommittally.

'Yes, a soldier,' the medium confirmed. A lone tear ran neatly through her mascara.

There were others in the room. Mademoiselle didn't have her clients sit about a table. She arranged them on stiff-backed chairs in a rough semi-circle and wandered theatrically among them, seizing with both hands the person to whom the spirit or spirits who spoke through her wished to address themselves.

Everyone was attentive. The medium put on a good show.

Mademoiselle Astarte's mother, a barrel-shaped lady draped in what might once have been a peculiarly ugly set of mid-Victorian curtains, let her fingers play over the keys of an upright piano, tinkling notes at random. It was supposed to suggest the music of the spheres, and put the spirits at ease. Catriona was sure the woman was playing 'Knocked 'Em in the Old Kent Road' very slowly.

Smoke filtered into the room. Not scented like incense, but pleasantly woody. It seemed to come from nowhere. The electric lamps were dimmed with Chinese scarves. A grey haze gathered over the carpet, rising like a tide.

'His passing was sudden,' the medium continued. 'But not

painful. A shock. He hardly knew what had happened to him, was unaware of his condition.'

Also calculated: no upsetting details – choking on gas while gutted on barbed wire, mind smashed by months of bombardment and shot as a coward – and a subtle explanation for why it had taken years for the spirit to come through.

There was a fresh light. It seemed sourceless, but the smoke glowed from within as it gathered into a spiral. A prominent china manufacturer gasped, while his wife's face was wrung with a mix of envy and joy – they had lost a son at Passchendaele.

A figure was forming. A man in uniform, olive drab bleached grey. The cap was distinct, but the face was a blur. Any rank insignia were unreadable.

Catriona's hands were almost bloodless. She had to steel herself to keep from yelping. Mademoiselle Astarte yanked her out of her chair and held tight.

The figure wavered in the smoke.

'He wants you to know . . .'

'. . . that he cares for me very much?'

'Yes. Indeed. It is so.'

Mademoiselle Astarte's rates were fixed. Five pounds for a session. Those whose loved ones 'made contact' were invariably stirred enough to double or triple the fee. The departed never seemed overly keen on communicating with those left behind who happened to be short of money.

Catriona peered at the wavering smoke soldier.

'There's something I don't understand,' she said.

'Yes, child . . .'

Mademoiselle Astarte could only be a year or two older than her.

'My soldier. Edwin.'

'Yes. Edwin. That is the name. I hear it clearly.'

A smile twitched on Catriona's lips.

'Edwin . . . isn't . . . actually *dead*.'

The medium froze. Her nails dug into Catriona's bare arms.

13

Her face was a study in silent fury. Catriona detached Mademoiselle Astarte's hands from her person and stood back.

'The music is to cover the noise of the projection equipment, isn't it?'

Mademoiselle's mother banged the keyboard without interruption. Catriona looked up at the ceiling. The chandelier was an arrangement of mirror pendants clustered around a pinhole aperture.

'There's another one of you in the room upstairs. Cranking the projector. Your father, I would guess. It's remarkable how much more reliable your connection with the spirit world has become since his release from Pentonville.'

She poked her hand into the smoke and wiggled her fingers. Greatcoat buttons were projected on to her hand. The sepia tint was a nice touch.

'You bitch,' Mademoiselle Astarte spat, like a fishwife.

The others in the circle were shocked.

'I really must protest,' began the china manufacturer. His bewildered wife shook her head, still desperate to believe.

'I'm afraid this woman has been rooking you,' Catriona announced. 'She is a clever theatrical performer, and a rather nasty specimen of that unlovely species, the confidence trickster.'

The medium's hands leaped like hawks. Catriona caught her wrists and held the dagger-nails away from her face. Her fringes writhed like the fronds of an angry jellyfish.

'You are a disgrace, Mademoiselle,' she said, coldly. 'And your sham is blown. You would do well to return to the music-halls, where your prestidigitation does no harm.'

She withdrew tactfully from the room. A commotion erupted within, as sitters clamoured for their money back, and Mademoiselle and her mother tried in vain to calm them. The china manufacturer, extremely irate, mentioned the name of a famous firm of solicitors.

In the hallway, Catriona found her good cloth coat and slipped it on over a moderately fringed white dress. It was daringly cut just above the knee, barely covering the rolled tops of her silk stockings. She fixed a cloche hat over her bobbed brown hair, catching sight of her slightly too satisfied little face in the hall mirror. She still had freckles, which made the carefully placed beauty mark a superfluous black dot. Her mouth was nice, though, just the shape for a rich red cupid's bow. She blew a triumphant kiss at herself, and stepped out on to Phene Street.

Her cold anger was subsiding. Charlatanry always infuriated her, especially when combined with cupidity. The field of psychical research would never be taken seriously while the flim-flam merchants were in business, fleecing the grieving and the gullible.

Edwin Winthrop awaited her outside, the Bentley idling at the kerb like a green and brass land-yacht. He sat at the wheel, white scarf flung over his shoulder, a large check cap over his patent-leather hair, warmed not by a voluminous car coat but by a leather flying jacket. The ends of his moustache were almost unnoticeably waxed, and he grinned to see her, satisfied that she had done well at the séance. Her soldier was seven years out of uniform, but still obscurely in the service of his country.

'Hop in, Catty-Kit,' he said. 'You'll want to make a swift getaway, I suspect. Doubtless, the doers of dastardly deeds will have their fur standing on end by now, and be looking to exact a cowardly revenge upon your pretty little person.'

A heavy plant-pot fell from the skies and exploded on the pavement a foot away from her white pumps. It spread shrapnel of well-watered dirt and waxy aspidistra leaves. She glanced up at the town house, noticing the irate old man in an open window, and vaulted into the passenger seat.

'Very neatly done, Cat,' Edwin complimented her.

The car swept away, roaring like a jungle beast. Fearful curses followed. She blushed to hear such language. Edwin sounded the bulb-horn in reply.

She leaned close and kissed his chilled cheek.

15

'How's the spirit world, my angel?' she asked.

'How would I know?' he shrugged.

'I have it on very good authority that you've taken up residence there.'

'Not yet, old thing. The Hun couldn't get shot of me on the ground or in the air during the late unpleasantness, and seven stripes of foul fellow have missed their chance since the cessation. Edwin Winthrop, Esquire, of Somerset and Bloomsbury, is pretty much determined to stick about on this physical plane for the foreseeable. After all, it's so deuced interesting a sphere. With you about, one wouldn't wish to say farewell to the corporeal just yet.'

They drove through Chelsea, towards St James's Park. It was a bright English autumn day, with red leaves in the street and a cleansing nip in the air.

'What do you make of this?'

One hand on the wheel, he produced a paper from inside his jacket. It was a telegram.

'It's from the Old Man,' he explained.

The message was terse, three words. Angel Down Sussex.

'Is it an event or a place?' she asked.

Edwin laughed, even teeth shining.

'A bit of both, Catty-Kit. A bit of both.'

3: *In the Strangers' Room*

Strictly speaking, the gentle sex was not permitted within the portals of the Diogenes Club. When this was first brought to Winthrop's attention, he had declared his beloved associate to be not a woman but a minx and therefore not subject to the regulation. The Old Man, never unduly deferential to hoary tradition, accepted this and Catriona Kaye was now admitted without question to the Strangers' Room. As she breezed into the discreet building in Pall Mall and sat herself daintily down like a deceptively well-behaved schoolgirl, Winthrop derived petty satisfaction from the contained explosions of fury that emanated from behind several raised numbers of *The Times*. He realized that the Old Man shared this tiny pleasure.

Though he had served with the Somerset Light Infantry and the Royal Flying Corps during the Great War, Edwin Winthrop had always been primarily responsible to the Diogenes Club, least-known and most eccentric instrument of the British Government. If anything, peace had meant an increase in his activities on their behalf. The Old Man – Charles Beauregard, Chairman of the Club's Ruling Cabal – had formed a section to look into certain matters no other official body could be seen to take seriously. Winthrop was the leading agent of that special section, and Catriona Kaye, highly unofficially, his most useful aide. Her interest in psychical research, a subject upon which she had written several books, dovetailed usefully with the section's remit, to deal with the apparently inexplicable.

The Old Man joined them in the Strangers' Room, signalled an attendant to bring brandy and sat himself down on an upholstered sofa. At seventy-two, his luxurious hair and clipped moustache were snow white but his face was marvellously unlined and his eyes still bright. Beauregard had served with the Diogenes Club for over forty years, since the days when the much-missed Mycroft Holmes chaired the Cabal and the Empire was ceaselessly harried by foreign agents after naval plans.

Beauregard complimented Catriona on her complexion; she smiled and showed her dimple. There was a satirical undercurrent to this exchange, as if all present had to pretend always to be considerably less clever than they were, but were also compelled to communicate on a higher level their genuine acuities. This meant sometimes seeming to take the roles of windy old uncle and winsome young flirt.

'You're our authority on the supernatural, Catriona,' said the Old Man, enunciating all four syllables of the name. 'Does Angel Down mean anything to you?'

17

'I know of the story,' she replied. 'It was a nine-day wonder, like the *Mary Celeste* or the Angel of Mons. There's a quite bad Victorian book on the affair, Mrs Twemlow's *The Girl Who Went With the Angels*.'

'Yes, our little vanished Rosie Farrar.'

Until today, Winthrop had never heard of Angel Down, Sussex.

'There was a wave of "angelic visitations" in the vicinity of Angel Down in the 1870s,' Catriona continued, showing off rather fetchingly. 'Flying chariots made of stars harnessed together, whooshing through the treetops, leaving burned circles in fields where they touched ground. Dr Martin Hesselius, the distinguished specialist in supernatural affairs, was consulted by the Farrar family and put the business down to a plague of fire elementals. More recently, in an article, Dr Silence, another important researcher in the field, has invoked the Canadian wendigo or wind-walker as an explanation. But in the popular imagination, the visitors have always been angels, though not perhaps the breed we are familiar with from the Bible and Mr Milton. The place name suggests that this rash of events was not unprecedented in the area. Mrs Twemlow unearthed medieval references to miraculous sightings. The visitations revolved around a neolithic circle.'

'And what about the little girl?' Winthrop asked.

'This Rosie Farrar, daughter of a farmer, claimed to have talked with the occupants of these chariots of fire. They were cherubs, she said, about her height, clad in silvery-grey raiment, with large black eyes and no noses to speak of. She was quite a prodigy. One day, she went into Angel Field, where the stones stood, and was transported up into the sky, in the presence of witnesses, and spirited away in a fiery wheel.'

'Never to be seen again?' Winthrop ventured.

'Until yesterday,' the Old Man answered. 'Rose has come back. Or, rather, a child looking exactly as Rose did fifty years ago has come back. In Angel Field.'

'She'd be an old woman by now,' Winthrop said.

18

'Providing time passes as we understand it in the Realm of the Angels,' said Catriona.

'And where exactly might that be, Cat?'

She poked her tongue out at him, just as the attendant, a fierce-looking Gurkha, returned with their brandy. He betrayed no opinion, but she was slightly cowed. Serve her right.

'The local rector made the report. One Bartholomew Haskins. He called the Lord Lieutenant, and the matter was passed on to the Diogenes Club. Now, I'm entrusting it to you.'

'What does this girl have to say for herself?' Catriona asked. 'Does she actually claim to be Rosie Farrar?'

'She hasn't said anything yet. Photographs exist of the real Rose, and our girl is said to resemble them uncannily.'

'Uncannily, eh?' said Winthrop.

'Just so.'

'I should think this'll make for a jolly weekend away from town,' Winthrop told the Old Man. 'Angel Down is near enough to Falmer Field for me to combine an investigation with a couple of sorties in *Katie*.'

Winthrop had kept up his flying since the War, maintaining his own aeroplane, a modified Camel fighter named *Katie*. She was getting to be a bit of an antique paraded next to the latest line in gleaming metal monoplanes, but he trusted her as much as he did Catriona or the Bentley. He knew the kite's moods and foibles, and could depend on her in a pinch. If she could come through the best efforts of the late Baron von Richthofen's Flying Circus, she could survive any peace-time scrape. If he were to tangle with 'chariots of stars', he might have need of the faithful *Katie*.

Catriona was thoughtful. As ever, she saw this less as a jaunt than he did. He needed her to balance him. She had a strong sense of what was significant, and kept him from haring off on wild streaks when he needed to be exercising the old brain-box.

'Has this miraculous reappearance been made public?'

19

The Old Man's brows knit. 'I'm afraid so. The Brighton *Argus* carried the story this morning, and the afternoon editions of all the dailies have it, in various lights. Haskins knows enough to keep the child away from the press for the moment. But all manner of people are likely to take an interest. You know who I mean. It would be highly convenient if you could come up with some unsensational explanation that will settle the matter before it goes any further.'

Winthrop understood. It was almost certain this business was a misunderstanding or a hoax. If so, it was best it were blown up at once. And, if not, it was sadly best that it be thought so.

'I'll see what I can do, Beauregard.'

'Good man. Now, you children run off and play. And don't come back until you know what little Rosie is up to.'

4: *A Demure Little Thing*

With Sam Farrar queerly reluctant to take his miraculously returned aunt into his house, Haskins had to put the little girl up at the rectory. He wondered, chiding himself for a lack of charity, whether Sam's hesitation was down to the question of the stake in Farrar Farm, if any, to which Rose might be entitled. It was also true that for Sam and Ellen to be presented in late middle age with a child they might be expected to raise as their own would be an upheaval in their settled lives.

The girl had said nothing yet, but sat quietly in an oversized chair in his study, huddled inside one of Haskins's old dressing gowns. Mrs Cully, his housekeeper, had got the poor child out of her filthy clothes and given her a bath. She had wanted to throw away the ruined garments, but Haskins insisted they be kept for expert examination. Much would hinge on those dirty rags. If it could be proven that they were of more recent provenance than 1872, then this was not Rose Farrar.

Haskins sat at his desk, unable to think of his sermon. His

glance was continually drawn to the girl. Now she had stopped keening, she seemed a demure little thing. She sat with one leg tucked up under her and the other a-dangle, showing a dainty, uncalloused foot. With her face clean and her hair scrubbed – she insisted on having her silver ribbon back – she could have been any well-brought-up child waiting for a story before being packed off to bed.

Telegrams had arrived all morning. And the telephone on his desk had rung more often than in the last six months. He was to expect a pair of investigators from London. Representatives from Lord Northcliffe's *Mail* and Lord Beaverbrook's *Express* had made competing overtures to secure the 'rights' to the story. Many others had shown an interest, from charitable bodies concerned with the welfare of 'a unique orphan' to commercial firms who wished 'the miracle girl' to endorse their soap or tonic. Haskins understood the girl must be shielded from such public scrutiny, at least until the investigators had assessed her case.

One telegram in particular stirred Haskins. A distinguished person offered Rose any service it was within his power to perform. Haskins had replied swiftly, inviting the author-knight to Angel Down. If anyone could get to the bottom of the matter, it would be the literary lion whose sharpness of mind was reputed to be on a par with that of the detective he had made famous and who had worked so tirelessly in his later years to demonstrate the possibility of the miraculous here on earth.

The girl seemed unaware of Haskins's fascination with her. She was a Victorian parent's idea of perfection – pretty as a picture, quiet as a mouse, poised as a waxwork. Haskins wondered about the resemblance to Sam Farrar. It had seemed so strong in the first light of discovery but was now hard to see.

He got up from his desk, abandoning his much-begun and little-developed sermon, and knelt before the child. He took her small hands, feeling bird-like bones and fragile warmth. This was a real girl, not an apparition. She had been vigorously bathed and spent the night in the guest bedroom. Ghosts did not leave dirty bathwater or crumpled sheets. She had consumed some soup last night and half an apple for breakfast.

Her eyes fixed his and he wanted to ask her questions.

Since she had stopped making her peculiar noise, she had uttered no sound. She seemed to understand what was said to her but was disinclined to answer. She did not even respond to attempted communication via rudimentary sign language or Mrs Cully's baby-talk.

'Rose?' he asked.

There was no flicker in her eyes.

Sam had produced pictures, yellowed poses of the Farrar children from the dawn of photography. One among a frozen gaggle of girls resembled exactly this child. Sam reluctantly confirmed the child in the portrait as his vanished Aunt Rose, the Little Girl Who Went With the Angels.

'What happened to you, Rose?'

According to the stories, she had been swept up to the Heavens in a column of starlight.

Haskins heard a buzzing. There was a wasp in the room!

He held the girl's hands too tightly. Her face contorted in pain. He let go and made an attempt to soothe her, to prevent the return of her screeches.

Her mouth opened, but nothing came out.

The wasp was still here. Haskins was horribly aware of it. His collar was damp and his stomach shifted.

There was more than one.

The buzzing grew louder. Haskins stood up and looked about for the evil black-and-yellow specks.

He looked again at Rose, suddenly afraid for her. The girl's face shifted and she was his sister, Jane.

It was like an injection of wasp venom to the heart.

Her mouth was a round aperture, black inside. The wasp shrill was coming from her.

Haskins was terrified, dragged back to his boyhood, stripped

22

of adult dignities and achievements, confronted with his long-dead victim.

He remembered vividly the worst thing he had ever done. The stick sinking into the nest. His cruel laughter as the cloud swarmed from the sundered ovoid and took flight, whipped away by strong wind.

Jane stood on the chair, dressing gown a heavy monk's robe. She still wore her silver ribbon. She wasn't *exactly* Jane. There was some Rose in her eyes. And a great deal of darkness, of something else.

She reached out to him as if for a cuddle. He fell to his knees, this time in prayer. He tried to close his eyes.

The girl's mouth was huge, a gaping circle. Black apparatus emerged, a needle-tipped proboscis rimmed with whipping feelers. It was an insectile appendage, intricate and hostile, parts grinding together with wicked purpose.

Her eyes were black poached eggs overflowing their sockets, a million facets glinting.

The proboscis touched his throat. A barb of ice pierced his skin. Shock stopped his heart and stilled his lungs, leaving his mind to flutter on for eternal seconds.

5: A Funny Turn

Angel Down Rectory was a nice little cottage close by the church, rather like the home Catriona had grown up in. Her kindly father was a clergyman in Somerset, in the village where Edwin's distant father had owned the Manor House without really being Lord of the Manor.

Colonel Winthrop had been literally distant for most of his later life, stationed in India or the Far East after some scandal which was never spoken of in the village. An alienist might put that down as the root of a streak of slyness, of manipulative ruthlessness, that fitted his son for the murkier aspects of his business. Recognizing this dark face, fed with blood in the trenches and the skies, as being as much a part of Edwin's personality as his humour, generosity and belief in her, Catriona did her best to shine her light upon it, to keep him fixed on a human scale. The Reverend Kaye mildly disapproved of her spook-chasing and changed the subject whenever anyone asked about his daughter's marriage plans, but was otherwise as stalwart, loyal and loving a parent as she could wish.

They had found the village with ease, homing in on a steeple visible from a considerable distance across the downs. For such a small place, Angel Down was blessed with a large and impressive church, which was in itself suggestive. If a site can boast an ancient stone circle and a long-established Christian church, it is liable to have been a centre of unusual spiritual activity for quite some time.

There was something wrong. She knew it at once. She made no claim to psychic powers, but had learned to be sensitive. She could almost always distinguish between an authentic spectre and a fool in a bedsheet, no matter how much fog and shadow were about. It was a question of reading the tiniest signs, often on an unconscious level.

'Careful, dearest,' she told Edwin, as they got out of the car.

He looked at her quizzically. She couldn't explain her unsettling feeling, but he had been with her in enough bizarre situations to accept her shrug of doubt as a trustworthy sign of danger ahead. He thrust a hand into his coat pocket, taking hold of the revolver he carried when about the business of the Diogenes Club.

She heard something. A sound like an insect, but then again not. It was not within her experience.

Edwin rapped on the door with his knuckles.

A round, pink woman let them in. Upon receipt of Edwin's card, the housekeeper, Mrs Cully, told them they were expected and that she would tell the rector of their arrival.

The narrow hallway was likeably cluttered. A stand was overburdened with coats and hats, boots lined up for inspection nearby, umbrellas and sticks ready for selection. A long-case clock ticked slow, steady seconds.

There was no evidence of eccentricity.

Mrs Cully returned, pink gone to grey. Catriona was immediately alert, nerves singing like wires. The woman couldn't speak, but nodded behind her, to the rector's study.

With his revolver, Edwin pushed open the door.

Catriona saw a black-faced man lying on the carpet, eyes staring. His hands were white.

Edwin stepped into the room and Catriona followed. They both knelt by the prone man. He had a shock of red-grey hair and wore a clerical collar, taut as a noose around his swollen throat.

The Reverend Mr Haskins – for this could be none other – was freshly dead. Still warm, he had no pulse, heartbeat or breath. His face was swollen and coal-coloured. His mouth and eyes were fixed open. Even his tongue was black and stiff. Droplets of blood clung to his hard, overripe cheeks.

'Snakebite?' she asked, shuddering.

'Could be, Cat,' he said, standing up.

She was momentarily troubled. Did she hear the soft slither of a dire reptile winding across the carpet? She was not fond of the beasts. A criminal mandarin-sorcerer had once tried to murder Edwin with a black mamba delivered in a Harrods' hamper. She had been unfortunate enough to be sharing a punt with him when the scheme came to hissing light. She had cause to remember that snakes can swim.

'And who have we here?' he asked.

She stood. Edwin had found the girl, sat calmly in an armchair, wearing a man's large dressing gown, leafing through a picture book of wild flowers. The supposed Rose Farrar was a tiny thing, too sharp-featured to be considered pretty but with a striking, triangular face and huge, curious eyes. Her expression was familiar to Catriona. She had seen it on shell-shocked soldiers coming home from a war that would always be fought in their minds.

She wanted to warn Edwin against touching the girl. But that would have been ridiculous.

'Little miss, what happened?' he asked.

The girl looked up from her book. For a moment, she seemed like a shrunken adult. The real Rosie would be almost sixty, Catriona remembered.

'He had a funny turn,' the child said.

That much was obvious.

'Do you have a name, child?' he asked.

'Yes,' she said, disinclined to reveal more.

'And what might it be?' she asked.

The little girl turned to look at her, for the first time, and said, 'Catriona.'

It was a tiny shock.

'I am Catriona,' Catriona said. 'And this is Edwin. You are . . . ?'

She held up her book. On the page was a picture of a wild rose, delicate green watercolour leaves with incarnadine petal splashes.

'Rose,' the girl said.

This was considerably more serious than a hoax. A man was dead. No longer just a puzzle to be unpicked and forgotten, this was a mystery to be solved.

A panicked cough from the doorway drew their attention. It was Mrs Cully, eyes fixed on the ceiling, away from the corpse.

'There's another come visiting,' she said.

Catriona knew they must have been racing newspapermen to get here. There would be reporters all over the village, and soon – when this latest development was out – front-page headlines in all the papers.

'Is it someone from the press?' Edwin asked.

The woman shook her head. A big, elderly man gently stepped around her and into the room. He had a large, bushy moustache and kindly eyes. She knew him at once.

'Sir Arthur,' said Edwin, 'welcome to Angel Down. I wish the circumstances of our meeting had been different.'

26

6: *Venomous Lightning*

Winthrop shifted his revolver to his left hand, so he could extend his right arm and shake hands with Sir Arthur Conan Doyle. The author was in his mid-sixties, but his grip was firm. He was an outdoor-looking man, more Watson than Holmes.

'You have me at a disadvantage, sir.'

'I am Edwin Winthrop, of the Diogenes Club.'

'Oh,' said Sir Arthur, momentously, '*them.*'

'Yes, indeed. Water under the bridge, and all that.'

Sir Arthur rumbled. He had clearly not forgotten that the Diogenes Club had once taken such a dim view of his mentioning their name in two pieces placed in the *Strand* magazine that considerable pressure had been brought to ensure the suppression of further such narratives. While the consulting detective was always slyly pleased that his feats be publicized, his civil servant brother – Beauregard's predecessor – preferred to hide his considerable light under a bushel. Sir Arthur had never revealed the exact nature of the Club and Mycroft's position within it, but he had drawn attention to a man and an institution who would far rather their names were unknown to the general public. No real lasting harm was done, though the leagues who followed Sherlock Holmes were tragically deprived of thrilling accounts of several memorable occasions upon which he had acted as an instrument of his older brother and his country.

'And this is Miss Catriona Kaye,' Winthrop continued.

'I know who she is.'

The sentence was like a slap, but Catriona did not flinch at it.

'This woman,' Sir Arthur said, 'has made it her business to harass those few unselfish souls who can offer humanity the solace it so badly needs. I've had a full account of her un-warranted attack this morning on Mademoiselle Astarte of Chelsea.'

27

Winthrop remembered Sir Arthur was a committed, not to say credulous, Spiritualist.

'Sir Arthur,' said Catriona, fixing his steely gaze, 'Mademoiselle Astarte is a cruel hoaxer and an extortionist. She does your cause – nay, *our* cause – no credit whatsoever. I too seek only light in the darkness. I should have thought, given your well-known association with the most brilliant deductive mind of the age, you would see my activities as a necessary adjunct to your own.'

She had him there. Sir Arthur was uncomfortable, but too honest a man not to admit Catriona was right. In recent years, he had been several times duped by the extraordinary claims of hoaxers. There was that business with the fairies. He looked around the room, avoiding Catriona's sharp eyes. He saw the body of Mr Haskins. And the girl curled up in the chair.

'Good Lord,' he exclaimed.

'This is exactly the scene we found,' Winthrop said.

'I heard a noise earlier, as we arrived,' Catriona revealed. 'Something like an insect.'

'It seems as if a whole hive of bees has stung him.'

Sir Arthur had trained as a doctor, Winthrop remembered.

'Could it have been poison?' he asked.

'If so, someone's tidied up,' Sir Arthur said, confidently turning the swollen head from side to side. 'No cup or glass with spilled liquid. No half-eaten cake. No dart stuck in the flesh. The face and chest are swollen but not the hands or, I'll wager, the feet. I'd say whatever struck him did so through this wound here, in the throat.'

A florin-sized red hole showed in the greasy black skin.

'It is as if he were struck by venomous lightning.'

Sir Arthur found an orange blanket in a basket by the sofa and spread it over the dead man. The twisted shape was even more ghastly when shrouded.

'The girl says he had a "funny turn",' Winthrop said.

For the first time, Sir Arthur considered the child.

'Is this Rose? Has she spoken?'

The girl said nothing. She was interested in her book again. At her age, she could hardly be expected to be much con-cerened with grown-up things.

If she was the age she seemed.

Sir Arthur went over to the chair and examined the girl. His hands, steady as a rock when patting down a gruesome corpse, trembled as they neared her hair. He touched fingertips to the silver ribbon that held back her curls, and drew them away as if shocked.

'Child, child,' he said, tears in his eyes, 'what wonders have you seen? What hope can you give us?'

This was not the dispassionate, scientific interrogation Winthrop had planned. He was touched by the old man's naked emotion. Sir Arthur had lost a son in the War, and thereafter turned to Spiritualism for comfort. He betrayed a palpable need for confirmation of his beliefs. Like the detective he had made famous, he needed evidence.

The possible Rose was like a child queen regarding an aged and loyal knight with imperious disdain. Sir Arthur literally knelt at her feet, looking up to her.

'Do you know about the Little People?' she asked.

7: A Gift From Faerie

Catriona had been given to understand that Rose did not speak, but she was becoming quite chatty. Sir Arthur quizzed her about 'the Little People', who were beginning to sound more like fairies than cherubs. She wondered if Rose were not one of those children who cut her personality to suit the adult or adults she was with, mischievous with one uncle, modest with the next. The girl was constantly clever, she felt, but otherwise completely mercurial.

It was only a few years since the name of Sir Arthur Conan Doyle, a watchword for good sense to most of Great Britain, had been devalued by the affair of the Cottingley Fairies. Two little girls, not much older than this child, had not only claimed to be in regular communion with the wee folk but produced photographs of them – subsequently shown to be amateur forgeries – which Sir Arthur rashly endorsed as genuine, even to the extent of writing *The Coming of the Fairies*, an inspirational book about the case. Though the hoax had been exploded a dozen times, Sir Arthur stubbornly refused to disbelieve. Catriona sensed the old man's *need* for faith, his devout wish for the magical to penetrate his world and declare itself irrefutably.

'I went away with them,' the girl told them. 'The Little People. I was in their home in the sky. It's inside of a cloud, and like a hollow tree, with criss-cross roots and branches. We could all fly there, or float. There was no up or down. They played with me for ever such a long time. And gave me my ribbon.'

She turned her head, showing the ribbon in her hair. Catriona had noticed it before.

'Rose, may I see your ribbon?' Sir Arthur asked.

Catriona wasn't comfortable with this. Surely something should be done for poor Mr Haskins before the girl was exhaustively interviewed.

Rose took the ribbon out of her hair solemnly and offered it to Sir Arthur.

'Extraordinary,' he said, running it through his fingers. He offered it to Catriona.

She hesitated a moment and accepted the thing.

It was not any fabric she knew. Predominantly silvery, it was imprinted with green shapes, like runes or diagrams. Though warm to the touch, it might be a new type of processed metal. She crumpled the ribbon into a ball, then opened her fist. The thing sprang back into its original shape without a crease.

'You're bleeding,' Edwin said.

The edges were sharp as pampas grass. Without feeling it, she had shallowly grazed herself.

'May I have it again now?' Rose asked.

Catriona returned the ribbon, which the girl carefully wound into her hair. She did not knot it, but *shaped* it, into a coil which held back her curls.

'A gift from faerie,' Sir Arthur mused.

Catriona wasn't sure. Her hand was beginning to sting. She took a hankie from her reticule and stemmed the trickle of blood from the scratch.

'Rose, my dear,' said Sir Arthur. 'It is now 1925. What year was it when you went away, to play with the Little People? Was it a long time ago? As long ago, ahem, as 1872?'

The girl didn't answer. Her face darkened, as if she were suddenly afraid or unable to do a complicated sum in mental arithmetic.

'Let's play a game,' Edwin suggested, genially. 'What's this?'

He held up a pencil from the rector's desk.

'Pencil,' Rose said, delighted.

'Quite right. And this?'

The letter-opener.

'A thin knife.'

'Very good, Rose. And this?'

He picked the telephone receiver up from its cradle.

'Telly Phone,' the girl said.

Edwin set the receiver down and nodded in muted triumph.

'Alexander Graham Bell,' he said, almost sadly. '1876.'

'She's been back two days, man,' Sir Arthur said, annoyed. He turned to the girl and tried to smile reassuringly. 'Did the rector tell you about the telephone? Did you hear it make a ring-ring noise, see him talk to friends a long way away with it?'

Rose was guarded now. She knew she had been caught out.

If this was a hoax, it was not a simple one. That ribbon was outside nature. And Haskins had died by means unknown.

'Why don't you use that instrument to summon the police?' said Sir Arthur, nodding at the telephone.

'Call the police?' Edwin said. 'Tut-tut, what would Mr Holmes say? This matter displays unusual features which the worthy Sussex constabulary will not be best equipped to deal with.'

'This man should at least have a doctor look at him.'

'He has had one, Sir Arthur. You.'

The author-knight was not happy. And neither was she.

8: A Changeling

Winthrop was satisfied that this girl was not the real Rose, and that an imposture was being planned – perhaps as part of a scheme to dupe the farmer, Sam Farrar, out of his property. The Reverend Mr Haskins must have stumbled on to the trick and been done nastily to death. From the look of the rector's throat, something like a poison-tipped spear had been used on him. It remained for the girl to be persuaded to identify the conspirators who had tutored her in imposture. She was too young to be guilty by herself.

'Now, missy, let's talk about this game you've been playing,' he said. 'The dress-up-and-pretend game. Who taught it to you?'

The girl's face was shut. He thought she might try crying. But she was too tough for that. She was like any adult criminal, exposed and sullen, refusing to cooperate, unaffected by remorse.

'It's not that simple, Edwin,' Catriona said. 'The ribbon.'

Winthrop had thought of that. Lightweight metallicized fabrics were being used in aircraft manufacture these days, and that scrap might well be an off-cut. It was a strange touch, though.

'There's something else. Look at her.'

He did. She had an ordinary face. There was something about the eyes, though. A violet highlight.

'There are Little People,' she said. 'There are, there are. They are bald, and have eyes like saucers, and no noses. They played with me. For a long time. And they have friends here, on the

32

ground. Undertakers with smoked glasses.'

'What is your name?'

'Rose,' she said, firmly.

Was she trying to get back to the story she had been taught? Or had she been hypnotized into believing what she was saying?

Suddenly, he saw what Catriona meant.

The girl's face had changed, not just its expression but its shape. Her nose was rounder, her chin less sharp, her cheekbones gone. Her mouth had been thin, showing sharp teeth; now she had classic bee-stung lips, like Catriona's. Her curls were tighter, like little corkscrews.

He stood back from her, worried by what he had seen. He glanced at the rector's body, covered with its orange blanket. It was not possible, surely, that this child . . .

. . . this angel?

'What is it, man? What is it?'

Sir Arthur was agitated, impatient at being left out. He must feel it humiliating not to have spotted the clue. Of course, he had come into it later and not seen the girl as she was when Winthrop and Catriona had arrived. It seemed now that her face had always been changing, subtly.

'Consider her face,' Winthrop said.

'Yes.'

'It changes.'

The violet highlights were green now.

Sir Arthur gasped.

The girl looked older, twelve or thirteen. Her feet and ankles showed under the dressing gown. Her shoulders filled the garment out more. Her face was thinner again, eyes almost almond.

'This is not the girl who was taken away,' Sir Arthur said. 'She is one of *them*, a Changeling.'

For the first time, Winthrop rather agreed with him.

'There are bad fairies,' Sir Arthur said. 'Who steal away children and leave one of their own in the crib.'

Winthrop knew the folk-tales. He wasn't satisfied of their literal truth, but he realized in a flash that this girl might be an instance of whatever phenomenon gave rise to the stories in the first place.

You didn't have to believe in fairies to know the world was stranger than imagined.

'Who are you, Rose?' Catriona asked, gently.

She knelt before the girl, as Sir Arthur had done, looking up into her shifting face.

Winthrop couldn't help but notice that the girl's body had become more womanly inside the dressing gown. Her hair straightened and grew longer. Her eyebrows were thinner and arched.

'Rose?'

Catriona reached out.

The girl's face screwed up and she hissed, viciously. She opened her mouth, wider than she should have been able to. Her incisors were needle-fangs. She hissed again, flicking a long, fork-tipped tongue.

A spray of venom scattered at Catriona's face.

9: 'Cruel Cunning'

The shock was so great she almost froze, but Catriona flung her hand in front of her eyes. The girl's sizzling spit stung the back of her hand. She wiped it instinctively on the carpet, scraping her skin raw. She had an idea the stuff was deadly.

The girl was out of her chair and towering above her now, shoulders and hips swaying, no longer entirely human. Her skin was greenish, scaled. Her eyes were red-green, with triangular pupils. Catriona thought she might even have nictitating membranes.

Catriona remembered the slither of the mamba.

She was frozen with utter panic, and a tiny voice inside nagged her for being weak.

Edwin seized the letter opener – the thin knife – from the desk and stabbed at the snake girl.

A black-thorned green hand took his wrist and bent it backwards. He dropped his weapon. Her hissing face closed in on his throat.

Catriona's panic snapped. She stuck her foot between the girl's ankles and scythed her legs out from under her.

They all fell in a tangle.

Rose broke free of them, leaving the dressing gown in a muddle on the floor.

She stood naked by Sir Arthur, body scaled and shimmering, as beautiful as it was horrid. She was striped in many shades of green, brown, yellow, red and black. She had the beginnings of a tail. Her hair was flat against her neck and shoulders, flaring like a cobra's hood. Her nose and ears were slits, frilled inside with red cilia.

Catriona and Edwin tried to get up, but were in each other's way.

Rose smiled, fangs poking out of her mouth, and laid her talons on Sir Arthur's lapels. She crooned to him, a sibilant susurrus of fascination. In the movements of her hips and shoulders and the arch of her eyes, there was a cruel cunning that was beyond human. This was a creature that killed for the pleasure of it, and was glad of an audience.

Sir Arthur was backed against a mantelpiece. His hand reached out, and found a plain crucifix mounted between two candlesticks. The Reverend Mr Haskins had evidently not been very High Church, for there were few other obvious signs of his profession in the room.

Rose's black-red lips neared Sir Arthur's face, to administer a killing kiss. Her fork-tipped tongue darted out and slithered between his eyes and across his cheek, leaving a shining streak.

Sir Arthur took the cross and interposed it between his face and hers. He pressed it to her forehead.

Rose reacted as if a drop of molten lead had been applied. She screeched inhumanly and turned away, crouching into a ball. The scales on her legs and back sizzled and disappeared, like butter pats on a hot griddle. Her body shrank again, with a cracking of bones.

'Oh my stars,' said someone from the doorway.

Two men, strangers, stood in the hall, amazed at the scene. The one who spoke was a prosperous-looking man, face seamed and clothes practical. Behind him was the silhouette of someone large, soft and practically hairless.

Rose looked up at the newcomers. Her eyes were round again, and full of puzzlement rather than malice. Catriona had a sense that the monster was forgotten.

The girl snatched up the dressing gown and slipped into it, modestly closing it over her body. Then she hurled herself at a window, and crashed through the panes into the gathering dusk outside.

She hit the ground running and was off, away over the fields.

'I knew that weren't Aunt Rose,' said the newcomer.

10: 'Anti-Christine'

'The Great Beast is among you,' announced the fat bald man, referring to himself rather than the departed Rose.

Sir Arthur still clung to the cross that had seen off the Rose creature.

'Of all things, I thought of *Dracula*,' he said, wondering at his survival. 'Bram Stoker's novel.'

Winthrop was familiar with the book.

'The cross had exactly the effect on that creature as upon the vampires in *Dracula*.'

'Ugh,' said the bald man, 'what a horrid thing. Put it away, Sir Arthur.'

Farrar had noticed the rector's body, and was sunk into a couch with his head in his hands. This was too weird for most people. The honest farmer would have to leave these matters for the experts in the uncanny.

The man who had arrived with Farrar wore a once-expensive coat. The astrakhan collar was a little ragged and his pinstripe trousers shiny at the knees. A great deal of this fellow's time was spent on his knees, for one reason or other. His face was fleshy, great lips hanging loose. Even his hands were plump, slug-white flippers. His great dome shone and his eyes glinted with unhealthy fire.

Winthrop recognized the controversial figure of Aleister Crowley, self-styled 'wickedest man in England'. Quite apart from his well-known advocacy of black magic, sexual promiscuity and drug use, the brewery heir – perhaps from a spirit of ingrained contrariness – had blotted his copybook in loudly advocating the Kaiser's cause during the War. In his younger days, he was reckoned a daring mountaineer, but his vices had transformed him into a flabby remnant who looked as though he would find a steep staircase an insurmountable obstacle.

'Aren't you supposed to be skulking in Paris?' Winthrop asked.

'Evidently, sir, you have the advantage of me,' Crowley admitted.

'Edwin Winthrop, of the Diogenes Club.'

The black magician smiled, almost genuinely.

'Charles Beauregard's bright little boy. I have heard of you, and of your exploits among the shadows. And this charming *fille de l'occasion* must be Miss Catriona Kaye, celebrated exposer of charlatans. I believe you know that dreadful poseur A.E. Waite. Is it not well past time you showed him up for the faker he is, dear lady?'

Crowley loomed over Catriona. Winthrop remembered with alarm that he was famous for bestowing 'the serpent's kiss', a mouth-to-mouth greeting reckoned dangerous to the receiving party. He contented himself with kissing her knuckles, like a gourmand licking the skin off a well-roasted chicken leg.

'And Sir Arthur Conan Doyle, whose fine yarns have given me and indeed all England such pleasure. This is a most distinguished company.'

Sir Arthur, who could hardly fail to know who Crowley was, looked at his crucifix, perhaps imagining it might have an efficacy against the Great Beast.

If so, Crowley read his mind. 'That bauble holds no terror for a magus of my exalted standing, Sir Arthur. It symbolizes an era which is dead and gone, but rotting all around us. I have written to Mr Trotsky in Moscow, offering to place my services at his disposal if he would charge me with the responsibility of eradicating Christianity from the planet.'

'And has he written back?' Catriona asked, archly.

'Actually, no.'

'*Quelle surprise!*'

Crowley flapped his sausage-fingers at her.

'Naughty, naughty. Such cynicism in one so young. You would make a fine Scarlet Woman, my dear. You have all the proper attributes.'

'My sins are scarlet enough already, Mr Crowley,' Catriona replied. 'And, to put it somewhat bluntly, I doubt from your general appearance that you would be up to matching them these days.'

The magus looked like a hurt little boy. For an instant, Winthrop had a flash of the power this man had over his followers. He was such an obvious buffoon one might feel him so pathetic that to contradict his constant declamations of his own genius would be cruel. He had seriously harmed many people, and sponged unmercifully off many others. The Waite he had mentioned was, like the poet Yeats, another supposed initiate of a mystic order, with whom he had been conducting an ill-tempered feud over the decades.

'The time for the Scarlet Woman is ended,' Crowley continued, back in flight. 'Her purpose was always to birth the perfect being, and now that has been superseded. I hurried here on the boat train when news reached me that *she* had appeared on Earth. She who will truly bring to an end the stifling, milk-and-water age of the cloddish carpenter.'

'I find your tone objectionable, man,' Sir Arthur said. 'A

clergyman is dead.'

'A modest achievement, I admit, but a good start.'

'The fellow's mad,' Sir Arthur blustered. 'Quite cuckoo.'

Winthrop tended to agree but wanted to hear Crowley out. He nodded towards the smashed window. 'What do you think she is, Crowley? The creature you saw attacking us?'

'I suppose Anti-Christ is too masculine a term. We shall have to get used to calling her the Anti-Christine.'

Catriona, perhaps unwisely, giggled. She was rewarded with a lightning-look from the magus.

'She was brought to us by demons, in the centre of a circle of ancient sacrifice, enlivened by blood offerings. I have been working for many years to prepare the Earth for her coming, and to open the way for her appearance upon the great stage of magickal history. She has begun her reign. She has many faces. She is the get of the Whore of Babylon and the Goat of Mendes. She will cut a swathe through human society, mark my words. I shall be her tutor in sublime wickedness. There will be blood-letting and licence.'

'For such a committed foe of Christianity, you talk a lot of Bible phrases,' Winthrop said. 'Your parents were Plymouth Brethren, were they not?'

'I sprang whole from the earth of Warwickshire. Is it not strange that such a small county could sire both of England's greatest poets?'

Everyone looked at him in utter amazement.

'Shakespeare was the other,' he explained. 'You know, the *Hamlet* fellow.'

Sir Arthur was impatient and Catriona amused, but Winthrop was alert. This man could still be dangerous.

'"The Great God Pan",' Catriona said.

Crowley beamed, assuming she was describing him.

'It's a short story,' she said. 'By Arthur Machen. That's where he's getting all this nonsense. He's casting Rose in the role of the anti-heroine of that fiction.'

'Truths are revealed to us in fictions,' Crowley said. 'Sir

Arthur, who has so skilfully blended the real and the imagined throughout his career, will agree. And so would Mr Stoker, whom you mentioned. There are many, indeed, who believe your employers, Mr Winthrop, are but the inventions of this literary knight.'

Sir Arthur grumbled.

'At any rate, since the object of my quest is no longer here, I shall depart. It has been an unalloyed pleasure to meet you at such an exhilarating juncture.'

Crowley gave a grunting little bow, and withdrew.

11: A Living Looking-Glass

'Well,' said Catriona, hardly needing to elaborate on the syllable.

'He's an experience, and no mistake,' Edwin admitted.

Having been yanked from horror into comedy, she was light-headed. It seemed absurd now, but she had been near death when the Rose Thing was closing on her throat.

'I see it,' said Sir Arthur, suddenly.

He lifted the blanket from the rector's head and pointed to the ghastly wound with the crucifix. Despite everything else, Sir Arthur was pleased with himself, and amazed.

'I've made a *deduction*,' he announced. 'I've written too often of them, but never until now truly understood. It's like little wheels in your head, coming into alignment. Truly, a marvellous thing.'

Sam Farrar looked up from his hands. He was glumly drained of all emotion, a common fellow unable to keep up with the high-flown characters, human and otherwise, who had descended into his life.

'The creature we saw had extended eye-teeth,' Sir Arthur lectured. 'Like a snake's fangs. Perhaps they were what put me in mind of Bram Stoker's vampires. Yet this wound, in the unfortunate Reverend Mr Haskins's throat, suggests a single stabbing implement. It is larger, rounder, more of a gouge than a bite. The thing we saw would have left two small puckered holes. Haskins was attacked by something different.'

'Or something differently shaped,' Edwin suggested.

'Yes, indeed. We have seen how the Changeling can alter her form. Evidently, she has a large repertoire.'

Catriona tried to imagine what might have made the wound.

'It looks like an insect bite, Sir Arthur,' she said, shuddering, 'made by . . . good lord . . . a *gigantic mosquito*.'

'Bart hated insects,' Farrar put in, blankly. 'Had a bad experience years ago. Never did get the whole story of it. If a wasp came in the room, he was froze up with fear.'

An idea began to shape in her mind.

The Reverend Mr Haskins hated insects. And she had a horror of snakes. Earlier, she had thought Rose was the sort of child who presented herself to suit who she was with. That had been a real insight.

'She's who we think she is,' she said.

Sir Arthur shook his head, not catching her drift.

'She is who we want her to be, or what we're afraid she is,' she continued. 'Sir Arthur wished to think her a friend to the fairies, and so she seemed to be. Edwin, for you it would be most convenient if she were a fraud; when you thought that most strongly, she made the slip about the telephone. The Reverend Mr Haskins was in terror of insects, and she became one; I am not best partial to crawling reptiles, and so she took the form of a snake woman. Every little thing, she reacts to. When I asked her what her name was, she quoted mine back to me. Sir Arthur, you thought of a scene in a novel, and she played it out. She's like a living looking-glass, taking whatever we think of her and becoming exactly that thing.'

Sir Arthur nodded, convinced at once. She was not a little flattered to detect admiration in his eyes. She had made a deduction too.

Edwin was more concerned.

'We've got to stop Crowley,' he said.

'*Crowley?*' she questioned.

'If he gets hold of her, she'll become what *he* thinks she is. And he thinks she's the end the world.'

12: *The Altar of Sex Magick*

There was only one place the Anti-Christine could have flown to: Angel Field, where once had stood a stone circle. Crowley knew Farrar Farm, since he had called there first, assuming the divine creature would be in the care of her supposed nephew. But Angel Field was a mystery, and there were no street-lights out here in the wilds of Sussex to guide the way.

Before departing, penniless, for England, he had telegraphed several of his few remaining disciples, beseeching funds and the loan of a car and driver. He was an international fugitive, driven from his Abbey of Thelema in Sicily at the express order of the odious Mussolini, and reduced to grubbing a living in Paris, with the aid of a former Scarlet Woman who was willing to sell her body on the streets to keep the magus in something approaching comfort.

He had left these damp, dreary islands for ever, he had hoped. He was no longer welcome in magical circles in London, brought low by the conspirings of lesser men who failed stubbornly to appreciate his genius.

No chauffeured car awaited him at Victoria, so he had hired one, trusting his manner and force of personality to convince one Alfred Jenkinsop, Esq., that he was good for the fee once the new age had dawned. As it happened, he expected the concept of money to be wiped away with all the other detritus of the dead past.

He found Jenkinsop in his car, outside Farrar Farm, reading *The Sporting Life* by torchlight. The fellow perked up to see him, and stuck his head out of the window.

'Have you seen a female pass this way?' Crowley asked.

Jenkinsop was remarkably obtuse on the point. It took him

some moments to remember that he had, in fact, happened to see a girl, clad only in a dressing gown, running down the road from the rectory and on to the farm.

'Which way did she go?'

Jenkinsop shrugged. Crowley made a mental note to erase his somewhat comical name from the record of this evening when he came to write the official history of how the Anti-Christine was brought to London as a protégée of the Great Beast.

'Come, man,' he said, 'follow me.'

The driver showed no willingness to get out of the car.

'It's a cold night, guv,' he said, as if that explained all.

Crowley left him to 'the pink 'un', and trudged through Farrar's open front gate. His once-expensive shoes sank in mud and he felt icy moisture seep in through their somewhat strained seams. Nothing to one who had survived the treacherous glacial slopes of Chogo-Ri, but still a damned nuisance.

If Farrar's vandal of a grandfather hadn't smashed the stones, it would have been easier to find Angel Field. It was a cloudless night, but the moon was just a shining rind. He could make out the shapes of hedgerows, but little more.

He had an alarming encounter with a startled cow.

'Mistress Perfection,' he called out.

Only mooing came back.

Finally, he discerned a fire in the night and made his way towards it. He knew his feet stood upon the sod of Angel Field. For the Anti-Christine was at the centre of the light, surrounded by her impish acolytes.

They were attendant demons, Crowley knew. Naked, hairless and without genitals. They had smooth, grey, dwarf bodies and large black insect eyes. Some held peculiar implements with lights at their extremities. They all turned, with one fluid movement, to look at him.

She was magnificent. Having shed her snakeskin, she had become the essence of voluptuous harlotry, masses of electric gorgon-hair confined by a shining circlet of silver, robe gaping open immodestly over her gently swelling belly, wicked green eyes darting like flames. Her teeth were still sharp. She looked from side to side, smile twisted off-centre.

This was the rapturous creature who would degrade the world.

Crowley worshipped her.

The occasion of their meeting called for a ceremony. The imps gathered around him, heads bobbing about his waist-height. Some extended spindle-fingered hands, tipped with sucker-like appendages, and touched him.

He unloosed his belt and dropped his trousers and drawers. He knelt, knees well-spaced, and touched his forehead to the cold, wet ground.

One of the imps took its implement and inserted it into Crowley's rectum. He bit a mouthful of grassy sod as the implement expanded inside him.

Crowley's body was the altar of sex magick.

The commingling of pain and pleasure was not new to him. This was quite consistent with the theory and practice of magick he had devised over many years of unparalleled scholarship. As the metallic probe pulsed inside him like living flesh, he was thrust forward into his new golden dawn.

The imp's implement was withdrawn.

Hands took Crowley's head and lifted it from the dirt. The Anti-Christine looked at him with loathing and love. Their mouths opened, and they pounced. Crowley trapped her lower lip between his teeth and bit until his mouth was full of her blood. He broke the serpent's kiss, and she returned in kind, nipping and nibbling at his nose and dewlaps.

Her lips were rouged with her own blood, and marked with his teeth.

Oh joy!

'Infernal epitome,' he addressed her, 'we must get you quickly to London, where you can spread your leathery wings, open your scaled legs and begin to exert a real influence. We shall start with a few seductions, of men and women naturally, petty and great persons, reprobates and saints. Each shall spread your glorious taint, which will flash through society like a new tonic.'

She looked pleased by the prospect.

'There will be fire and pestilence,' he continued. 'Duels and murders and many, many suicides. Piccadilly Circus will burn like Nero's Rome. Pall Mall will fall to the barbarians. The Thames will run red and brown with the blood and ordure of the King and his courtiers. We shall dig up the mouldy skeletons of Victoria and Albert and revivify them with demon spells, to set them copulating like mindless mink in Horse Guard's Parade. St Paul's shall be turned into a brothel of Italianate vileness, and Westminster Abbey made an adjunct to the London Zoological Gardens, turned over to obscene apes who will defecate and fornicate where the foolishly pious once sat. The London *Times* will publish blasphemies and pornography, illustrated only by the greatest artists of the age. The Lord Mayor's head will be used as a ball in the Association Football Cup Final. Cocaine, heroin and the services of child prostitutes will be advertised in posters plastered to the sides of all omnibuses. Willie Blasted Yeats shall be burned in effigy in place of Saint Guy Fawkes on every November 5th, and all the other usurpers of the Golden Dawn laid low in their own filth. All governments, all moralities, all churches, will collapse. The City will burn, must burn. Only we Secret Chiefs will retain our authority. You shall beget many children, homunculi. It will be a magnificent age, extending for a thousand times a thousand years.'

In her shining, darting eyes, he saw it was all true. He buttoned up his trousers and spirited her away to where Jenkinsop waited with the car, unwitting herald of welcome apocalypse.

13: 'The Fire-Wheel'

Winthrop held *Katie*'s stick forward, flying at an angle, nose into the wind, so the dark, shadowed quilt of Sussex filled his view. The dawn light just pricked at the East, flashing off ponds and streams. Night-flying was tricky in a country dotted with telegraph poles and tall trees, but at least there wasn't some Fokker stalking him. He tried to keep the Camel level with the tiny light funnels that were the headlamps of what must be Crowley's car.

They had got to Farrar Farm just after Crowley's departure with Rose or Christine or whatever the girl chose to be called. He had set Catriona and Sir Arthur on their tail in the Bentley, and borrowed Sir Arthur's surprisingly sprightly runabout to make his way to the airfield at Falmer, where his aeroplane was hangared. It was like the War again, rousing a tired ground staff to get him into the air within minutes of his strapping on helmet and boots.

He had assumed few automobiles would be on the roads of Sussex at this hour of the morning, but had homed in on a couple of trundling milk trucks before picking up the two vehicles he assumed were Crowley's car and his own Bentley. He trusted Catriona at the wheel, though Sir Arthur had seemed as startled at the prospect of being driven by a woman as he had when confronted by the girl's monstrous snake-shape. When Winthrop had last seen them, Sir Arthur was still clutching his crucifix and Catriona was tucking stray hair under her sweet little hat.

He wished he had time to savour the thrill of being in the air again. He also regretted not storing ammunition and even a couple of bombs with *Katie*. Her twin machine-guns were still in working order, synchronized to fire through the prop blades, but he had nothing to fire out of them. His revolver was under his jacket, but would be almost useless: it was hard to give accurate fire while flying one-handed, with one's gun-arm flapping about in sixty-mile-an-hour airwash.

Suddenly, the sun rose. In the West.

A blast of daylight fell on one side of Winthrop's face. He felt a tingle as if he were being sun-burned. For a moment, the air currents were all wrong, and he nearly lost control of *Katie*.

The landscape below was bleached by light. The two cars were quite distinct on the road. They were travelling between harvested wheat-fields. There were circles and triangles etched into the stubble, shapes that reminded Winthrop of those on Rose's silver ribbon.

Winthrop looked at the new sun.

It was a wheel of fire, travelling in parallel with *Katie*. He pulled back the stick and climbed up into the sky, and the fire-shape climbed with him. Then it whizzed underneath the Camel and came up on his right side.

He looped up, back and below, feeling the tug of gravity in his head and the safety harness cutting into his shoulders. It would take a demon from hell to outfly a Sopwith Camel in anger, as the fire-wheel recognized instantly by shooting off like a Guy Fawkes rocket, whooshing up in a train of sparks.

Katie was now flying even, and sparks fell fizzing all around. Winthrop was afraid they were incendiaries of unknown design, but they passed *through* his fuselage and wings, dispersing across the fields.

His eyes were blotched with light-bursts. It was dark again and the fire-wheel gone. Winthrop recalled the stories of the signs in the sky at the time of Rose Farrar's disappearance. He assumed he had just had personal experience of them. He would make sure they went into the report.

Proper dawn was upon them.

A long straight stretch of road extended ahead of Crowley's car. They were nearing the outskirts of the city. Crowley's driver must be a good man, or possessed of magical skills, since the Bentley was lagging behind.

He knew he had to pull a reckless stunt.

Throttling *Katie* generously, he swooped low over the car and headed off to the left, getting as far ahead of Crowley as possible, then swung round in a tight semi-circle, getting his nose in alignment with the oncoming vehicle. He would only get one pass at this run.

He took her down, praying the road had been maintained recently.

Katie's wheels touched ground, lifted off for a moment, and touched ground again.

Through the whirling prop, Winthrop saw Crowley's car. They were on a collision course.

The car would be built more sturdily than the canvas and wood plane. But *Katie* had whirling twin blades in her nose, all the better to scythe through the car's bonnet and windshield, and severely inconvenience anyone in the front seat.

Crowley might think himself untouchable. But he wouldn't be doing his own driving.

Winthrop hoped a rational man was behind the wheel of Crowley's car.

The distance between the two speeding vehicles narrowed.

Winthrop was oddly relaxed, as always in combat. A certain fatalism possessed him. If it was the final prang, so be it. He whistled under his breath.

It had been a good life. He was grateful to have known Cat, and the Old Man. He had done his bit, and a bit more besides. And he was with *Katie* at the last.

Crowley's car swerved, plunging through a hedgerow. Winthrop whooped in triumph, exultant to be alive. He cut the motors and upturned the flaps. Wind tore at the wings as *Katie* slowed.

Another car was up ahead.

The Bentley.

14: 'I believe . . .'

Catriona pressed down on the foot-brake with all her strength. She was not encouraged by Sir Arthur's loud prayer. The aeroplane loomed large in the windshield, prop blades slowing but still deadly. She couldn't remember whether they were wood or metal, but guessed it wouldn't make much difference.

The Bentley and the Camel came to a halt, one screeching and the other purring, within a yard of each other. She recommenced breathing and unclenched her stomach. That was not an experience she would care to repeat.

Somewhat shaken, she and Sir Arthur climbed out of the car. Edwin was already on the ground, pulling off his flying helmet. He had his revolver.

'Come on, you fellows,' he said. 'The enemy's downed.'

She helped Sir Arthur along the road. The car they had been pursuing had jumped the verge and crashed into a hedge. Crowley was extricating himself from the front seat with some difficulty. A stunned driver sat in the long grass, thrown clear of his car, shaking his head.

The rear door of the car was kicked open and a female fury exploded from it.

Rose was in mostly human shape, but Catriona could tell from her blazing snake-eyes she had been filled with Crowley's cracked fancies. She was transformed into a species of demonic Zuleika Dobson, set to enslave and conquer and destroy London and then the world. As the dawnlight shone in the Anti-Christine's frizzy halo of hair, Catriona believed this creature was capable of fulfilling Crowley's mad prophecies. She was a young woman now, still recognisably the child she had been, but with a cast of feature that suggested monumental cruelty and desperate vice. Her hands were tipped with claw-nails.

Her inky eyes radiated something. Hypnotic black swirls wound in her pupils. She was humming, almost sub-audibly, radiating malicious female energy. Sir Arthur gasped. And Edwin skidded to a halt. The revolver fell from his hand.

Catriona was appalled. Even these men, whom she respected, were struck by Rose. Then, she was fascinated. It was alien to her, but she saw what magnificence this creature represented. This was not madness, but . . .

No, she decided. It was madness.

'You are powerless to stop her,' Crowley yelled. 'Bow down and worship her filthiness!'

Catriona fixed Rose's eyes with her own.

She took Sir Arthur's hand and reached out for Edwin's. He hesitated, eyes on Rose's body, then clutched. Catriona held these men fast.

It was Sir Arthur who gave her the idea. And, perhaps, another distinguished author-knight, J.M. Barrie.

'Do you believe in fairies?' she asked.

Crowley looked aghast.

Sir Arthur and Edwin understood.

With all her heart, she imagined benevolence, worshipped purity, conceived of goodness, was enchanted by kindly magic. As a child, she had loved indiscriminately, finding transcendent wonders in sparkling dew on spun webs, in fallen leaves become galleons on still ponds.

'*I* believe in fairies,' she declared.

She recognized her kinship with the kindly knight. She was a sceptic about many things, but there was real magic. She could catch it in her hand and shape it.

The English countryside opened up for her.

She truly believed.

Rose was transfixed. She dwindled inside her dressing gown, became a girl again. Dragonfly wings sprouted from her back, and delicate feelers extended from her eyebrows. She hovered a few inches above the grass. Flowers wound around her brow. She shone with clean light.

Sir Arthur was tearful with joy, transported by the sight. Edwin squeezed her hand.

Spring flowers sprouted in the autumn hedgerow.

Crowley was bewildered.

'No,' he said, 'you are scarlet, not watercolour.'

He was cracked and had lost.

'Come here,' Catriona said, to the girl.

Rose, eight years old again and human, skipped across the road and flew into her arms, hugging her innocently. Catriona

50

passed her on to Sir Arthur, who swept her up and held her fiercely to him.

'I think your new age has been postponed,' Edwin told Crowley.

'Curse you,' Crowley swore, shaking his fist like the melo-drama villain he wished he was.

'You're going to pay for the car, sir,' said the driver. 'Within the hour.'

Crowley was cowed. He looked like a big baby in daylight. His bald head was smudged and his trousers were badly ripped and stained.

There were new people on the scene. She supposed it was inevitable. You couldn't land a biplane and crash a car without attracting attention.

Two men stood on the other side of the road. Catriona didn't know where they could have come from. She had heard no vehicle and there were no dwellings in sight.

Rose twisted in Sir Arthur's hug to look at the men.

Catriona remembered what the girl had said about the friends of the Little People. Undertakers in smoked glasses.

The two men were the same height, tall even without their black top hats. They wore black frock coats, black trousers, black cravats, black gloves. Even black spats and black-tinted glasses that seemed too large for human eyes. Their faces were ghost-white, with thin lips.

'They've come for me,' Rose said. 'I must go away with them.'

Gently, Sir Arthur set her down. She kissed him, then kissed Catriona and Edwin, even Crowley.

'Don't worry about me,' she said, sounding grown-up, and went to the undertakers. They each took one of her hands and walked her down the road, towards a shimmering light. For a while, the three figures were silhouetted. They they were gone, and so was the light.

Edwin turned to look at her, and shrugged.

51

15: *The Vicinity of the Inexplicable*

The Old Man nodded sagely when Winthrop concluded his narrative. He did not seem surprised by even the most unusual details.

'We've come across these undertakers before,' Beauregard said. 'All in black, with hidden eyes. They appear often in the vicinity of the inexplicable. Like the Little Grey People.'

They were back in the Strangers' Room.

'I suppose we should worry about Rose,' Winthrop mused, 'but she told us not to. Considering that she seems to be whatever we think she is, she might have meant that it would be helpful if we thought of her as safe and well since she would then, in fact, be so. It was Cat who saw through it all, and hit upon the answer.'

Catriona was thoughtful.

'I don't know, Edwin,' she said. 'I don't think we saw a quarter of the real picture. The Little Grey People, the fire-wheel in the skies, the Changeling, the undertakers. All this has been going on for a long time, since well before the original Rose was taken away. We were caught between the interpretations put on the phenomena in the last few days by Sir Arthur and Crowley, fairies and the Anti-Christine. In the last century, it was angels and demons. Who knows what light future researchers will shine upon the business?'

Withrop sipped his excellent brandy.

'I shouldn't bother yourself too much about that, old thing. We stand at the dawn of a new era, not the apocalypse Crowley was prattling about but an age of scientific enlightenment. Mysteries will be penetrated by rational inquiry. We shall no longer need to whip up fairy tales to cope with the fantastical. Mark my words, Catty-Kit. The next time anything like this happens, we shall get to the bottom of it without panic or hysteria.'

THE END OF THE PIER SHOW

Icy winds barrelled in off the sea, lashing the front like an invisible tidal wave. Fred Regent shoved his fists deeper into the pockets of his yellow silk bomber jacket.

Apart from keeping his hands out of the cold blast, Fred was trying to prevent himself from constantly fingering the bee-fuzz on his scalp where he used to have hair like Peter Noone's. If his bonce went blue, it'd look like a copper's helmet and that'd be the end of this lark. Going undercover with the Boys now seemed a lot less like a comfortable way out of uniform and more like a protracted invitation to a busted mug and a cryo-dunking in the channel.

'It's April,' said Jaffa, the Führer Boy. 'Whatever happened to spring?'

'New ice age, mate,' said Oscar, the 'intellectual' of the Boys. 'Hitler's astrologers said it'd happen.'

The Boys clumped along the front, strutting in their steel-toed, cleat-soled Docs. They shivered as a razor-lash of wind cut through turn-up jeans, Fred Perry shirts and thin jackets. Only Oscar could get away with a duffel coat and Jaffa sometimes sneered 'mod' at him. The Boys were skins and hated mods; not to mention hippies, grebos, Pakkis, queers, students, coons, yids, chinks, car-park attendants, and – especially – coppers.

Fred wondered if the others felt the cold on their near-

53

exposed skulls the way he did. If so, they were too pretend-hard to mention it. Skinhead haircuts were one of the worst ideas ever. Just as the Boys were some of the worst people ever. It'd be a pleasure putting this bunch of yobs inside. If he lived that long.

The point of this seaside excursion was for Fred to get in with Jaffa. A bag of pills, supposedly nicked with aggro from a Pakistani chemist's, had bought him into the Boys. But Kevin Jaffa, so-called King Skin, didn't trust anyone until they'd helped him put the boot into a third party. It was sort of an initiation, but also made all his mates accomplices in the event of legal complications.

It had seemed a lot simpler back in London, following DI Price's briefing on King Skin and the Boys, getting into the part, learning the lingo ('Say "coon", not "nigger"') from a wheelchair-bound expert nark, picking out the wardrobe, even getting the haircut. Steel clippers snicking over his head like an insectile lawnmower. Now, barely two months out of Hendon, he was on his own, miles away from an incident room, with no one to shout for if he got on the receiving end of an unfriendly boot.

What was he supposed to do? How far was he supposed to go?

For the Boys, this was a pleasure trip, not business. And Fred was supposed to be stopping Jaffa's business.

On the train down, Jaffa had taken over a compartment, put his Docs up on the seat to defy British Rail, and encouraged everyone to pitch in ideas for entertainment. Nicking things, smashing things, getting plastered and snatching a shag were the most popular suggestions. Petty stuff, day-outing dirty deeds. Fred was supposed to let minor offences slide until he had the goods on one of Jaffa's Big Ideas, but he supposed he'd have to draw a line if it looked like some innocent was going to get hurt.

'Everything's bloody shut,' Doggo whined. 'I could do with six penn'orth of chips.'

Jaffa cuffed the smaller skin, who couldn't be older than fourteen.

'All you bloody think of is chips, Doggo. Set your sights higher.'

The shops along the front were mostly boarded over, battered by wind-blown sand and salt. Stacks of deckchairs down on the beach were chained down under tarpaulins. A few hardy dog-walkers were out and about. But no one else. The whole town was shut up and stored away.

They came to the pier.

'Let's take a look-see,' Jaffa suggested, climbing over a turnstile. There was a booth nearby but it wasn't manned. The Boys trooped after their leader, clumping on to shaky boards. They fought the wind, walking towards the pagoda-like green structure at the end of the pier.

On a board in the shape of an arrow was written *This way to "The Emporium", Palace of Wonders, Arcade of Education, Variety Nitely. Admission: 6d.* There was no admission price in new money.

As he clambered over the turnstile, Fred noticed a poster on the side of the booth. A comical drunk in a long army greatcoat sat in a pub with a slinky blonde draped round him. Half the woman's face was covered by a wave of hair; she was smoking a cigarette in a holder, the smoke forming a skull with swastika eye-sockets. The slogan was *Careless Talk Costs Lives.* The poster might have been up since the War.

No, the colours were too bright, as if just from the printer's. It must be part of an exhibition.

'Come on, Fred,' said Oscar. 'Last one in's a sissy.'

Seamouth wasn't big enough to support the pier these days, but it had been a fashionable resort around the turn of the century. Seventy-odd years of decline hadn't yet dragged the attraction into the sea. The structure projected out from the beach, struts and pillars temporarily resisting the eternal push and pull of the waves. It couldn't stand up on its own much longer. Everything creaked, like a ship at sea.

Looking down, Fred saw churning foam through ill-fitting, water-warped boards. He thought he saw crabs tossed around in the water.

They reached the Emporium. It was turquoise over gun-metal, the paint coming off in swathes. Ingraham put a dent in a panel with his armoured toe. Freckles flew off.

'This shed looks about ready to collapse,' Oscar said, shaking a loose railing. 'Maybe we should give it a shove.'

Oscar hopped from one foot to another, looking like a clog-dancer, shoulders heaving.

'Everything's shut,' Doggo whined.

Jaffa sneered with pity at the kid. A three-inch orange line on the King Skin's scalp looked like a knife scar but was a birth malformation, skull-plates not knit properly. It was probably why he was a psycho nutter. With an elbow, Jaffa smashed a pane of glass and reached inside. He undid a clasp and pulled a door open, then stood aside like a doorman, indicating the way in.

Doggo straightened himself, took hold of his lapels, and strutted past. Jaffa tripped him and put a boot on his backside, shoving the kid into the dark.

Doggo whined as he hit the floor.

Jaffa went inside and the Boys followed.

Fred got out his lighter and flicked on a flame. The Emporium seemed bigger inside than it had on the outside, like Doctor Who's police box. There were posters up on free-standing boards, announcing shows and exhibitions that must have closed years ago, or attractions that were only open in the two weeks that passed for Summer on the South Coast. *Mysteries of the Empire, Chu Chin Chow, Annual Talent Contest.*

'Don't think anyone's home,' Oscar said.

Fred noticed Jaffa was interested in the pier, but couldn't understand why. There was nothing here to nick, no one to put the boot into, nothing much worth smashing, certainly no bints to shag. But Jaffa had been drawn here. The King Skin was on some private excursion in his own head.

Was there something going on?

Stepping into the Emporium, Fred felt a sense of being on edge, of something just out of sight watching. The atmosphere was heavy, between the smell of the sea and the mustiness of damp and forgotten exhibits. There was a greenish submarine glow, the last of cloudy daylight filtered through painted-over glass.

'I don't like it,' whined Doggo.

Jaffa launched a half-strength kick into the kid's gut, curling him into a fetal horseshoe around his boot. Doggo's lungs emptied and his face shut. He was determined not to cry, poor bastard.

If there wasn't a Pakki or a hippie or a queer about, Jaffa was just as happy to do over one of his mates. DI Price thought there might be something political or big-time criminal about the Boys, but it was just brutishness, a small-minded need to hurt someone else.

Fred's fists knotted in his pockets. He wanted this over, and Jaffa put away.

It was getting dark outside and it couldn't be later than seven. This was a weird stretch of the coast.

Oscar was looking at the posters.

'This sounds great,' he said.

Hitler's Horrors: The Beasts of War.

The illustration was crude, circus-like. A caricature storm-trooper with fangs, machine-gun held up like an erection, crushing a map of Europe under jackboots.

He remembered the *Careless Talk Costs Lives* poster. This looked like a propaganda show left over from the War. Twenty-five years too late to scare the kiddies, but too bloody nasty to get nostalgic about. Fred's parents and their friends were always on about how it had been in the War, when everyone was pulling together. But Fred couldn't see it. He came along too late, and only just remembered when chocolate was rationed and half the street was bomb sites.

57

Ingraham clicked his heels and gave a Nazi salute. He was the pretend fascist, always reading paperbacks about the German side of WWII, ranting against Jews, wearing swastika medallions. He talked about 'actions' rather than 'aggro', and fancied himself as the Boys' Master Planner, the Goebbels of the Gormless. Not dangerous, just stupid.

Fred's lighter was getting hot. He let the flame shrink. The stormtrooper's eyes seemed to look down as the light went away.

There was a gushing trickle and a sharp smell. One of the skins was relieving himself against a wall.

'Dirty beast,' Oscar sneered.

'Don't like it here,' whined Doggo.

Fred knew what the kid meant.

'Doggo's right,' Jaffa said. 'Let's torch this shithole. Fred, you still got fluid in that lighter?'

If he helped, he'd be committing a crime, compromising any testimony he gave.

'It's out, chum,' he said.

'I got matches,' said Ingraham.

'Give the boy a prize,' said Jaffa.

Ingraham passed over the Swan Vestas. Jaffa had the others scout for newspapers or anything small that would burn. After hesitating a moment, Fred started ferreting around too. Arson, he could just about live with. At least it wasn't duffing up some corner shop keeper or holding a bint down while the others shagged her. And there was something about the pier. He wouldn't mind if it burned. By sticking out from the shore, it was inviting destruction. Fire or water, it didn't make much difference.

They split up. Though the Emporium was partitioned into various spaces, the walls only reached just above head height. Above everything was a tent-like roof of glass panels like Crystal Palace, painted over with wavy green.

He found a row of penny-in-the-slot machines, lit up by tiny interior bulbs. He had three big dull old pennies mixed in with the shiny toy money that now passed for small change, and felt compelled to play the machines.

In smeary glass cases were little puppet scenes that played out tiny dramas. The theme of the collection was execution. A French Revolution guillotining: head falling into a basket as the blade fell on the neck of a tin aristocrat. A British public hanging: felon plunging on string through a scaffold trap-door, neck kinking with the drop. An Indian Mutiny reprisal: rebel strapped over the end of a cannon that discharged with a puff to blow away his midriff.

When he ran out of proper pennies – d. not p. – he wasn't sorry that he couldn't play the Mexican firing squad, the Spanish garrotting or the American electrocution. The little death scenes struck him as a funny sort of entertainment for kiddies. When the new money had completely taken over, penny-in-the-slot machines would all get chucked out and that would be the end of that.

Round the corner from the machines was a dark passage. He tripped over something. Someone. Scrambling up, he felt the bundle. He flicked on his lighter again. The flamelight was reflected in a bloody smear that had been a face. From the anorak, Fred recognized Oscar. He was still barely alive, cheeks seeping in time with his neck-pulse. Something had torn the hood of flesh from his skull, leaving a ragged line along his chin. He wasn't a skinhead any more; he was a skinned head.

Fred stood. He hadn't heard anything. Had Jaffa done this, somehow? Or was there someone else in here?

'Over here,' he called. 'It's Oscar.'

Doggo was the first there. He took one look and screamed, sounding very young. Ingraham slapped him.

Jaffa had a flick-knife out. Its blade was clean, but he could have wiped it.

'Did you do this?' Jaffa asked Fred.

Fred heard himself whimpering.

'Fuck me,' someone said. Everyone shouted, talked and moaned. Someone was sick.

'Shut up,' said Jaffa.

In the quiet, something was moving. Fred turned up the flame. The Boys huddled in the circle of light, scared cavemen imagining spirits in the dark beyond the fire. Something heavy was dragging itself, knocking things aside. And something smaller, lighter, pattered along on its own. They were circling the skinheads, getting closer.

The lighter was a hot coal in Fred's fingers. They all turned round, peering into the dark. There were partitions, covered with more posters, and glass cases full of battlefield dioramas. Nearest was a wall-sized cartoon of a bug-eyed demon Hitler scarfing down corpses, spearing a woman on his red, forked tail.

The heavy thing held back and the light thing was getting closer. Were there only two? Fred was sure he heard other movements, other footfalls. The steps didn't sound like shod feet. But there was more than an animal purpose in the movement.

Doggo was whimpering.

Even Jaffa was scared. The King Skin had imagined he was the devil in the darkness; now that was a shredded illusion. There were worse things out there than in here.

Fred's fingers were in agony but he didn't dare let the flame fall.

The Hitler poster tipped forwards, cracking down the middle. Hitler's face broke in half. And another Hitler face – angry eyes, fleck of moustache, oiled hairlick – thrust forward into the light, teeth bared. A child-sized figure in a puffy grey Hitler mask reached out with gorilla-length arms.

Fred dropped the lighter.

Something heavy fell on them, a living net of slithering strands.

There was screaming all around.

He was hit in the face by a dead hand.

The net cut against his palm like piano-wire. Seaweed wound between the strings stung, like nettles. A welt rose across his face.

The net was pulled away.

Warm wetness splashed on his chest, soaking in. Something flailed in the dark, meatily tearing.

Someone was being killed.

He blundered backwards, slamming into a partition that hadn't been there, a leathery elephant's hide that resisted a little, and shifted out of the way. His palm was sandpapered by the moving, living wall.

There was a gunshot, a fireflash and a loud report. Fred's eyes burned for a moment but he wasn't hit. Someone else had taken a bullet.

In the momentary light, he'd seen things he didn't believe. Uniformed creatures falling upon the Boys with human intellect and demon savagery. Doggo's head a yard from his body, stringy bone and muscle unravelling between his neck and shoulders. On his chest squatted something with green wolf-eyes and a foot of lolling tongue.

Fred bolted and collided with someone.

'Fucking hell,' said Jaffa, gripping Fred's arm.

They ran together, skinhead and copper, fleeing the other things. They made for a cold indraught of outside air.

Something came after them.

Jaffa pushed ahead and was first through the door.

None of the others was with them.

Fred stumbled out of the Emporium. They couldn't have been inside more than fifteen minutes, but night had fallen. There was no light from the town, no yellow street lamps, no electric glow from homes up on the hill. The shapes of buildings were just discernible, but it was as if no one was home.

Jaffa turned to Fred, knife raised.

An orange tendril snaked out of the Emporium at chest height and brushed Jaffa's head. It was like a squirt of living flame. The King Skin's eyes widened and mouth opened, but the fire took hold inside his skull and poured out.

He was still recognisable, still alive. Fred ran away, encumbered by the heavy boots he wasn't used to. Jaffa, a living candle, stumped after him. Fred vaulted the turnstile and looked back. Jaffa's head was a pumpkin lantern, rushing forwards in the dark.

Fred tripped and fell to his knees. He looked back, not believing what he saw.

'Oi you,' someone shouted, at Jaffa.

The man in uniform stood near Fred, shaking his fist. He had a tommy's tin helmet, but wore police-style blue serge. An armband bore the letters ARP. He was in his sixties, and had no chin to speak of, just a helmet strap under his lower lip.

Fred was near fainting.

The King Skin stopped, flame pluming six or seven feet above his head, and howled.

'Oi you,' the ARP man shouted again, *'put that bloody light out!'*

'Then Jaffa was blown to one side, as if the wind had caught hold of his fire. He was pitched against the loose railings and went over the side, trailing orange and red flames. He hit the sea with a hiss. Then everything went completely black. When I woke, it was early in the morning. The bloke in the tin hat was gone. I hot-footed it for the station and got the first train back here.

'There's something not right in Seamouth.'

As he told his story, Fred concentrated on Euan Price's cold eyes. The Detective Inspector asked few questions and took no notes. He didn't interject exclamations of disbelief, or shout at him that he was a nutter or on drugs or just plain lying.

Yesterday, Constable Fred Regent had lived in a world with law and order. Now, there was only anarchy.

He sat at the desk in the interview room, feeling himself under the spotlight, cold cup of New Scotland Yard tea in front of him. Price sat opposite, listening. The strangers leaned on the sound-proofed walls, half in and half out of the light.

It disturbed him that Price could accept the horror story with such serious calm. Either his superior believed him, or the consultants were psychiatrists in disguise.

There were two of them, dressed like peacocks.

The woman was in her early twenties and could have been a model: seamless mane of red hair down to her waist; Italian mouth, painted silver; Viking cheekbones; unnaturally huge, green eyes. She wore a purple leather miniskirt and matching waistcoat with a blinding white roll-neck pullover and knee-length high-heeled white boots. Her only visible jewelry was an Egyptian-looking silver amulet with an inset emerald. A red scar-line cut through one fine eyebrow, a flaw to set off perfection.

The man was even more striking. He could have been anywhere between thirty and fifty. A coal-black mass of ringlets spilled on to his shoulders, Charles II style, and he wore a pencil-line Fu Manchu moustache. His face was gaunt to the point of unhealthiness and dark enough to pass for a Sicilian or a Tuareg. Thin and tall and bony, he wore a fluorescent green velvet jacket with built-up lapels and collar, tight red Guardsman's breeches with a yellow stripe up the sides and stack-heeled, elastic-sided, banana-coloured boots. A multi-coloured explosion of a scarf was knotted round his neck, and his shirt was rippling mauve silk. He had several rings on each finger, a silver belt-buckle in the shape of a demon face with a curvy dagger thrust through its eyes, and a single gold hoop on his right ear.

As he listened to Fred's story, he played with a wide-brimmed fedora that matched his jacket, slipping long fingers in and out of a speckled snakeskin band. He looked as if he'd be equally happy on the foredeck of a pirate ship or in a coffee bar on the King's Road.

The contrast with Euan Price in his Marks & Sparks mac was vivid. Whoever these consultants were, they were not with the police.

Though they were the sort he had been taught at Hendon to

regard as suspicious, Fred had a warm feeling from these two. They might dress strangely, but did not look at him as if they thought he were a maniac. As he went through it all, starting with his undercover job but concentrating on the happenings at Seamouth Pier, the woman nodded in sympathy and understanding. The man's violet eyes seemed to glint with tiny fireflies.

Fred had expected to be dismissed as a madman.

After the story was done, Price made introductions.

'Constable Regent,' he said, 'this is Mr Richard Jeperson.'

The man fluttered a hand and curved his thin lips into a smile. As his frilly mauve cuff flapped, Fred caught sight of tiny blue marks on his wrist. Some sort of tattoo.

'I represent the Diogenes Club,' Jeperson drawled, voice rich and deep as a BBC announcer. 'A branch of government you won't have heard of. Now you have heard of it, you'll probably be required to sign the Official Secrets Act in blood. Our speciality is affairs like this, matters in which conventional methods of policing or diplomacy or defence come up short. I gather you are still reeling from the revelation that the world is not what you once thought it was.'

Fred thought the man had read his mind.

'You can take some comfort from the fact that the Diogenes Club, which is a very old institution, has always known a little of the true state of things. There has often been someone like me on the lists of HM Government, a private individual with a public office, retained for circumstances like this.'

'This has happened before?' Fred asked.

'Not *this*, precisely. But things *like* this, certainly. Impossible obtrusions into the mundane. Vanessa and I have pursued several of these tricky bits of business to more or less satisfactory conclusions.'

The woman – Vanessa – smiled. Her teeth were dazzling.

'With your help, we shall see what we can do here,' said Jeperson.

'With my help?'

A spasm of panic gripped him.

'You're detailed to work with Mr Jeperson,' Price told him. 'Out of uniform.'

'Topping,' Jeperson said, holding out his hand.

Fred stood up and shook Jeperson's hand, feeling the smoothness of his rings and the leather of his palm. This was a man who had done hard outdoor work.

Looking down, he noticed the blue marks again. A row of numbers.

'We should probably take a spin down to the coast,' Jeperson said. 'Take a look at Seamouth.'

Fred was suddenly cold again.

'It'll be fun to go to the seaside.'

It didn't take detective work to deduce which of the vehicles in the New Scotland Yard car park belonged to Richard Jeperson. It was a silver-grey Rolls-Royce the size of a speed-boat, bonnet shaped like a cathedral nave, body stream-lined to break land speed records.

Fred whistled.

'It's a ShadowShark, you know,' Jeperson said, running his fingers across the RR Spirit of Ecstasy symbol. 'They only made five. I have three.'

Parked among the panda cars and civilian Minis, the car was a lion in a herd of deer.

'Hop in the back, Fred,' Jeperson said, with easy familiarity, opening the rear door. Fred slipped on to soft black leather and inhaled luxury. Two fresh roses were propped in sconces. Surprisingly, Jeperson joined him. Vanessa got into the driver's seat.

'Vanessa'd win Brooklands if they'd let her enter. She can drive anything.'

'I'm learning to fly a jump jet,' she said, over her shoulder. 'Perk of the position.'

She disengaged the hand-brake and turned the key. The engine purred and she manoeuvred the ShadowShark out of the car park. Fred noticed her confidence at the wheel. He doubted if he'd be as blithe handling such a powerful (and expensive) car.

'Don't hurry,' Jeperson told her. 'I want to stop for a pub lunch on the way. Have a spot of rumination.'

Vanessa headed for the South Coast road, cruising through the thinning traffic. Fred found himself relaxing, enjoying the head-turns of other motorists. Jeperson obviously didn't believe in blending in with the crowd.

'A sort of uncle of mine lives in Seamouth,' Jeperson said. 'Brigadier-General Sir Giles Gallant. We'll have to look him up. He sat on the Ruling Cabal with Jeffrey Jeperson.'

'Your father?' Fred asked.

Jeperson's eyes were unreadable.

'Adoptive,' he said. 'Picked me out. In the War.'

'And this Sir Giles?'

'Also with our mob, I'm afraid. Diogenes Club. At least, he was once. Retired now. You'll find, now you know to look, that we pop up all over the board. Unless I very much miss my guess, Sir Giles will know something about your End of the Pier Show. He's too sharp to live near an incident like this jaunt without feeling tingles in the cobweb. We'll probably set up camp at his house.'

Everything since the pier seemed unreal. Only now that he was on the road back to Seamouth did Fred realize quite how the pattern was broken. He had been handed over into the care of this odd stranger, almost palmed off on the man. What disturbed him most was that Jeperson actually seemed to know what was going on, to accept the insanity without question, without even registering shock or disbelief.

It would be easy to be afraid.

'What about the Seamouth police?' Fred asked.

'Tell you what, I don't think we'll trouble them until we have to. I like to keep my involvement with the authorities limited to a few enlightened souls like Euan Price. Too many plods have the habit of not seeing what they don't want to. No offence, Constable Regent. Your mob like to tie up neat little parcels and sometimes all we can give them is a dirty great mess.'

If he shut his eyes for a moment, Fred saw what the gun-flash had shown him on the pier. A hellish scene, impossible to understand, hideously vivid. Real, and yet . . .

'What was the first thing?' Jeperson asked, quickly. 'The first thing that told you things weren't in whack. Don't think, answer.'

'Careless Talk Costs Lives,' he said, just seeing it.

'And Loose Lips Sink Ships.'

'It was a poster. An old one, from the War. But it wasn't old, faded. It had been put up recently.'

'Bingo, an apport!'

'What's an apport?'

'Something which shouldn't done ought to be there but bloody well just is. Mediums often materialize the fellahs, but this isn't like that. Nothing consciously evoked. This came with the house, like wallpaper.'

'I thought there might be an exhibition.'

'There's always that possibility. Prosaic, but nonetheless not out of the question.' Jeperson seemed a little disappointed. 'Any funny smell? Ozone?'

'Just the sea.'

'The sea, my dear Fred, is not in the "just the" category. It's the oldest living thing on the planet. It abides, it shifts, it shrinks, it grows, it senses, it hints.'

They were out in the country now, bombing through winding lanes at ninety. Fred gripped the armrest on the door, reacting to the rush.

'We have a dispensation,' Jeperson explained. 'Speed limits do not apply to us. We take great risks for our country, so the least the Queen can do is exempt us from a few of the pettier regulations that bind the rest of her subjects. With Vanessa at the wheel, we needn't worry about accidents.'

They took a blind corner at speed. The road ahead was clear. 'She has second sight, poor love.'

The country pub where Jeperson had hoped to lunch was gone, knocked down and replaced by a Jolly Glutton. Fred had been in these places before; they were popping up beside motorways and A roads all over the country. Everything was brand new but already tarnished. A big cartoon Friar Tuck was the place's mascot and the struggling waitresses dressed as monkettes with hooded robes and miniskirts. The fare was flat pies and crinkle-shaped chips, hot enough to disguise the lack of taste, and tea worse than the stuff served at the Yard out of a machine.

Jeperson was disappointed, but decided to sample the place anyway.

As he looked at his Jolly Fare, the man from the Diogenes Club slumped in dejection. He lifted a sprig of plastic parsley from his wriggly chips and dropped it into the full tin ashtray on the formica-topped table.

'What's the world coming to?' he asked, eyes liquid with pain.

The Jolly Glutton catered to shabby couples with extremely loud children. In the next booth, a knot of youths with Jaffa haircuts messed around with the plastic tomatoes of ketchup, and tried to get their hands up the waitresses' skirts.

'I wonder what happened to the regulars? Did they find another pub somewhere? With decent beer and proper food? Or did the fat Friar have them hanged in the forest to silence their poor plaints?'

Jeperson knit his brows, and concentrated.

Suddenly, Fred smelled beer, heard the clink of glasses, the soft grumble of rural accents, saw the comforting smoky gloom of the snug. Then, it was all snatched away.

'What did you just do?' he asked Jeperson.

'Sorry,' Jeperson said. 'Didn't mean to impose. It's a nasty little knack sometimes. Call it wishful thinking.'

'I knew what you were seeing.'

Jeperson shrugged, but the tiny glints in his eyes were not apologetic. Fred had a sense of the man's power.

'I don't fancy the one with the 'tache,' a voice said, 'but 'er with the legs'd do for a shag.'

It was the skinheads in the next booth. They were propped up on the table and seats, leaning over the partition, looking down at Vanessa, who was sitting opposite Fred and Jeperson.

'Bloody hippie,' said the kid who had spoken. His left eye twitched. 'Hair like a girl's.'

Jeperson looked at the skin almost with pity.

'You should have seen this place the way it was,' he said. 'It was a comfort in a cold world.'

The skin didn't understand.

'What are you doing with this pouf?' Twitch asked Fred.

For a moment, he was confused. Then he remembered what his head looked like.

'I'm taking your girlfriend,' Twitch said.

Fred didn't know whether the skin meant Vanessa or Jeperson.

Twitch, who was smaller and duller than Jaffa, put his hand on Vanessa's neck, lifting aside her hair.

Jeperson nodded, almost imperceptibly, to the girl.

Vanessa reached up, swiftly, and took Twitch's ear in a firm grip. She pulled him off his perch and slammed his face into her plate of uneaten chips.

'You can look but you better not touch,' she whispered into his red ear.

Twitch's friends, an older bloke with a Rupert scarf and a wide-shouldered hulk, were astonished.

Vanessa pushed Twitch off the table and dropped him on the chessboard-tiled floor. He had maggot-shaped mashed chips all over his face.

Everyone in the Jolly Glutton was paying attention.

Twitch pulled out a sharpened screwdriver but Jeperson

stepped on his wrist, bringing down a blocky yellow heel on crunching bones. The pig-sticker rolled away.

'I'll have that,' Jeperson said, picking up the homemade shank with distaste. 'Nasty thing.'

Fred was penned into the booth – these bolted-down plastic chairs and tables were traps – but Vanessa stood up and slipped out. All her movements were effortless; she wasn't just made for show.

'I'd advise you to pick up your friend and get back to your delicious fare,' Jeperson said, to Rupert Scarf and Shoulders. 'My associate doesn't want to hurt you.'

The two skins looked Vanessa up and down, and made a mistake.

Shoulders clumped forward, big hands out, and was on the floor before Fred could work out what Vanessa had done to him. She seemed to have stuck her fingers into his throat and sternum, making a cattle prod of her hand. Shoulders made a lot of noise about going down and rolled over Twitch, groaning that he was crippled.

Rupert Scarf spread his hands and backed away. The message had got through.

Shoulders, still moaning, got up on his hands and knees, snarled and made another grab at Vanessa. She whirled like a ballet dancer and stuck the white point of her boot into his ear, lifting him off the floor for a moment and laying him flat out. Her hair spun round with her and fell perfectly into place. She was smiling slightly, but didn't seem to feel the strain.

Rupert Scarf pulled Twitch up, and together they picked up Shoulders.

'You're a dead dolly-mixture,' Twitch said, retreating.

Vanessa smiled, eyebrows raised.

The skins left the restaurant. All the other customers, and the waitresses, applauded. Vanessa took a bow.

'Three more friends for life,' she said.

They continued by B roads. After the Jolly Glutton, Jeperson slumped into a fugue of despair. He said nothing, but his mood was heavy. Fred was beginning to sense that the man from the Diogenes Club was remarkably open. A changeable personality, he felt things so deeply that there was an overspill from his head, which washed on to anyone around him. Just now, Fred was lapped by the waters of Jeperson's gloom. It was the loss of his beloved country pub as much as the encounter with the yobs, maybe the loss of his beloved country.

Vanessa kept away from the main road, casually driving through smaller and smaller villages. Greenery flashed by, stretches of thickly wooded land alternating with patchwork-quilt landscapes of fields and hedgerows. Brooks and stiles and tree-canopied roads. Tiny old churches and thatched cottages. A vicar on a bicycle.

This didn't seem to be the same world as the Jolly Glutton. No formica, no plastic tomatoes, no crinkle-cut chips.

Jeperson stirred a little and looked through the tinted window.

'Spring seems to have sprung,' he announced.

It was true. This was a fresh season.

The ShadowShark crested a hill. The road gently sloped down towards sparkling sea. Seamouth was spread out, sun shining on red tile roofs. Gulls wheeled high in the air. A small boat cut through the swell, tacking out in Seamouth Bay.

It was very different from the dull day with the Boys, when the sea had been churning grey soup.

Fred saw the pier, a finger stretched out into the sea. He had another flash. Jeperson shivered.

'Looks like a picture postcard,' he said. 'But we know something nasty is written on the back. There are things moving under the surface.'

Fred tried to conquer his fear.

'Drive on, Vanessa love,' Jeperson said.

Seamouth spread up away from the front on to the rolling downs, bounded to the East by the cliffs and to the West by a stretch of shivering sands. Overlooking the sea were serried ranks of whitewashed villas, at least a third called Sea View.

The ShadowShark attracted some friendly attention. Folks looked up from their gardening to wave and smile. A postman paused and gave a smart salute. Fred was almost touched.

'It's nearly four o'clock,' he said. 'That postie should have finished work hours ago.'

'Second afternoon post?' Jeperson suggested.

'Not in this decade.'

'I suppose not.'

Vanessa found Raleigh Avenue, where Brigadier-General Sir Giles Gallant lived. His villa was called The Laurels. Rich green bushes, planted all around, did their best to seem like trees.

The cars outside the villas were all well-preserved but out-of-date. There wasn't a Mini or an Imp in sight, just big, elegant machines, polished to perfection, invisibly mended where they'd pranged.

They parked in the driveway of The Laurels and got out. Fred's legs had gone rubbery on the long drive and he stamped a bit on the gravel to get his circulation back.

'Good afternoon,' said a man in overalls, looking up from his spade-work. 'Here to see the Brig?'

'Yes, indeed,' said Jeperson.

'Top hole,' said the neighbour. 'I'm Marshall Michaelsmith. Two names, not three.'

Michaelsmith was a game old bird of perhaps seventy, with snow-white hair and red cheeks. He had been digging vigorously, turning over a flower-bed. A stack of pulled-up rose-bushes lay discarded on the lawn. There were a few plants left, tied to bamboo spears.

'I'm with the Brig on the Committee,' Michaelsmith said.

He tore up another rose-bush by the roots and threw it away, momentarily sad.

'Shame to do it,' he said. 'The missus loves these blooms, worked at them for years. But one has to do one's bit. I'm putting in potatoes, cabbages, rhubarb. Dig for Victory, eh?'

The last of the roses was gone.

'The missus has taken to her bed. For the duration, probably. Still, she'll be up and about in the end.'

Michaelsmith stood on his ravaged flower-bed.

'The Brig's in town, on official business. I'll see if we can scrounge you some tea in the meantime. Come into my parlour. This way, miss.'

Michaelsmith escorted Vanessa, extending a courteous arm to steady her across the rough earth. Fred and Jeperson followed.

'I hear you girls are doing your bit too,' Michaelsmith said to Vanessa. 'Before it all got too much, the missus was the same. Backs to the land, girls. Jolly good show. We must all pull together, see it through. Right will prevail, my dear. Oh yes it will. Always does in the end. Never doubt it for a moment.'

Fred gathered Marshall Michaelsmith was a bit potty. Slung on the old man's back was a khaki satchel. Fred recognized the shape. His Dad had kept his gas mask well past the Festival of Britain. Michaelsmith's looked to be in good order, ready to pull on in an instant.

Jeperson hung back a little, looking around.

Mrs MacAlister, Marshall Michaelsmith's Scots housekeeper, brought in a silver tea-service, and Michaelsmith poured them all cups of Lipton's. He made a ritual of it, using a strainer to catch the leaves, apologising for the thinness of the brew and the condensed milk.

Michaelsmith talked about the half-brick in his cistern, to cut down on the water flushed away, and the line drawn in his bath to keep the level down to four inches. He seemed proud of his austerity measures.

Fred supposed the old man had got into the habit during the War and never let up.

Michaelsmith's reception room was cosily cluttered, with a

73

view of the back garden through french windows. There was a black-bordered photograph of a young man in naval uniform on the piano.

'Mitch, my brother,' Michaelsmith explained. 'Went down at Jutland. In the last show.'

Jeperson sipped his tea and breathed in the atmosphere.

Somehow, even in banana-coloured boots, he fitted in the room. Fred supposed he was such an odd sort that he'd do anywhere. Since arriving here, Jeperson had been paying close attention. It wasn't just a question of one dotty old man.

Michaelsmith was taken with Vanessa, and no wonder. He was explaining all the family photographs. There were a great many of 'the missus', following her from long-faced youth through middle-aged elegance to painful frailty.

The french windows opened and a man in uniform stepped into the room. Michaelsmith stood to attention.

'Richard,' the newcomer exclaimed. 'This is a surprise. What brings you to this backwater?'

'The usual thing, Giles.'

The man – Sir Giles Gallant – was suddenly serious.

'Here? I don't believe it.'

Jeperson stood up and embraced Gallant, like a Frenchman.

'The lovely Vanessa, you know,' Jeperson said. Sir Giles clicked his heels and Vanessa demurely bobbed. 'And this is Fred Regent. He's the new bug.'

'Pleased to meet you,' Sir Giles said, inflicting a bone-crushing handshake. 'We need all the good men we can get.'

Brigadier-General Sir Giles Gallant must have been about the same age as Michaelsmith, but his manner suggested a much younger man. He was iron, where his friend was willow. His grey hair was still streaked with black and his hawk eyes were bright. He wore no rank insignia, but his perfectly pressed khakis denoted obvious officer status. He struck Fred as a very determined man.

'It's your pier we're interested in, Giles,' Jeperson said. 'Seems to be infested with apports. And other nastinesses.'

'The pier?' Sir Giles was taken aback. 'Should have blown it up years ago. Damn thing's a shipping hazard.'

'But it's not just the pier,' Jeperson said.

'No,' Sir Giles said, 'you're quite right, Richard. I should have called Diogenes myself.'

Fred remembered Richard had said Sir Giles would know what was going on.

'I thought I could cope on my own. I'm sorry.'

'No apologies, Giles.'

'Of course not.'

'We'll set up HQ at your place. I'll go over the whole thing with you. Vanessa, take the worthy Fred for a walk along the front, would you? I needn't tell you to stay away from the pier, but keep an eye out for oddities.'

Fred was alarmed, but at least he knew Vanessa could take care of herself. And him too, probably, though that hardly did anything for his confidence.

'It's a mild evening,' Jeperson said. 'You might go for a paddle.'

They walked down towards the front, zig-zagging downwards through neat, quiet roads. The sky darkened by degrees.

'Have you noticed?' Vanessa said. 'No one's turning their lights on.'

Fred looked at the windows of the villas.

'If they did, you couldn't tell,' he said. 'The houses all have those thick black curtains.'

'I knew people were conformists in these parts, but it's beyond the bounds of probability that every Sea View should have the same curtains. Whatever happened to white net?'

They looked over rows of roofs, towards the sea.

'There's something missing,' Vanessa said.

Fred saw it.

'Television aerials. There aren't any.'

'Well spotted, that man.'

'Time seems to stand still. I noticed it the first time.'

75

He didn't want to think further on that line.

'I feel I've come in on the last act of the panto,' he said. 'How did you get into this business?'

'Like you. I took a turn off the road, and realized things were not as they seem.'

'Meaning?'

'Have you ever heard of demonic possession?'

'I think so.'

'I don't recommend it.'

'Mr Jeperson is an exorcist?'

'Not quite. He's trickier than that. At heart, he's a sensitive.'

'He seems a funny bloke.'

'He's had a funny life.'

They were at the front. There were people around. The locals smiled and bade them good evening, but hurried on their way. The streetlamps did not come on.

'On his wrist,' Fred began.

'The numbers? They're what you think.'

'Concentration camp?'

'Death camp, actually. His foster father and Sir Giles were with the unit that liberated the place. They pulled him out. He was just a kid then.'

'Is he Jewish?'

'Almost certainly not,' she said. 'He doesn't actually know. He has no memory of anything before the camp. I've always assumed he was born a gypsy. But he's as British as you can get.'

'And this club?'

'The Diogenes Club. They collect useful people. They've been doing it for centuries. Richard's talents were obvious, much showier then than now, if you can credit it. Probably why he was in the camp. Old Mr Jeperson – he died a few years ago – adopted the boy, sent him to his old school, brought him up. Shaped him and trained him. That wasn't easy for either of them. Richard's no one's cat's paw. He's a free agent.'

'What about you?'

'I've been collected too. And now, so have you.'

A chill breeze made him hug his jacket. He still wore his skinhead outfit. He was getting used to it. The Peter Noone haircut had made him look as big a prat as . . . well, as Peter Noone. It was time someone reclaimed the skin look from thugs like Jaffa.

They had been ambling along the front, deliberately walking away from the pier. Now, they stopped, leaned on railings, and looked out to sea.

Waves rolled in, lapping the sands. Wreaths of kelp tangled on rocks. A man in a straw hat, barefooted with his trousers rolled up to the knee, pottered among the pools, collecting seashells.

'It's an idyll,' Vanessa said. 'You'd never think there was a war on.'

'What war?' Fred asked, shocked.

'There's always a war, Fred.'

Back at The Laurels, they found Jeperson and Sir Giles in a book-lined study, snifting brandy from glasses the size of human heads.

'How's town?' Jeperson asked.

'Quiet,' Vanessa commented.

'Always the way.'

'I've decided to bring the pier up on the Committee,' Sir Giles said. 'It's been shut down for years. Time to get rid of it altogether.'

'Let's not be too hasty,' Jeperson said. 'Our problem may not be the pier itself, but something that happens to be there at the moment. If you get rid of the structure, the problem might deem it an opportune moment to move inland.'

Sir Giles offered Fred, but not Vanessa, a drink. He thought it best not to accept.

'I'll call the Committee anyway,' Sir Giles said. 'Best to alert them all to the danger. Shan't be a sec.'

Jeperson smiled and sipped as Sir Giles left the room. Once the door was closed, his face shut down.

'We must get out of this house,' he said, serious.

Vanessa accepted without question.

The windows were fastened and barred. The study door was locked. Fred was surprised.

He didn't ask what was going on.

Vanessa handed Jeperson a hairpin. He unbent it and picked the lock. It was done in seconds. Jeperson was pleased with himself and not in too much of a hurry to take a bow. He opened the door a crack. Sir Giles was in the hallway, on the telephone.

'We must act fast,' Sir Giles was saying. 'You don't know this man.'

Their host was between them and the front door.

Jeperson stepped silently out into the hallway.

'Giles,' he said, sharply.

Sir Giles turned, face guilty. He muttered something, and hung up.

'Richard.' He attempted a genial smile. Without much success. Brigadier-General Sir Giles Gallant was sweating and shifting.

Jeperson bent the hairpin back into shape and returned it to Vanessa.

'We should do each other the courtesy of being honest,' Jeperson said. 'You of all people know how difficult it is to deceive someone like me.'

'I would have told you,' Sir Giles said. 'I wanted you to hear it from the whole Committee.'

The door opened and uniformed men came in. With guns. Six of them. All middle-aged or older, but hard-faced, smart in khakis. Bright eyes and clipped moustaches. Proper soldier boys. Rifles were levelled.

'This is for the best, Richard.'

'Who decides?' Jeperson asked.

'We do,' Sir Giles claimed. 'We've earned that right.'

Fred was lost. He didn't know who was who and who was on whose side.

Jeperson sank to the floor, knees bowing outwards as he fit into a lotus position. The rifle barrels followed him. Fred saw the tension in his back. He pressed his palms together, shut his eyes, and hummed almost below the threshold of hearing.

Sir Giles looked torn. For an instant, Fred thought he was about to order his men to fire. Instead, he stepped forwards, raising the telephone receiver like a club, aiming a blow at Jeperson's head.

It never connected.

Sir Giles was caught – by Jeperson's humming? – and froze, receiver held above his head, cord dangling. His face showed a struggle.

The humming was louder, machine-like, insectile.

What was Jeperson doing?

The men with guns took their directions from Sir Giles. They were spectators. Sir Giles was fighting. He wrestled the receiver, trying to bring it down. Jeperson rose as he had sunk, unbending himself. He was projecting something from inside. Static electricity crackled in his hair.

Vanessa took Fred's arm and tugged him along, in a cone of protection that emanated from the man from the Diogenes Club. As long as he could hear the humming, he felt safe.

They passed Sir Giles, whose face was scarlet. The old soldiers fell back to either side, lowering their weapons. There was a clear route out of The Laurels.

Jeperson seemed to glide across the carpet, eyes still shut, still radiating noise. The hum was wavering.

'Stop them,' shouted Sir Giles.

A rifle was raised, its barrel-end dragging up Fred's leg. Without thinking, he knocked the gun aside and shoved its owner – the chinless ARP man – backwards.

They were on the porch of The Laurels.

Vanessa was in the Rolls, turning over the engine.

Someone fired a wild shot, into the air.

The humming snapped off and Jeperson stumbled. Fred caught him, and sensed that all the strength had gone out of the man. He helped him into the car.

'You don't understand,' shouted Sir Giles. 'It's for the best.'

'Drive,' breathed Jeperson.

Fred pulled the car door closed. A gun went off. He saw the muzzle-flash. He looked out of the window, and something struck the pane, making him go cross-eyed. He should have been shot in the face, but the round was stopped in a web of cracks.

'Bullet-proof glass,' Vanessa said.

'Thank God for that,' Fred said.

He was shaking.

Sir Giles's men didn't waste any more ammunition. The Rolls pulled away, down Raleigh Road.

Jeperson sprawled on the seat, exhausted. He seemed thinner, less substantial. Whatever resource he had summoned up was spent and its exercise had taken a toll.

'What was that all about?' Fred asked.

'We're on our own,' Jeperson croaked.

The ShadowShark wasn't easy to hide, so they just parked it in the open and walked away. Of course, the three of them were also pretty difficult to miss. As they walked back towards the front, Fred had a sense that the whole town was watching them from behind their blackout curtains, and that Sir Giles's Committee knew exactly where their three troublemakers were. More old soldiers would be despatched after them.

Jeperson had needed to be supported for a while but soon got his strength back.

'Giles couldn't have managed anything on this scale on his own,' he said. 'He must have a powerful source somewhere. But not a first-rate one. The casting isn't pure, or we'd have been absorbed at once.'

Fred understood maybe one word in three.

Vanessa didn't ask questions. He decided just to go along with it all.

'At first I thought it was your pier, but Giles's Committee hadn't reckoned on whatever you ran into. Whatever they've done here hasn't taken in the way they hoped.'

They were in the middle of the dark town.

'Fred, I'm afraid we're going to have to go to the pier.'

He had known it would come. So much else had got in the way, so much else that was impossible to follow, that he had almost put it out of his mind.

Now it hit him again.

There were monsters.

'Maybe we can get to the bottom of it all by morning.'

They were on the front. The pier was in sight.

Because of the lack of street lighting, it was easy to creep up on the pier. A checkpoint was set up by the turnstile. Three men in uniform manned the point. Barbed wire was strung around the admissions booth. The soldiers were smoking cigarettes. From somewhere, Vera Lynn sang 'We'll Meet Again'.

An aeroplane whine sounded overhead.

There was a shrill whistle.

'An air raid,' Jeperson said. 'I doubt if that was part of the intended casting. It just came along with the package.'

A plane flew in from the Channel, a dark shape against black clouds, pregnant with bombs.

Jeperson signalled that they should proceed.

Fred tried to think away the painful tightness in his gut. If Jeperson and Vanessa weren't afraid, he shouldn't be. Of course, they hadn't been here before.

A column of fire rose from up among the villas. It burned his eyes. Then the sound of the explosion hit. It was strong enough to make him stagger.

They walked rapidly towards the checkpoint.

The soldiers were craning, looking up at the fire.

'Jerry blighter,' one sneered.

'Our ack-ack'll bring him down,' his mate said.

As if in reply, the crump of ground guns sounded. The earth

81

was shaking. There were shellbursts in the sky, silhouetting the plane.

Fred was surprised by the soldiers' faces.

They were not old, like the men at the villa. They were young, familiar. The three yobs from the Jolly Glutton. Rupert still had his yellow scarf tucked into the neck of his khaki jacket. Twitch was sucking on his cigarette, eye in motion. Shoulders awkwardly unslung his rifle.

'Who goes there?' he barked.

Vanessa stepped forward.

'Remember me?'

'It's a dangerous night to be out, miss,' said Rupert Scarf, politely. 'Best get down in the shelters.'

'Are you in the theatre?' Twitch asked, looking at her legs.

The three didn't remember Vanessa. Fred thought they might not remember their own names, whatever they were.

'We're with the Ministry,' Jeperson said, holding out a folded newspaper picked from a rubbish bin.

Rupert Scarf took the paper and looked at it.

Jeperson hummed again, a different pitch. Rupert Scarf looked at the paper and at their faces.

'All in order, sir,' he said, smiling, saluting.

Jeperson took back the paper and tucked it under his arm.

'Let's take a look at the problem then, shall we?' he said. 'If you could let us through.'

The three smartly dismantled the barrier.

'Shan't be a jiffy,' Jeperson said, stepping on to the pier.

Fred looked at the Emporium, dimly outlined at the end of the promenade. Its glass roof had a slight greenish glow. He had a 'Go Back Now' feeling.

'Are you coming?' Vanessa asked.

'Yes,' Fred said, resolving.

They strolled towards the Emporium.

'It feels as if we're miles from the shore,' Jeperson said.

He was right. Fred looked back. The fire up in the villas was under control. The bomber seemed to be gone. There was still a flicker from where the bomb had fallen.

'What about those skinheads?' Fred asked.

'Caught up in the casting. Weak minds are prone to that. It's like a psychic press-gang. It turns people into costume extras.'

'I can't say I miss the old versions.'

The sea sounded beneath them. An ancient susurrus.

The pier was such a fragile thing, an umbilicus connected to the shore.

Fred had to overcome an urge to bolt back.

'This is definitely it,' Jeperson said. 'The flaw in the pattern. You can feel the atoms whirling the wrong way.'

Vanessa nodded.

They were at the Emporium. There was the dent where Ingraham had kicked. And the pane Jaffa had smashed. If it were daylight, he was sure he'd see the scorch-trail Jaffa left before he went over the side.

'I don't have to tell you to be careful, do I?' Jeperson said, reaching in through the broken pane, opening the door. '*Excelsior*.'

Fred looked into the darkness. He followed Jeperson and Vanessa inside.

'Someone's cleared up,' he said. 'There should be bodies all over the place.'

Vanessa had a slim torch. She played light around the space. There were scrubbed and bleached patches on the floor. And some of the exhibits were under dust-sheets.

Jeperson looked at the storm-trooper poster.

'It's all to do with the War,' he said.

'Even I'd worked that out,' Fred said. 'It's been a while since anyone bombed the South Coast from the air.'

'A lot of people liked the War,' Jeperson said, scratching his wrist. 'I don't think I did, though. I can't actually remember much of it. But it wasn't anything I'd want to bring back.'

'I can understand that.'

Vanessa ran torchlight across the exhibits. She spotlit a display Fred hadn't noticed on his first visit. It was a set of caricature figures of Hitler, Goebbels and Mussolini. Hitler was child-sized and cut off at the waist, Goebbels a rat-bodied pet in Hitler's top pocket, and Mussolini a towering fat clown with an apple-sized red head and a conical Punchinello hat.

'These fellows, for instance,' Jeperson said. 'I don't miss them one bit.'

Hitler's mask crinkled in a scowl as its wearer escaped from the display. The creature walked very rapidly on its hands, detaching itself from the base. It was a legless torso.

Half-Hitler brushed past Vanessa, screeching, and slid through a panel. It had left Rat-Goebbels behind, rodent feet curled up, horrid little eyes glittering.

Man Mountain Mussolini quivered, a ton of jelly poured into a barrage balloon-uniform. His belly rumbled, and a falsetto laugh emerged from his circular lipsticky mouth.

Fred looked around. Vanessa moved the torchlight. Panels were sliding upwards. Boots shone. Black jackboots. Then grey-uniformed knees. There were half a dozen panels. Behind them were men – mannequins? – in Nazi uniform.

Rat-Goebbels right-sided himself and scurried towards a pair of boots, nestling between them like an affectionate pet.

The panels were above leather belts. Swastikas and Iron Crosses showed on grey chests. Luger pistols and Schmeisser machine-guns were pointed.

Man Mountain Mussolini, still laughing like a eunuch, rolled back and forth on his belly. His legs were normal-sized, useless with his gut-bulk, and stuck out of his egg-shaped body like broken tree-branches.

Faces showed. Faces Fred knew. The Boys. Jaffa's nose was smudged with soot, his cheeks burned to the bone, his eyes dead under the rim of his storm-trooper helmet. The others were similarly transformed. Ingraham in an SS uniform, Doggo a regular soldier. Oscar's face was crudely stitched back on, forehead sewn to his Afrika Corps cap, skin hanging slack like a cloth mask.

Half-Hitler advanced from between two rows of Nazi skins, using its arms like crutches, inching forwards its truncated torso. Its face was not a mask, but coated in a transparent fungus that exaggerated the familiar features. The homunculus set itself down and crossed its arms, tottering back and forth a little. The storm-troopers snapped off perfect Nazi salutes.

'*Sieg Heil*,' they shouted, '*Heil Hitler*.'

'You'll excuse me if I don't respond in kind,' Jeperson said. 'But I could never stand you, you little sneak.'

He drew back his banana boot as if converting a rugby try and kicked Half-Hitler in the face. The diminished Führer tipped over backwards, outsize hands slapping the floor, and overturned completely like a chimpanzee on a trapeze, winding up face down and arms flailed out.

Safety catches clicked off. Guns fired.

Fred grabbed Vanessa round the waist and threw himself at the floor. Together, they rolled behind the row of penny-in-the-slot machines, inches ahead of the line of bullet-pocks that raked the floorboards.

The space was too enclosed for the Nazi zombies to get much accurate use of their guns. Bullets ricocheted and spanged around. Doggo took a hole in his face and staggered back. Black goo leaked from inside him, but he wasn't seriously hurt.

Ingraham kicked aside the penny-in-the-slot machines.

Fred tried to put his hands up.

Ingraham raised his Luger.

The gun writhed. Its metal parts contracted as if the mechanism were about to sneeze. It was partly a gun, but infused with the life of a small rodent.

The gun-thing coughed. Fire belched. Slow enough to see, a bullet squeezed out of the barrel and sped towards them, a blob of flaming jelly.

It spattered against his chest, stinging through his shirt. He brushed the fiery glop away, feeling the flames curling around his fingers, and scraped it off on to the floor.

Ingraham's pistol growled at them.

Jaffa came over. He held Jeperson by one arm twisted playground-bully-style up behind his back. A silver-bladed dagger was held at Jeperson's throat, steel quivering with a life of its own. The zombie indicated Fred and Vanessa should surrender. Fred stood up, trying to keep his body in front of Vanessa.

Jaffa smiled. His burned lips made an expression Fred remembered from when the Nazi was King Skin.

'You're enjoying this, aren't you, Kevin?'

In the burned-out eyes anger glowed.

Half-Hitler scuttled over, and bit Jeperson's leg like a terrier. Its teeth couldn't get through the banana boot.

At a nod from the Führer, Fred was pulled away. The Nazi homunculus looked Vanessa over, little black eyes excited. She tried not to show disgust.

'Eva,' Half-Hitler breathed, besotted.

Man Mountain Mussolini rolled over to look. Other fascist freaks came out of the shadows. A pig-faced Goering, warty wings folded over his Luftwaffe tunic. Himmler-and-Hess Siamese twins, joined at the waist, heiling with all available arms. A snake-bodied, fork-tongued Martin Bormann. An armoured Rommel, bony tank-plates coating his body, desert camouflage smearing his face. A werewolf Heydrich, cheeks and hands pierced by dozens of hooks.

They all gathered, looking at Vanessa.

Half-Hitler crawled around her legs, as if inspecting a horse. Vanessa looked down at the little creep. It retreated and barked an order.

The Nazi Boys raised their machine-guns. Fred opened his mouth to protest. Guns chattered, pouring liquid fire out of hosepipe barrels. It washed against Vanessa, burning swatches of her clothing, hanging around her hair.

Where the fire burned, she was transformed. A cloak of

flame enveloped her. White boots became black. Straps grew around her chest. A jewelled swastika hung at her throat. Her hair, a living thing, coiled into a braid, clinging to the back of her head like a cap. She twisted as she turned, resisting the metamorphosis, but the zombies kept pouring the changing fire at her.

Half-Hitler's eyes shone.

The light went out in Vanessa's face. The flame fell away from her. She was the same woman, but turned into a Nazi pin-up.

Jeperson was mumbling furiously, trying to call up some counter-charm.

Half-Hitler gave another order.

Eva-Vanessa uncoiled a short whip and struck Jeperson in the face, breaking his concentration. The Nazi monsters laughed. Jeperson went limp, and Jaffa dropped him.

Half-Hitler jumped up and down on its waist-stump, chortling with glee. Eva-Vanessa picked it up as if it were a child, and hugged it. They kissed. Fred felt sick.

'Today the pier,' Goebbels snickered; 'tomorrow the world.'

Jeperson got up on to his knees. As he fell, he had snatched something from Jaffa's belt. Now he opened his hand. It was a grenade. He opened his other hand. There was the pin.

Time froze.

Then everyone was scrambling out of the way.

Jeperson let the grenade roll on the floor.

Fred was kicked about by Nazi boots. He found himself behind the execution machines again.

The grenade didn't so much explode as suck light and matter in from all around. It gathered into a heavy black ball and fell through the floor.

Fred saw the dark sea frothing below. Jeperson stood over the lip of the hole and stepped into it, plunging towards the water.

Gunfire raked the room.

Fred followed Jeperson, without thinking.

SEVEN STARS

He tumbled badly and hit the sea as if it were a tossing sheet of iron. Cold water slammed him in the face and tried to shove him under.

He woke up on the beach, with water being forced out of his lungs. His mouth was full of the sick taste of too much salt. And he was as cold as he had ever been, racked with spasms of shivering.

'Welcome back,' Jeperson said. 'Thought you'd upped stumps for a minute.'

Fred rolled over on the sand and water poured out of him.

Looking out to sea, Fred saw that the Emporium at the end of the pier was lit up with fairy lights. It seemed like a jewelled palace in the darkness.

'The ARP won't like that,' Jeperson commented.

'What is going on here?' Fred asked.

'A very bad business,' Jeperson said, concerned. 'Very bad business indeed.'

People stood around, with rifles.

A man came forwards, wearily. Sir Giles.

'Oh dear,' he said. 'We shall have to get you two dried off.'

Fred was picked up. He recognized the ARP man he had shoved earlier. He was too weak to resist.

'A cup of tea might help,' said Sir Giles.

They were back in the study at The Laurels. All that could be found for Fred was a naval uniform, left behind by Michaelsmith's brother. Jeperson had a change of clothes (or a dozen) in the Rolls. He now wore a tiger-striped frock coat and aquamarine knee-breeches, a violet kaftan shirt, and red riding-boots. His hair was still damp.

Sir Giles sat in his favourite armchair while Marshall Michaelsmith, in an orderly's uniform, served mugs of hot tea. Fred was grateful for that. Jeperson leaned forwards, eyes blazing, fixing Sir Giles with a stern schoolmaster's gaze.

'What were you thinking of, Giles?'

The old soldier shrivelled in his chair.

Finally, feebly, he said, 'It was decimalization.'

'What?' Jeperson shouted.

Sir Giles was embarrassed, but a little defiant.

'Decimal coinage, you know. The new money. I can never get it straight, all these pence and no shillings. The new coins don't *mean* anything. They're like counters in a child's game. That was the last straw. Not just changing the money, of course. But everything it meant. All the other changes. The Common Market coming up. Motorways. Everything plastic. High-speed inter-city trains. Racialist violence. Hotpants. Instant soup. Hire purchase. Everything's cheapened, somehow. Since the War.'

'Regrettable, perhaps. But what about heart transplants? A man on the moon?'

'The pill?'

Jeperson sat back, and shook his head. 'Have you forgotten how you felt in 1930? That deadening weight of history, of the way things have always been. Why do you think Mr Jeperson chose me, passed on the responsibilities? Because I can still embrace the change, the chaos. I can still accommodate.'

'This is different,' Sir Giles said.

'No, it's the same. It's just that you have resources. How wide is the casting?'

'Just the town.'

'Who is the focus?'

Sir Giles hesitated. But Michaelsmith said, 'The missus.'

Jeperson looked at the man.

'She dreams of the old times,' Michaelsmith explained.

'Effective dreams? Reality-changing dreams?'

Sir Giles nodded.

'You know how dangerous that game is. And you had to pick the War.'

'Why not?' Sir Giles's defiance was growing. He needed to defend himself. 'We were all working together, all differences

SEVEN STARS

set aside. Everyone was prepared to sacrifice for everyone else.
It was our finest hour.'

Jeperson thought for a moment.

'And what about the air raids? The pier?'

'An impurity in the casting,' Sir Giles said. 'It will be
rectified.'

'No,' Jeperson said. 'Not an impurity, not a mistake. It was
inevitable. You can't just have back the things you liked about
the War. You want *ITMA* on the wireless and duchesses
cosying up to shopgirls in the shelters, but that means you have
to have the monsters. Can you really have forgotten what the
War was like for most of Europe? For Britain, even.'

Jeperson rolled up his cuff to show his camp tattoo.

Sir Giles looked down at the carpet, ashamed.

Jeperson was contemptuous. 'And all because you didn't
want to learn decimal coinage?'

Fred thought of Vanessa, transformed and perhaps lost.

'Couldn't we just wake his wife up?' he suggested.

Sir Giles, Michaelsmith and Jeperson looked at him,
surprised that he had spoken.

'That might seem on the surface to be the best bet,' said
Jeperson, 'but there are people alive in the vortex of evil at the
end of the pier. We can banish the dream with a hearty
breakfast, but they'll all be sucked back into whatever nether-
world Giles and his Committee called the War up from.'

Fred could well do without Jaffa and the Boys.

But Vanessa?

'I'm very much afraid that we're going to have to go back to
the Emporium.'

'We got hammered last time.'

'That was an exploratory mission. This time, we'll be
prepared.'

Sir Giles looked up.

'We'll do what we can, Richard.'

'I should think you will,' said Jeperson, chipper but stern.
'First, you must have some young persons about town?'

90

Sir Giles nodded.

'Excellent. You Committee men will need to loot your sons' wardrobes. And you'll have to hook up the air-raid sirens to a gramophone. Oh, and no Vera Lynn.'

The dawn was beginning to pink the horizon, outlining the sea beyond the pier.

'What year is it, soldier?' Jeperson asked Twitch.

The skinhead couldn't remember.

'Don't say 1941,' Jeperson prompted.

Twitch looked from Jeperson to the Committee.

The street-lamps came on, two by two, lighting up the seafront. Twitch's eyes widened.

Brigadier-General Sir Giles Gallant wore pink loon pants, a paisley tie the shape of a coat-hanger and a rainbow-knit tank top. Marshall Michaelsmith was squeezed into a pair of ripped drainpipe jeans held up by wide tartan braces, a T-shirt with Bob Marley's face on it, and an oversize flat cap with a swirl pattern.

The rest of the Committee, and their wives, were similarly kitted up. It was uncomfortably like fancy dress, a ridiculous pantomime vision of mock trendiness.

But it rang bells.

Twitch remembered, a trace of his old viciousness cutting through his artificial politeness.

'Gits,' he spat.

Ending this casting wouldn't be entirely a good thing.

'It's not then,' Twitch said. 'It's now.'

'That's right,' said Jeperson. 'The War's been over for twenty-five years.'

Twitch undid his uniform. Rupert Scarf and Shoulders looked bewildered at their posts, but caught on slowly.

'You may not like these people,' Jeperson said to the Committee. 'In fact, I can almost guarantee you won't. But you had no right to take their personalities away. Besides, a lot of tommies were more like them than you want to think. You tried to bring back the War as you remembered it, not as it was. Just imagine what would have happened if I had been your focus. Just think what the War I can't remember – which is still inside my skull – would have been like spread over your whole town. The pier wouldn't have been an impurity. It would have been the whole show.'

Sir Giles looked chastened, and not a little ridiculous. Fred guessed that was part of the idea.

'This is the future,' Jeperson announced. 'Learn to live with it. Come on, Fred.'

He started walking down the pier.

'The point is to undo the casting from the inside,' Jeperson said. 'Just think of the 1970s. Fix in your mind all the things that furnish the present.'

They stood outside the Emporium. A swastika flag flew from the summit.

'Colour television, Post Office Tower, frozen peas, Milton Keynes,' Fred chanted.

Jeperson shook his head. 'I hope we're doing the right thing.'

'Multi-storey car parks, inflatable chairs, Sunday supplements, *Top of the Pops* . . .'

Jeperson sighed and kicked the door open.

'Wakey-wakey, Nazis!'

They passed undisturbed through the exhibition and found the theatre. A miniature Nuremberg rally was in process. Columns of light rose from the stage. Half-Hitler was propped up on an up-ended dustbin, ranting in German. His monster ministers stood at attention. Eva-Vanessa stood beside her Führer, eyes blank with fanaticism. A map of Seamouth was lit up on the wall, with red swastika-marked arrows on it. An audience of Nazi zombies was arranged before the stage.

'We're just in time,' Jeperson whispered. 'They're planning an invasion.'

The zombies were rapt, intent on their leader's speech.

'They must intend to attack at dawn. How traditional.'

Half-Hitler seemed stronger than before, more substantial. It wasn't growing legs, but was secure in its perch. The more followers it had, the more power gathered in its hateful torso. The homunculus's voice was deeper, more purposeful.

The swastika arrows moved on the map, stabbing into town.

This mob looked grotesque, but Fred had a sense of the immensity of the damage they could do. The map suggested that this 'casting' was out of the control of Sir Giles's Committee, and that these creatures would soon be able to manipulate the spell, and spread it along the coast and inland, striking towards London like the Nazi invasion that hadn't come in 1940. What was wrong here, at the end of the pier, could blanket the country, drawing strength from the millions sucked into what Jeperson had called a 'vortex of evil'.

Today the pier; tomorrow the world.

Jeperson strode into the audience, down the centre aisle. He was apparently calm, but Fred caught the wiry intensity under his languid pose. This man was a warrior. The Nazis noticed the intruder, and with a liquid motion turned to look. Guns were raised.

Jeperson held up a small, shiny object.

'By this totem, I banish you,' he said.

The tiny light caught the audience's attention.

It was a seven-sided coin, one of the new fifty-pence pieces. And it shone like a star.

Half-Hitler snarled. The map shrivelled like ice on a griddle.

'All of you, turn out your pockets,' Jeperson barked. Nazis were used to obeying orders. 'If you find one of these, you'll know you've been fooled. These creatures lost their chance years ago. And a good job too. You have been sucked into someone else's nightmare.'

Goebbels chittered. Himmler-and-Hess fought over their single side-arm. Mussolini leaked jelly at his uniform neckline.

The zombies were exploring their own pockets. Fred did the

93

same and found a fifty-pence piece. He gripped the emblem of modernity.

'Simon Dee, Edward Heath, Germaine Greer, George Best, Cilla Black,' he shouted.

More than one of the zombies had found new money in his pockets. Jaffa tore open his uniform to reveal his scorched Fred Perry. He roared.

'Rise up,' Jeperson said, 'and be free!'

Music began to play from an ancient horn Victrola. 'The Horst Wessel Song'. It quieted the zombies for a moment. The Nazi freaks stood at attention.

Half-Hitler pulled out a pistol, settled on its waist-stump, and shot at Jeperson's hand. A squirt of slow flame lashed out, and tore the fifty-pence piece away, robbing Jeperson of his totem.

Jeperson held his stinging hand. Half-Hitler managed a smug smile. With the Nazi anthem filling the room, it seemed to swell, to float above its bin on a carpet of air.

Jeperson closed his eyes, and began to hum.

Then another sound obliterated the marching band.

It was the Beatles, singing 'Let It Be'.

Half-Hitler dropped its pistol and covered its ears.

The air raid siren PA was broadcasting at a million decibels. The song filled the theatre.

Fred saw Vanessa's eyes register reality. The Beatles reached inside and got to her.

She kicked Half-Hitler's bin out from under it.

'*Oh Lord*,' Fred yelled, '*let it be . . .*'

The zombies swayed with the all-pervasive, all-powerful sound of the 1970s. Jaffa and the Boys wouldn't have liked this music when they were alive, but it was a part of them, imprinted on their minds and on the minds of everyone who had paid attention for the last ten years.

Fred thought the Fab Four had been going downhill since *Revolver*, but this once conceded that there might be something in the Maharishi music-hall stuff.

The zombies began firing their guns. At the stage. The Nazi freaks exploded like ectoplasm balloons. Mussolini went off like a hydrogen bomb, fountaining gallons of green froth that washed off the stage and into the audience.

The song changed to 'Here Comes the Sun'.

Dawn broke over the sea, pouring daylight into the Emporium. Goebbels was smoking, and burst into blue flames, screeching like a dying rodent.

Vanessa, herself again, picked her way elegantly through the gunfire and the deliquescing phantoms.

Though most of the Boys were struck by the music, Jaffa was apparently immune – were his ears burned away? He reached out for Jeperson, snarling.

Fred leaped on the zombie's back, getting an armlock round his neck, and pulled him back. Jaffa's clutching hands failed to get a grip on Jeperson's hair. Fred felt the zombie's skull loosening on his neck.

Jeperson got up on the stage, borrowed rifle in his hands, and stuck a bayonet through Half-Hitler, pinning the homunculus to the boards. The creature deflated, leaking ecto-ichor through gashes in its uniform tunic.

As their *Führer* fell apart, the others were sucked out of the world, leaving behind only a scatter of medals and coins.

The zombie twisted in Fred's grip, eyes sparking with the last of life. Then he was gone, just a corpse dressed up in an old uniform. At the very last, Fred fancied Kevin Jaffa, King Skin, was briefly himself again, not ungrateful to be set free from the casting.

He didn't know how to feel.

The struggle was over.

Jeperson left the rifle stuck into the stage, pinning the empty jacket. He took Vanessa's hands, and kissed her. She turned her face up to the light, reborn as a Sun Goddess, hair loose and shining like burnished copper.

They sat on the beach. The Committee were still broadcasting, condemned to play every single in Sir Giles's eleven-year-old grand-daughter's collection. Currently, Sergio Mendes was doing Joni Mitchell's 'Chelsea Morning'. Clean sunlight shone on the beach, as if it were newly sown with fresh sand.

They were still taking bodies off the pier, dead for days. All that was left of the freaks was the occasional streak of drying slime. They were phantasms, Jeperson explained, conjured up with the casting.

'They weren't real, but they would have been.'

Twitch and his cronies, themselves again with blank spots in their short-term memories, were playing football on the beach, slamming into each other, swearing loudly.

Jeperson looked down, ashamed for the skinheads.

'Welcome back to the 'Seventies,' Fred said.

'We can't pick and choose what we accept from the present,' Jeperson admitted, tossing a pebble at the sea.

'White Horses', by Jacky, was playing.

Vanessa had taken her shoes off, and was wiggling her toes in the sand. She seemed unaffected by her brief spell with the End of the Pier Show.

'Young Fred,' Jeperson said, 'you did well when things got weird. You might have an aptitude for this line of strangeness. I've requested you be transferred off the beat. I think you might come in handy at the Diogenes Club. Interested?'

Fred thought about it.

YOU DON'T HAVE TO BE MAD . . .

Prologue: A Graduate of the Laughing Academy

He arrived bright and early in the morning. At eight o'clock, the entire workforce was assembled in the open air. The managing director introduced him as an outside consultant with bad news to deliver and handed him the loud-hailer. Barely restraining giggles, Mr Joyful announced the shipyard would close down at the end of the year and they were all sacked.

Escorted off site by armed guards, ignoring the snarls and taunts of to-be-unemployed-by-1971 workmen, he was back in his bubble car, stomach knotted with hilarious agony, by eight-fifteen. He managed to drive a few miles before he was forced to pull over and give vent to the laughter that had built up inside him like painful gas. Tears coursed down his cheeks. The interior of his space-age transport vibrated with the explosions of his merriment.

At nine o'clock, chortling, he told a young mother that her son's cancer was inoperable. At ten, snickering, he informed the founder of a biscuit factory that he'd been unseated in a boardroom coup and would be lucky to escape prosecution over a series of mystery customer ailments. At eleven, in full view of a party of schoolboys, he wielded a length of two-by-four to execute an aged polar bear that a small zoo could no longer afford to feed. At twelve, almost unable to hold the saw steady for his shaking mirth, he cut down a seven-hundred-year-old oak tree on the village green of Little Middling by the Weir, to make way for a road-widening scheme. The chants of the protesters were especially rib-tickling.

From one until two, he had a fine lunch in a Jolly Glutton motorway restaurant. Two straight sausages and a helping of near-liquid mash. An individual apple pie with processed cream. It was a privilege to taste this, the food of the future. Each portion perfect, and identical with each other portion. That struck him as funny too.

At two-thirty, controlling himself, he murdered three old folk in a private home, with the hankie-over-the-mouth-and-nose hold. Their savings had run out and this was kinder than turning them loose to fend for themselves. His five o'clock appointment was something similar, a journalist working on a news item about hovercraft safety for the telly programme *Tomorrow's News*.

'I've got some bad news for you,' he told the surprised young woman.

'Who are you?' she demanded.

'I'm Mr Joyful. Aren't you interested in my news?'

'Why are you grinning like that? Is this a joke?'

He was about to go off again. Amused tears pricked the backs of his eyes. Laughter began to scream inside his brain, clamouring for escape.

'Your contract is cancelled,' he managed to get out.

It was too, *too* funny.

He produced the silenced pistol. One quick *phut* in the face and he could knock off for the day.

He was laughing like a drain.

What this woman didn't know – but would find out unless stopped – was that the Chairman of the Board of Directors of her employer, Greater London Television, was also responsible for Amalgamated British Hoverlines, and had authorized the cost-cutting scheme that resulted in the deaths of twenty-eight day-trippers.

His gun barrel shook as it pointed.

The look on the woman's face was too much. He barked laughter, like the policeman in the comedy record. His sides literally split, great tears running down from his armpits to his hips.

His shot creased the woman's shoulder.

That was funny too. People held him down, wrestling the gun out of his grip. Someone even kicked him in the tummy. It was too much to bear.

He kept on laughing, blind with tears, lances of agony stabbing into his torso. Then he stopped.

Act I: Vanessa is Committed

She was comfortably lotused among orange and purple scatter-cushions in the conference room of the Chelsea mansion, rainbow-socked feet tucked neatly into the kinks of her knees. Vanessa wore a scarlet leotard with a white angora cardigan. Her long red hair was in a rope-braid, knotted end gripped in a giant turquoise clothespeg. Fred Regent sat nearby, on a wire-net bucket chair, in his usual jeans and jean jacket, square head almost shaven.

Jazz harpsichord tinkled out of the sound system concealed behind eighteenth-century wood panelling. Matched Lichten-stein explosions hung over the marble mantelpiece. A bundle of joss sticks smoked in a Meissen vase on a kidney-shaped coffee table.

Richard Jeperson, silver kaftan rippling with reflected light, nested cross-legged in a white plastic chair that hung from the ceiling on an anchor chain. It was shaped like a giant egg sliced vertically, with yolk-yellow padding inside.

He showed them a photograph of a happy-looking fat man. Then another one, of the same man, lying on the floor in a pool of mess.

'Jolyon Fuller,' he announced.

Vanessa compared the shots. Fuller looked even happier in the one where he was dead.

'He made his living in an interesting way,' Richard said. 'He delivered bad news.'

'I thought that was Reginald Bosanquet's job,' put in Fred.

'Fuller doesn't look gloomy,' Vanessa ventured.

'Apparently, he wasn't,' Richard said. 'He laughed himself to death. Literally. Matters you or I would consider tragic were high comedy to him. His wires were crossed somewhere up here.' He tapped his head.

Taking back the pictures, hawkbrows momentarily clenched, he gave them consideration. Shoulder-length black ringlets and the mandarin's moustache gave his face a soft, almost girlish cast, but the piercing eyes and sharp cheekbones were predatory. After all they'd been through together, Vanessa still hadn't got to the bottom of Richard Jeperson.

It had been weeks since the last interesting problem had come along, the business of the Satanist Scoutmaster and his scheme to fell the Post Office Tower. Richard had summoned his assistants to announce that they were to investigate a string of strangenesses. This was often the way of their affairs. At the Diogenes Club in Pall Mall, a group of clever and wise minds – under the direction of Edwin Winthrop, Grand Old Man of the Ruling Cabal – constantly sifted through court records, police reports, newspapers and statements from members of the public, ear-marking the unusual and red-flagging the impossible. If the inexplicabilities mounted up, the matter was referred to one of the Club's Valued Members. Currently, Richard was reckoned the Most Valued Member.

'Here's another pretty fizzog. Harry Egge.'

Richard showed them a glossy of a boxer, gloves up, bruises on his face.

'He was supposed to be the next 'Enery Cooper,' said Fred, who followed sport. 'He could take the Punishment for fifty rounds. Couldn't feel pain or didn't care about it. No matter how much battering he took, he kept on punching.'

'I read about him,' Vanessa said. 'Didn't he die?'

'Indeed he did,' Richard explained. 'In his home, in a fire caused by faulty wiring.'

'He was trapped,' she said. 'How horrible.'

'Actually, he wasn't trapped. He could have walked away, easily. But he fought the fire, literally. He punched it and battered it, but it caught him and burned him to the bone. Very odd. When you put your hand in a flame, you take it out sharpish. It's what pain is for, to make you do things before you think about them. Nature's fire alarm. Harry Egge kept fighting the fire, as if he could win by a knock-out.'

'Was he kinky for pain?'

'A masochist, Vanessa? Not really. He just wasn't afraid of being hurt.'

'And that makes him barmy?'

'Quite so, Fred. Utterly barmy.'

Vanessa wondered what Jolyon Fuller and Harry Egge had in common, besides being mad and dead.

'There are more odd folk to consider,' Richard continued, producing more photographs and reports. 'Nicholas Mix-Elgin: head of security at a multi-national computer firm. He became so suspicious that he searched his children's pets for listening devices. Internally. Serafine Xavier: convent school-teacher turned high-priced callgirl, the only patient ever hospitalized on the National Health with "clinical nympho-mania". We only know about her because several male patients on her ward died during visits from her. Lieutenant Commander Hilary Roehampton: a naval officer who insisted on volunteering for a series of missions so dangerous only a lunatic would consider them.'

'Like what?' asked Fred.

'Sea-testing leaky submarines.'

'Cor blimey!'

Vanessa had to agree.

'These people held more or less responsible positions. It's only by chance that their files were passed on to us. The *grande horizontale* was, I believe, retained by the FO for the intimate entertainment of visiting dignitaries.'

'They all sound like loonies to me,' Fred said.

'Ah yes,' Richard agreed, extending a finger, 'but their lunacies *worked* for them, at least in the short term. You are familiar with that allegedly humorous mass-produced plaque you see up in offices and other sordid places? "You Don't Have To Be Mad To Work Here" – asterisk – "But It Helps." Sometimes being mad really does help. After all, a head of security should be a bit of a paranoiac, a boxer needs to have a touch of the masochist.'

'Don't most firms and all government agencies make prospective employees take a battery of psychiatric tests these days? To weed out the maniacs?'

'Indeed they do, my dear. I have copies here.'

He indicated a thick sheaf of papers. She reached out.

'Don't bother. All our interesting friends were evaluated within the last three years as one hundred per cent sane.'

'The tests must be rigged,' Fred said. 'You don't just go bonkers overnight. This lot must have been in and out of nut-hatches all their lives.'

'As a matter of fact, they were all rated with Certificates of Mental Health.'

Fred didn't believe it.

'And who gave out the certificates?' she asked.

Richard arched an eyebrow. She'd asked the right question. That was the connection.

'Strangely enough, all these persons were certified as sane by the same practitioner, one Dr Iain Menzies Ballance. He is Director of the Pleasant Green Centre, near Whipplewell in Sussex.'

'Pleasant Green. Is that a private asylum?'

'Not officially,' he told her. 'It offers training courses for executives and other high-earners. Like a health farm for the mind. Sweat off those unsightly phobias, that sort of thing.'

She looked at a glossy prospectus that was in with all the case files. A Regency mansion set among rolling downs. Dr Ballance smiling with his caring staff, all beautiful young women. Testimonials from leaders of industry and government figures. A table of fees, starting at £500 a week.

'Let me get this straight,' said Fred. 'Sane people go in . . .'

'And mad people come out,' Richard announced.

She felt a little chill. There was something cracked in Dr Ballance's half-smile. And his staff couldn't quite not look like the dolly bird wing of the SS.

'The question which now presents itself, of course, is which of us would most benefit from a week or two under the care of the good Dr Ballance.'

Richard looked from Fred to her. Fred just looked at her.

'You're the sanest person I know, Ness,' Fred said.

'That's not saying much,' she countered.

Richard was about to give a speech about knowing how dangerous the assignment would be and not wanting her to take it unless she was absolutely sure. She cut him off. After all, she owed him too much – her sanity, at least, probably her life – to protest.

'Just tell me who I am,' she said.

Richard smiled like a shark and produced a folder.

In the garage of the Chelsea house, her white Lotus Elan looked like a Dinky toy parked next to Richard's Rolls-Royce ShadowShark but it could almost match the great beast for speed and had the edge for manoeuvrability. She should get down to Sussex inside an hour.

Fred was already in Whipplewell. If asked, he was a bird-watcher out after a look-see at some unprecedented avocets. Richard had given him an *I-Spy Book of Birds* to memorize. He would watch over her.

Richard had turned out to see her off. He wore an orange frock coat with matching boots and top hat, over a psychedelic waistcoat and a lime-green shirt with collar-points wider than his shoulders. He fixed her with his deep dark eyes.

'My love, remember who you are.'

When they met, she'd been a different person, not in command of herself. Something it was easiest to call a demon had her in a thrall it was easiest to call possession. He'd been able to reach her because he understood.

'We have less memory than most. That's why what we have, what we are, is so precious.'

Richard was an amnesiac, a foundling of the War. He had proved to her that it was possible to live without a past that could be proved with memory. Once, since the first time, she had come under the influence of another entity – she shuddered at the memory of a pier on the South Coast – but had been able to throw off a cloak dropped over her mind.

'You'll be pretending to be a new person, this Vanessa Vail. That's a snakeskin you can shed at any time. While the act must be perfect, you must not give yourself up to it completely. They can do a great deal to "Vanessa Vail" without touching Vanessa the Real. You must have a core that is you alone.'

She thought she understood.

'Vanessa,' he repeated, kissing her. 'Vanessa.'

She vaulted into the driving seat of the Lotus.

'What's your name?' he asked.

She told him, and drove off.

'You are an army officer?' Dr Ballance asked, looking up from the folder. He had a hard Scots accent of the sort popularly associated with John Laurie, penny-pinching, wife-beating and sheep abuse.

Vanessa nodded. She was supposed to be a paratrooper. Looking at her long legs and big eyes, people thought she must be a fashion model, but she had the height to be a convincing warrior woman. And she could look after herself in hand-to-hand combat. It wasn't a great snakeskin but it was wearable.

'Things have changed since my day, Lieutenant Vail.'

She hated her new name. The double V sounded so cartoony. But you couldn't be in the army without a surname.

'Were you in the services, Dr Ballance?'

He nodded and one side of his mouth smiled. The left half of his face was frozen.

She imagined him in uniform, tunic tight on his barrel chest, cap perched on his butter-coloured cloud of hair, tiger stripes on his blandly bespectacled face. She wondered which side he had been on in whichever war he had fought.

'You will be Lieutenant Veevee,' he said. 'For "vivacious". We rename all our guests. The world outside does not trouble us here in Pleasant Green. We are interested only in the world inside.'

She crossed her legs and rearranged her khaki miniskirt for decency's sake. Dr Ballance's one mobile eye followed the line of her leg down to her polished brogue. She was wearing a regimental tie tucked into a fatigue blouse, and a blazer with the proper pocket badge. Richard had suggested medal ribbons, but she thought that would be over-egging the pud.

'I'll have Miss Dove show you to your quarters,' said Dr Ballance. 'You will join us for the evening meal, and I shall work up a programme of tests and exercises for you. Nothing too strenuous at first.'

'I've passed commando training,' she said.

It was true. Yesterday, getting into character, she had humped herself through mud with an incredulous platoon of real paratroopers. At first, they gallantly tried to help her. Then, when it looked like she'd score the highest marks on the course, they did their best to drag her back and keep her down. She gave a few combat-ready squaddies some nasty surprises and came in third. The sergeant offered to have her back to keep his lads in line.

'Your body is in fine shape, Lieutenant Veevee,' said Dr Ballance, eye running back up her leg, pausing at chest level, then twitching up to her face. 'Now we shall see what we can do about tailoring your mind to fit it.'

Dr Ballance pressed a buzzer switch. A young woman appeared in the office. She wore a thigh-length flared doctor's coat over white PVC knee-boots, a too-small T-shirt and hot pants. Her blonde hair was kept back by an alice band.

'Miss Dove, show Lieutenant Veevee where we're putting her.'

The attendant smiled, making dimples.

Vanessa stood and was led out of the office.

Pleasant Green Manor House had been gutted, and the interior remodelled in steel and glass. Vanessa took note of various gym facilities and therapy centres. All were in use, with 'guests' exercising or playing mind games under the supervision of attendants dressed exactly like Miss Dove. They looked like Pan's People rehearsing a hospital-themed dance number. Some processes were obvious, but others involved peculiar machines and dentist's chairs with straps and restraints.

She was shown her room, which contained a four-poster bed and other antique furniture. A large window looked out over the grounds. Among rolling lawns were an arrangement of pre-fab buildings and some concrete-block bunkers. Beyond the window was a discreet steel grille, 'for protection'.

'We don't get many gels at Pleasant Green, Lieutenant Veevee,' said Miss Dove. 'It's mostly fellows. High-powered executives and the like.'

'Women are more and more represented in all the professions.'

'We've one other gel here. Mrs Empty. Dr Ballance thinks she's promising. You'll have competition. I hope you'll be chums.'

'So do I.'

'I think you're going to fit in perfectly, Lieutenant.'

Miss Dove hugged her.

Vanessa tensed, as if attacked. She barely restrained herself from popping the woman one on the chin. Miss Dove air-kissed her on both cheeks and let her go. Vanessa realized she had been very subtly frisked during the spontaneous embrace. She had chosen not to bring any obvious weapons or burglar tools.

'See you at din-din,' Miss Dove said, and skipped out.

Vanessa allowed herself a long breath. She assumed the wall-size mirror was a front for a camera. She had noticed a lot of extra wiring and guessed Dr Ballance would have a closed-circuit TV set-up. She put her face close to the mirror, searching for an imaginary blackhead, and thought she heard the whirring of a lens adjustment.

There was no telephone on the bedside table.

Her bags were open, her clothes put in the wardrobe. She hoped they had taken the trouble to examine her marvellously genuine army credentials. It had taken a lot of work to get them up to scratch, and she wanted the effort appreciated.

She looked out of the window. At the far end of the lawns was a wooded area and beyond that the Sussex downs. Fred ought to be out there somewhere with a flat cap, a thermos of tea and a pair of binoculars. He was putting up at the Coach and Horses in Whipplewell, where there were no bars on the windows and you could undress in front of the mirror without giving some crackpot a free show.

Where was Richard all this time? He must be pulling strings. He was supposed to be following up on the graduates of Pleasant Green.

She felt sleepy. It was late afternoon, the gold of the sun dappling the lawn. She shouldn't be exhausted. There was a faint hissing. She darted around, scanning for ventilation grilles, holding her breath. She couldn't keep it up, and if she made an attempt the watchers would know she was a fake. She decided to go with it. Climbing on to the soft bed, she felt eiderdowns rise to embrace her. She let the tasteless, odourless gas into her lungs, and tried to arrange herself on the bed with some decorum.

She nodded off.

Something snapped in front of her face and stung her nostrils. Her head cleared. Everything was suddenly sharp, hyper-real.

She was sitting at a long dinner table, in mixed company, wearing a yellow-and-lime striped cocktail dress. Her hair was done up in a towering beehive. A thick layer of make-up – which she rarely used – was lacquered over her face. Even her nails were done, in stripes to match her dress. Overhead fluorescents cruelly illuminated the table and guests, but the walls were in darkness and an incalculable distance away from the long island of light. The echoey room was noisy with conversation, the clatter of cutlery and The Move's 'Fire Brigade'. She had a mouthful of food and had to chew to save herself from choking.

'You are enjoying your eyeball, Lieutenant?'

The questioner was a slight oriental girl in a man's tuxedo. Her hair was marcelled into a Hokusai wave. A nametag identified her as 'Miss Lark'.

Eyeball?

Chewing on jellying meat, she glanced down at her plate. A cooked pig's face looked back up at her, one eye glazed in its socket, the other a juicy red gouge. She didn't know whether to choke, swallow or spit.

The pig's stiff snout creaked into a porcine smile.

Vanessa expectorated most of the pulpy eye back at its owner.

Conversation and consumption stopped. Miss Lark tutted. Dr Ballance, a tartan sash over his red jacket, stared a wordless rebuke.

The pig snarled now, baring sharp teeth at her.

A fog ocean washed around Vanessa's brain. This time, she struggled. Flares of light that weren't there made her blink. Her own eyeballs might have been Vaselined over. The room rippled and faces stretched. The guests were all one-eyed pigs.

Some eye slipped down her throat. She went away.

This time, the smell of cooking brought her to. She was in an underground kitchen or workshop. Sizzling and screeching was in the air. Infernal red lighting gave an impression of a low

108

ceiling, smoky red bricks arched like an old-fashioned bread-oven.

In her hands were a pair of devices which fitted like gloves. Black leather straps kept her hands round contoured grips like the handles of a skipping rope, and her thumbs were pressed down on studs inset into the apparatus. Wires led from the grips into a junction box at her feet.

She was wearing black high-heeled boots, goggles that covered half her face and a rubber fetish bikini. Oil and sweat trickled on her tight stomach, and down her smoke-rouged arms and calves. Her hair was pulled back and fanned stickily on her shoulders.

Her thumbs were jamming down the studs.

Jethro Tull was performing 'Living in the Past'.

And someone was screaming. There was an electric discharge in the air. In the gloom of the near distance, a white shape writhed. The goggles were clouded, making it impossible to get more than a vague sense of what she was looking at.

She relaxed her thumbs, instantly. The writhing and screaming halted. Cold guilt chilled her mind. She fought the fuzziness.

Someone panted and sobbed.

'I think you've shown us just what you think of the cook, Lieutenant Veevee,' said Dr Ballance.

He stood nearby, in a kilt and a black leather Gestapo cap. A pink feather boa entwined his broad, naked chest like a real snake.

'Have you expressed yourself fully?' he asked.

She could still taste the eyeball. Still see the damned pig-face making a grin.

Red anger sparked. She jammed her thumbs down.

A full-blooded scream ripped through the room, hammering against the bricks and her ears. A blue arc of electricity lit up one wall. The white shape convulsed and she kept her thumbs down, pouring her rage into the faceless victim.

No. That was what they wanted.

109

She flipped her thumbs erect, letting go of the studs.

The arc stopped, the shape slumped.

Half Dr Ballance's face expressed disappointment.

'Forgiveness and mercy, eh, Lieutenant? We shall have to do something about that.'

Attendants took down the shape – was it a man? a woman? an animal? – she had been shocking.

Vanessa felt a certain triumph. They hadn't turned her into a torturer.

'Now cook has the switch,' said Dr Ballance.

She looked into the darkness, following the wires.

Shock hit her in the hands and ran up her arms, a rising ratchet of voltage. It was like being lashed with pain.

Her mind was whipped out.

She was doing push-ups. Her arms and stomach told her she had been doing push-ups for some time. A voice counted in the mid-hundreds.

Staff Sergeant Barry Sadler's 'The Ballad of the Green Berets' was playing.

She concentrated on shoving ground away from her, lifting her whole body, breathing properly, getting past pain. Her back and legs were rigid.

Glancing to one side, she saw a polished pair of boots.

Numbers were shouted at her. She upped the rate, smiling tightly. This, she could take. She was trained in dance (ballroom, modern and ballet) and oriental boxing (judo, karate and *jeet kune do*), her body tuned well beyond the standards of the commandos. She reached her thousand. Inside five seconds, she gave ten more for luck.

'On your feet, soldier,' she was ordered.

She sprung upright, to attention. She was wearing fatigues and combat boots.

A black woman inspected her. She had a shaved head, three parallel weals on each cheek, and 'Sergeant-Mistress Finch' stencilled on her top pocket.

Her tight fist jammed into Vanessa's stomach.

She clenched her tummy muscles a split second before hard knuckles landed. Agony still exploded in her gut, but she didn't go down like a broken doll.

Sergeant-Mistress Finch wrung out her fist.

'Good girl,' she said. 'Give Lieutenant Veevee a lollipop.'

Miss Dove, who was dressed as a soldier, produced a lollipop the size of a stop sign, with a hypnotic red and white swirl pattern. She handed it to Vanessa.

'By the numbers,' Sergeant-Mistress Finch ordered, 'lick!'

Vanessa had a taste-flash of the pig's eyeball, but overcame remembered disgust. She stuck her tongue to the surface of the lollipop and licked. A sugar rush hit her brain.

'Punishments and rewards,' commented a Scots voice.

She woke with the taste of sugar in her mouth and a gun in her hand. She was wearing a kilt, a tight cut-away jacket over a massively ruffled shirt, and a feathered cap. Black tartan tags stuck out of her thick grey socks and from her gilt epaulettes.

Sergeant-Mistress Finch knelt in front of her, hands cuffed behind her, forehead resting against the barrel of Vanessa's pistol.

'S-M Finch is a traitor to the unit,' said Dr Ballance. Vanessa swivelled to look at him. He wore the full dress uniform of the Black Watch.

They were out in the woods, after dark. A bonfire burned nearby. Soldiers (all girls) stood around. There was a woodsy tang in the air and a night chill settling in. A lone bagpiper mournfully played 'Knock Knock, Who's There?', a recent chart hit for Mary Hopkin.

'Do your duty, Lieutenant Veevee.'

Vanessa's finger tightened on the trigger.

This was a test. But would she pass if she shot or refused to shoot? Surely, Dr Ballance wouldn't let her really kill one of the attendants. If he ran Pleasant Green like that, he would run out of staff.

111

The gun must not be loaded.

She shifted the pistol four inches to the left, aiming past the Sergeant-Mistress's head, and pulled the trigger. There was an explosion out of all proportion with the size of the gun. A crescent of red ripped out of Finch's left ear. The Sergeant-Mistress clapped a hand over her spurting wound and fell sideways.

Vanessa's head rang with the impossibly loud sound.

She looked out through white bars. She was in a big crib, a pen floored with cushioning and surrounded by a fence of wooden bars taller than she was. She wore an outsized pinafore and inch-thick woollen knee-socks. Her head felt huge, as if jabbed all over with dental anaesthetic. When she tried to stand, the floor wobbled and she had to grab the bars for support. She was not steady on her feet at all. She had not yet learned to walk.

Veevee crawled. A rattle lay in the folds of the floor, almost too big for her grasp. She focused on her hand. It was slim, long-fingered. She could make a fist. She was a grown-up, not a baby.

A tannoy was softly broadcasting 'Jake the Peg (With an Extra Leg)' by Rolf Harris.

She picked up the rattle.

The bars sank into the floor and she crawled over the row of holes where they had been. She was in a playroom. Huge alphabet blocks were strewn around in Stonehenge arrangements, spelling words she couldn't yet pronounce. Two wooden soldiers, taller than she was, stood guard, circles of red on their cheeks, stiff Zebedee moustaches on their round faces, shakoes on their heads, bayonet-tipped rifles in their spherical hands.

Plumped in a rocking chair was Dr Ballance, in a velvet jacket with matching knickerbockers, a tartan cravat frothing under his chin, a yard-wide tam o'shanter perched on his head.

'Veevee want to play-play?' he asked.

112

She wasn't sure any more. This game had been going on too long. She had forgotten how it started.

There were other children in the playroom. Miss Dove and Miss Lark, in identical sailor suits. And others: Miss Wren, Miss Robin and Miss Sparrow. Sergeant-Mistress Finch was home sick today, with ear-ache.

The friends sang 'Ring-a-ring-a-roses' and danced round Veevee. The dance made her dizzy again. She tried to stand, but her pinafore was sewn together at the crotch and too short to allow her body to unbend.

'You're it,' Miss Dove said, slapping her.

Veevee wanted to cry. But big girls didn't blub. And she was a very big girl.

She was a grown-up. She looked at her hand to remind herself. It was an inflated, blubbery fist, knuckles sunk in babyfat.

The others were all bigger than her.

Veevee sat down and cried and cried.

Act II: Richard is Rumbled

Alastair Garnett, the Whitehall man, had wanted to meet in a multi-storey car park, but Richard explained that nothing could be more conspicuous than his ShadowShark. Besides, two men exchanging briefcases in a car park at dead of night was always suspicious. Instead, he had set a date for two in the morning in the Pigeon-Toed Orange Peel, a discotheque in the King's Road.

He sat at the bar, sipping a tequila sunrise from a heavy glass shaped like a crystal ball. An extremely active girl in a polka-dot halter and matching shorts roller-skated behind the long bar, deftly balancing drinks.

Richard was wearing a floor-length green suede Edwardian motorist's coat over a tiger-striped orange-and-black silk shirt, zebra-striped white-and-black flared jeans and hand-made zig-zag-striped yellow-and-black leather moccasins. In place of a tie, he wore an amulet with the CND peace symbol inset into the eyes of a griffin rampant. In his lapel was a single white carnation, so Garnett could identify him.

He lowered his sunglasses – thin-diamond-shaped emerald-tinted lenses with a gold wire frame – and looked around the cavernous room. Many girls and some boys had Egyptian eye motifs painted on bare midriffs, thighs, upper arms, throats or foreheads. The paint was luminous and, as the lights flashed on and off in five-second bursts, moments of darkness were inhabited by a hundred dancing eyes.

A band of long-haired young men played on a raised circular stage. They were called The Heat, and were in the middle of 'Non-Copyright Stock Jazz Track 2', a thirty-five-minute improvised fugue around themes from their début album, *Neutral Background Music*.

A pleasantly chubby girl in a cutaway catsuit, rhinestone-studded patch over one eye, sat next to Richard and suggested they might have been lovers in earlier incarnations. He admitted the possibility, but sadly confessed they'd have to postpone any reunion until later lives. She shrugged cheerfully and took his hand, producing an eyebrow pencil to write her telephone number on his palm. As she wrote, she noticed the other number tattooed on his wrist and looked at him again. A tear started from her own exposed eye and she kissed him.

'Peace, love,' she said, launching herself back on to the dance floor and connecting with a Viking youth in a woven waistcoat and motorcycle boots.

Across the room, he saw a thin man who wore a dark grey overcoat, a black bowler hat and a wing-collar tight over a light grey tie, and carried a tightly furled Union Jack umbrella. Richard tapped his carnation and the man from Whitehall spotted him.

'What a racket,' Garnett said, sitting at the bar. 'Call that music? You can't understand the words. Not like the proper songs they used to have.'

'"Doodly-Acky-Sacky, Want Some Seafood, Mama"?'

'I beg your pardon?'

'A hit for the Andrews Sisters in the 1940s,' Richard explained.

'Harrumph,' said Garnett.

A boy dressed in tie-dyed biblical robes, with an enormous bush of beard and hair, paused at the bar while buying a drink and looked over Garnett. The Whitehall man held tight to his umbrella.

'That's a crazy look, man,' the boy said, flashing a reversed V sign.

A crimson flush rose in Garnett's face. He ordered a gin and tonic and tried to get down to business. Though The Heat were playing loud enough to whip the dancers into a frenzy, there was a quiet-ish zone at the bar which allowed them to have a real conversation.

'I understand you're one of the spooks of the Diogenes Club,' the Whitehall man said. 'Winthrop's creature.'

Richard shrugged, allowing the truth of it. The Diogenes Club was loosely attached to the Government of the Day and tied into the tangle of British Intelligence agencies, but Edwin Winthrop of the Ruling Cabal had kept a certain distance from the Gnomes of Cheltenham since the War, and was given to running Diogenes more or less as a private fiefdom.

It was said of one of Winthrop's predecessors that he not only worked for the British Government but that under some circumstances he *was* the British Government. Winthrop did not match that, but was keen on keeping Diogenes out of the bailiwick of Whitehall, if only because its stock in trade was everything that couldn't be circumscribed by rules and regulations, whether the procedures of the Civil Service or the laws of physics. Richard was not a Civil Servant, not beholden to the United Kingdom for salary and pension, but did think of himself as loyal to certain ideals, even to the Crown.

'I'm afraid this is typical of Diogenes's behaviour lately,'

Garnett said. 'There's been the most almighty snarl-up in the Pleasant Green affair.'

Garnett, Richard gathered, was one of the faction who thought the independence of the Diogenes Club a dangerous luxury. They were waiting patiently for Winthrop's passing so that everything could be tied down with red tape and sealing wax.

'Pleasant Green is being looked into,' Richard said.

'That's just it. You're jolly well to stop looking. Any expenses you've incurred will be met upon production of proper accounts. But all documentation, including notes or memoranda you or your associates have made, must be surrendered within forty-eight hours. It's a matter of national security.'

Richard had been expecting this curtain to lower.

'It's ours, isn't it?' he said, smiling. 'Pleasant Green?'

'You are not cleared for that information. Rest assured that the unhappy events which came to your notice will not reoccur. The matter is at an end.'

Richard kept his smile fixed and ironic, but he had a gnawing worry. It was all very well to be cut out of the case, but Vanessa was inside. If he wanted to extract her, there would be dangers. He had been careful not to let Garnett gather exactly what sort of investigation he had mounted, but it had been necessary to call in favours from the armed forces to kit the girl up with a snakeskin. Garnett might know Vanessa was undercover at Pleasant Green, and could well have blown her cover with Dr Iain M. Ballance.

Garnett finished his g.-and-t. and settled the bar bill. He asked the surprised rollergirl for a receipt. She scribbled a figure on a cigarette paper and handed it over with an apologetic shrug.

'Good night to you,' the Whitehall man said, leaving.

Richard gave Garnett five minutes to get clear of the Pigeon-Toed Orange Peel and slipped out himself.

The ShadowShark was parked round the corner. Vanessa

usually drove for him, and Fred was occasionally allowed the wheel as a treat, but they were both down in darkest Sussex. He slid into the driver's seat and lowered the partition.

'You were right, Edwin,' he told the man in the back seat.

Winthrop nodded. Though he wore a clipped white moustache and had not bulked out in age, there was a certain Churchillian gravity to the Old Man. He had fought for King and Country in three world wars, only two of which the history books bothered with.

'Ghastly business,' Winthrop snorted, with disgust.

'I've been asked to cease and desist all investigation of Pleasant Green and Dr Ballance.'

'Well, my boy, that you must do. We all have our masters.'

Richard did not need to mention Vanessa. Winthrop had made the call to an old army comrade to help outfit 'Lieutenant Vail' with a believable life.

'The investigation was a formality, anyway,' Winthrop said. 'After all, we knew at once what Ballance was up to. He drives people off their heads. Now, we know who he mostly does it for. He has private-sector clients but his major business is to provide tailor-made psychopaths who are placed at the disposal of certain official and semi-official forces in our society. It's funny, really. The people behind Ballance are much like us, like the Diogenes Club. Governments come and go, but they're always there. There are times when any objective observer would think them on the side of the angels and us batting for the other lot. You know what our trouble is, Richard? England's trouble? We won all our wars. At great cost, but we won. We needed a new enemy. Our American cousins might be content to clash sabres with the Soviets, but Ivan was never going to be our dragon. We made our own enemy, birthed it at home, and raised it. Maybe it was always here and we are the sports and freaks.'

Richard understood.

'I know what Garnett wants me to do,' he said. 'What does Diogenes want?'

'Obviously, you are to stop investigating Dr Ballance's business. And start dismantling it.'

Act III: Vanessa is Valiant

In the morning room, comfortable armchairs were arranged in a circle. Group sessions were important at Pleasant Green.

In the next seat was a middle-aged man. Dr Ballance asked him to stand first.

'My name is Mr Ease,' he said.

'Hello, Mr Ease,' they all replied.

'. . . and I cheat and steal.'

'Good show,' murmured an approving voice, echoed by the rest of Group. She clapped and smiled with the rest of them. Dr Ballance looked on with paternal approval.

He was a businessman. It had apparently been difficult to wash away the last of his scruples. Now, after a week of Pleasant Green, Mr Ease was unencumbered by ethics or fear of the law. He had been worried about prison, but that phobia was overcome completely.

'My name is Captain Naughty,' said a hard-faced man, a uniformed airline pilot. 'And I want to punish people who do bad things. Firmly. Most of all, I want to punish people who do nothing at all.'

'Very good, Captain,' said Dr Ballance.

Next up was the patrician woman who always wore blue dresses, the star of Group.

'My name is Mrs Empty,' she announced. 'And I feel nothing for anyone.'

She got no applause or hug. She earned respect, not love. Mr Ease and Captain Naughty were clearly smitten with Mrs Empty, not in any romantic sense but in that they couldn't stay away from the sucking void of her arctic charisma. Even Dr Ballance's staff were in awe of her.

'My name is Rumour,' drawled a craggy Australian. 'And I

want everything everyone thinks to come through me.'

'Good on you, sir,' Captain Naughty said, looking sideways to seek approval, not – like everyone else in Group – from Dr Ballance but from Mrs Empty.

'My name is Peace,' said a young, quiet Yorkshireman. 'I like killing women.'

Peace, as always, got only perfunctory approval. The others didn't like him. He made them think about themselves.

She was last. She stood, glancing around at the ring of encouraging faces.

The Group was supportive. But this would be difficult.

'My name is Lieutenant Veevee,' she said.

'Hello, Veevee,' everyone shouted, with ragged cheer.

She took a deep breath, and said it.

'. . . and I will kill people.'

There. She felt stronger, now.

Mr Ease reached up, took her hand and gave a friendly squeeze. Miss Lark gave her a hug. She sat down.

'Thank you all,' said Dr Ballance. 'You are very special to Pleasant Green, as individuals and as Group. You're our first perfect people. When you leave here, which you're very nearly ready to do, you'll accomplish great things. You will take Pleasant Green with you. It won't happen soon, maybe not for years. But I have faith in you all. You are creatures of the future. You will be the Masters of the 1980s.'

Already, complex relationships had formed within Group. Mr Ease and Captain Naughty competed to be friends with Mrs Empty, but she liked Rumour best of all. Peace was drawn to Veevee, but afraid of her.

'Would anyone like to tell us anything?' Dr Ballance asked.

Captain Naughty and Mr Ease stuck hands up. Mrs Empty flashed her eyes, expecting to be preferred without having to put herself forward.

'It's always you two,' Dr Ballance said. 'Let's hear from one of the quiet ones.'

He looked at her, then passed on.

'Peace,' the doctor said. 'Have you thoughts to share?'

The youth was tongue-tied. He was unusual here. He had learned to accept who he was and what he wanted, but was nervous about speaking up in the presence of his 'betters'. Whenever Mrs Empty made speeches about eliminating laziness or what was best for people, Peace opened and closed his sweaty hands nervously but looked at the woman with something like love.

'I was wondering, like,' he said. 'What's the best way to a tart's heart. I mean, physically. Between which ribs to stab, like?'

Captain Naughty clucked in disgust.

Peace looked at her. She lifted her left arm to raise her breast, then tapped just under it with her right forefinger.

'About here,' she said.

Peace flushed red. 'Thank you, Veevee.'

The others were appalled.

'Do we have to listen to this rot?' Captain Naughty asked. 'It's just filth.'

Peace was a National Health referral, while the others were Private.

'You've just run against your last barrier, Captain,' Dr Ballance announced. 'You – all of you – have begun to realize your potential, have cut away the parts of your personae that were holding you back. But before you can leave with your Pleasant Green diploma, you must acknowledge your kinship with Peace. Whatever you say outside this place, you must have in your mind a space like Pleasant Green, where you have no hypocrisy. It will ground you, give you strength. We must all have our secret spaces. Peace will get his hands dirtier than yours, but what he does will be for Group just as what you do will be for Group.'

Mrs Empty nodded, fiercely. She understood.

'That will be all for today,' Dr Ballance said, dismissing Group. 'Veevee, if you would stay behind a moment. I'd like a word.'

The others got up and left. She sat still.

She didn't know how long she had been at Pleasant Green, but it could have been months or days. She had been taken back to the nursery and grown up all over again, this time with a direction and purpose. Dr Ballance was father and mother to her psyche, and Pleasant Green was home and school.

Dr Ballance sat next to her.

'You're ready to go, Veevee,' he said, hand on her knee.

'Thank you, Doctor.'

'But there's something you must do, first.'

'What is that, Doctor?'

'What you want to do, Veevee. What you like to do.'

She trembled a little. 'Kill people?'

'Yes, my dear. There's a "bird-watcher" on the downs. Fred Regent.'

'Fred.'

'You know Fred, of course. A man is coming down from London. He will join Fred in Whipplewell, at the Coach and Horses.'

'Richard.'

'That's right, Lieutenant Veevee. Richard Jeperson.'

Dr Ballance took a wrapped bundle out of his white coat and gave it to her. She unrolled the white flannel, and found a polished silver scalpel.

'You will go to the Coach and Horses,' he told her. 'You will find Fred and Richard. You will bring them back here. And you will kill them for us.'

'Yes, Doctor.'

'Then, when you have passed that final exam, you will seek out a man called Edwin Winthrop.'

'I've met him.'

'Good. You have been brought up for this purpose specifically, to kill Edwin Winthrop. After that, you can rest. I'm sure other jobs will come up, but Winthrop is to be your primary target. It is more important that he die than that you live. Do you understand?'

She did. Killing Winthrop meant more to her than her own life.

'Good girl. Now, go and have dinner. Extra custard for you today.'

She wrapped the scalpel up again and put it in her pocket.

'You've been in there five days, Ness,' Fred told her.

'It seems longer,' she said. 'Much longer.'

Richard nodded sagely. 'Very advanced techniques, I'll be bound.'

They were cramped together in her Elan. She drove carefully, across the downs. After dark, the road could be treacherous.

'I was close to you in the wood on the first night,' Fred said. 'For the soldier games. What was that all about?'

She shrugged.

Richard was quiet. He must understand. That would make it easier.

She parked in a lay-by.

'There's a path through here,' she said. 'To Pleasant Green.'

'Lead on,' Richard said.

They walked through the dark wood. In a clearing, she paused and looked up at the bright half-moon.

'There's something,' Fred said. 'Listen.'

It was the bagpiper, wailing 'Cinderella Rockefeller'. Dr Ballance stepped into the clearing. Lights came on. The rest of the Pleasant Green staff were there, too: Miss Lark, Miss Wren, and the others. To one side, Mrs Empty stood, wrapped up in a thick blue coat.

'It seems we're expected,' Richard drawled.

'Indeed,' said Dr Ballance.

Fred looked at her, anger in his eyes. He made fists.

'It's not her fault,' Richard told him. 'She's not quite herself.'

'Bastard,' Fred spat at Dr Ballance.

Mrs Empty cringed in distaste at the language.

Dr Ballance said 'Veevee, if you would . . .'

She took her scalpel out and put it to Richard's neck, just behind the ear. She knew just how much pressure to apply, how deep to cut, how long the incision should be. He would bleed to death inside a minute. She even judged the angle so her ankle-length brown suede coat and calfskin high-heeled thigh boots would not be splattered.

'She's a treasure, you know,' Dr Ballance said to Richard. 'Thank you for sending her to us. She has enlivened the whole Group. Really. We're going to have need of her, of people like her. She's so sharp, so perfect, so pointed.'

Richard was relaxed in her embrace. She felt his heart beating, normally.

'And quite mad, surely?' Richard said.

'Mad? What does that mean, Mr Jeperson? Out of step with the rest of the world? What if the rest of the world is mad? And what if your sanity is what is holding you back, preventing you from attaining your potential? Who among us can say that they are really sane? Really normal?'

'I can,' said Mrs Empty, quietly and firmly.

'We have always needed mad people,' Dr Ballance continued. 'At Rorke's Drift, Dunkirk, the Battle of Britain, the Festival of Britain, we must have been mad to carry on as we did, and thank mercy for that madness. Times are a-changing, and we will need new types of madness. I can provide that, Mr Jeperson. These women are perfect, you know. They have no conscience at all, no feeling for others. Do you know how hard it is to expunge that from the female psyche? We teach our daughters all their lives to become mothers, to love and sacrifice. These two are my masterpieces. Lieutenant Veevee, your gift to us, will be the greatest assassin of the era. And Mrs Empty is even more special. She will take my madness and spread it over the whole world.'

'I suppose it would be redundant to call you mad?' Richard ventured.

Dr Ballance giggled.

Vanessa had Richard slightly off-balance, but was holding

123

him up. The blade of her scalpel was pressed against his jugular, steady.

'Ness won't do it,' Fred said.

'You think not?' Dr Ballance smiled. 'Anybody would. You would, to me, right now. It's just a matter of redirecting the circuits, to apply the willingness to a worthwhile end. She feels no anger or remorse or hate or joy in what she does. She just does it. Like a tin-opener.'

'Vanessa,' Richard said.

Click.

That was her name. Not Veevee.

Just his voice and her name. It was a switch thrown inside her.

Long ago, they had agreed. When she first came to Richard, under the control of something else, she had been at that zero to which the Pleasant Green treatment was supposed to reduce her. She had escaped, with his help, then built herself up, with his love and encouragement. She was the stronger for it. Her name, which she had chosen, was the core of her strength. It was the code-word which brought her out of a trance.

Everything Pleasant Green had done to her was meaningless now. She was Vanessa.

Not Veevee.

She didn't change, didn't move.

But she was herself again.

'That's all it takes,' Richard said, straightening up. 'A name. You don't really make people, Doctor. You just fake them. Like wind-up toys, they may work for a while. Then they run down. Like Mr Joyful ... Mr Achy ... Mr Enemy ... Miss Essex ... Lieutenant-Commander Hero?'

He enunciated the names clearly. Each one was a jab at Dr Ballance. The living half of his face froze, matching the dead side.

'This Group is better than them.'

'No more crack-ups, eh? They're just mad enough, but not

too broken to function?'

Mrs Empty's cold eyes were fixed on them.

'To survive in the world we are making,' Dr Ballance said, 'everybody will have to be mad.'

He reached into his coat and brought out a gun. In a blink, Vanessa tossed her scalpel. It spun over and over, catching moonlight, and embedded its point in Dr Ballance's forehead. A red tear dripped and he crashed backwards.

When he had gone for the gun, he had admitted defeat. He had doubted her. At the last, he had been proved wrong.

It all came crashing in. The programming, the torture, the disorientation – there had been drugs as well as everything else – fell apart.

With a scream, Miss Dove flew at her. She pirouetted and landed a foot in the attendant's face. The girl was knocked backwards and sprawled on the ground. She bounced back up, and came for her.

It was no match. Miss Dove was a master of disco-style roughhouse. All her movements came from her hips and her shoulders. Vanessa fell back on the all-purpose *jeet kune do* – the style developed by Bruce Lee which was starting to be called kung fu – and launched kicks and punches at the girl, battering her on her feet until she dropped.

The others backed away. Mrs Empty walked off, into the dark.

Fred checked Dr Ballance, and shook his head.

'Well done,' Richard said. 'I never doubted you.'

She was completely wrung out. Again, she was on the point of exploding into tears.

Richard held her and kissed her.

'I trusted you here, rather than go myself or send Fred, because I know your heart,' he said, kindly. 'Neither of us could have survived Pleasant Green. We're too dark to begin with. We could be made into killers. You couldn't. You can't. You're an angel of mercy, my love, not of death.'

Over his shoulder, she saw Ballance stretched out with a

stick of steel in his head. She loved Richard for what he felt about her, but he was wrong. The Pleasant Green treatment might have failed to make her a malleable assassin, but Dr Ballance had turned her into a killer all the same. After his doubt, had he known a split-second of triumph?

'It was about Winthrop,' she said. 'After you and Fred, he wanted me to kill Winthrop. It was part of some plan.'

He nodded grimly, understanding.

Coda: Mrs M.T.

On the croquet lawn of the Pleasant Green manor house, Richard found an oriental woman feeding a bonfire with an armful of file-folders. Fred wrestled her to the ground, but she had done her job with swift efficiency. Filing cabinets had been dragged out of the pre-fab buildings and emptied. Documents turned to ash and photographs curled in flame.

Vanessa, cloaked with her coat, was still pale. It would take a while for her to recover fully, but he had been right about her. She had steel.

The oriental – Miss Lark – produced a stiletto and made a few passes at Fred's stomach, forcing him back. Then she tried to slip the blade into her own heart. Vanessa, snapping out of her daze, grabbed the woman's wrist and made her drop the knife.

'No more,' she said.

Miss Lark looked at them with loathing. Dr Ballance would never have approved of an emotion like that.

The rest of the staff had vanished into the night, melting away to wherever it was minions languished between paying jobs. Bewildered folk in dressing gowns, among them the electric-eyed woman who had been in the wood, had drifted out to see what the fuss was all about and found themselves abandoned. The other members of the Group.

Car headlamps raked the lawns, throwing shadows against

the big house. Doors opened and people got out. They were all anonymous men.

'Jeperson,' shouted Garnett.

The Whitehall Man strode across the lawns, waving his umbrella like a truncheon.

Richard opened his hands and felt no guilt.

'I think you'll find Dr Ballance exceeded his authority, Mr Garnett. If you look around, you'll find serious questions raised.'

'Where is the Doctor?' demanded Garnett.

'In the wood. He seems to be dead.'

The civil servant was furious.

'He has a gun in his hand. I think he intended to kill someone or other. Very possibly me.'

Garnett obviously thought it a pity Ballance hadn't finished the job. It was a shame this would end here, Richard thought. Important folk had been sponsoring Dr Ballance, and had passed down orders to act against the Diogenes Club. Winthrop would be grimly amused to learn he was the eventual target of the plan.

'It wasn't working, though,' Richard said.

'What?' Garnett said.

'The Ballance Process or whatever he called it. He was trying to manufacture functioning psychotics, wasn't he? Well, none of them ever functioned. Didn't you notice? Look at them, poor lost souls.'

He indicated the people in dressing gowns. Ambulances had arrived, and the Pleasant Green guests were being helped into them.

'What use do you think they'll be now?'

By the ambulances was parked a car whose silhouette Richard knew all too well. There were only five Rolls-Royce ShadowSharks in existence; and he owned three of them, all in silver. This was painted in night black, with opaque windows to match. A junior functionary like Garnett wouldn't run to this antichrist of the road.

He would know the machine again. And the man inside it, who had ordered his death and Edwin's.

Garnett turned away and scurried across the lawn, to report to the man in the ShadowShark. The woman from the wood firmly resisted orderlies who were trying to help her into an ambulance. She asked no questions and made no protests, but wouldn't be man-handled, wouldn't be turned.

'Who is that?' he asked Vanessa.

'Mrs Empty,' she said. 'The star pupil.'

He shuddered. Mrs Empty was quite, quite mad, he intuited. Yet she was strong, mind unclouded by compassion or uncertainty, character untempered by humour or generosity. In a precognitive flash that made him momentarily weak with terror, he saw a cold blue flame burning in the future.

She was assisted finally into an ambulance, but made the action seem like that of a queen ascending a throne, surrounded by courtiers.

The ambulances left. The ShadowShark stayed behind a moment. Richard imagined cold eyes looking out at him through the one-way black glass. Then the motor turned over and the Rolls withdrew.

He looked at Fred and Vanessa.

'Let's forget this place,' he said.

'That might not be easy,' Vanessa said.

'Then we shall have to try very hard.'

WHERE THE BODIES ARE
BURIED 3: BLACK AND WHITE
AND RED ALL OVER

He thought his wide suit made him look like a useless boyfriend in a Seventies sit-com. Not Scobie's idea of a good time but Harry insisted his reporters be smart. 'We're a local paper,' Harry always said, 'we have to be acceptable to local people.' The editor also insisted his reporters' hair be neither too short nor too long. Working for the *Herald* was like doing National Service.

At his desk, playing cat's cradle with elastic bands, Iain Scobie dreamed of Fleet Street. Rather, he dreamed of London Docklands. Most nationals had quit the Street. Papers like the *Comet* and the *Argus* were published from the Docklands Pyramid of Leech International.

He was resigned to serving out years in this West Country backwater before he was summoned by Derek Leech to join the thrusting dynamo of the *Comet*. Unless a horse came along: a story he could ride all the way to the finish line.

The *Herald*'s one eccentricity, which no one dared joke about to its editor's face, was Harry's enthusiasm for stories about the Girl Guides. An edition never passed without a picture of some pigtailed pixie covered in mud for charity creeping into the first three pages.

Scobie had recently manoeuvred a promotion from fêtes and

129

school pantos to crime. In this town, crime meant broken pub windows, missing bicycle lamps and scrumped apples. When a New Age convoy crept near, he'd thought it might be his horse, but the police diverted the travellers into swamp moorland with no fuss at all.

'Time for a cup of Rosie Lee,' Harry announced, having finished his editorial about council car parks. He looked about for someone who could be forced into tea-making. Scobie let go and bands twanged into space, stinging his fingers.

'Iain,' Harry said, pronouncing the second 'i' which often got left out of Scobie's by-line, 'could you bestir yourself kettle-wards?'

Scobie's telephone rang.

'Important call, Harry,' Scobie said, picking it up. Actually, the call was unlikely to be anything. Another cow wedged in a ditch. A bid to twin the town with a pile of war-torn rubble in the former Soviet Union. A cancelled Carnival concert.

It was Greg Dunphy, a police constable Scobie bought pints for. Both liked to pretend Scobie was a journalist and Dunphy a valuable source.

'I've got summat,' Dunphy said.

From the lack of preliminary when-is-the-next-skittles-match-and-piss-up? farting-around, he could tell Dunphy really had something he was forced to take seriously. Scobie heard the faint neighing of a wild horse, ready to be roped and broken and rough-ridden to the *Comet*.

On the Achelzoy road, about two miles beyond the town limits, Scobie found the car, an anonymous white Honda. It looked to have been badly parked rather than crashed. Its front stuck over the roadside ditch, wheels in mud. Dunphy's bike leant against the phone box. The policeman stood by the car. The girl sat on the grass, as if for a picnic. Dunphy must have radioed the station before he called Scobie – it took a lot more rounds to earn the kind of loyalty that made coppers call a reporter before his sergeant – but Scobie had arrived first.

He parked the Skoda – the *Herald*'s car, not his choice – and got out. Dunphy, almost hopping, was relieved to see him. The constable was completely out of his depth, terrified of messing up.

'Iain, watch this girl.'

She was under twenty and wore a white dress. Blonde hair pinned back. Pretty without being sexy. Wholesome. Harry would love to run a picture of her in a Girl Guide uniform.

Dunphy hopped towards a bush. The policeman had been bursting for a pee. Scobie looked at the girl, who smiled openly, then at the car.

'I wasn't careless,' she said. 'Swerved to miss a rabbit.'

A police car, siren shrilling, drew up next to Scobie's Skoda. Sergeant Sloman had his driver cut off the racket and walked over, not pleased to see Scobie. Dunphy came back, relieved, but was shaken at his sergeant's arrival when he was off the scene.

'You,' Sloman said, pointing. 'Go home.'

Scobie got out his press card.

'That doesn't say "Get Out of Jail Free" scumshine.'

He backed off but did not make a move towards the Skoda. Sloman stood by the girl and thought things over.

Scobie recognized her. School nurse at Ash Grove Comprehensive. He'd interviewed her about a rumoured epidemic of headlice. It had come to nothing. Her name was Elizabeth Yatman.

'Where are the others, Elizabeth?' asked Sloman.

She said nothing.

Sloman's driver poked around Elizabeth's car. He opened the passenger door and a bundle fell out. A white face stuck out of blanket swaddling. The bundle looked like a big baby.

Sloman's driver was sick.

'Where are the others, Elizabeth?'

The Honda was ringed with police cars, as if an armed terrorist were at the wheel. The road was coned across in both directions. Diversion signs were up. Sloman had the cordon established so quickly Scobie was trapped *inside* rather than kept out. Not wanting to admit a mistake, Sloman (also out of his depth) let him stick around providing he didn't get in the way.

There was confusion about what to do. Sloman felt Elizabeth's car and the horrid bundle shouldn't be moved until a lot more policemen had looked them over, but that still left him with Elizabeth herself. She was smiling and cooperative unless asked a direct question. Anyone coming on the scene would assume she was a victim or a witness . . .

That would be a good first line. 'Anyone coming on the scene would assume Elizabeth Yatman was a victim or a witness, not the alleged murderer of one child and a suspect in the disappearance of eight others . . .' Not 'assume'. That wasn't a newspaper word.

As afternoon faded, gloom gathered. It was quite warm for autumn, but a chill was coming. Policemen milled about, directionless. The Backwater Plods were waiting for the Pros from Dover.

Scobie slid into the Skoda and locked the doors. He bent low and dug out his cellular phone. He could dictate to the *Herald*'s copy-taker. Even Harry would tear the car park decision off the front page to make room for Elizabeth Yatman.

He stabbed Autodial #1, then cut off half-way through the clicks. This was his horse. He shouldn't lead it to the wrong stable. Loading his phone's memory with numbers, he'd been able to think of only nine he used regularly. The extra space, he hopefully filled with a number he would like to use regularly. He stabbed Autodial #0.

The phone was instantly answered.

'*Daily Comet*, how may I help you?'

At first, the *Comet* wanted to send down their own stringer from Bristol, but Scobie bargained hard. He was on the spot and had a head start. Unless he got to file his own copy, he'd

132

go to the next tabloid on the list. The phone-answerer transferred him up through several desks to Ronald Clewes, the *Comet*'s crime editor.

Clewes quickly cut a deal and passed him to a copy-taker. 'Anyone coming on the scene would think Elizabeth Yatman, 19, was a victim or a witness . . .'

He dictated a 300-word front-page story off the top of his head. He felt a buzz of non-chemical high as he compressed the horror into ready-formatted prose.

'What about pictures?' Clewes asked.

Scobie had that covered. 'I could ask multiple k for a pic, but I want your word you'll let me stay on the story. I won't let you down.'

'People don't let me down,' Clewes said. 'People don't let *Derek* down.'

'A pic will be wired.'

Scobie hung up and called the *Herald*. He got Gemma, the two-day-a-week picture editor, and asked her to look out the shots of Elizabeth (overexposed in a blinding white uniform) taken for the aborted lice feature and wire them to the number Clewes had given him. Gemma chuckled at the mystery but did not ask what was going on.

If Scobie stayed on this bronco, everything would change.

Within a day, he was no longer the only reporter on Elizabeth Yatman. But he was first. The *Comet* broke the story – 'SISTER OF MURDER: INNOCENT FACE OF MONSTER NURSE' – and Elizabeth's now-chilling perky smile was plastered over 30 million newspapers.

The hordes of New Grub Street descended on the West like a New Age convoy, booking every hotel room in Somerset, pestering every Ash Grove pupil, parent and teacher. There was little new stuff to pick over, so everyone dug for background.

No one had suspected anything. She seemed such a nice girl. There was no explanation.

Because he could afford to be generous, Scobie acted as a native guide to the nationals, telling them which pubs to haunt. His exclusive with Greg Dunphy was enough to get him another *Comet* front page.

On the third day, he remembered to call Harry and resign.

Evidence suggested Crispin Toomey, 13, had reported to Elizabeth Yatman with a twisted ankle after a morning-break soccer game. The nurse offered to drive him home. Instead, she took him to an unknown location (her car was too clean to have been used) and spent five hours killing him. Then she drove back to town and, sighting a rabbit, had her accident.

Eight other children, aged between eleven and fifteen, were missing. Hitherto, it had been presumed they had run away to join the travellers. All but one were pupils at Ash Grove. Four of them, it turned out, were last seen on their way to the nurse for minor treatment. Elizabeth did not say anything about the missing children. It was assumed they were dead, but Scobie wrote a story about the search, holding out the slim hope they might show up alive. It was as well to leaven horror with hope. Scobie had an instinctive understanding of that. Clewes commended him for it and looked forward to meeting him when he relocated to London and took his job on the *Comet*.

This was the most exciting time of his life.

The Monster's parents were dead. The only thing resembling a boy-friend who had turned up was Toby Combs, a shocked youth who helped her cater school outings. There was a much-reprinted photograph, taken at a Hallowe'en social, of Toby and Elizabeth dressed as witches, doling out punch from a bowl labelled with crossbones and the word 'POISON'.

On the fifth day, with Elizabeth still not talking, the *Comet* ran a story about an adulterous pop star on its front page. A sidebar promised more inside on the Monster Nurse, but Scobie had only been able to secure and sell interviews with a former Head who remembered Elizabeth as a pupil at Ash Grove. It turned out she had been a Girl Guide. Harry financed a holiday to Majorca selling file photos of her accepting a Life-

Saving Award from a *Blue Peter* presenter.

Scobie felt betrayed. Looking at the star, caught in a flash glare with the sort of microskirted blonde Scobie hoped to associate with when he moved to London, he was panic-stricken. What if tomorrow's *Comet* didn't even have a sidebar?

The first reporters had already drifted back to Bristol and London. The story was still big – television news always put it just after the big international events – but it dwindled daily.

He worried that his horse might be ready to throw him.

Dunphy met him for a pint. Though he had taken a mighty bollocking from Sloman for calling Scobie in the first place, he *was* the copper who had caught the killer, even if by accident. Dunphy just about realized what Scobie had known from the first: that getting off his bike to check that Honda in the ditch was the most important thing he'd do in his entire life.

'This is the medical report,' Dunphy said, pulling a folder out of his anorak. 'I did a photocopy.'

Scobie looked down the report. Naturally, Elizabeth was put through an exhaustive series of tests. Her skull was X-rayed in the hope of finding a tumour that might 'explain' her behavioural lapses.

He skimmed a lot of technical detail and hit on something.

'I have a call to make,' he said.

The next day's *Comet* front page carried his story... 'VIOLENT VIRGIN: MONSTER NURSE HAS NEVER HAD IT'.

Heavily coated policemen spread out in a straggly line and waded across the soggy moor, looking for freshly turned sod. Grey sky threatened drizzle.

The man from the *Mirror* complimented Scobie on his 'Violent Virgin' piece. Now, all the other press – even the BBC – called Elizabeth the 'Virgin Monster Nurse'.

'Do you think they'll find anything?' Scobie asked the older journo, a Welshman with a nose raspberried by too many whiskies.

'Let's hope not. This is good for another month. Better than an escaped puma or a little girl down a well.'

'What makes this happen?'

'It's in the air. In the Seventies, violent crime – rapes, murders, muggings – rose by ten per-cent every year. In the 'Eighties, it was 23 per cent. Now, it's 31. It's like a bug in society, a 'flu going round. People just catch it and go out and . . . kill.'

'Is that going to be the angle you write up?'

The journo laughed. 'Lord, no. Punters don't want blather about philosophical illnesses. They want something to blame. It's usually in the water. Maybe Satanic Heavy Metal.'

Elizabeth's CD collection was small and conventional: Andrew Lloyd Webber musicals, light classics used in TV adverts, Take That. Nobody could claim owning both the Broadway and West End cast recordings of *Cats* drove them to kill nine children.

It seemed the line of police had found something, but it was just an old bucket lodged in a ditch.

'Is there a nasties connection?' Clewes asked.

Scobie had thought of that.

'Elizabeth doesn't have a video.'

'Pity. What about the boy-friend?'

Talking on the phone, he imagined the editor pacing his bustling office, sleeves rolled up, minions approaching with proofs and urgent messages.

Scobie tried to remember Toby Combs's front room. The youth had refused to talk with him since the 'Violent Virgin' headline. He wondered if being branded a monster's boy-friend was worse than the revelation that he hadn't even had sex with her.

'Her boy-friend has a video,' Scobie said. 'I'm sure of it.'

'Well, find out if they watched nasties. Or porn. Or anything.'

Scobie imagined Toby and Elizabeth sitting demurely at either end of the sofa watching *Lassie Come Home*. Maybe holding hands during the sad bits.

'It's all on the computer,' Mrs Morris told him. 'I can tell you exactly what any member has rented out. The figures go into a pile at the head office and make up the charts.'

Mrs Morris's shop used to be called Valerie's Videos. Now it was part of a big chain. The place looked like a fast-food outlet, with cassettes instead of burgers.

The charts were propped up on the counter. This week at Number One was *Where the Bodies Are Buried 3*. A poster for the horror film trumpeted its '3-D trip to Hell'. Special glasses were provided with each rental.

'Could you tell me what Toby Combs has rented?'

'If I can work this menu properly,' Mrs Morris said, stabbing keys. 'Ah, victory.'

A sheet of paper printed out.

'He's not a very regular renter. Less than one a month.'

Scobie read the list. The only real surprise was the *Comet Knock-Outs Bouncing Beachballs Bonanza*, which featured the topless girls who appeared on the inside pages of the *Comet* playing volleyball in slow motion. Scobie wondered if Toby had asked Elizabeth round that evening, and imagined the youth's violet blushes.

Otherwise, it was all mainstream: *Problem Child, Blame It on the Bellboy, Cocoon, Top Gun, The Little Mermaid*. At the bottom of the list was another title that didn't quite fit: *Where the Bodies Are Buried 3*.

'Did he really take this out?'

Behind the counter towered a cardboard cut-out of Rob Hackwill, the monster from the *Where the Bodies Are Buried* films, single eye flashing red, silver-foiled claws glinting.

'It's a huge rental. We stock copies in depth. Everybody has taken it out. Kids love horror films. I prefer musicals myself.'

'Why would anyone want to pay to be horrified?'

'Have you got a girl-friend? Couples like these films because they're an excuse to cuddle during the scary scenes.'

Scobie imagined Toby putting on *Where the Bodies Are Buried 3* and edging nearer Elizabeth's end of the sofa, arm creeping along cushions behind her back, itching to pounce, like Rob Hackwill on a cheerleader. He saw the reflection of the monster in Elizabeth's wide blue eyes.

The *Comet* headline read: 'TWO FACES OF EVIL'. Below were the familiar shot of a smiling Elizabeth in her nurse's hat and a still of the fang-baring monster from one of the *Where the Bodies Are Buried* films. In the article, Scobie asked if *Where the Bodies Are Buried 3* had snapped Elizabeth Yatman's mind, if she had asked Rob Hackwill into her life, if she had acted on orders from the Hollywood bogeyman? He asked the questions: 33 million *Comet* readers answered with a series of decisive 'yeses'.

That night, Cloud 9, the satellite channel owned by Derek Leech, the *Comet*'s proprietor, cancelled the *première* of a comedy action film called *Surfin' CIA* to broadcast *Where the Bodies Are Buried 3*. After the transmission, which drew the highest rating of the year, viewers voted by calling one of two numbers: one for those who felt the film definitely caused Elizabeth Yatman's crimes and should be withdrawn, one for those who believed violent films had no effect on society. Leech promised to abide by the results: when 78 per cent of calls said no to Rob Hackwill, he withdrew *Where the Bodies Are Buried 3* from Cloud 9 and promised never to show it again, or any of the other films in the series. At least, not after the Cloud 9 Hallowe'en Midnight-till-Dawn marathon advertised as 'the last chance to see' all five *Where the Bodies Are Buried* films. The marathon, which followed a news special on the Yatman case, also drew record ratings.

On the suggestion of the *Comet*, video shops reluctantly pulled *Where the Bodies Are Buried 3* off the shelves – since Scobie's story, it was the most popular title in the horror section – and tried to return them to the distributor. When the company wouldn't buy back the tapes, the *Comet* quietly bought a job lot and organized parents' groups and moral crusaders into a mass burning on the rec ground where Elizabeth's victims had once played football. The family of Crispin Toomey were too stricken to attend, but several parents of still-missing children showed up and were photographed throwing cassettes into the flames. Faces contorted, either with loathing or in the natural expression of someone who has inhaled a lungful of burning videotape.

Cloud 9 interviewed Scobie at the burning. He was beginning to wonder whether his future was in print journalism after all. Maybe he could vault from the *Comet* into television.

'These evil films must be stopped,' Scobie said, sincerely. 'How long can we afford to pour filth into weak minds and not expect them to become clogged with insanity?'

Some bystanders cheered him. He was already a local celebrity. Soon he would be a national figure.

The next day, Sloman turned up at his flat, swallowing his dislike. Elizabeth Yatman wanted to see him. She had something to say she would only say to him.

He was alone with the Monster. A matron who resembled Dolph Lundgren was just outside the door, beyond a peephole. Elizabeth's prison dress looked like a dyed-blue nurse's uniform. Anything she wore looked like a nurse's uniform.

'You've made me famous, Mr Scobie. Thank you.'

'You made yourself famous, Elizabeth.'

'I never miss the *Comet*. When I were little, I wanted to be a *Comet* Knock-Out. I didn't grow the chest for it.'

If she posed nude now, she could command a bigger fee than Princess Di. People would be interested.

Scobie did not know what to ask. Asked thousands of questions in the past weeks, she had kept her secrets. In person, she was even more ordinary than in the pictures that had to be doctored to make her eyes shine like evil neon. Her blonde eyebrows were almost invisible.

'Do you watch horror films?'

Elizabeth made a face. 'I get scared. I saw half of *Carry On Screaming* on the telly box once and had nightmares for months.'

'Do you remember *Where the Bodies Are Buried 3*?'

'The film Toby rented?'

'Yes.'

'I read about it in the *Comet*. Sounds horrid.'

'Did you see it?'

She didn't say anything. To the *Herald*, Toby claimed he had been given the film by mistake. He had wanted to rent *When the Whales Came*. None of the nationals picked up that twist on the story.

'Did Rob Hackwill, the monster, make you do . . . the things you did?'

Elizabeth smiled. 'If it helps the *Comet*, Mr Scobie.'

For the first time, he found her frightening.

'I've a tape of the film, Elizabeth. I've been watching it. Trying to understand.'

'I hope you don't watch it on your own. You'll scare yourself to death.'

It was just a silly horror film. A rubber monster leaping out of the dark, drawing lines of ketchup on aerobicized teenage bodies. Loud noises and bad music. Explosive death and bad jokes. Pathetic.

'There hasn't been so much in the *Comet* lately.'

Elizabeth was off the front page. The search for the missing children had gone on too long to be interesting. Psychiatrists gave interviews with too many polysyllables to be usable.

'It's all Baby Milena and Barry Gatlin.'

Baby Milena was a Bosnian orphan flown to London at Derek Leech's expense for plastic surgery on her badly burned face. Barry Gatlin was an American comedian who got into a shoot-out with the Los Angeles police after a traffic offence.

140

'I'd like to help the *Comet*, Mr Scobie. I'd like to tell you where to find . . .'

She giggled like a thirteen-year-old.

'Let me put it this way,' she adopted a gruff American movie trailer horror voice, 'I'd like to tell you *Where the Bodies Are Buried* . . .'

If he didn't tell the police, he could get into trouble. But if he told the police, he'd have to share. He thought of a way of telling the police and keeping his exclusive.

He called Greg Dunphy.

The constable met him for a lunchtime drink at the Valiant Soldier, a pub in Alder. The village was nine miles outside town. Dunphy returned one of the *Comet*'s copies of *Where the Bodies Are Buried 3* to him.

'Couldn't get through it,' he admitted. 'Jimmy and Mandy loved it, though. Horror don't bother them.'

Dunphy's kids went to Ash Grove. Jimmy was in the football team with Crispin Toomey.

Scobie slipped the video into his coat pocket.

'She told me where she did it.'

'Christ!'

'The kids are still there, she says.'

'Christ oh Christ!'

'You and me, we'll beat the detectives from Bristol. We'll find the place. I'll write it up as if we worked out the clues. I'll say she dropped hints.'

Dunphy gulped his pint.

Elizabeth's parents had run a small farm in Alder. With the recession, they'd been badly behind on the mortgage payments when they died in a car crash. Now the bank had the place up for sale. Even with the notoriety of being the childhood home of the Monster Nurse, the farm wasn't shifting.

'The Bristol CID boys were all over,' Dunphy said.

'Elizabeth had a secret den.'

'We dug bloody holes everywhere.'

'It's not under the ground.'

They dragged open the gate and walked up the muddy track towards the house and a barn.

'I should call Sloman.'

'Let's make sure Elizabeth isn't playing us for twazzocks first. Mass murderers have been known to lie.'

The barn-door was open. They went inside. Bare, the barn still smelled of hay and dung. Scobie looked up at the flat wooden roof. Outside, the roof was corrugated iron and curved.

He searched for the rope Elizabeth had told him about.

'Bingo.'

It was wound round a skewer in the ground. Anyone not in the know would assume it was just part of the webbing hay bales were to be fixed to. He untied the rope and gave a strong tug. A trapdoor creaked upwards and a rope ladder fell on Dunphy. The constable yelped and cringed.

'Magic,' Scobie said.

A nasty smell seeped out of the cavity in the roof. He knew the next minutes would be unpleasant.

'Did you bring a torch?' he asked.

'On my bike?'

Scobie fished out his cigarette lighter and made flame. 'This will have to do.'

'You're going up there?'

'Tell you what, you call Sloman.'

Scobie checked the flash on his camera. He would get his own pictures. Exclusive. Official. 'VIRGIN MONSTER NURSE'S HORROR LAIR'.

Dunphy backed away, towards the barn door. Afternoon light spilled around him. Scobie climbed up to the darkness. He lifted his lighter in through the trapdoor and poked his head into Elizabeth's hidey-hole.

Stench flailed about his face like a chain.

His hand brushed something stiff and crinkly on the surface but soft, moist and giving underneath. He nearly lost his footing on the ladder. A small face, as twisted as anything in *Where the Bodies Are Buried 3*, was close to his own. His flickering lighter gave its shadow-etched features movement. He pulled himself into the low space. There was a gap of about four feet between the wooden floor and the tin ceiling.

How had Elizabeth persuaded the kids to climb the ladder? For the younger ones, it might have been a game. For the older ones, the boys at least, it might have been a promise.

His head spun as he sat in the hidey-hole, surrounded by dead kids. A paraffin lamp stood by the trapdoor. The lighter burned his fingers. Maybe seeing it properly would be better than imagining it from outlines. He lit the lamp and turned up the wick.

Every inch of the hole – tin roof, stone walls, the wooden beams – was collaged with paper. The black and white wasn't red all over, but it was speckled with dark brown that must have been red when fresh. Elizabeth had cocooned herself with newspaper cuttings. *Comet* Knock-Outs, interchangable breasts and smiles, were plastered throughout news pictures and headlines. From the Knock-Outs' hairstyles, Scobie knew Elizabeth had been papering this den since the early Eighties, since before she was ten years old.

There were famous headlines. 'GERTCHA GAUCHOS!', from the Falklands War. 'HANG HUSSEIN!', from the Gulf War. 'DID ELVIS DIE OF AIDS?: OUR PSYCHIC REVEALS THE TRUTH'. 'HAIRY PASSAGE: HAMSTER IN HOLLYWOOD HUNK'S BACK ENTRANCE'. 'BUGGER OFF, BRUSSELS!' 'PAY YOUR POLL TAX AND WIN A FORD MONTEGO'. A run-down of Derek Leech's evolving political position: 'MAGGIE WALLOPS KINNOCK', 'MAGGIE RULES', 'MAGGIE MUST STAY', 'MAGGIE MUST GO', 'MAJOR WALLOPS KINNOCK', 'MAJOR RULES', 'MAJOR MUST STAY', 'MAJOR MUST GO'. Wars, football, riots, bingo. Royal romances, royal weddings, royal divorces. Strikes, scandals, silly season dog-biting, sex, soap, satellite TV.

All the cuttings were from the *Comet*.

Myra Hindley, Peter Sutcliffe, Dennis Nilsen, Jack the Ripper, the Krays, the Black Panther, Ted Bundy, Jeffrey Dahmer, David Koresh, Ivan the Terrible, Frederick West. Murderers and criminals stared out of dozens of *Comet* front pages. Headlines spoke of Monster Manors, Horror Houses, Axe Atrocities, Gun Sieges, Terror Lairs, Human Fiends, Pitiless Gazes, Killer Smiles, Death Cars, Satin Satans.

When she was little, Elizabeth Yatman wanted to get into the *Comet* by posing topless, but she didn't grow the chest for it. She'd found another way to get her wish.

This was not a story which would sell.

With decisive certainty, Scobie plucked clippings from surfaces where they had been gummed. The old paper tore and crumbled.

He stayed away from the corpses as he ripped. A mossy clump of Knock-Out pin-ups, moulded together by damp, came off in a great rip. Stabs of daylight came through joins between the tin sheets of the roof. The space was small enough to be cleared completely in enough time. He would be done before Dunphy got back with Sloman.

He scrunched the clippings into a ball the size of a pillow and dropped it through the trapdoor. The ball came apart on the bare earth floor of the barn. He could easily scoop it together and get it to the car. It would all burn later.

A last look-around showed him he had done a good job. Nothing remained of Elizabeth's tabloid collage.

One more touch. He took the *Where the Bodies Are Buried 3* video out of his pocket and propped it against a beam. Rob Hackwill's rubber snarl caught his eye. The monster, framed on the cover, seemed to be swearing vengeance.

The next day's *Comet* headline was obvious: 'MONSTER NURSE: WHERE THE BODIES WERE BURIED'.

Elizabeth's lawyers started bleating about the evil influences of Rob Hackwill. In Hollywood, Allan Keyes, English creator of *Where the Bodies Are Buried*, had no comment. Snordlij Svensson, the Icelandic movie brat who directed *Where the Bodies Are Buried 3*, was too busy on *Cretaceous Cop*, the 100-million-dollar summer blockbuster he had landed on the strength of his work on the horror sequel, to say anything quotable.

Cloud 9 staged a debate about the effects of horror violence on impressionable minds, between Morag Duff, a right-wing Labour MP and 'moral crusader', and Shelley Carlisle, a film critic who edited *Rabid*, the 'International Magazine of Cine-Terror'. Scobie, plugged into the information super-highway, chaired the show.

'I think the pressure should be on those who claim film violence *doesn't* have an effect to prove their case,' said the politician. 'Lives are at stake. It seems strange to plead freedom of speech when kids are being killed. If one life is saved, surely it's worth getting rid of a load of pernicious rubbish.'

The studio audience agreed with her. Someone got up and said, 'Even if horror films don't cause real horror, we can do without them. Let's ban the bastards to be on the safe side.'

Shelley Carlisle, who was quite attractive in a Goth sort of way, looked disgusted and got flustered. She tried to make a point but he cut in.

'Shelley,' he began, heavily, 'if you'd been in that barn, you'd never be able to watch a horror film again.'

On the first day of the trial, the judge commented he thought it 'quite likely' Elizabeth had been influenced by *Where the Bodies Are Buried 3*. In the *Comet*, Scobie wrote 'JUDGE BLAMES NASTY: OFFICIAL'.

The next day, Valerie's Video, which had binned its entire stock of horror films, was broken into by vandal vigilantes who piled cassettes of animal comedies on the floor and set a fire. Mrs Morris, who lived in a flat upstairs, was stricken by smoke inhalation but rescued in time to survive. The *Comet* called her 'another victim of the curse of Rob Hackwill'.

In parliament, Morag Duff called for a crack-down on 'horror books and videos' and received cross-party support for a bill which would bring in stringent new regulations. The British Board of Film Classification withheld certificates from films by Wes Craven, Quentin Tarantino and Martin Scorsese. Johnny Faith, an unemployed fitter caught while holding up his fifth post office, claimed he was ordered to a life of crime by Rob Hackwill. Madame Tussaud's Chamber of Horrors and the London Dungeon were picketed by the Concerned Parents' Group. Scobie and Morag Duff addressed the CPG rally.

'Christmas With Frank and Drac', a holiday season of Hammer Films, was announced by BBC1, then pulled after a wave of public protest. A chain of newsagents, one of Derek Leech's holdings, refused to stock *Rabid*, which ceased publication. Libraries took books by Shaun Hutson, Allan Keyes and James Herbert off their shelves, lending them by written request only to those who could prove they were over eighteen. Publishers rejacketed the backlists of Stephen King and Clive Barker, tagging the authors as 'the master of dark suspense' and 'the prince of *fiction magique*'. Cloud 9 broadcast *Apocalypse Now* with the swearing and violence left in, but the line 'the horror . . . the horror' removed from the soundtrack.

Peter Paul Patrick, a convicted arsonist, set off a fire bomb in a private club where old horror films were shown. Five people died in reel two of the 1943 *Henry Aldrich Haunts a House*. Patrick claimed it was time 'to rid the world of Rob Hackwill and the perverts who are his disciples'. Fifty-seven per cent of *Comet* readers agreed with him.

Throughout her trial, Elizabeth Yatman was polite but said very little. She never exactly claimed to have been influenced by, or even seen, *Where the Bodies Are Buried 3*, but she didn't deny it either. Her lawyers argued she was driven by the phantasm of Rob Hackwill, and that she should not be blamed for her actions. She was committed to Broadmoor, presumably for the rest of her life. In his summing-up, the judge reiterated his remarks about the *Where the Bodies Are Buried* films. The Prime Minister promised action.

He was too busy to settle properly into his new flat, so everything sat in boxes. Scobie was earning more in a month on the *Comet* than he had in a year on the *Herald*. Harry and Gemma and other Backwater bods clubbed together and bought him a big dictionary as a leaving present. He had used it once, while deciding whether to label a Cabinet Minister a 'pedophile' or a 'paedophile'. In the end, a sub altered it to 'child molester'.

He started going out with Lizzie Trilling, who had come second in the Knock-Out of the Year contest. Her breasts were strange, like giant haemorrhoids. She had no feeling at all in her nipples. When she told him she had originally wanted to be a nurse, he lost an erection.

Clewes used him only for major stories: the private indiscretions of public figures, and violent crime. As the *Comet* spokesman in the campaign against horror, Scobie became a public figure himself. Some journos even started sniffing around his private life, but the *Comet* – which had unusual resources – frightened them off.

When a drugs war broke out in a North London estate, Scobie was the first reporter on the scene. In a flak jacket, he dragged a photographer through small-arms fire.

'This way, Mr Scobie,' said the deferential police sergeant. The *Comet* was very law and order. A lot of policemen read it. 'We've cleared out the trouble-makers.'

The house had iron shutters over the windows. The door had been kicked in. An armoured policeman stood guard like a knight outside a castle. Scobie noticed bullet-pocks in the stone cladding.

'This was the field headquarters of the zonk gang.'

Zonk, a new cocaine derivative, was just filtering through into the British market. Competition between dealers was leading to many skirmishes.

Scobie stepped over the welcome mat. The hallway was still smoky. There were blood-squirts on the flock wallpaper. The fitted stair carpets had been raked with gunfire.

The photographer took pictures of Scobie striding around.

'This was their command centre,' the sergeant said, indicating the lounge. 'It's a bit of a mess.'

There were corpse outlines on the lino. Blood spattered on a scrunched carpet of newspapers, all recent editions of the *Comet*. Elizabeth smiled from several of his front-page stories. The room was full of expensive equipment: computers, a fax, a HDTV screen, a video. Stapled to the walls were *Comet* Knock-Outs. Lizzie's full lips, as siliconed as her chest, kiss-mouthed off half a dozen full-colour shots.

'What's in the video?' he asked.

A policeman tried to press buttons with thick-gloved fingers. A tape ejected.

'Something nasty, I'll bet,' the sergeant said.

The policeman looked at the spine and read, '*The* Comet *Official History of the Gulf War.*'

'Taking tips on bombing, I'll be bound.'

The sergeant opened his crime-scene briefcase and pulled out a cassette.

'Shove this in, sonny. The chief likes it tidy.'

The sergeant handed his man a copy of *Where the Bodies Are Buried 3* and gave Scobie the wink.

'Has to be an explanation for all this crime and violence, eh?'

Unable to drift off, Scobie left Lizzie open-mouthed on her back – for her, there wasn't any other way to sleep – and padded into his bare front room. He didn't have any chairs yet, but the Home Entertainment System was fully installed. It was a present from Derek Leech, a perk of the new job. He sat on the carpet and watched *Where the Bodies Are Buried 3*. He still had several copies left.

Know Your Enemy, he thought.

Every time he watched the film, it was different. It must be an illusion. Some scenes he remembered being subtle were explicit. Some actors' faces changed. The tapes were like siblings, alike but not identical. Each copy had its own peculiarities.

This was the Tiffany Tape. The scene with Tiffany, Hackwill's first victim, having sex with her boy-friend before he turns into the monster, was minutes longer and more graphic than in any of his other copies. Tiffany was a nurse. In sex-play, her boyfriend mapped her pleasure centres with acupuncture needles. Hackwill turned them into syringes and filled her with hellfire. She expanded with pleasure, veins popping all over her nude body, and exploded in orgasm.

Scobie found the Tiffany Tape more disturbing than other variations: the Adam Kiss Tape (more talk scenes), the Raving Rob Tape (more screaming monster) and the Loud Shit Tape (more heavy metal). He watched it more often.

Tiffany looked a little like Elizabeth Yatman. Almost all women, and some men, looked a little like Elizabeth.

If Morag Duff's unopposed Private Member's Bill passed, Scobie would be liable to pay a £50 fine for every tape of *Where the Bodies Are Buried 3* he owned. He thought of disposing of them, but that might leave him in the dark, unprotected. As long as he kept looking at *Where the Bodies Are Buried 3*, Rob Hackwill was prevented from looking at him.

He frame-advanced through Tiffany's death scene, trying to discern the movie magic used to make her die.

Real Press, Derek Leech's publishing firm, signed him to do a quickie book on the Monster Nurse and the Evil Effects of Horror Videos. It would be called, of course, *Where the Bodies Were Buried*. Letters of support poured in from the CPG and ordinary citizens. Morag Duff, who agreed to write a preface to the book, took him and Lizzie out to dinner at Langan's and gave him sound-bites all evening. Everything she said was strident and quotable.

Fifth-generation copies of any of the *Where the Bodies Are Buried* films changed hands on the black market for up to £500. Customs reported they seized more Dutch-subtitled horror movies than porn. Peter Paul Patrick was remanded into psychiatric care. Scobie discovered Patrick was a survivor of child abuse and that the grandparents who had tormented him in childhood were both lookalikes, at least in photographs, for Boris Karloff.

Scobie knew *Where the Bodies Are Buried 3* so well he could dream it, with endless variations. Sometimes he was Adam Kiss, the journalist hero tormented by the ghost of the murderer he had written about. Sometimes he was Rob Hackwill, clacking claws as he sought revenge. Sometimes, Tiffany was Lizzie, every part of her body but her breasts rippling during the sex scenes. Sometimes, Tiffany was Elizabeth, filling hypos from a punch-bowl marked POISON.

At the office, Clewes handed him an envelope. 'A letter from your girl-friend.'

It was a note from Elizabeth, offering to help with his book. She was looking forward to reading more about herself. Scobie showed it to Clewes.

'Publicity junkie. That's why she let herself get caught.'

Scobie wasn't sure it was that simple.

'Think about it. She left eight kids in the loft where she killed them but drove into a ditch with Crispin in the passenger seat. Why didn't she leave him with the others?'

'I don't get it.'

'It had gone on too long. She wasn't enjoying anonymity. She didn't even enjoy killing the little brats. She was waiting for you to come along and make her famous.'

'It didn't have to be me.'

Clewes shrugged. 'No, but you're her Dr Watson, her

Boswell. She's as much a creature of the *Comet* as Lizzie Trilling or Princess Di or Morag Duff. Or me.'

In the office, Scobie was called 'Monster Hunter'. The nickname stuck and was used by his police contacts.

'You'll need a strong tummy for this, MH,' said Detective Inspector Hollis. 'It's carnage on a carpet.'

They were on a staircase in a Soho walk-up, outside a flat used as a place of business by a young woman who called herself 'Ariane'. Her real name was June Lowther.

The DI pushed the open door. The familiar stench hit Scobie. Death always smelled like Elizabeth's barn loft.

'Hacked up like a jigsaw.'

This was the third. Like the others, Ariane was a prostitute, but not a streetwalker. No card downstairs offered 'busty model' or 'Miss Strict'. Her clients had to know her address. Her murderer was probably one of them.

Theresa Gottschalk, the first victim, called herself 'Tiffany'. That set wheels in motion. The story Scobie wrote about the Gottschalk murder was headlined 'DOES A REAL ROB HACKWILL STALK LONDON TARTS?' He expected the second victim to be a Nancy, like Hackwill's second victim in *Where the Bodies Are Buried 3*, but she was called Muriel Bone. Nevertheless, the connection was made in the public mind. All coverage of the crimes called the unknown murderer 'the real Rob Hackwill'.

Scobie stepped carefully round Ariane, who was cut up and spread out on the floor. A polythene sheet was laid over her, but splotches of blood showed where it pressed an open wound. A black rag of hair was like a pond plant trapped under ice.

'This Hackwill is one sick puppy,' said Hollis.

'It's the same man?' Scobie asked.

'Left his calling card.'

Stuck to a mirror with bloodspots was a *Comet* Knock-Out. It wasn't Lizzie, but might have been. The killer had biroed

151

dotted lines across the smiling pin-up's body. He might as well have inked in little scissors with 'cut here' instructions.

At the Tiffany crime scene, it *had* been a picture of Lizzie.

With tweezers, Hollis removed the Knock-Out and slipped it into a clear plastic envelope. The police agreed with Scobie that this detail be kept back from the official press releases, so copycat crimes could be excluded from the investigation.

'Any luck on a little black book?'

Searches of the other victims' flats had not turned up any sort of address book or client list. The assumption was that the killer took away anything that might give away his name.

'Our laddie likes the ladies,' said Hollis. 'You should have him judge the Knock-Out of the Year Contest.'

A rasping came from the flat's tiny kitchen. Scobie and Hollis jumped.

Stacy Cotterill pushed through the bead curtain. The Detective Constable looked too young to get into an 18 certificate film.

'She had a computer, sir,' Cotterill said. 'I found a file named KISSES. It's printing out names and addresses.'

Hollis grinned. 'Just like Crippen. Caught because he didn't keep up with new technology.'

'The list is annotated, sir. Explicitly.'

The DI looked down at Ariane. 'Who's a clever girl, then?'

As Clewes finished his speech, Scobie and Hollis stood at the back of the room. They were near the apex of the Derek Leech Enterprises Pyramid in London Docklands. Clewes was addressing a seminar on the marketing of the *Comet*, which Leech wanted replicated throughout his media empire.

'The *Comet* was a dead duck when Derek bought it out,' Clewes said. 'It was the most boring tabloid in Britain. It was more boring than most of the heavies . . .'

There was dutiful laughter from the suits.

Ariane's client list included a few familiar names: Alistair Garnett, a high-ranking civil servant who had helped draft

Morag Duff's anti-horror bill, liked 'the usual' but always 'got it over with quickly'. Scobie was surprised to discover Morag herself couldn't 'get enough fist' and 'needs it up to the elbow'. None of these was a real Rob Hackwill suspect. An assortment of alibis, unearthed in embarrassing interviews, checked out.

Among a lot of anonymous suits whose performance rated demeaning remarks, the only one who seemed a likely prospect was Ronald Clewes. Ariane noted he got 'rough, then weepy'.

DI Hollis asked Scobie to smooth the way. Scobie was well aware how difficult this would be to write up. No blame must attach to the *Comet*. But Ronald Clewes *was* the *Comet*. He was Derek Leech's blue-eyed editor. He had risen from the subs' pits on the strength of 'GERTCHA GAUCHOS!'.

'Derek thought of the Knock-Outs,' Clewes continued. 'Derek thought of everything. In the Seventies, circulation rose an average of 10 per cent each year after Derek became proprietor. In the Eighties, it was 23 per cent. In the Nineties, 31.'

The figures were creepily familiar.

In a shadowed corner stood a tall figure, himself shadowed. Scobie thought it might be Derek Leech, whom he had never met face to face, but he was turned away, unrecognizable. Unusually, he wore a black slouch hat indoors, and a long black coat.

Clewes stood before a panoramic window which was turned to mirror by nightfall. His reflection mimicked his gestures. The reflection looked like Rob Hackwill. Scobie knew his boss was the murderer.

Cotterill sidled in and leaned close to Hollis.

'We've been through his desk, sir,' she said, nodding at Clewes. 'He kept *souvenirs*.'

Hollis made a face.

Polite applause concluded the seminar. The suits left. Clewes looked at Scobie and the detectives. The shadowman was still there, watching.

'Ronald . . .' Scobie began.

Clewes turned and looked at his face in the window mirror. It contorted, teeth bared, eyes red.

'He's Hackwill,' Hollis said.

Clewes head-butted the window. It cracked across and night-wind whistled through.

Hollis waded through chairs. Scobie just watched. Clewes launched himself through the window.

Officially, the real Rob Hackwill was still at large. Leech cut a deal with Hollis. Since his divorce, Clewes had filled his house with contact sheets from the Knock-Out shoots. He must have obsessed about the girls for years.

Lizzie wasn't around much. She got a part as a tart in a film about Jack the Ripper, but production was shut down when the video distributors, afraid of the 'horror' tag, pulled out their money. She settled instead for a *Comet* Knock-Out tape called *Wet Melons*. It wasn't the same.

At every crime scene he visited, Scobie found the *Comet*. Used to wrap fish 'n' chips. A headline pasted to a wall. A face or a pair of breasts cut out of a picture. The royal divorce colour pull-out special. The police tidily disposed of the evidence, always leaving a cassette of one of the *Where the Bodies Are Buried* films in place of the newspaper.

The tapes were getting quite rare. His own stash was dwindling: the machine ate the Adam Kiss tape, he had to give the Loud Shit Tape to Hollis to leave under the dangling feet of a teenage suicide. He mainly watched the Tiffany tape.

He felt as close to Rob Hackwill as to a brother.

The week the *Comet* reacted to an EU scare about BSE with a series of recipes making use of 'Best British Beef', Scobie received a food parcel from Broadmoor. Elizabeth sent him a *Comet*-approved 'cow pie' she had made herself. In her note, she asked how the book was coming on.

He sat and stared at the pie, wondering.

In the month after Morag (Glove Puppet) Duff's Private Member's Bill became law, there were mass burnings of horror videos, books, comics and magazines in all major British cities. The editors of a series of paperback original horror anthologies were convicted under the Duff Law and served three weeks in prison. A bespectacled writer, hailed as the leading light of the 'miserabilist' horror movement, chained himself to railings outside the Houses of Parliament and was pelted with rubbish by a mob. The police staged a series of dawn raids on the homes of horror book and video collectors, parading sorry culprits before their neighbours as quantities of material were shovelled out of their houses.

While covering the ongoing campaign against horror, the *Comet*'s circulation rose by 44 per cent. As zonk became the drug of choice for the unemployed and Rob Hackwill imitators committed strings of murders in Cardiff and Manchester, violent crime also rose by 44 per cent.

Scobie began to avoid interview requests. He put on his telephone answering machine and never returned calls from the media.

Every night, he watched the Tiffany tape. It might be the last copy of *Where the Bodies Are Buried 3* in Great Britain. He knew now that the film was innocent: the Monster lived somewhere nearer.

One night, the film was interrupted by a commercial break which had never been there before.

Two *Comet* Knock-Outs jiggled in bikini bottoms around a seated figure reading the newspaper. The headline read 'HACKWILL MUST GO'. From behind the paper peeped a snarling face. A single red eye winked at Scobie. Rob Hackwill said, 'You have to have a giggle, don't you?'

The girls cuddled close to the monster, who stuck his claw-hands into their soft bellies and poked sharp fingers out through their breasts. They bled silicon.

'What's black and white and red all over?' the monster asked. 'A newspaper.'

Hollis didn't say who he was but Scobie recognized the voice.

'Pick up, MH,' he said. 'It's about the Real Rob.'

Scobie took the phone and identified himself.

'Ariane had a copy of her list. It's gone to another paper. They'll make the Clewes connection. Tell Leech I can't cover for the *Comet* this time.'

The policeman hung up.

On the screen, Hackwill stalked Adam Kiss through an intestinal corridor. Scobie knew there wasn't time to get round to Clewes's still-sealed house, dispose of the Knock-Outs and leave the Tiffany tape. The connection would be made.

It was his own fault. He had embedded in the public mind the notion that violent crime was caused by something in the media. Now horror was gone, something else would take its place.

Something like the *Comet*. The newspaper, a Derek Leech product, had seeped out and touched people: people like Elizabeth, Peter Paul Patrick, Clewes, the zonk gangs.

The phone rang again. Scobie picked up before the answering message could cut in.

'You know who this is,' the voice said. It was deep, almost American. Scobie couldn't be sure whether it was Derek Leech or Rob Hackwill. 'And you know what to do.'

On the screen, Hackwill closed on Adam Kiss, mouth expanding to fasten round his head.

The darkness wasn't in the film. It was in the Docklands Pyramid. Scobie was its servant, just as Elizabeth and Clewes had been its servants. He had no choice about his future.

Scobie rooted through unopened house-warming presents. Clewes had given him just the thing. A cordless electric carving knife. Probably the same model Clewes used himself.

It took half an hour to work out the instructions. The appliance had to be plugged in for three hours before it was powered. It would have been frustrating, but he timed the period by playing the Tiffany tape twice. What he was planning would mean the extinction of the film and its like. He was absent-mindedly sorry for the loss, but the *Comet* must go on.

At a button touch, the blade buzzed. He touched it experimentally to the polystyrene packaging, which flew with a shriek into hundreds of tiny snowballs.

He took out his address book and ordered a Spicy Hawaiian Pizza from a firm that used girls as despatch riders. Then he called an 'oriental masseuse' who gave home service and asked her to come over immediately. He left a message with Lizzie's answering service asking her to call in person as soon as possible to pick up a contract marked 'urgent' which had come from her agent. Then he telephoned DC Cotterill's answering machine and asked if she could come over this evening to do an interview for his book.

That, he decided, was enough. Four possibles.

He sat in the recliner in front of the television, electric knife in one hand, video remote in the other. He gave an experimental buzz into the air, fascinated by the whirring blade, then rewound *Where the Bodies Are Buried 3*. He should watch the Tiffany tape through at least one last time before any of his callers came.

WHERE THE BODIES ARE
BURIED 2020

Spring Meadow, Illinois. Anytown, USA, in the Middle America of the mind. A night in fall, a full moon.

Chantal, consciousness uneasily nestled within the Tina simile, looked through the viewpoint character's eyes. As Tina, she stood alone in a patch of fenced-in park.

The verdigrized town founder, a crooked politician two centuries gone, posed on a pedestal. The statue was in sharp focus, richly dimensional, palpably solid.

Mimesis was generations beyond Virtual.

Dreamwelt was indistinguishable from Actual, affording complete sensory interface. Through the Tina construct, Chantal heard cicadas chirrup on the backtrack; felt crisp cold, to the bone; saw breath clouding in damp whispers; smelled grass, after rain.

The indistinct receptors VR did not connect with were active. Her backbrain was absorbing infobits it would take conscious effort to scroll. A million tiny subliminals supported the dream.

Spring Meadow *tasted* real.

INITIATE TITLE SEQUENCE

Disembodied words ghosted in front of the statue, filling the night with letters of jagged green newsprint.

WHeRE tHE BodiES Are BurlEd

The words came apart like mist. She wasn't sure how to make the dream RUN. She couldn't swivel her neck – 'her' neck – to shift viewpoint.

PAUSE

'Don't try to think what it's *like*, Sister Chantal. Just let it happen.'

Jerome's voice seemed to come from empty air, blotting out all other sound and sense. Merely by giving the advice, he made it impossible for her to take it. Aural bleed-through wavered the dreamwelt, shattering the statue into pixels.

Behind the bead curtain of dreamnight, Chantal saw spectre-shapes. Jerome Rhodes and Roger Duroc were watching over her, monitoring her progress.

What was she doing really? Sitting on the couch or standing like Tina, a puppet jerked along by the program?

She felt the weight of the hoodset, the pull of her regular body, the gravity of realwelt.

The curtain hung still, the statue reformed.

STILL PAUSE

She felt the cold again, and heard insects. The spectres were hidden. Calming, she tried to accept the dream. She recognized that she found it hard to surrender to Mimesis.

People do this for *fun*, she reminded herself. For *entertainment*.

A smart program probed for a way around her mental block. She tried not to feel violated.

Chantal did not trust stories, but they still fascinated her. She was not sure which of her conflicting reactions was wrong.

As Tina, her viewpoint was fixed. It was like – 'Don't try to think what it's *like*' – wearing a thick suit of too-tight clothes wired rigid by an armature sewn into the lining. She could feel everything, but do nothing.

Her itch to move her neck affected the dreamscene, shifting the visionfield.

180° PAN

The movement was part of the dream, not of her volition. She saw more of the square. Carefully-trimmed trees. A white-painted bench. Abandoned civic buildings. A black cat – very convincing, lithely alive – slunk through bushes, cringing in moonlight. Something dark wafted across the penny-bright face of the moon.

Atmos, atmos.

Despite blurbclaims, it was not like *being* the viewpoint. Chantal wore Tina's dreambody, but was a *dybbuk*, a passenger in her – its – 'mind'.

She could resist the dream, but impetus was to carry on with the story.

Something gave.

RUN

Under the wind, chords sounded, building, suspenseful. Her heart – hers or Tina's? – pounded faster. That cat was gone, melding with liquid shadows. The moon was clear.

The viewpoint looked around. Not the smooth pan of the last movement, but quick, birdlike darts. The pan was to get the dreamer accustomed to visionfield shifts. This was how people saw realwelt; through a skull-camera mounted on a neck-gyro, blurring transitions between shaky half-hemispheres of SurroundSound CineRama.

Tina was waiting, expectant and a little afraid, for someone. There was to be a meeting at midnight. By the old clock on the town hall – something of a cliché – it was a breath away from twelve.

Tina was maybe fifteen years younger than Chantal, in her late teens. She wondered who the girl was.

The dream reacted: a 'Tina Singleton' packet opened, downloading infodump. Flash-images of parents and friends, establishing relationships. A rolling scroll of backstory. Facts and figures about Spring Meadow. Blips of childhood, blats of school, blurts of domestic terror. Tina was a good student, popular at Spring Meadow High. Her home life was uncertain, locked between feuding parents. Sometimes, Mom – reversal of expectations – got zonked and hurt her. Dad didn't want to notice.

Technically, Mimesis was impressive. But not real, any more than reading a book or watching a motion picture. It was just a story.

The wind raised a flurry of leaves, which swirled around the statue, drifted against her legs. She snatched an oak leaf, held it up. Through the viewpoint's fingers, it seemed absolutely real. She crunched it up and threw it away.

How much information had she just converted?

The park was deserted. Chantal stubbornly sensed Jerome and Duroc, tuning in from outside dreamwelt. And something else.

Another presence.

Tina's nerves frazzed in fearful anticipé. Chantal was puzzled. This sharing of mindspace was not what she expected. Tentatively, she clicked on Tina, allowing more seepthrough.

Tina had been receiving Valentines, collaged of newsprint like blackmail notes. At first, sweet.

THeeNk*ng of U, allwAyS.

Then sinister, intimating secret knowledge.

HoW'S MoMMY's leeTle guRL?

Why didn't this twittette go to her School Confessor? There were so many safety nets.

Of course, Chantal knew why:

This is just a stupid story. Logical behaviour would spoil it.

161

Today's note:

> MEaT ME, ToWN $quAre @ MEEDNiGHT.

Unlike the others, it was signed; in an arachnoidal scrawl:

> Rob Hackwill.

The name triggered an eerie melody that rose and fell with the swirl of leaves.

Another information package appeared, sealed for the now. Chantal intuited more backstory.

Rob Hackwill was the villain, the killer, the monster. A blackmailer, tortured to death by his corrupt victims; back from the grave for revenge on hypocrite and innocent alike; an agent of the Devil Princess of Hell, tormented and tormenting; a franchise from the last century, still lurking in the collective pop-unconscious.

While preparing her thesis on the Hackwill Effect, Chantal had seen *Where the Bodies Are Buried*, the original motion picture, over and over. Before that, Hackwill had haunted her childhood nightmares. When her Confessor suggested the academic work was an attempt to deal with earlier terrors, he had not told her anything she had not intuited for herself.

Why did the first wide-release Mimesis production have to be a dremake of *Where the Bodies Are Buried*? Why not *Little Women* or *La dolce vita*?

Tina looked around nervoso. She was sure it was all skit. Stacey Snyder, her bestest ammi, projected she was *sooooo* funny. This was muchissimo. There would be payback in school tomorrow.

Or maybe it was Jimmy Traynor. One of the Hackwill notes was about him:

> Yr SeeCret's saFE, I KnOW U ♥ ♥ ♥ ♥ JiMMy T.

She had no secret crush on Jimmy. No, she was lying to herself. Tina dezzed desperé that Jimmy would glom her.

Chantal was frustrated. The teenthink was difficult to follow. She tried to take over viewpoint, cutting the slango, communicating danger.

From the back of Tina's cramped mind construct, she shouted: look behind you, run away, go home, pull up the covers, call the cops! She caught herself trying to influence a fictional character. She had not expected to be fooled in quite this way. It was absurd.

Jimmy and Stacey were guilty, Tina was pozz. Stacey had snitched her crush to Jimmy. They were gagging together, in the bushes. Her heart would fraction again. There was no Secret Admirer. That scut was only in bad movies – Hah! – and daydreams. There was no Rob Hackwill.

Hadn't Tina registered the name? Didn't this town remember? There had been a dozen sequels. It was impossible that no one knew. After thirteen murder-filled films, Rob Hackwill should be as famous in the storywelt as in the real.

Of course, the Mimesis wasn't so much sequel as remake. According to the blurb, this was supposed to 'reinvent the mythos', to take Hackwill 'back to his festering origins' and make him 'a monster for the new millennium'.

Something barrelled at her. A clawed hand grasped her shoulder. Music leaped like a jaguar. Her throat opened in scream. She was pulled around and knocked down.

Gotcha!

Even *knowing* this would happen did not make it less of a shock.

Pressed into soft grassy earth, she sensed the weight of the dark shape pinning her. She smelled a foul breath. She heard muttering.

'I know . . . Robbie knows . . . Robbie has always known . . . *where the bodies are buried*!'

Her coat ripped at shoulder-seam, sliced by a razor-edged clawnail. There was something like pain and something like warmth – few want to be hurt in a dream, though the option's there – as the nail pierced Tina's shoulder.

Why would anyone want to pay for this?

Chantal wanted STOP, but had no control. Tina could not

struggle; the monster had her. Chantal was completely sucked in by the viewpoint. There was no Chantal Juillerat, S.J.; only Tina Singleton, doomed girl.

The nail grew in her shoulder-wound, scraping past bone, through ligament. Everything distorted. Pain substitute flooded her mind.

The viewpoint was on her back, looking up. The statue stood above, like a towering gravestone. A face thrust close to her, eclipsing the statue and the moon. Sharp teeth clacked, several centimetres of enamel exposed. A single red eye gleamed.

An ice fist took her heart . . .

'*The Hack is back!*'

. . . and squeezed.

STOP EJECT

The dreamwelt vanished like ice on a griddle, but there were after-sensations. Chantal still felt Tina's terror.

She needed a moment to reorient.

She was on the couch, as when she had initiated **RUN**. Physically, she had not moved.

Jerome fussed at the dreamdeck. He had ordered **STOP** – didn't he think she could take it? – and was extracting the dreamsphere from its tray. Eyepieces receded into her hoodset.

It took moments for hearing to return. Her brain had to recalibrate for reality, after only minutes of Mimesis.

'Sister, art thou all right in thyself?' asked Duroc.

She nodded and lifted off the hoodset. She shook her hair out – as if she had Tina's shoulder-length blonde fall rather than her own black bob – and scanned the inside of the contraption. Transparent padding protected a neural network of wires and crystal chips.

The Mimesis Process was, in the end, only light. Dreams reached the brain through the optic nerves, duping neural receptors into interpreting nanoflashes as sight, sound, smell, taste, pain, pleasure. But it was hard to remember the tech when a monster was kissing you to death.

She waved Duroc away and looked a question at Jerome.

'I thought you were losing yourself,' he answered.

'I'd have preferred to make the decision from the inside.'

'You're right, Sister. I'm sorry.'

Both Duroc and Jerome used the archaic form, 'Sister'. At the Euro-Commission press conference in Brussels, she had been required to wear full habit for the cameras. She was embarrassed by the penguin costume, which made her a sexless nonperson. She preferred a plain dark singlepiece with a discreet roman collar.

The floor swayed slightly: the ship easing on its moorings, not her strings being snipped. Her spinal spirit level was settling. She had her weltview back. She returned the hoodset to its cradle.

The Eunion Parliament had argued in circles about where to site the Euro-Commission on the Model-Duff Amendment. Brussels had superior facilities, but a policy of positive anti-bias against second-generation members meant they were in Prague.

The influx of Eurocracy with Czechia's two-year chairing of EU put office space at a premium. E-Com wound up with the *Gustav Meyrink*, a riverboat at permanent anchor near the Charles Bridge. Subotai, the Mongol indentured to E-Com as minion, joked that the ship constituted the Bohemian Navy.

Her quarters, one deck down, were not much smaller than her cell in Castel Sant'Angelo. Jerome, unused to the cenobite life, nagged admin into getting him a hotel suite. Duroc seemed not to mind his cabin. He had little baggage.

'Thoughts, Sister?'

Tina haunted her. And the stab of Hackwill's claw was a phantom twinge in her shoulder.

'Not yet, Duroc. This will take time. The tech has outpaced the psych. There'll have to be long-term studies.'

'That's what the Industry says,' put in Jerome. 'But they

regard mass audiences as a field test. We've too much gen on Mimesis, not enough cognition.'

Jerome Rhodes was English, an Information Analyst. Chantal was Swiss, a Media Psychologist. Their skills were supposed to be complementary. They had not worked together before E-Com seconded them.

'Then again, the Industry has been co-operative. Pyramid are allowing us dreams well before the public. *Bodies* hasn't been theatrical in the States, much less cleared for Home Mimesis.'

He was in his late twenties, which gave her a year or so on him. He cultivated a slender boyishness she was not yet pozz – a stray Tina word – suited him. He might be a template for her in-progress/back-burnered bookfile on Information Children: a global generation whose personality, values and culture were shaped by mediamass rather than religion, family background, social class or nationality.

Something had made him **STOP** and pull her out.

'The Industry wants absolution, Jerome,' she said. 'Just as Model-Duff – offence none, Duroc – want us to condemn Mimesis. Everybody deems it in their interest to co-operate. It gets them to where they cognit they can influence us.'

Pyramid Releasing was part of the Derek Leech Group. The multi-media mogul had offered to underwrite the study, but E-Com could not directly accept credit from a source with such a stake in Mimesis, any more than from lobbyists who wanted the Model-Duff Amendment passed into Euro-Law. Leech had been working towards Mimesis since the turn of the century.

'There is Evil around,' Duroc said. 'The Reverend Model has warned us.'

Roger Duroc was a Hardline Christian Zealot, a French follower of Joseph Model, the Liechtensteinian Euro-Vangelist. A big man in his forties, he was a veteran of the Basque Insurrection of '09. While Jerome wore Oxford bags and a tartan *Gorille* jacket, Duroc dressed like a nineteenth-century ascetic: black suit fastened with pegs, white shirt pinned at the throat. Like other extreme sects, Modelists abjured buttons.

With Britain's Prime Minister Morag Duff, Model proposed the Third Amendment to the Eunion's Revised Criminal Code. E-Com was supposed to give its recommendation to Parliament before the Code was enforced throughout the EU on 1 January 2020.

'It is the work of the Devil. This is a Holy Crusade.'

She couldn't quite scan Duroc. Sometimes, he seemed to assume comradeship with her as a fellow religious, though Modelists – especially ex-Catholics – were obliged to damn Pope Georgi as 'dangerously soft on Hellfire'. Sometimes, she was sure Duroc put on an Ominous Warning act, subtly mocking those who expected 'thou' and 'thine' of him.

'The Reverend has decreed we must put away Evil Things.'

Duroc was an ex-cop: after the Europa Defence Forces, he had been with Interpol, specializing in transnational serial murder. He had put away three of the Hackwill Killers: Pietro Moschone, Nadja Thiel, Hugh Best.

Duroc's law-enforcement background, not his standing in the Modelist Church, earned him his place on E-Com. Jerome's company had informal ties with media consortia, which meant he balanced Duroc. As of now, the vote was split: Duroc for, Jerome against; like any Swiss, she was neutral.

Though resident in Vatican City, she did not hold an EU passport. Whatever E-Com recommended, the Amendment would not apply in her homeland.

'It's not like Virtual Reality,' she said. 'Except in the generic way television is like theatre.'

'The Industry cognits Mimesis is the Real Thing,' said Jerome, holding the dreamsphere. It was a pleasing bauble, a flawless silver pearl. 'VR was a side-track. All you could do was chuck things at customers' heads or let them wander around CGNvironments. Remember when "interactive" was the buzz? That was Big Mistake Uno. Punters want *stories*, not choices. Once they got past redoing *This is Cinerama!* and zotzing aliens, everyfool zoned out of VR. That's why it's taken two decs to develop Mimesis. When all those Millennium VR parlours went belly-up, research funding dried. If not for Derek Leech's deep pockets, we wouldn't have the tech. And if Mimesis rockets faster than zonk cocaine, it still won't show a profit before 2050. Then again, Leech can afford it.'

'This is like being someone else, Jerome. No, not like being. Like being in someone else's head.'

The stick figure of Tina Singleton came to mind.

'Same effect reading *Pamela* two-point-five centuries back, Sister Chan. Or auditing an Oedipus or Hamlet soliloquy. The diff is it isn't just words now. You're not on the outside, empathizing. You're on the inside, sharing.'

'It's the work of the Devil,' said Duroc.

'Or Derek Leech, which Mum says is the same thing,' said Jerome. 'Then again, Leech's Cloud 9 Satellite Net carries Reverend Model's tele-ministry.'

Though there were no mirrors in the scene she had dreamed through, the viewpoint carried a self-image icon. Beneath the Hollywood cheerleader face, Chantal intuited a template with which she was familiar.

'Tina looks like Marthe Wink, don't you think?'

Marthe Wink was the Hamburg victim.

Jerome was startled. 'There are resemblances; then again, there are differences.'

Duroc said nothing.

Chantal found the file on the desk. She flipped it on and called up post-mortem glossies.

The phantom intrusion in her shoulder matched a wound in Marthe's shoulder. The gouge was a 3-D rose through the wrong side of a stereoscope, a hole ribbed with red folds.

'We mustn't be too dazzled by the tech or the aesthetic,' she said. 'Mimesis is just breaking. There's so much to cognit about how it works, what its potential might be. What we have to decide is whether it turns dreamers into murderers.'

After two years studying *Where the Bodies Are Buried* kill clusters, Chantal was still unsure of the Hackwill Effect.

In Vatican screenrooms, she refamiliarized herself with all thirteen films; meanwhile, tapping into archives, she immersed herself in seemingly every incidence of homicide that occurred during the fifteen-year run of the series.

The Hackwill Effect began as a newsnet scare patterned on long-running tabloid rumours that certain blues or heavy metal audio-tracks were conducive to suicide, but evidence accrued like coral. Some people who watched *Bodies* films went out and committed atrocities. Rob Hackwill reached out from screens to warp minds, making monsters of random members of the audience. Undeniably, there were murders. Equally undeniably, following a newsbite lead, it was claimed in court – by prosecution and defence – that murderers were under the influence of the bogeyman.

She scrolled through a mediamorass of interviews with 'Hackwill Killers'. The most interesting was the most talkative: Elizabeth Yatman gave a bookfile of detail about how Hackwill had turned her into a mass murderess. But Chantal intuited in Yatman's references an evasiveness that suggested only sketchy, second-hand knowledge of the films. No Hackwill fanatic would confuse Tina Singleton with Stacey Snyder, but Beth Yatman did.

Yatman, nearly fifty, was thriving in England's Broadmoor Facility, happily claiming 'Hackwill made me do it' to Backchat Sites, making encouraging noises to the pressure group campaigning for her release. An accomplished cook, she sent cakes to supporters, and also to Relatives of Hackwill Victims spokesfolk. RHV hardly needed to campaign for her continued incarceration.

Chantal was inclined to class the Hackwill Effect a modern instance of Loudun or Salem Hysteria, an arbitrary shifting of guilt on to something beyond self. Instead of the Devil, a string of tame horror films were singled out and blamed for atrocities conceived and executed by apparently normal people. The oldest, saddest excuse of all: 'I was only obeying orders.'

Cardinal Kevin Menzies, her supervisor, allowed her thesis

to be a first public acknowledgement that the Vatican had ever considered the Hackwill Effect. She seconded the findings of a *sub rosa* 2004 inquiry which recommended Yatman's request for exorcism be ignored. Not refused, *ignored*. The plea was one of Yatman's increasingly bizarre attempts to remain Site Prime News. Besides, Rob Hackwill was not officially recognized as a demon, nor was ever likely to be.

There was still *something* about the *Bodies* films. Something unhealthy, if not unholy.

Yatman, like two other Hackwill Killers – one of whom was never caught – murdered in and around the English backwater where Allan Keyes, writer-director of the original *Where the Bodies Are Buried*, had grown up. Lesley Conyers, victim of the unsolved Hackwill killing, was once Keyes's girlfriend. Another murderer was *called* Robert Hackwill. His name had lodged in Keyes's memory from childhood, resurfacing arbitrarily in his fiction.

Could it be something in the water?

Or maybe the popularity of the *Bodies* films was not causal to the Hackwill Killings but parallel with them. Both might be symptoms of something else.

It was not Hackwill that unnerved her: once she was past adolescence, he struck her as an obvious loser with a stale repertoire. More disturbing was the Devil Princess, Hackwill's infernal mistress. It said much about Keyes's psyche that he chose to depict Ultimate Evil as a provocative teenage fillette who wore black leather and chains or a scarlet nun's habit.

Maybe it was the medieval architecture around her as she worked, but at the root of the Hackwill Effect was something that made her yearn to leave the Post-Modern Papacy of Genial Georgi and take refuge in a Vatican which believed in physical war with the armies of the Devil.

While working on the thesis, she dreamed often.

Her conclusion, deleted from the final draft at Menzies's request, was that the Church should not rely on psychology in dealing with the resurgent Hackwill Effect, but should fall back on ancient, spiritual resources.

Her now-cautious thesis was modestly posted on the Vatican branch of the World-Tree just as Morag Duff, on the point of yielding the EU chair to Czechskanzler Martina Drnkova, set down the Amendment as a parting gift to her successor.

'For century kiddettes like me, Information is Air, Chantal. We breathe it in from birth.'

Jerome had finally not called her Sister. For her, a little triumph.

'Actually, Mum's a Nouveau Luddite. Won't have a flatscreen in the apartment. Never downloads newsbits.'

'You're probably reacting to her.'

'She taught me not to surrender to white noise, to scan only for what matters. Then again, usually I intuit *when* gen matters but not *why*. That, I cognit, is your job description.'

They were at a pavement café in the Ghetto. An electric brazier melted the thin snow back metres away from their table, and created a bubble of warmth. A mâché golem, creaking with every move, served tall glasses of hot tea. Jerome played with his Kafka Salad, picking out chocolate roaches.

The tottering Expressionist walls and tiny alleyways were processed styro, spray-coated to mimic ancient stone. Cabalist graffiti art covered every surface. The place was less than ten years old, an exact recreation of an original razed early in the last century.

All the capitals of Eunion were becoming theme parks; even the Vatican. Sub-national congresses passed laws requiring citizens to wear 'traditional' costume in public. Australasian tourists expected it.

Nearby, *Robotas* – in the original Czech sense, indentured workmen, not machines – were restoring the frontage of a vandalized Synagogue Gift Shop by abrading deep-etched, luminous Anti-Semitic slogans. Throughout the Ghetto, there were rumours of a *pogrom* coming. Few Jews lived here, but misethnicists had as much contempt for the Mongols and

171

Kurds collected in the beehive-cell apartments stacked above these streets.

A giant head popped into being above a public holo-plate. Waves of white hair around a withered angel face, eyes augmented by burning azure overlays.

'It's Roger's boss,' Jerome commented. 'The Model Man.'

Joseph Model was the most successful E-Vangelist. He synthesized saleable qualities perfected by US tele-ministries of the last century, but preached Old World Puritanism and a Work Ethic that verged on slavery. Doctrinally, an economic Calvinist; politically, a Mussolini fascist; he liked to compare himself with Savonarola, Malcolm Muggeridge and Rush Limbaugh.

The holo began speaking, simultaneously in Hebrew and Czech, about the uprising in Cádiz. Model harshly criticized EU refusal to let his relief-workers deploy in combat zones. In a rare moment of passion, Pope Georgi had described Modelist Rapid Response Teams as 'spiritual looters'. During the Basque Insurrection, RR Teams dispensed medical help and subsistence food only in exchange for signatures on lifetime contracts with the Modelist Ministry.

'I can't scan Roger,' Jerome admitted. 'Why is he with Model? He seems too clued to be a Zombie.'

'I've heard that said about me.'

'Georgi's made it snazz to be a nun, Chan. His renunciation of the doctrine of Papal Infallibility is a major break with deadhead tradition. Then again, liberalism might erode core strengths.'

'Strictly speaking, I'm a priest, not a nun. That's another Georgi reform for you.'

'I'm sorry. It's hard sometimes to rewrite the program.'

'Worry not. Many in the Church have the same problem.'

Model was talking about the Amendment now, another declaration of intent with case histories. She caught the name 'Marthe Wink'.

'Scans like Roger reported back.'

She agreed.

'Then again, I imagine the Modelists have access to as much gen as we do.'

It turned out Marthe was one of a group of tech-buff teens who had rigged up their own dreamdeck and got hold of bootleg dreamspheres from the States. The night before her murder, the girl had dreamed *Where the Bodies Are Buried*. Model made much of the similarities between Tina Singleton's encounter with Hackwill and the actual killing.

'He's distorting the story,' Jerome said. 'Tina's the viewpoint throughout. Hackwill doesn't kill her in the first scene, just marks her.'

Model announced that Marthe's parents were co-chairing the revived Relatives of Hackwill Victims Group and supporting the Model-Duff Amendment. The financial recompense to which they would be entitled if the Amendment became law was unimportant, the E-Vangelist said, because the Winks were independently wealthy. They just wanted those responsible for their daughter's death to be held culpable. Any settlement received from Pyramid Releasing – Model actually named the Leech Company – would be donated to the Ministry's Spiritual War Chest.

'So if his law gets passed, Model is in line for a credit injection. Then again, he's already independently wealthy too.'

In its fifteen years' existence, Modelism had become the second richest Church in the world. If his petition to assume temporal leadership of Liechtenstein was allowed, Model would be in a position to challenge Rome. Cardinal Menzies, only half joking, suggested the Vatican develop First Strike capability against the day the Modelist standard went up in Vaduz.

She found Eurocash in her purse and settled the addition. Swiss francs or Australasian dollars would be more welcome, but Eurocrats could not afford to betray the currency.

Model was harping on 'malign Asiatic influences'. One of the *robotas* heaved a bucketful of styrodust and grubby frozen snow into the Model head, disrupting the holo-link. Patches of see-through speckled the head like measles. The *robota* was a Mongol, one of the Genghis Khan trail refugees produced by the Sino-Tibetan crisis. His gesture was cheered by many by-standers, but a black-suited 'missionary' at the next table looked on grimly, noting faces.

The holo-head kicked into its pre-programmed appeal for all the Faithful to dedicate their worldly goods to Modelism, noting both the Biblical exhortation to 'lay up for yourselves treasures in Heaven' and Liechtenstein's liberal tax regime. At the same time, Model scorned the poor, the sick, the stricken. If God made some people victims, then that was His business and should not be argued with. In His wisdom, God had set up tollgates on the road to Heaven.

'I love God so much, Jerome,' she said, surprised at her-self. 'Through my life, that has been my strongest relation-ship. It's never gone away. I've never doubted, not for a second . . .'

Model offered sacraments of wealth and immortality. A credit card hotline number flashed on his forehead.

'. . . so why do I find it so easy to hate religion?'

In the dream, Tina survived but the Mark of Hackwill was on her shoulder. She alone in Spring Meadow knew the monster's face. Chantal was almost used to riding viewpoint now; comfortable in the dreambody, lulled along.

Mind-chewing over her midnight encounter, Tina walked down the corridor towards the lockers. The set was dressed with posters for the Junior Prom. Kids passing by wore 2019 fashions – box suits and skunk-stripes – and toted set books, but the dreamscene was classically archetypal. Tina – tartan skirt, white blouse, ankle socks – would pass as a teen queen in any of the last eight decs.

A hand fell on her aching shoulder. Chantal's heart leaped as Tina jumped. She whirled, prepared to face Hackwill, and was relieved to see her best friend, Stacey Snyder.

'What's word, humming-bird?' Stacey chirruped.

'What's tale, nightingale?' Tina replied.

Arm-in-arm, the girls walked to their lockers, turning boyheads as they passed. Chantal's own secondary school in Geneva had been shaped by US mediamass into a multilingual imitation of Spring Meadow High. Some of the extras wore the faces that furnished her memories.

'You scan devastaté, Teen. Hard night with Jimmy T?'

'One hopes.'

Chantal looked side-on at Stacey. Like all the supporting characters, she was almost totally convincing. An actress would have leased herself as a template for CGIdentity, converting her likeness and the character tics of a specific performance into a stream of infobits. Now the dream, orchestrated by a computer-assisted Talent, was recycling information as a semi-autonomous illusion.

'Serious, girlchik. You scan like Death on Drugs.'

'I had . . . bad dreams.'

'Condolences.'

'Processed and perfected.'

Chantal was fluent in French, Italian, English, German, Latin and Japanese; and had a working knowledge of a dozen other tongues. She found Hollywood teenspeak hard to follow.

Processed and perfected.

Tina's locker, where Hackwill notes had been delivered, loomed large in visionfield. A subliminal thrum of dread built up suspense as she approached.

Stacey blithely opened her locker and pulled out her set-book. She shook it, disrupting the fog-pattern on the screen, and tapped in the code for the biology text.

'Ugh,' she said. 'It's anelids.'

Tina looked at her locker. She tapped entrycode on the keypad and the lock clicked free.

'S'matter, Teen? You got Jimmy's severed head stashed?'

Tina took out her set-book. The message icon was blinking at her. She meant to stab DELETE, but knew she would spend the day wondering. She accessed the message and the cut-up letters appeared on the set-book's screen.

2-niTE's Sta-C's NIGHT.

'What's it process, Teen?'

Tina looked at Stacey. A superimposition skull flashed on her pretty-pretty face. In Tina's head, Hackwill's laugh sounded.

'Absolute Secret, huh?'

Tina hugged Stacey, hard.

'Care, Stace. Take chance none. For me, please.'

'Nichevo, Teen. It's only anelids. I can process and perfect.'

'No, not that. Really care.'

A frozen moment: Tina pulled back and looked again at Stacey's open face, fixing it poignantly in memory.

From the original film – where the notes were on paper not screen – if not this heavy foreshadowing, Chantal knew Stacey would be Hackwill's next victim.

She told herself Stacey was a simulacrum wearing the face of a woman now auditioning for better roles, but it was still a wrench: tonight, this girlchik would die.

TRANSITIONAL FADE

Even Mimesis could not make it scan as real. When Tina shut her eyes, she was in school in the morning, warmed by sunlight glimmering through windowwalls; when she opened them a subjective blink later, it was after dark and she was outside her house, wearing a heavy coat against the cold.

Like theatre and cinema, Mimesis cut and pasted bits of narrative into scenes unfolding faster than life. The irony was that it was technically easier to provide convincing, unedited actuality, but there wasn't a market. In realwelt, too much time is wasted getting from place to place, feeding and cleaning, doing nought. This was reality edited for length, doled out in suspenseful slices.

Here, the dremake was departing from the first *Where the*

Bodies Are Buried. The old film cut from the locker scene to Stacey later that day, receiving her own suggestive note, taking a lengthy – gratuitous – shower before dolling up for a date. In a dark scary house, she was stalked by Hackwill and turned limb by limb into a mannequin. A classic image from the film was her living eyes, trapped in a smooth plastic face, tears trickling down unfeeling cheeks.

Mimesis required the story be perceived from a single viewpoint. No cutting away to other characters, no privileging the audience with information withheld from the heroine. Right now, it was a first-person medium. Jerome reported the Industry was experimenting with allowing the dreamer to hop from viewpoint to viewpoint, even choosing whom to ride through the plot. That was a generation or two down the line.

As Tina trotted nervously through the night, constantly scanning behind her, Chantal realized the dream was taking the easiest possible alternative. Tina was going to sneak into the dark scary house – the Old Hackwill Place, naturally – and witness the monster's torment of her friend.

When she wondered how Tina knew where Stacey was being lured, there was an annoying misty patch in the mind construct. Chantal recognized a program flaw. Whenever the dreamer spotted a logic lapse, the viewpoint threw up a strategic memory blank.

The Old Hackwill Place loomed. Tina stopped to look up at it, giving a visionfield of the major locale. It was a tridvid synthesis of every haunted house in every horror movie: from the rusted gate hanging by one hinge to the single light in a gable window, the stone eagle over the doorway to the bricked-up room in its own turret.

Beyond the house was the graveyard where Hackwill had been caught and tortured by the mob. Chantal was getting ahead of the story; presumably, that flashback would come later, when Tina got suspicious enough to track down Judge Jonathan and get the story out of him.

Chantal's impatience made Tina walk fast forward. The

front door opened by itself and she stepped inside the house. A scream abused her ears.

ERROR

The scream caused some kind of playback fault. Chantal lost Tina and found herself back in realwelt. The heavy hoodset was giving her a crick in the neck.

This time, she was alone. But she had the sense someone had been in the cabin with her and just stepped out.

More authentically spooked at that than by the cliché horror house, she considered getting up and looking into the walkway outside. It ran the length of the *Meyrink*. Her visitor – if visitor there had been – should still be in sight.

Could it be Jerome? Subotai?

The hoodset was too heavy. A design fault. She didn't want to get up. She twisted around, looking for the remote, and found it clipped to her breast pocket.

She tapped **RUN**.

Tina stood, fear-frozen, in the doorway. Before her was a tableau.

On the stairs Stacey writhed, dead legs dragging. On the landing, looking down, was Rob Hackwill.

Tina watched the transformation continue. Stacey's elbows kinked the wrong way and became notched-and-pinned joints. She held fingers to her face and gasped as they became bone-like chunks of wood, strung together on wires.

Stacey looked to her friend for help.

Tina was rigid. Chantal was irritated at the dream's assumption of girly uselessness. Tina made no move to help or comfort Stacey.

Stacey's face stiffened and drained of colour. It was the crying mannequin image, recreated in tridvid. Chantal realized the moment was somewhat thrown away.

Mimesis distanced her from Stacey, trapping her in Tina. In

the original, there was a powerful sense of loss. Not least because the actress playing Stacey was better than the inept ex-model cast as Tina. As a viewer, Chantal knew that with Stacey's death her pleasure in the balance of the film would be limited by the lack of the character.

Now, Chantal was confused. She couldn't be frightened for Tina because she realized, even if the dremake diverged radically from Allan Keyes's old script, she was fundamentally safe. If the viewpoint died, the dream would end.

Suddenly, she realized she was invincible in the dreamwelt. With a surge of courage, she looked up at Hackwill, knowing him for a cardboard fiend. He had no power over her, in realwelt or this shoddy simile.

The monster stepped into the light. He moved like a human snake, hissing through lipless smile, red eye winking. Talons grooved scratches in the banister.

Hackwill prodded the Staceyquin with a toe-point. In a tangle of loose limbs and twisted clothes, the dummy rolled downstairs. Twisted round, the head looked up, eyes pools of anger, face cracked across. A beetle crawled out of the fissure, a gratuitously icky touch.

Tina stood her ground. Chantal wondered if she had short-circuited the dream by spotting the logic lapse. Would her realization that the viewpoint could never be in mortal peril trigger a fast-forward to plot resolution?

'You think Robbie has no surprises left, don't you?' said the monster.

He stepped down to Tina and reached out. His claw-fingers lightly touched her face. His nailpoints were cold and sharp.

'We're to be great friends and collaborators, dearest. This rag doll is only the beginning. There'll be many others. And the work we have to do is such fun.'

Hackwill wasn't like Stacey. Up close, he had a different texture. There was something super-real about him, a fuzziness in the detail. He shifted through levels of reality, catching the light differently from moment to moment, like silk or falling rain. He was not like an actor in a close-fitting latex monster mask, any more than he was like a real disfigurement victim.

Hackwill leaned close to her and whistled softly through his bare teeth. She saw his red eye up close, and intuited something unique in its depth. She caught a whiff of gravemould under a strong cologne.

'We're partners, Sister . . .'

The sibilants of *ssissster* were razor kisses. Panic seized her. Everything spun out of control.

'Come now,' Hackwill chided. 'Did you think I wouldn't recognize you, Chantal? We're old friends.'

STOP BREAK

'He calls her "Tina"', Jerome said. 'Well, he calls me "Tina" when I dream it. Then again, there are playback variants. It's to do with the interface between Mimesis and your back brain. It's always been metaphorically true; now it's literally so. Consciousness is inescapably subjective. We all see things differently: a tree, a painting, a girl.'

'Hackwill knew me,' Chantal insisted.

Jerome had dreamed through the scene carefully. He was genuinely concerned. He trusted her word. The monster had talked to her. Not to Tina, to her. Like a good information-processor, Jerome was not denying the input but trying to interpret it.

In its blackwood and red velvet box, the dreamsphere was inert. Chantal's reflection distorted in its curved surface.

She was not quite ready to go back and dream the Dark Scary House scene again.

'Maybe it's a programming glitch. *Bodies* is pre-release. This is only a test impression.'

'I didn't feel alone in there.'

'You're intuiting the presence of the Talent. It's impossible to erase entirely.'

'Who is the Talent?'

'Ultimately, Allan Keyes. He's the dreamshaper. Augmented by tech-assists. Maybe he's just a marquee name, and subsidiary Talents do the actual shapework. Not everyone can be a Talent. It's inborn.'

Chantal knew about Allan Keyes. Rob Hackwill was his life's work. Obviously, he was still with the program.

'We'll have to take testimony from him.'

Jerome smiled. 'It's fixed. Pyramid are setting up a Virtual Pow-Wow. Us here, Keyes in La-La Land. Wonders of Modern Science.'

She got up and looked out of the porthole. A restaurant floated by, trailing balloons under the Charles Bridge. On each balloon was the face of the Dalai Lama over crossed Armalite-99 rifles. It was a fund-raiser for yet another Church Militant.

'Where's Duroc?' she asked.

'He left a holonote. His Interpol sources slipped him pre-release news and he's hared off to Barcelona. Dark hints, hush-hush. He says it's a relevant mission.'

'Relevant to us, or Model?'

'Mr and Mrs Wink, the Euro-Commission extends deep con-dolences for your loss.'

'Thank you, Sister,' said Herman Wink.

Chantal wished Duroc were here. Herman and Monika Wink, flanked by Modelist bodyguards, spoke mostly through a lawyer whose singlepiece was fastened by tiny tags.

The couple did not strike Chantal as especially upset, but people took losses in their own way. Most of the other parents were unable to give testimony, spasming with uncontrolled grief or mind-blanked by sedation. The Winks were the official spokesfolk of Relatives of Hackwill Victims. Their Pro-Amendment petition was still downloading.

'We take comfort that Marthe was of the Last Generation,' Monika Wink said. 'Her transgression was justly rewarded, but her lapse will guide others.'

Jerome covered the audio and talked to Chantal, 'I'm not understanding this. Transgression? Lapse?'

As Modelists, the Winks believed their daughter had marked herself for death simply by sampling the dream. By being murdered, she had cleansed herself and would be redeemed. Model always used the analogy of investment, referring to those judged favourably by the Lord as wise savers whose investment had matured. Those who sinned were spendthrifts whose earthly poverty would extend into the afterlife. Extreme suffering of the flesh could, in certain cases, wipe out the heaviest of debts.

'It is certain Marthe dreamed *Where the Bodies Are Buried*?'

Herman nodded. Chantal thought a flicker of genuine hurt crossed Monika's face.

'This is so,' Herman admitted. 'She was led into Evil Ways by unhealthy associations. The Reverend Model has proscribed Mimesis as a Tool of the Devil, but Marthe would not see the wisdom. She was wilful.'

Marthe's murderer was still unknown and at large. I-Pol established he was the same person known to be responsible for at least sixteen other killings, throughout the Eunion, within the last two years. The newsnets inevitably tagged him as a Hackwill Killer. The murders began at about the time Pyramid announced *Bodies* would be remade in Mimesis. Three of the last five victims had, like Marthe, had contact with bootlegs.

'We comfort ourselves that our daughter's death serves a high purpose, Sister,' Herman Wink said. 'This Evil Thing will be destroyed.'

'We thank you,' said Jerome.

The Winks' lawyer broke the link. The holo-projections of the witnesses and their entourage vanished.

Chantal and Jerome sat alone in the hearing room. She loosened her collar.

'They were a piece of work,' Jerome said.

She flipped on Marthe Wink's file, scrolling through the

forensics, calling up pre-death clips. She had looked like her mother.

'This isn't about them, Jerome. This is about Marthe. And the others.'

She was on deck, reading her breviary. After fourteen years, daily duty came easily. As a novice, she had scrubbed cell floors between masses and her secular studies. Though clerical celibacy was abolished, it was no wonder few priests married. Who had the time?

'Chan, excuse me . . .'

It was Jerome, with something important. He knew the breviary was her one inescapable daily commitment.

'Some Czechs have come aboard. They want to throw Subotai over the side.'

She had been aware, distantly, of the commotion.

'Modelists?'

'No, regular fascisti.'

'How many?'

'Three.'

They walked around the deck. The fascisti – teenagers with Rommel coats, swastika-tat scalps and top hats – had Subotai up against the rail. The E-Com cook and one of the secretaries – both Czechs who openly despised the Mongol – were watching, not making a move.

She tried to conquer her anger.

Obviously, the fascist not holding Subotai, prepared to let her comrades do the tossing-overboard for her entertainment, was leaderine. She was a heavy-set girlchik with steroid biceps and blonde Viking plaits.

Without saying anything, Chantal walked into the situation and angled a high kick at the underside of leaderine's chin, sticking the point of her pump into softness.

The fascist staggered, dizzy, gulping. Jerome was equally astonished. The girlchik growled – she had a jewel skull inset in an incisor – and Chantal ducked under an attempted

183

wrestling-grasp. She heaved up, thumping the Valkyrie's sternum with her shoulder.

The leaderine went over the side with a satisfying splash, crashing through a thin ice-lily.

'As Devil Princesses go, not very impressive, *hein*?'

Chantal chided herself for enjoying the moment.

The other two let Subotai go.

'My vows oblige me to forgive you your sins, but not forget them. You may leave by the gangway and fish out your wet friend. Good day.'

The kids bolted. Subotai nodded impassive thanks and returned to whatever he had been doing.

'We were lucky,' she told Jerome. 'Modelists wouldn't have been seen off so easily. Religion gives a lot of idiots strength.'

Jerome was admiring her.

'Chan, I can't decide whether you remind me more of Audrey Hepburn in *The Nun's Story* or Diana Rigg in *The Avengers*. I'm sorry. Those references don't mean anything to you, do they?'

She laughed. He always forgot her field was pop culture.

'In Switzerland, *The Avengers* is called *Bowler Hat and Kinky Boots*. It was on all the time when I was little. And every woman with the calling has to see *The Nun's Story* when she's nine. I saw it back-to-back with *The Red Shoes* and was torn between becoming a saint or a prima ballerina.'

Duroc's head sat on the plate. Chantal and Jerome held still, so their faces were caught in the link-beams. Agitated talkers lost ears and noses over holo.

'The Hackwill Killer is in the city,' Duroc said.

'We're conferencing with Keyes tomorrow,' Jerome said. 'Can you tap in from Barcelona?'

'It is not likely,' Duroc replied. 'Thy report will be accepted.'

His face was blank. He accepted holo but Virtual Conference was too close to Mimesis. She wondered if he was tempted to sample a dream. She and Jerome dipped in and out of *Where the Bodies Are Buried* all the time, but Duroc was required by contract with the tele-ministry to abjure Mimesis. The Modelist must at least be curious. He was still human.

The head vanished.

'His cop genes are taking over,' Jerome said. 'These cases were his speciality.'

With his background, I-Pol Barcelona must be glad to have Duroc. From his involvement with the Moschone, Thiel and Best cases, he was up to speed on Hackwill Killers.

'He knows about us,' she said.

'Duroc?'

'The killer. He's following E-Com. The first murder was just after the Model-Duff Amendment was proposed. Jeanine Csathó, the Budapest victim. All the killings have been inside the Eunion. If Model-Duff becomes law, it will only be enforced within the EU.'

'Gets bigger every year. If Libya is admitted, it'll open up the rest of North Africa. The only hold-out is your place.'

'There are no Swiss victims. He's killed from Gibraltar to Greenland, from Ankara to Yeltsingrad. Why not Zurich, or Tel Aviv, or Cuba? The *day* after Bermuda came in, he killed there. It's as if he's drawing a map.'

'He doesn't want to go through passport control.'

'He'd have needed a passport to get to Bermuda before killing McCharen.'

'You're beginning to sound like a Hackwill Killer yourself. Do you really think Rob Hackwill is talking to you?'

'This is realwelt, Jerome.'

'I'm sorry, Chan. I'll have to process this. You have to admit it scans paranoid at first scroll-through.'

'You, me and Duroc. We're between two huge grinding cliffs of credit. On the one side, a hugely wealthy Industry: the Derek Leech Group is richer than most countries. On the other, the Relatives of Hackwill Victims, underwritten by the Modelist tele-ministry. These killings have been going on since the last century. If Model-Duff gets on the statutes in the EU, RHV will bring multiple suits. If cases go their way, there'll be a credit transfer bigger than the one that caused the Nikkei Crash of 2014.'

'I know all this, Chan. We have to focus on micro-issues. The Amendment. We recommend or not on its own merits. Think of the victims. Think of the victims who are still alive, who haven't been born yet.'

The idea wasn't original to Joseph Model and Morag Duff: it had been proposed in America as early as the 1990s. It was to do with blame and compensation: if murderers were shaped not born, then the forces which influence them should share culpability. If a rapist's mind was warped by pornography, then a rape victim should be able to sue pornographers. The Model-Duff Amendment proposed moral guilt be brought under a legal remit.

It was a simple, appealing idea. Yet it frightened her.

The Barcelona Victim was called Armando de Castro Oros. Duroc downloaded stats before the newsnets got them.

Hours before the scheduled Virtual Conference, Chantal was praying for guidance. No matter how she tried to clear her mind, de Castro Oros remained.

The boy was found dressed as a schoolgirl, face coated with asphyxiating plastic. Post mortem, his murderer had cracked the fast-setting mask and jammed in a chocolate beetle. The victim's tears were trapped bubbles in the plastic.

He was a Stacey. Like Victor McCharen, Saira Matsoela and Laure Petietich.

The killer was repeating victim types: Tinas, Staceys, Jimmy Traynors, Judge Jonathans, Boss Hoopers. All the characters from the dream.

There was no other connection between de Castro Oros and *Where the Bodies Are Buried*. If there was a black market dreamsphere in Barcelona, I-Pol had not found it.

Duroc was returning to Prague by way of Bermuda, where

he wanted to follow up on McCharen. An American tourist, the Bermuda Victim might have been a smuggler, responsible for getting the dreamspheres into the EU in the first place.

For Chantal, prayer was a communion. Like Jerome processing random infobits, she could sometimes run through the elements of a problem and be led to a conclusion in something approaching a vision.

Not today.

Chantal would have been satisfied with a holo-link, swapping tridvid with Beverly Hills. Pyramid, wanting to impress E-Com with tech, insisted on a fancier Virtual Conference.

They were to meet Allan Keyes in Spring Meadow. Jerome, excited, explained the *Bodies* dreamwelt could be accessed as a non-narrative CGNvironment. It was a supplementary feature of Home Mimesis dreamspheres, along with a bound copy of the script and collector's cards.

Jerome sat on the couch, adjusting his hoodset. He had already helped her plumb in.

'You won't be a *dybbuk* this time, Chan. You'll have autonomy.'

'But I'll still be Tina.'

Jerome nodded, hoodset bulbous. 'Since *Bodies* is a single viewpoint dream, so will I.'

Her eyepieces descended, blanking her vision. A test signal blipped into her brain.

'Ready?' Jerome asked.

She was back in the park, standing before the statue, waiting for midnight. As she slipped into the Tina simile, Chantal prepared for a mindlink that did not come. For a moment, she thought the puppet's strings were cut and she would fall in a tangle. Then she was in control.

She was herself, but with Tina's dreambody.

By the statue stood a pretty girl in a heavy coat and a wool scarf. She smiled and shrugged.

'Weird,' Jerome commented, through the pretty girl's mouth. 'This gets stranger.'

Jerome-as-Tina looked a little different from the self-image of Chantal-as-Tina. She saw Jerome's slenderness in his simile, even an underlay of his cheekbones in the Tina face.

She wondered if Allan Keyes and the Pyramid CEO would also be forced to be Tinas. Probably not; at their end, they would have more sophisticated dreamtech and should be able to select viewpoints to suit themselves.

She looked around, dreamflesh creeping.

'What's up, Chan?'

'There's someone here.'

'They're not online yet.'

'No, not them.'

He glanced about too, and shrugged again. His distinctive smile stretched the Tina face.

'It's the first-scene feeling, from the dream,' she explained. 'When Hackwill is creeping up on Tina.'

'The story isn't in RUN. For once, there's no Robbie here.'

'"There's always a Hackwill in Spring Meadow."'

'A-ha. Judge Jonathan's speech. You're a *Bodies* buff. I keep forgetting.'

Beeptone came from their coats. Jerome found his set-book before Chantal found hers. Both lit up with identical messages.

ThE olD HaCKwill playCE.

'Do you want to walk, or . . .?'

'Skip that,' she said. They both blinked . . .

TRANSITIONAL FADE

. . . and were outside the Dark Scary House. Stacey, a walking mannequin, was waiting for them on the porch. She had blots of rouge on white plastic cheeks.

'Mr Rhodes, Ms Juillerat,' she said through stiff, barely parted lips. 'I'm Medea Calm, of Pyramid Releasing. We're proud to have you in Spring Meadow.'

188

The similes shook hands. Medea's fingers were hard and unmoving.

'Sorry about this. I had hoped to rep myself as the Stacey of her cute scenes, not the Staceyquin. I actually look a little like the babe version. But we had a simile transfer glitch. The bugs will be worked out prontissimo. It's cutting-edge tech.'

Chantal had expected a Pyramid exec to be more like the Devil Princess.

'Allan is inside, waiting.'

Medea hobbled lop-sided into the mansion. Jerome hung back a little to let Chantal in first. The hallway was as it was in the finale, Hellfire burn-marks on the wall.

Someone stood in the dark at the top of the stairs.

'Allan,' said Medea-as-Staceyquin, 'Mr Rhodes and Ms Juillerat are from the Euro-Commission on the Model-Duff Amendment.'

'I've scrolled your thesis, Sister,' said Keyes. 'You make some points.'

He stepped forward into the light.

Chantal had expected Keyes to be Hackwill, but the Talent was in the simile of Japheth Jonathan, the corrupt judge who explains Hackwill's origins. Thankfully, he was not as last seen in the dream – head exploded by his own tongue swollen to the size of a watermelon – but as in his intro scene. Keyes must be about Jonathan's age, but newssims did not suggest other resemblance. The Judge was an impressively eyebrowed character actor; Keyes was one of those nondescript Englishmen, Jerome grown not old but faint.

One of the Hackwill Victims was Keyes's own girlfriend: it must take something to continue weaving nightmares after that. Originally a novelist, Keyes had turned himself into a motion picture director and then a Mimesis Talent, extending the reign of Hackwill into fresh media.

'How does a Jesuit get to know so much about horror films?' he asked.

'My field of study is Media Influence. Genre horror is central

189

to the discipline. The pioneer work of Martin Barker and Julian Petley in the 1990s . . .'

'But do you *like* horror? Do you like what *I* do?'

She tried to give an honest answer. 'While working on my thesis, I became so familiar with the material that I lost perspective on aesthetic or entertainment quality. But I first decided to be a Jesuit because of *The Exorcist*. As a child, I saw the original *Where the Bodies Are Buried* – it was made the year I was born – on Cloud 9 TV. It gave me nightmares for weeks, but I pleaded with my parents to let me watch it again.'

'Your thesis could do with input from the little girl you once were. I intuit you regret a weakness for the films. Because of the Hackwill Effect.'

'Pyramid Releasing does not acknowledge the existence of the so-called Hackwill Effect,' Medea cut in. 'Many studies – including your own, Sister Juillerat – question a hypothesized causal relationship between fictional and realwelt violence.'

'Our guests aren't interested in blipquotes, Medea,' Keyes said. 'Credit them with that.'

Medea continued, 'If you lump together so-called Hackwill Killings over the last twenty-five years, including those later established as unconnected, you have at most 400 murders. Five times that many died in the Reverend Model's Warsaw *pogrom* last year. And what about British Druids mustard-gassed by Special Branch in the solstice of '17? Joseph Model and Morag Duff should look to their own consciences.'

The lecture was pointed, but sounded strange from a life-sized broken doll.

'You've obviously given the Hackwill Effect thought,' Chantal said to Keyes. 'Yet you've continued with *Bodies*. It can't just be for the credit. Why do you do it? Why do you create only horrors?'

Keyes smiled sadly. 'What makes you think I have a choice?'

All around, Hellfire exploded.

INTERFERENCE

The similes could be hurt. These flames bit harder than the pain analogues usual in dreams. Consciousness unfiltered through viewpoint, she was immersed in intense heat, blinding light, choking stench, nipping agony.

Jerome was patting out the flames on her arm. Medea had vanished, presumably breaking the link. Half of Jerome's Tina hair was singed off.

A burning beam fell between them and Keyes. He stood still in the inferno. She wondered if his simile was an empty freeze-frame. But his eyes moved.

The laughter of the Devil Princess poured out of the air, setting fires wherever it was heard. In the original, only the mansion was destroyed; in the dremake, most of Spring Meadow was consumed.

Windows burst outwards. Draughts of cold air whipped flames into spirals that entwined the two Tinas. Chantal and Jerome hugged, as if the heroine wanted to reunite her divided self.

'Another glitch?' Jerome asked.

In the fire behind Keyes, a black shape coalesced, rearing up over him, arms enfolding the Talent. Bands of clawed shadow held him fast. A single red eye shone, a crystal of fire in a man-shaped patch of night.

'Keyes!' she shouted.

Jerome thumped his own forehead, where the hoodset panel was in realwelt. He disappeared.

She was alone in Spring Meadow with Keyes and the Hackwill Effect. Fire rushed to fill the space where Jerome's Tina had been.

Allan Keyes – she could swear – smiled with almost relief as the shadow and flame wrapped round him. This was the end of his private dreamstory.

STOP

Jerome was pulling the hoodset off her. Half his face was an angry red.

She looked at her hands and saw white spots where cinders had scalded her in Spring Meadow.

Subotai was checking the fixed-up link, genuinely concerned for his temporary masters.

She intuited she had just experienced the downside of cutting-edge tech.

'Do we still have audio-link?' she asked Subotai.

The *robota* stood aside and gave her the handset.

Jerome was swearing profusely in English, touching his pain patches. He was burned under unsinged clothes.

'Hello,' she said to the handset. 'Ms Calm? Keyes?'

There was a commotion at the other end.

'Ms Juillerat,' came a voice. A woman, shaky.

'Medea?'

'Uh, yes. We have no rationale for that . . . uh . . . incident.'

'Is Keyes out of the dream?'

'We've cut him off. He's here . . . his body's here . . . but there's nobody home.'

It was Site Prime in the weeks leading up to Hallowe'en: Allan Keyes, the Hackwill Man, was the latest victim of the Hackwill Effect. His body might live but he was mindwiped, a human blank. Medicos theorized that if he came out of coma, he might develop from mental infancy, growing a new personality. But it was a moot point: he had suffered 78 per cent burns in the Virtual Conference; if he came round, he would probably die from paintrauma.

From the deck, Chantal looked down on grey waters. A drift of ground-hugging riot gas seeped down from the bridge, floating on the surface of the Vltava. She felt after-sting in her nostrils, even through the domino mask she wore when the pollution count was high.

Where the Bodies Are Buried had been recalled – E-Com had to surrender their dreamsphere to a notarized messenger – and Mimesis was on hold 'until bugs can be ironed out'. Whatever the truth of the Hackwill Effect, Keyes was proof that Mimesis could be hazardous to dreamers' health, mental and otherwise.

E-Com's ground was out from under them. The original inexpressed purpose of the enquiry, beyond even the Amendment, was to determine whether Mimesis be allowed unrestricted into Eunion. Now, Mimesis was withdrawn by the Industry: if Model-Duff passed, it would apply only to old-fashioned mediatech like motion pictures, tele and VR. Not newsworthy, but still a major legislative shift.

Using the railing as a *barre*, Chantal ran through ballet moves, stretching her legs until they felt real, making points of her toes. With the Troubles, she was advised not to go jogging up to the Castle and back, as she had in E-Com's early days in the city. The *Meyrink* sometimes felt like a prison. She needed to maintain strength and suppleness. Exercise was a courtesy to God: it was her duty to maintain in peak condition the wonderful gift of a body her soul had been given.

As she felt the knots popping in her muscles and joints, she thought it over.

Duroc, back from his travels, was meticulously assembling an infodump about the current Hackwill Killings. He had taken their report of the Conference on board but had no ideas about it. To him, Mimesis dreams were Hell equivalents even without brimstone.

Jerome thought it a glitch – bleedthrough from the narrative of *Bodies* – but Chantal was convinced there had been another presence in Spring Meadow. It was hard not to think of it as Rob Hackwill.

On the Charles Bridge, the demonstration turned ugly. Students, supporting persecuted refugees, clashed with Modelists, and armed police were caught between them. People fell or were tossed off the bridge, splashing into gas-covered water. Throwing malcontents into the river was a traditional Prague response to trouble; just as throwing bureaucrats out of windows was a traditional Prague way of making trouble. Last night, the head of the local Modelist Congregation had been defenestrated.

She stopped her programme of kicks, and towelled her sweaty forehead. Through the domino, she breathed deeply.

The McDonald's Airport was shut down, transnational holo-links were out. After the Ghetto riots, Modelist Advance Teams combed the ruins, offering salvation with share options and low monthly payments. Subotai had heard a whisper that E-Com would have to share the *Meyrink* with a Europa Defence Force response unit straight from Cádiz.

Jerome came up on deck, looking sheepish. Turfed out of his hotel by a newsnet anchor, he was mooching around the ship, face glistening from the healing gel he had to wear until his burns faded.

'Chan, I've made my decision.'

She had expected this. The Spring Meadow Incident had shaken him. And the December deadline was approaching. She pulled off her domino so she could speak with him.

'I'm voting the Amendment be attached to the Revised Criminal Code,' he said. 'That aligns me with Roger.'

'I see.'

It didn't have to be unanimous. She still felt the enquiry should be pursued: Mimesis might even prove a side-issue to the greater question.

'As of now, I can't change my position,' she said.

'Still Swiss?'

She took the railing and kicked in the air, above Jerome's head. She had always had trick hips.

'I abstain. You know why.'

'I'm sorry, Chan.'

She went belowdecks to tell Duroc. At her knock, he unlocked his door.

Aside from the bunk, his cabin was furnished only with a flatscreen and a knee-rest. An official holo-bust of Reverend Model hovered under the bare lightstrip. Duroc worked always under the blind gaze of his master.

He stood aside to let her in. They both had to bow slightly

because of the low ceiling. Duroc blithely dipped his head through Model, but Chantal avoided the holo as if it were a solid.

Duroc, alarmingly, was stripped to the waist. His back was striped with scars, some fresh. He had a scourge in his hand, a wicked cluster of studded flails with a riding crop grip.

She had not known he was a flagellant.

On the flatscreen were images Chantal recognized. A field laid out neatly with corpses. Black-clad Modelists prowling among the dead.

'The Basque Insurrection?' she asked.

Duroc nodded.

Most who had served in the Insurrection were soured on Modelists for life. There was a famous incident in which a non-com had been court-martialled for disobeying orders and intervening to cut short a massacre supervised by elders of the tele-ministry.

Duroc must be Model's only convert from the EDF. No wonder he felt the need to whip himself.

'Jerome's changed his vote. To Yes.'

Duroc nodded, understanding.

'I'll prep a formal statement for Brussels. We all put our signatures to it. Then, we can go home.'

'Hast thou changed thy vote?'

'It doesn't have to be unanimous.'

'I know.'

He looked at her. She saw something hanging back in his eyes, but could not process it.

'Yes,' she admitted, 'I have changed my vote. From Abstention to No.'

She did not ask if Duroc wished to change his Yes to Abstention or No. That would have been futile.

'I'm sorry, Sister. We must all act in accordance with our conscience.'

He looked sideways at the Model head, as if seeking higher approval.

The decision was communicated on a priority line to Brussels, and the Model-Duff Amendment was attached to the Revised Criminal Code.

On New Year's Eve, Joseph Model held a celebratory rally in Vaduz. In his speech, he personally commended Chantal Juillerat, Jerome Rhodes and Brother Roger Duroc as Good Credit Christians. He claimed their Heavenly Portfolios were maturing exceptionaly well, throwing off high-yield interests. He also promised arms to the Advance Teams in Prague, and accused Tel Aviv of inciting ghetto-dwellers to murder their Modelist rescuers.

The E-Com, officially dissolved, was still in Prague. Travel restrictions were in force until the fighting died down. On New Year's Day, there was a Hackwill Killing outside the Castle. Pavel Zahradnik, a Boss Hooper, head burned to the skull. His wife signed up with RHV. The Model-Duff Amendment – no, the Model-Duff Law – was retroactive: Petra Zahradniková would have to join a queue of grieving, suing relatives.

The conglomerated lawsuit was already issued, and Pyramid's corporate attorneys were resisting attempts to bring the case to the European Court in Kiev.

Morag Duff, under fire for imposing an extension of the term between general elections to ten years, gloried in the success of her Amendment – she carefully never mentioned Model in public – and announced she would now devote herself to removing nudity from art galleries, and British World Tree Sites. With lewdness and licence expunged, she claimed – repeating her last electoral slogan – 'everything will be nice again'.

Chantal kept her cabin when the EDF unit moved in, but Duroc and Jerome had to bunk together. Subotai was pounced upon in the Square and severely beaten by Modelists. He was then removed to a camp in the Carpathians, where Czechskanzler Drnkova claimed refugees could be protected from violent mobs. Duroc did not want to take part in any of his Church's activities in the city, and shutters came down whenever the soldiers talked about the militia missionaries against whom they expected to be deployed.

Cardinal Menzies communicated that she was expected back in Rome when restrictions were lifted. She passed time with her breviary, unable to shift her mind from the dead issue of E-Com to her next task, finishing her Information Children bookfile.

She still sensed, just out of sight, the creature of flame and darkness that had attacked Allan Keyes in Spring Meadow.

'What are you scanning?' Jerome asked.

On deck, the EDF were doing push-ups. Duroc, twenty years older than most of the soldier kids, was earning respect by matching them thrust for thrust.

Jerome was frustrated; he missed spending the holidays with his mother. It seemed he would not get out of Czechia before Spring. Also, he was off-salary.

'I'm going through our logs, checking the hours we've put in at terminals and in meetings.'

'You think we've been rooked on our expenses?'

'Something nags.'

'Close it down, Chan. It's processed and perfected. We did our bit. Now it's up to lawyers.'

On St Valentine's Day, Subotai escaped from the Relocation Centre and made his way to Prague where, according to the newsnets, he was waylaid by the Hackwill Killer. He was a Judge Jonathan, head burst by a pressure capsule – intended for instant liferaft inflation – forced into his mouth.

Chantal was shocked and depressed. She had liked and trusted the *robota*. Subotai's scattered family – and several women who repped themselves as his wives, but whose claims were instantly disproved – joined the RHV and added their lawsuits to the others. She intuited the case would not reach Kiev until the Hackwill Killer was caught.

Allan Keyes's condition remained stable.

On the *Meyrink*, it was hard to concentrate. She kept going over the logs of the E-Com. Jerome, suffering cabin fever, had taken to complaining about foreigners. The EDF – mostly Turks and Swedes – were growing nervy as their deployment was put off. Everyone was getting irritable.

Except Duroc. He exercised, read Modelist screentexts, and showed no interest in the world outside his faith.

It was Jerome who pointed out the anomaly.

'It's odd. Roger traipsed from Spain to Bermuda on the trail of the Hackwill Killer, but hasn't crossed the river to join the hunt now the murderer is in Prague. I'm surprised I-Pol haven't conscripted him to head the investigation.'

Just around midnight on 1 March, the alarum sounded. One moment, Chantal was in the *Meyrink*'s mess hall, improving her Swedish by chatting with a non-com from Malmö; then she was surrounded by *Mary Celeste* detritus of abandoned card games and unfinished mugs of recaff.

The clattering of boots was a brief thunder. The ship actually rocked as the EDF unit assembled on one side of the deck. They yomped out, weighed down by weaponry, towards the Ghetto. She prayed for their safety. And for those they would be fighting.

Through the mess windows, she saw a glow in the sky. She had a flash of the Old Hackwill Place.

'They're burning the Ghetto,' Jerome said. 'The bloody fools. Modelist maniacs.'

Duroc was with them, showing no emotion.

Jerome turned on the Modelist. 'How can you be with those bloodthirsty credit-grubbers?'

'The Reverend Model tells us we must terminate un-rewarding investments. Only radical measures will serve.'

'You can't really believe that scut!'

Duroc went up on deck.

In prayer, it came to her. The discrepancy that had been nagging was Duroc's trip to Barcelona.

She had to check first.

'Where are you going, Chan?'

She left Jerome in the mess hall and made her way down a deck.

The office was sealed but she still had a viable entry-code. She called up the logs on the terminal and scrolled them side by side with a newsnet chronology of the killings.

Jerome was in the doorway, puzzled. She was glad he had followed her. The ship lurched. A noise hammered: an explosion ashore, nearby. There was the popping of gunfire.

She concentrated on the screen, shutting out the macro-issues.

'Chan, what is it?'

'Look. Duroc arrived in Barcelona *before* Armando de Castro Oros was murdered.'

'He had an I-Pol tip-off?'

'No, he's the Hackwill Killer.'

There was a thump.

She turned from the screen and looked at Jerome's face. He was open-mouthed and wide-eyed, stunned. A trickle of blood came from his hairline. He stood statue-still, then pitched forwards.

Duroc, spanner in hand, stepped over Jerome and looked at her.

'I'm not a Hackwill Killer,' he said. 'There are no Hackwill Killers.'

As a teenager, ballet had led for a while to martial arts. She saw the point in the centre of Duroc's solid chest where she should kick.

She stood slowly, tense but trying to calm herself. She knew she had no chance. Besides being a trained soldier, policeman and fanatic, Duroc was a practised murderer. She could not hope to fight him.

'I'm doing the Lord's work,' he said, deadpan. 'As revealed

to me by the Reverend Model. We must put away Evil Things.'

Was he mocking her?

He held the spanner loosely, thwacking his open palm with the heavy instrument.

Would she be a Tina or a Stacey?

He was a barrier in the doorway. That left her with one other option.

She made her move, grabbing the terminal chair and rolling it across the deck towards Duroc. It slammed him, not hurting at all, but distracting.

Chantal jumped and grasped with both hands a pipe that ran across the ceiling. She swung back and forth twice like an aerialist, feeling the *wrench* in her shoulders, then aimed herself feet-first at the porthole.

She was – thank God – wearing sensible shoes and a singlepiece. Her points punched the circle of glass out of the hole and she followed through, body like a dart, praying hips or shoulders would not catch.

Fire raked her back as she plunged through the porthole, scraping herself on the rim. Her whole body was out in cold night when her wrists were grabbed.

Her shoulders exploded. Angry ants ate at the muscles from inside. For an instant, she thought her arms had come off.

Duroc held her, but her whole weight dragged her down. She slammed against the *Meyrink*'s steel hull. Bursts of shadow and flame obscured her visionfield.

This time, she was not a viewpoint. This was realwelt, with real pain and real death.

Her weight and momentum hauled Duroc partially out of the porthole. She looked up at his face and saw only shadow. The sky above the ship was crimson-streaked.

Somewhere else, guns were going off.

Duroc held her by the wrists, but couldn't haul her up without adjusting his grip.

'You never dreamed *Where the Bodies Are Buried*,' she said, through pain. 'You told me you never even saw the old film.'

'That is true.'

'Was it the Hackwill Killers you caught? You've been recreating their crimes?'

'There are no Hackwill Killers.'

It hit her that Pietro Moschone, Nadja Thiel and Hugh Best were innocent. Roger Duroc had framed them for earlier murder clusters.

'Roger, why?'

A fireburst illuminated the side of the ship, casting their harsh shadows on the hull. In red light, she glimpsed an upside-down smile playing around Duroc's lips.

'Sister, the Lord showed me the Way. Through Joseph Model.'

He dropped her.

She plunged into the filthy Vltava and touched bottom before air in her lungs buoyed her. She struggled up through thick, freezing water. The ripples above were blobbed with reflected firebursts.

When she broke the surface, her ears were roaring. She swam to the bank, found an iron ring inset in a concrete wall, and pulled herself up, sopping, on to a jetty. Her singlepiece stuck to her like a layer of clogged ice.

She wanted to curl up and get warm.

But she had left Jerome with Duroc.

She found the gangplank and ran up it, leaving dripping footsteps.

'Duroc!' she shouted.

A bullet spanged against the hull of the *Meyrink*. A power-boat passed by, raising a white froth of wake. Someone fired another wild shot, not at her but at the sky.

'Praise the Lord and shoot the sinners,' shouted the boatman.

She had no idea what that was about.

She looked around for a weapon as she made her way down

to the office deck. All she could find was a solid-body guitar. One of the Turkish soldiers had left it behind.

The corridor was quiet. She saw Jerome's legs, stuck out of the doorway. They shifted, as he was turned over.

Heart clenched, she ran to the office.

Duroc squatted by Jerome, examining his head wound.

'He'll be all right, Sister.'

She held the guitar by the neck, hefting it like a bludgeon.

'I've called the police. They're busy.'

With all her strength, she smashed the guitar into Duroc, lifting him off the floor.

As Duroc fell backwards, Chantal stepped through the door. The lights went out and a chill fell on her. She blinked and held on to the neck of the broken guitar.

She was not in the office, with its burst porthole and dreamdeck, but back in the park in Spring Meadow. Duroc was sprawled at the base of the statue of the town founder.

He was not Duroc, but Hackwill.

Yet she was not Tina, but Chantal.

She stood over the monster, wondering whether to end it by driving the guitar-neck through his heart. You could not kill Hackwill; he always came back for the sequel.

For some reason, the Modelist had been committing murders for years. Initially, he had used his position in I-Pol to frame others, tagging them as Hackwill Killers. It couldn't be the Hackwill Effect, unless it were a new strain, a Hackwill Effect By Proxy.

The monster was hurt, trying to lift himself.

'I said we had work to do, sissster,' he said.

She held the guitar-neck out like a crucifix to ward off Evil. Duroc supported himself by clinging to the pedestal. Bloody spittle hung from his mouth.

She guessed Duroc had intervened in the Virtual Conference, projecting into the dreamwelt through the thing of shadow and fire. He was playing out some immense game-plan.

And she had a horrid intuition that mass murder and E-Com and Model-Duff were merely facets of an intricate device whose purpose was not yet apparent.

Darkness and fire were contained in Duroc's thick chest, entwining his body with ropes of wavering black and red. He wore a transparent Hackwill mask. Behind it, his face was set.

She tossed the guitar-neck away and braced herself to fight.

In this waking dream, she was herself. She was still wet and hurt.

Pirouetting, she slammed her foot into his chest, imagining it a blunt knife, focusing her all into the kick.

Duroc coughed and thumped back against the statue.

Her ankle was badly jarred, but she ignored pain. Making triangular wedges of her fingers, she jabbed Duroc's torso where she had kicked, probing for broken spots.

Despite her blows, he stood up.

'I do the Lord's work,' he repeated.

He was completely shrouded in flame and shadow. Heat seared and cold stung her hands as she hit him. His Hackwill mask was illuminated from within, as if his skull were red hot beneath translucent flesh.

'May the Lord forgive you,' she said.

She punched him in the face and danced back away from him, knowing she couldn't keep this up much longer.

At the edges of the park, the dead gathered. The dead of *Where the Bodies Were Buried*: Stacey, Jimmy, the Judge, even Tina. And the dead of realwelt: Jeanine Csathó, Subotai, Marthe, McCharen, Zahradnik, de Castro Oros. Mannequin-like, the broken witnesses hobbled together.

Duroc stood still, relaxing, head hung slightly. She felt her anger fading.

Horror-movie dead closed in, a shambling noose tightening round Chantal and Duroc. Allan Keyes was there, a ghost in his own dreamwelt, drifting above the grass. And the Devil Princess, hair like white flame spilling from her scarlet wimple.

The dream was running down.

'Where are we?' she asked.

'Outside, Sister,' the Devil Princess purred. 'In Spring Meadow, where the bodies are buried.'

Duroc spread his arms in surrender. Feathers of flame ran along their undersides. Fire and darkness gathered in Duroc's torso and coursed through his arms, exploding from his fingers, channelling into the dead, dissipating in the dream.

Duroc, empty, sagged at the knees, slumped at the feet of the statue. His face was pathetic, a childish plastic mask, broken across. His claws had come off too.

Rob Hackwill was only Roger Duroc dressed up.

Chantal stood over the murderer, feeling the tug of the realwelt beginning.

She knew now there was no Rob Hackwill. Just a man who had killed in the monster's name.

Suddenly, a laugh fell upon her from above, a laugh like a rain of hot pebbles. She knew instantly the cackle of the Real Rob. The pure evil of the old movies thrived. Hackwill still lurked in dreamspheres, scratching inside silver eggshell, to be born into the realwelt.

She looked up from the fallen Duroc to the greened bronze boots of the town founder. The statue creaked to life. A clawed hand raised a sword.

The burning red eye, the gnashing bloody teeth, the pouring laughter. Raised on his pedestal, Rob Hackwill ruled Spring Meadow.

Chantal fell to her knees and locked her hands in prayer.

She was back on the *Meyrink*, kneeling by the fallen Duroc, praying fiercely.

She must work swiftly.

As she tied Duroc up with cables from the dreamdeck, she worried at it in her mind. If it had been a vision, she intuited Duroc had shared it. Some of the dream had stuck in her mind and enveloped them both. Through Rob Hackwill, she was trying to tell herself something, trying to understand a mystery.

Duroc, unconscious, was heavy and awkward. He came round while she was binding him, but did not struggle or try to talk.

It was not over.

When she was finished with Duroc, she checked on Jerome. He was breathing but asleep. She sat, exhausted and shivering, against a bulkhead. Duroc watched her, as inexpressive as ever.

'The Lord's work,' he repeated.

She tried to stop her teeth chattering.

For the first time in fifteen years, the Reverend Joseph Model was unavailable for comment.

In the Castle, Czech I-Pol interrogated the accused. Chantal and Jerome stood in the dark beyond the mirror, watching. Duroc was co-operative, giving convincing detail. He had precise recall of what he claimed were 156 homicides going back to 2010. He insistently referred to 'the Lord's work' and respectfully claimed that the Lord's needs were revealed to him by the teachings of the Reverend Model.

'I say, he's going to be a Model Prisoner,' snorted Jerome.

Through one-way glass, Duroc seemed to be looking at her. He explained how he had schooled Hugh Best to make a confession, claiming five murders. He took no delight in his crimes but was punctilious in corroborating his claims. She was sure even a cursory check would confirm everything he said.

Jerome's forehead was disfigured by a splotch of hardened healing gel. He was certainly taking his knocks.

She was all right, but her shoulders felt as if she had been racked and her back was scraped raw. She was a real Tina. She had faced the monster and won. She would be around for the sequel.

All her hurt was inside.

Rob Hackwill was laughing in her dreams, exulting in a victory she did not yet understand. And his Devil Princess whispered to her. She looked sometimes like Stacey, sometimes like Beth Yatman. And sometimes, horribly, like Chantal Juillerat, S.J.

'It was too easy,' Chantal said. 'He got away with it for too long to be stopped by us.'

'He doesn't seem upset or unhappy.'

Duroc politely refused an offer of recaff or a cigarette. His faith required him to abjure stimulants. He explained the electro-magnetic pulse he had used to mindwipe Allan Keyes. Model called the Talent 'the author of Maximum Evil', and Duroc had been the instrument of the Lord's vengeance.

'This is like everything else Duroc ever did. Part of his program.'

The ghetto was clear of Modelists. Prague was pacified for the moment, the price being armoured EDF goons on every corner. As Eunion servants, Chantal and Jerome would have priority when travel restrictions were lifted. For every week their flights were delayed, they were given McDonald's scrip redeemable for a Happy Meal at any airport in the world.

They were alone on the *Meyrink*. The EDF Rapid Response team was redeploying to Dublin, where the factionalized followers of so-called Anti-Pope James Bacon were fire-bombing each other.

Duroc was all over the newsnets, nicknamed 'the Scourge of God', 'Model's Murder Messiah' or 'Holy Hackwill'. He was likely to end his days in the Eunion Penal Therapy Colony on Sicily, shackled in an *oubliette*. Pyramid announced a drama-docudream about his killing spree.

In Broadmoor, Beth Yatman changed her plea from 'Hackwill made me do it' to 'God told me to'. In Kiev, the Relatives of Hackwill Victims – reconstituted as the Relatives of Victims of Religious Fanaticism – changed their lawsuit. Pyramid Releasing and Derek Leech Enterprises were no longer indicted. The new defendants were the Reverend Joseph Model, the Modelist Tele-Ministry and the State of Liechtenstein.

If, under the Model-Duff Law, the case was decided in favour of RVRF, Model and his church would be bankrupt, forced to bestow settlements on upwards of 25,000 claimants. Purge survivors all over the Eunion were bringing their own suits against Model.

All because of Roger Duroc.

Jerome importuned her for spiritual advice she could not give. Her own faith was not shaky, but she sensed a precedent being established: if religions were responsible legally for violence done in God's name, what Church would still stand in ten years' time?

On the deck of the *Meyrink*, she walked with Jerome. Suddenly, he kissed her.

'That was for coming out of the river for me. I've never thanked you.'

'I don't think Duroc would have killed you.'

'That's not what either of us thought then.'

She had been going over Duroc's bio, following everything that came out on the newsnets. It was important that she understand. It was the same old question: what makes a monster of a man?

'It started in the Basque Insurrection,' she thought out loud. 'He saw what the Modelists were capable of in that carnage, then joined their Church.'

'He was a murderer. Modelism was made for him.'

'He wasn't a murderer then. He didn't kill – even in battle – until after he joined the Church.'

'Model brought out something in him. Medea Calm was right. The Reverend should have looked to his own house. The Amendment is based on the theory that people can be warped by mediamass, that dreaming of Hackwill turns you into him. Duroc proved the theory sound, but established that what we had to worry about was not what came out of the mind of Allan Keyes but what we heard in the pulpit and read in the Bible. You can weigh fifteen supposed Hackwill Killers against

207

thousands of murderers who fancy themselves instruments of a vengeful God. They all learned madness in a church somewhere.'

'Exactly. And I intuit that's the position Duroc wants us to take. Or, worse, the truth he wants us to face. He's spent ten years and 156 lives on his design. And he's going to bring down a Church that could have counted itself among the world's great powers.'

'Your lot will probably canonize him.'

'If God's ministers can be brought to trial for the crimes of His followers, Modelism will be only the first Church to fall.'

This morning, Cardinal Menzies had reported that the first lawsuits were being laid against the Vatican. RVRF expanded their claims, charging not only Modelists but seventeen other major churches. Georgi was not handling the impending crisis well. Menzies wanted her in Vatican City. She was their expert on what made people murder.

It began to rain, gently at first.

'I was once told raindrops were God's tears,' Jerome said. 'He has a lot to cry about.'

Prague rain was rusty, laced with pollutants from seventy-five years of unregulated factory smokestacks. The Vltava was choppy today. The deck shifted under them.

She took Jerome's hand. She needed human contact, something to fix on, some outward manifestation of God's goodness. Though His servants were flawed, Creation was a marvel.

'I'm afraid, Jerome . . .'

'Chan?'

'Churches are built on corpses. Mine most of all.'

If Kiev upheld Model-Duff, the great wealth of the Roman Catholic Church – of all Churches within the Eunion – was in peril. There were incalculable economic consequences.

'I liked him, Chan. I thought he liked us. Despite all the pegs and abjuring, I truly intuited he was a solid fellow. Was he really mad all along?'

'He was trying to teach us a lesson. Maybe he would have had to be mad to try. Maybe, after all, there was a little of Rob Hackwill in him. It's all been about attribution of guilt. It's all been about where the bodies are buried.'

She gripped Jerome's hand until her knuckles hurt. Soon, she would let go, let him go, let Duroc go, let Hackwill go. Soon, she would return to Rome, to her cell, to her faith, to fighting for her Church.

Soon.

The rain began to pelt. Drops drummed the deck like liquid bullets, driving them below.

SEVEN STARS

Prologue: In Egypt's Land   1302 BC

All Thebes, all *Egypt*, was filled with the stench. Pai-net'em
had bound up his head with linen, bandaging nose and mouth
as if wrapping himself for interment. The stench got through,
filling his nostrils and throat, curling his tongue.

His eyes were swollen almost shut by weeping boils. Insects
clumped around his bloody tears, regathering every time he
wiped them away. Eggs laid in the gum around his eyes
hatched hourly. New-born flies chewed with tiny teeth.

Progress through the city was slow. The roads were filled
with the dead, animals and men. Darkness was relieved only by
the spreading fires. Most of the people were too concerned
with private griefs to lend their hands to fighting the fires.

Truly, this was the time of calamities.

A priest, a man of science, Pharaoh's closest adviser, he was
brought as low as a leper. He could not hold in his mind all
that had happened in the last month. Looking at the mottled
swellings and punctures on his body, he could not tell the
marks of sickness from insect bites, even from the scars left by
hailstones.

The Gods must hate Egypt, to let this happen.

Pai-net'em could not number the dead of his household. His

grief had been spent on lesser catastrophes, sickening cattle and rioting slaves. Now, with brother and son struck down, his wife dead by her own hand, servants' corpses strewn like stones about his estates, he had no more grief, no more feeling, in him.

A stream of blood trickled past Pharaoh's Palace. Tiny frogs hopped in the reddened water. A living carpet – millions of locusts, flies and gnats – covered the streets, slowly reducing the fallen to skeletons. Insects assaulted the feet of those like Pai-net'em who waded perversely about, fixed like stars on their own courses.

The guards lay dead at their posts, wavering masks of flies on their faces. Pai-net'em passed through the open doors. Even here, inside Pharaoh's house, insects swarmed and gnawed. With the crops and the cattle blasted, many more would die of famine even after the darkness abated.

Lightning was striking all through the city.

Pai-net'em found Pharaoh in his morning room, hunched on his day-bed, face as swollen and distorted as the lowest slave's. The great were not spared; indeed, Pharaoh seemed to suffer more than his subjects, for he had far more to lose. If all who lived under him were obliterated, his name would pass from memory.

The old Pharaoh had done much to preserve his name, built many temples, left many writings. This younger man, so addicted to luxury that he neglected public works, had taken to having his name inscribed on tablets over those of his predecessors. It was a desperate act, a cry against the advance of oblivion.

'Pai-net'em,' Pharaoh said, mouth twisting, tongue swollen, 'what has brought these curses upon Egypt?'

Pai-net'em found he did not have the strength to rise from his knees.

'The Israelites claim responsibility, sire.'

'The *Israelites*? The conquered people?'

'Yes. They say their God has visited his wrath upon Egypt.'

211

Pharaoh's eyes widened.

'Why?'

'They are a sorcerous people. But their claims are fatuous. They have but one God, a child beside our Gods.'

'This is not the work of the Gods.'

Pai-net'em agreed with Pharaoh.

'We both know what is at the bottom of this.'

'You have it here, sire?' Pai-net'em asked.

Pharaoh got off his day-bed, flies falling from his robes. Blood streaked his legs. His chest was sunken, his skin rubbed raw or bloated with sickness.

Pai-net'em stood, coughing fluid into his mouth-linen.

Pharaoh opened a wooden box. The darkness of the morning room was assaulted by red light. Pai-net'em remembered the first time he had seen the glow. Then, Pharaoh had been slim and swift and powerful. And he had been secure in his health, his position.

Bravely, Pharaoh took the object of out the box. It was as if he had dipped his hand into fire and pulled out a solid lump of flame.

Pai-net'em got closer and looked at the jewel. A ruby as big as a man's fist. Inside glinted seven points of red light, in the shape of the seven stars of the night sky. It had fallen into the Nile, from the stars themselves, and turned the river to blood. It was not a jewel, given in tribute to Pharaoh. It was a curse, spat from above at Egypt. It was the source of all miseries, of the insects and the lightning, of the darkness and the death.

'Such a beautiful thing,' Pharaoh mused, 'to contain such curses.'

Pai-net'em saw the beauty, yet the jewel was hideous, crawling with invisible filth.

He shook his head, thinking with bitter humour of the Israelites' claim. This was beyond the Gods of any people. This was death made into an object. It could not be destroyed – that had been tried, with chisels and fire – only passed on, to the unwitting.

212

'Take it,' Pharaoh said, tossing the jewel to Pai-net'em.

He caught the thing, feeling its horrid pulse.

'Take it far from here.'

Pai-net'em bowed his head.

He would die in the execution of this task. But he had no other purpose. His name would be remembered for this sacrifice. As long as Egypt endured, so would Pai-net'em.

Outside the Palace, he held the jewel to his chest, cupping it with his hand. He thought himself the calm centre of a storm. All around, insects and death whirled in bloody darkness. Evils flowed from the stone, but he was shielded from them. It was as if he were inside it rather than it inside his fist.

Everything was tinted red, as though he were looking through the ruby. His limbs were heavy and he felt trapped.

He started to run, away from the Palace.

A burning began in his chest, where the jewel was clutched, as if a blob of molten metal had struck him and was eating its way towards his heart.

He let his hand fall, but the jewel was stuck to his torso, sinking in. Agony filled his chest, and he tore the linen from his face, screaming.

But he still ran, wading through the streams of frogs and locusts. The weakness of his legs was washed away. He no longer felt anything.

He knew he was dying, but that the jewel kept his body from falling. He shrank inside himself, withdrawing into the ruby, suspended among the seven stars. This was not death as he knew it, a calm passage into a dignified afterlife where his family and servants awaited, but a change of perception. He would remain in the world, but be apart from it. As he had served Pharaoh, so would he now serve the Seven Stars.

From the heart of the red night, he looked down on the devastation that was the Land of Egypt.

And could not weep.

SEVEN STARS

Episode 1: The Mummy's Heart   *1897*

It was the size of a human heart. Charles Beauregard let his hand hover over it, fingers outstretched. He shut one eye but could not quite blot out the jewel.

'Aren't rubies generally smaller than this?' he asked.

Professor Trelawny shrugged. 'So I believe. I'm an Egyptologist, not a geologist. Strictly, a ruby is a pure transparent red corundum, though the term is loosely applied to merely red gemstones, like certain varieties of spinel and garnet. In rock-tapping circles, there's an argument that this isn't a ruby proper. Corunda, as you know – sapphire, emery and so on – are second only to diamond in hardness. The Seven Stars is at least as hard as diamond.'

Trelawny tapped the Seven Stars with a knuckle, touching it with a diamond ring. He did not try to scratch the priceless artefact. Presumably for fear of breaking his ring.

'So it's a red diamond?' Beauregard assumed.

Trelawny's huge eyebrows wriggled. 'If such exists, it may well be. Or mighthap a gemstone unknown to modern science. A variety perhaps once familiar to the Pharaonic Kings, lost to obscurity and now rediscovered, for the glory of our own dear Queen.'

Ever since the cloth was unfolded and the jewel disclosed, Beauregard had felt an urge to touch the stone. But he kept his fingers away. Though it was absurd, he had the impression the jewel would be hot as fire, as if just coughed from a volcano.

'Why is it called the Seven Stars?'

Trelawny smiled, weathered face crinkling.

'Turn up the gaslight, would you?'

Beauregard obliged. The flame grew with a serpent's hiss, casting more light. The basements of the British Museum were divided into dozens of store-rooms, offices and laboratories. Trelawny's lair, a surprisingly uncluttered space, was currently devoted to the study of the Jewel of Seven Stars.

Trelawny pulled on a white cotton glove and lifted the stone.

He had to stretch his thumb and little finger to get a secure grip.

'Look *through* the jewel, at the flame.'

Beauregard stepped around the table. Trelawny held the gemstone like a lens. In the red depths, seven fires burned. Beauregard shifted position and the fires vanished. He moved back, and they shone again. Seven pinpoints of light, in a familiar pattern.

'Ursa Major,' he commented.

Trelawny set the jewel down again.

'The Great Bear, Charlemagne's Wain, the good old Plough. Also known, I understand, as the *Septentriones*, the Seven Ploughing Oxen, and, to the Hindoo, the Seven *Rishis* or Holy Ancient Sages. Or, as our American cousins would have it, the Big Dipper. What in Hades do you think a dipper is, by the way?'

'A ladle. Do you take an interest in astronomy, Professor?'

Trelawny laughed and indicated the jewel.

'I take an interest in this. The rest of it I got from an encyclopedia.'

'Is it a natural effect?'

'If not, Ancient Egyptian jewellers were possessed of secrets lost to memory. Which is, incidentally, not an entirely unlikely hypothesis. We still don't really know how they managed to build pyramids. I incline, however, to consider the stars a natural, or supernatural, phenomenon.'

'Supernatural?'

Trelawny's eyebrows waved again.

'There's a curse, you see.'

'Of course there is.'

Without the light behind it, the jewel seemed a dead lump, a giant blood clot. There was certainly blood in its history.

'I can't take curses too seriously,' Trelawny announced. 'Every ancient site has been at least thrice-accursed. If you consider its collection of maleficent objects from unhallowed graves, you'd have to deem the British Museum the most curse-plagued spot in the Empire. But hundreds of visitors traipse around upstairs every day without suffering ill-effects. Unless, of course, they've first stopped at the pie stall in Great Russell Street.'

Beauregard thought the professor might be whistling in the dark.

'And yet,' Trelawny mused, 'this little item has its secrets.'

'I assure you, professor, I should not be here if those secrets were not taken very seriously by eminent persons.'

'So I understand.'

Trelawny was an open man, not at all the stuffy professor. He had spent more years in deserts and digs than in classrooms and store-rooms. Beauregard had liked him at first sight. However, the professor was wary of him.

Beauregard must seem mysterious: not a policeman or a diplomat, yet given charge of this delicate matter. When called upon to explain his position, he was supposed to describe himself as a servant of the Queen and not mention the Diogenes Club, the adjunct of the Crown to which he was attached.

'Since the Seven Stars was discovered . . .'

'In the Valley of the Sorcerer, two years ago,' Trelawny footnoted.

'Nine men have died. In connection with this stone.'

Trelawny shrugged. Beauregard knew most of the dead had been the professor's colleagues.

'Nothing mysterious in that, Beauregard. The jewel is of enormous academic interest but also great value. The traditional tomb-robbers believe Egyptologists are, so to speak, poaching on their preserve. To us, these remnants of the past are miraculous glimpses of lost history, but generations of *fellahin* have seen the tombs of the long-dead as a field of potatoes, to be dug up and sold.'

Beauregard's gaze kept returning to the jewel. It was one of those objects that had the power of fascination. Even without the light behind it, there was a fire there.

'It was found, I understand, *inside* a mummy?'

Trelawny nodded. 'Not common practice, but not unknown. The mummy was that of Pai-net'em, of the household of Meneptah II. From the fragmentary records, it seems Pharaoh relied on him much as our own dear Queen relies on Lord Salisbury. An influential adviser. Meneptah, a wastrel, left the duller administrative chores to men like old Pai-net'em.'

'Was he the sorcerer for whom the valley was named?'

'Almost certainly not. Pai-net'em was squeezed in among many tombs. His place of interment is modest, especially considering his importance. By rights, he should have been buried in the Theban version of Westminster Abbey. At first, we believed the mummy to be one of Pai-net'em's servants but evidence – not least, the Seven Stars – later revealed him as the man himself.'

'The jewel?'

'We shipped the mummy here for examination. When Sir Joseph Whemple and I supervised the unwrapping, it was as if fire exploded from its chest. A trick of the light, but startling. It's a unique find. The Cairo Museum of Antiquities started hemming and hawing and asking for "their" mummy back – oh, and the the jewel of course. Lord Cromer convinced the *khedive* the most apt course of action would be to make a gift of the Seven Stars to the Queen, in honour of her Jubilee.'

'Sir Joseph was subsequently murdered?'

Trelawny nodded.

'Some devil cut his throat. In his office. Four doors down the corridor. With a dull knife. It was as if his neck were clawed open.'

'But the jewel was safe?'

'*In* a safe, actually. We have vaults for items of especial value.'

Beauregard had seen the police reports. Half the Egyptian scholars in London had been urgently interrogated, suspected of membership of some fanatic cult. No arrests had been made.

The death of Sir Joseph brought the Seven Stars to the notice of the Diogenes Club. Mycroft Holmes, of the Ruling Cabal, had clipped the report from *The Times* and predicted the affair would be forwarded to his department.

'Has the mummy been returned to Cairo?'

Beauregard was relying on a favourite tactic, asking a question to which he knew the answer. Mycroft taught that facts themselves were often less significant than the way facts were presented by individuals.

'Now there's a question,' Trelawny said, brow crinkled. 'Whoever killed Sir Joseph stole the mummy. It was a light enough carcass. Still, not an easy item to get past our stout night-watchmen. And of little worth in monetary terms. Mummies are ten a penny. Most were robbed of their funerary ornaments thousands of years ago. If the jewel hadn't been *inside* Pai-net'em, the robbers would have had it along with the rest of his grave goods.'

'Certain occult practitioners have use for the ancient dead,' Beauregard commented.

'Good Lord, what for?'

'Charms and potions and totems and such. Ingredients in arcane rituals.'

Trelawny said nothing. At Oxford, he had been a member of an occult society, the Order of the Ram.

'"Eye of mummy, toe of dog", that sort of thing,' Beauregard prompted.

Eventually, Trelawny snorted.

'Some dunderheads do take an interest in that sort of rot,' he admitted. 'In my student days, I ran into a pack of them myself. The sons of the clods I knew probably still pay through the nose for crumbled horse manure passed off as the ashes of the mages of Atlantis. Pai-net'em's poor bones might fetch something on that singular market. I trust the police are pursuing that avenue of inquiry.'

'So do I.'

Beauregard looked back at the Seven Stars.

'I shan't entirely be sorry to see the jewel go to the Tower,' Trelawny said. 'The death of Sir Joseph rattled me, I don't mind telling you. The scientist in me says I should cling to the stone until its mysteries are exhausted. But the cautious man tells me to let the next fellow worry about it.'

'And I'm the next fellow?'

Trelawny smiled, sadly. He dropped a cloth over the Seven Stars.

'From Meneptah to Pai-net'em,' the professor said. 'And now from Abel Trelawny to Queen Victoria. From pharaoh to sovereign in just three thousand years. Perhaps that'll be the end of it. For my part, I certainly hope so.'

Beauregard made his way upstairs. Late in the afternoon, the crowds were thinning. He touched his hat-brim to Jenks, the Diogenes man who wore the uniform of an attendant and had been working here, keeping an eye out, ever since the murder of Sir Joseph.

The Hall of Egyptian Antiquities, always popular, was almost empty. A noseless giant head dominated the room, eyes eerily impassive. Beauregard wanted to take a look at some mummies, to get an idea of what was missing.

Under glass was the bandage-wrapped corpse of a young girl.

He thought of his late wife, Pamela. She was buried in the hill country of India, a world away. Would she find herself on display millennia hence, a typical specimen of the nineteenth century Anno Domini?

He felt an instant of connection. With the girl.

The plaque said she was unknown, but the daughter of wealth. *Ushabti* mannikins were found in her grave, to be her servants in the afterlife. Her bindings were an intricate herringbone. Her nose still had definition under ancient cloth.

Beauregard had a sense that he was a moment in history, a pause in a story which had begun long before him and would continue well past his death. People came and went, but some things remained, eternal.

He thought of the Seven Stars, undisturbed for three thousand years. And who knew how old the jewel had been when buried inside Pai-net'em?

A chill crept up his spine. He felt eyes upon his back, but the only reflection in the glass of the display case was that of the blind stone head.

He turned, and saw a woman with a pale face and smoked glasses. Almost a girl, fair and fragile. He thought for a moment she might be blind too, but she was watching him.

He almost said something, then, very swiftly, she was gone.

In another life . . .

He looked at the mummy again, wondering why he was so stirred inside.

He bade Jenks a good day and left the museum.

Pall Mall was half decorated. London was disappearing under cheerful swathes of patriotic bunting in honour of the Queen's Diamond Jubilee. Her sixty years on the throne had seen unimaginable changes in Britain and her Empire. The Queen had weathered constitutional crises, setting an example in conduct that many of her subjects, from her own children down, could not match.

He had taken an open cab from the British Museum, enjoying the early June evening. The Jubilee, not yet fully upon the city, encouraged an opening-up. People wore sashes and ribbons in celebration of a Queen who ruled through love, not the fear Meneptah and his like had wielded like a lash.

In years of service, he had seen the Empire at its best and worst. He hated the pettiness and cruelty that existed as much in this city as in the farthest outpost, but admired fiercely the aspirations to decency and honour embodied in Victoria's great heart. To him, the Union Jack was not the trade-mark of some gigantic financial concern or the territorial stink of a bristling bulldog but a banner which meant the innocent were protected and the helpless defended.

He entered the lobby of the Diogenes Club and was

discreetly admitted to the chamber of the Ruling Cabal. Mycroft Holmes, the huge spider at the centre of the nation's intelligence web, sat in his custom-made leather armchair, plump fingers pyramided, brows knit in thought. He did not greet Beauregard for a full minute, as he finished some mental calculation.

'Beauregard,' he said. 'This is a delicate business.'

Beauregard agreed.

'You've seen the bauble?'

'It's considerably more than that, Mycroft. A ruby as big as my fist.'

'It's not a ruby.'

'I fail to see how the geology is germane to the affair.'

'One should consider a jewel from all angles, the better to appreciate its many facets. This is a jewel like no other.'

'I couldn't agree more.'

'It won't attract as much attention as the *Koh-i-Noor* or the Moonstone or the Eye of the Little Yellow God. But it's more remarkable.'

'It's washed in blood.'

'All great gems are.'

'This one looks like it.'

'Tell me, Beauregard, what of the points of light?'

'The Seven Stars. Exactly in the configuration of Ursa Major. That's an uncanny feature. As if the stone were a star map.'

'Stent, the Astronomer Royal, has suggested the Seven Stars fell to Earth as a meteor. Maybe it is a message from those stars.'

Beauregard shuddered. He didn't like to think of a red streak nearing the Earth, millennia ago.

'It's a strange thing,' he admitted.

'And what of the murder of Sir Joseph Whemple and the theft of the mummy?'

Beauregard considered the little he had learned.

'Trelawny went out of his way to pooh-pooh a suggestion that the mummy might have been stolen for use in magical rituals. Yet he was, admittedly as a youth, involved in such rites himself. It's my consideration that he suspects as much, but does not dare propose the theory strongly lest his past be looked into too closely.'

Mycroft's fat face crumpled in mild irritation. 'We know much about Abel Trelawny and the Society of the Ram. Have you heard of Declan Mountmain?'

'The Fenian?'

'Not strictly. We came close to gaoling him for that dynamite business at Lord's but he slipped through the net, found subordinates to take the blame.'

Beauregard remembered the atrocity. It was a wonder no one had been killed.

'Mountmain is a crank,' declared Mycroft, 'but a dangerous one. Most advocates of Irish Home Rule distance themselves from him. The Fenian Brotherhood regard him as a loose cannon of the worst sort. He wrote a pamphlet which was suppressed as obscene, alleging prominent cabinet ministers and churchmen constitute a cult devoted to the pagan worship of a goddess incarnated as our Queen. Apparently, we are given to snatching drabs from the alleys of the East End and ritually disembowelling them in a temple beneath Buckingham Palace.'

Beauregard found the suggestion disgusting.

'Mountmain himself believes none of it. He is merely trying to project his own methods and manners on those he deems his foemen. He is an adept in occult sciences, and remains the Great Pooh-Bah of the Order of the Ram. His beliefs are a mixture of paganism and Satanism, with a little Hindoo or Ancient Egyptian tosh thrown in. He blathers about Atlantis and R'lyeh and the Plateau of Leng, and Elder Gods from the Stars. All very arcane and eldritch, no doubt.'

'You believe this Mountmain to be behind the attempts on the Seven Stars?'

'I believe nothing that cannot be proven. Mountmain has an old connection with Trelawny. He is a collector of weird

222

artefacts. He has a fortune at his disposal, augmented by funds extorted from supporters of his dubious political cause. He is by no means the only blackguard of his stripe – you've heard me remark that the mountaineer Aleister Crowley is a young man worth watching – but he is currently the worst of his shabby crowd.'

'Should I make some discreet inquiries about Declan Mountmain?'

'If you think it worthwhile.'

As usual with Mycroft, Beauregard felt he had been led through a maze to a foregone conclusion. It was the Great Man's knack to draw his own ideas out of other people.

'Very well. I think I know where to start.'

A mere hundred yards from the Diogenes Club were the offices of the *Pall Mall Gazette*. He strolled casually, pondering the two sides to his immediate problem.

When Mycroft mentioned Declan Mountmain, Beauregard knew he would have to bring Katharine Reed into it. She was a reporter, the sole woman in regular employment at the *Gazette*, at least when she wasn't in jail for suffragette agitations. Kate knew as much about the Irish Home Rule movement as any man, probably because she was in it up to her spectacles. She also had a knack for finding out things about prominent personages that did them no credit. He was certain Kate would know about Mountmain.

The other side of the coin was that Kate was insatiably curious and as tenacious as a tick. Every time she was asked a question, she asked one back. And traded answer for answer. With her disarming manner and steel-trap mind, she might latch on, and follow him to what she imagined was a story worth printing. The Diogenes Club prided itself on being the least-known arm of the British Government. Mycroft had a positive distaste for seeing the organization's name, let alone his own, in the papers. Such things he left to his more famous, though less acute, brother.

Kate had been a friend of Pamela's. She shared with his late wife a trick of seeing through Charles Beauregard as if he were a pane of glass. And he was about to recruit her for a confidential mission.

He thought, not for the first time, that he must be mad.

He knew where Kate's cubby-hole was, but would have been able to identify it anyway. By the shouting.

A large, well-dressed man, neck scarlet, was blustering.

'Come out from that desk and be thrashed!'

He recognized Henry Wilcox, the financial colossus.

He guessed at once that the *Gazette* must have carried a story under Kate's by-line that revealed an irregularity on Wilcox's part.

'Shift yourself, coward,' the colossus roared.

Wilcox was standing over a sturdy desk. He lashed it with a riding-crop.

The desk shook.

Kate, Beauregard gathered, was underneath.

He wondered whether he should intervene, but thought better of it. Kate Reed didn't care for it if other people fought her battles for her, though she was herself practised at pitching in to any brawl that came along.

Wilcox savagely whipped a type-writing apparatus.

The desk heaved upwards and a small woman exploded from her hiding-place.

'How dare you!' she shouted. 'Henry Wilcox, you have a great deal to be ashamed of!'

The colossus, as imposing physically as he was financially, was given pause. Kate, red-haired and freckled and often hesitant in polite company, was in a fine fury. Up on her toes, she stuck her face close to Wilcox's and adjusted her thick spectacles.

'This piece which names me,' he began.

'Do you deny the facts?'

'That's not the point,' he snarled.

'I rather think it is. Maybe we should print a follow-up article. You want your side of it to be given. Well, Mr Wilcox, now is your chance.'

Kate set her chair upright and fed a sheet of paper into her type-writer.

'First of all, there's the question of the girl's age. What was your initial estimate?'

'I didn't come here to be insulted.'

'Really? Where do you go to be insulted? I understand the house that employs your young associate offers many varieties of satisfaction.'

'Your manner does not become your sex.'

Kate Reed looked as if she was about to breathe fire.

'I suppose seeking Biblical knowledge of children is a noble and worthy occupation for the mighty male gender.'

'That's libel.'

'No, that's slander. It is only libel if we print it. And if it's proven untrue.'

'She'd never furnish proof.'

'Your soiled dove? How much would you wish to wager on that?'

Wilcox's entire face was red. Beauregard wondered if the colossus were not on the verge of a coronary. From what he gathered, the man was an utter swine.

Kate typed rapidly, fingers jabbing like little knives.

'Would you care to take the address of the *Gazette*'s solicitors with you? Your own can get in touch with them when this piece runs.'

Wilcox muttered a word Beauregard had hoped never to hear in a lady's presence. Kate, unblushing, kept on typing.

The financial colossus put on his hat and withdrew, pushing impatiently past Beauregard.

'Stupid little tart,' he said.

'The girl or me?' Kate shouted after him.

Beauregard replaced Wilcox in Kate's line of fire, standing by her desk. She looked up, smiled a little, and kept on typing.

225

'Charles, good day to you. What trouble am I in now?'

'You seem more than able to find enough on your own.'

'That man buys children for unspeakable purposes. And yet he'll probably wind up with a knighthood.'

'I doubt that.'

'Others have before him.' She broke off typing, and looked at him. 'Oh, I see. Words in the right ears. A name crossed off a list. Closed ranks. Nothing in the open, you know, where it might upset the rabble. Just an understanding. Some things aren't done, you know. He has money all right, and the house, and the prospects. But he's not a *gentleman*. You can probably do it. I don't underestimate your shadowy influence. But getting him blackballed isn't the scope of my ambitions for the monstrous thug. I'd rather see him de-balled.'

Beauregard was shocked. Kate was habitually forward, but he'd never heard her voice such an extreme sentiment.

She softened and rested her elbows on her desk. Her hair had come undone.

'I'm sorry. I shouldn't rail at you. It's not your fault.'

Beauregard pulled the paper from the typewriter. Kate had been typing a nursery rhyme.

'Mr Stead won't publish anything more about Wilcox,' she admitted, referring to the editor. 'He's a crusading soul, hot on exposing the "maiden tribute of modern Babylon", but to be frank, our solicitors aren't up to the level Wilcox can afford. Stead wants to stay in business.'

Kate took the sheet of paper, crumpled it into a ball, and missed a wicker basket.

Beauregard wondered how best to broach the subject.

'What are your plans for the Jubilee?' he asked.

'Are you offering to escort me to that little ceremony at the Tower I'm not supposed to know you're arranging? If you were, I'd suspect you were only luring me there so I could be clapped in irons and penned in the deepest dungeon.'

'I thought, as a reporter, you might be interested.'

'She's a nice enough old girl, the Queen. But I don't think she

226

ought to be ruling over my stretch of the world. Or quite a few other patches of red on the map. I was imagining I'd celebrate the Jubilee by cosily chaining myself to some nice railings and being spat on by patriotic crowds.'

Beauregard couldn't miss the seam of self-doubt in Kate's calculated outrageousness.

'Can I depend on your discretion?'

She looked at him with comical pity.

'Of course I can't,' he said, smiling. 'However, needs must when the Devil drives. What do you know about Declan Mountmain?'

Anything comical was wiped from Kate's face.

'Charles, *don't*.'

'I don't understand.'

'Whatever involves Mountmain, don't pursue it. There are fools and blackguards and rogues and monsters. He's all of them. Beside Mountmain's sins, Henry Wilcox's are mere errors of judgement.'

'His name has come up.'

'I want nothing to do with it. Whatever it is.'

'Then you won't want to be my guest at the Tower. To see the Jewel of Seven Stars.'

'That's different. I accept that invitation. Thank you, kind sir.'

She stood up and leaned over the desk to kiss his cheek.

'What shall I wear? Something green?'

He laughed. 'Don't you dare.'

She giggled.

The deepness of her feelings about Mountmain shadowed their gaiety. Uncomfortably, Beauregard suspected Mycroft had set him on the right road, and that he would not like where it was leading.

There were policemen in the courtyard of the British Museum. And a light burning behind one set of tall windows. He realized that the illuminated room was the Hall of Egyptian Antiquities.

He had been summoned from his house in Chelsea by a cryptic message. Before being shaken awake by his man-servant, Bairstow, he had been dreaming an Egyptian dream, floating down the Nile on a barge, pursued by the hordes of the Mahdi – which had actually happened to him in this life – and of the Pharaoh of Exodus – which certainly hadn't.

In the Hall, caped constables stood over a sheeted form. A small, whiskered man in a bowler hat, fretted.

'Good morning, Lestrade.'

'Is it?' the policeman asked. Dawn was pinking the windows. 'Seems like the start of another long bloody day to me.'

There was a lot of damage about. The case of the mummy he had looked at earlier was smashed in, broken shards of glass strewn over the Egyptian girl. Other exhibits were knocked over and scattered.

'I needn't tell you how unpleasant this is,' Lestrade said, nodding to a constable, who lifted the sheet.

It was Jenks, throat torn away.

'We thought he was just a keeper,' Lestrade said. 'Then we found his papers, and it seems he was one of your mob.'

'Indeed,' Beauregard said, not committing himself.

'Doubtless poking around into the last business. The Whemple murder. Behind the backs of the hard-working police.'

'Jenks was just watching over things. There's a crown jewel in the basement, you know.'

'There was.'

The phrase was like a hammer.

'The vault was broken into. Nothing subtle or clever. Looks like dynamite to me. The blast woke up every guard in the building. The ones who slept through this.'

'The Jewel of Seven Stars is gone?'

'I should say so.'

Beauregard looked at Jenks's wound.

'Is this what Whemple looked like?'

Lestrade nodded. 'Ripped from ear to ear, with something serrated and not too sharp.'

Beauregard had seen tiger-marks in India, crocodile attacks in Egypt, lion maulings in the Transvaal, wolf victims in Siberia and the Canadian Northwoods.

'Could have been an animal,' he said.

'We thought of that. With Whemple, there was nothing missing, if you get my drift. Ripped this way and that, but not chewed, torn off, or eaten. Animals don't do that. They always at least try to eat what they've killed.'

For some reason, he thought of the woman in smoked glasses who had been here when last he saw Jenks. In his memory, she had teeth like a dainty cannibal, filed to points.

'It's unusual.'

'I don't like the unusual ones, sir. They always mean that poor old coppers like me get pushed aside and clever fellows like you or the chap from Baker Street are let loose on my patch. What I like is a murderer who gets drunk and takes a cudgel to his wife, then sits down blubbing until the police turn up. That's a proper murder. This is just fiendishness.'

'Your murderer has made two bad mistakes tonight, Lestrade. In taking the Seven Stars, he has robbed the Queen. And in killing Jenks, he has aroused the ire of the Diogenes Club. I should not care to exchange places with him.'

Declan Mountmain's London address was a Georgian mansion in Wimpole Street. Just the lair for a viper who wished to nestle close to the bosom of Empire.

He deemed it best to make a direct approach. It would be interesting, considering last night's business at the Museum, to gauge Mountmain's condition this morning. Were his ears ringing, as if he had been in the vicinity of an explosion in a confined space?

He knocked on Mountmain's sturdy front door, and waited on the step for the butler to open up.

'Mr Mountmain isn't receiving visitors, sir,' said the sharp-faced servant. 'He has taken to his bed.'

'He'll see me,' Beauregard said, confidently.

The butler hesitated.

'Are you the doctor, sir? The *confidential* doctor?'

Beauregard looked up and down the street, as if suspecting he was being followed. As it happened, there was a suspiciously human-sized bundle in a doorway a dozen houses distant. This was not a district in which gentlemen of the road sleeping under the stars were much tolerated.

'Do you think you should mention such matters out on the street where anyone might hear you?'

The butler was chastened, and – unless Beauregard wildly missed his guess – terrified.

The door was pulled open wide, and Beauregard allowed in. He tried to project from within the impression that he was a disgraced physician on a hush-hush mission of dark mercy. Such impersonations were surprisingly easy, especially if one didn't actually claim to be who one was pretending to be but merely let others make assumptions one did not contradict.

Mountmain's hallway was dark. The windows were still curtained. A line of wavering light under a door revealed that one of the rooms was occupied, and low voices could be made out. The butler led Beauregard not to that door but to another, which he opened.

A single lamp burned, a dark lantern set upon a table. A man lay on a divan, a sheet thrown over him. He was groaning, and a black-red stain covered a full quarter of the sheet.

The butler turned up the lamp and Beauregard looked at the man. He was deathly pale beneath grime, teeth gritted, pellets of sweat on his forehead.

Beauregard lifted the sheet.

A gouge had been taken out of the man, ripping through his shirt, exposing ribs.

The wounded man gripped Beauregard's arm.

'A priest,' he said. 'Get a priest.'

'Come now, Bacon,' boomed a voice. 'Have you so easily turned apostate and reverted to the poor faith of your feeble fathers?'

Beauregard turned.

In the doorway stood the man he knew to be Declan Mountmain. Short and stout, with a high forehead growing higher as his black hair receded from the point of his widow's peak, Mountmain was somehow an impressive presence. He wore a Norfolk jacket and riding boots, unmistakably blooded. Not the sort of outfit for lounging around the house before breakfast, but ideal wear for an after-midnight adventure in larceny and murder.

Bacon's wound was irresistibly reminiscent of the fatal injuries suffered by Jenks and Whemple.

'Who might you be, sir?' Mountmain asked. 'And what business have you poking around in young Bacon's open wound? You're no damned doctor, that's certain.'

Beauregard handed over his card.

'I wished to consult you in your capacity as an expert on occult matters.'

Mountmain looked at the card, cocked a quizzical eyebrow, then landed a slap across the face of his butler, slamming him against the wall.

'You're a worthless fool,' he told his servant.

'This man needs medical attention,' Beauregard said. 'And, by his admission, spiritual attention too.'

Mountmain strode over.

Beauregard felt Bacon's grip strengthen as Mountmain neared. Then it was suddenly limp.

'No, he needs funerary attention,' Mountmain said.

Bacon's dead hand fell. There was blood on Beauregard's sleeve.

'Very tragic,' Mountmain said, deliberate despite his rage. 'A carriage accident.'

According to Mycroft, people who volunteer explanations as yet unasked-for are certain to be lying. Beauregard realized Mountmain's contempt for others was such that he did not even take the trouble to concoct a believable story.

Mountmain's jacket was dusty and odiferous. He recognized

231

the Guy Fawkes Night smell that lingers after a dynamite blast.

'There will now be tedious complications as a result of my charitable taking-in of this stranger. I should be grateful if you quit this house so I can make the proper, ruinously costly, arrangements.'

Beauregard looked at the dead man's face. It was still stamped with fear.

'If I can be of assistance,' he ventured, 'I shall report the matter to the police. I am in a small way officially connected.'

Mountmain looked up at Beauregard, calculating.

'That will not be necessary.'

'The young man's name was, what did you say, Bacon?'

'He blurted it as he was carried into the house.'

Mountmain spread his arms and looked down at his blood- and dirt-smeared clothes. He did not say so outright, but implied he was in this condition because he had hauled an injured passer-by off the street. Now his rage was cooling, he showed something of the canniness Beauregard expected of such a dangerous man.

'The business upon which I called . . .'

'I can't be expected to think of that,' Mountmain said. 'There's a corpse ruining the furniture. Put your concerns in writing and send them to my secretary. Now, if you will be so kind as to leave . . .'

Mountmain's door slammed behind Beauregard. He stood outside the house, mind swarming around the problem.

He glanced at the doorway where the vagrant had been earlier but it was unoccupied. He half thought the bundle might have been Kate, pursuing a story. She was certainly not above disguising herself as an urchin.

A man had died in his presence.

No matter how often it happened, it was shocking. Death struck deep in him, reaching that portion of his heart he thought buried with Pamela. All death took him back to the hill country, to his wife bathed in blood and their stillborn son.

Then, he had wept and raged and had to be restrained from taking a sabre to the drunken doctor. Now, it was his duty to show nothing, to pretend he felt as little as Mountmain evidently did. Death was at worst a rude inconvenience.

He concentrated. His hands did not shake. He walked away from the house with even steps. An observer would not think he was about business of great moment.

Mountmain and Bacon, and who knows how many confederates, had been at the Museum last night, and had certainly set the charges that blew the safe. The man had a habit of meddling with dynamite. He must be after the Seven Stars, though it was not yet clear whether Mountmain's interest in the stone was because of its monetary value, its political import or an as-yet unknown occult significance.

He paused casually and took a cigar from his case. He stepped into the shelter of a doorway to light the cigar, turning and hunching a little to keep the match-flame out of the wind. He paused to let the flame grow the length of the match, and lit up the doorway. A scrap of rag wound round the boot-scraper, some grey stuff brittle with dust.

He puffed on his fine cigar and picked up the rag, as if he had dropped it when taking his matches from his pocket. It almost crumbled in his hands and he carefully folded it into his silver cigar case.

A hansom cab trundled by, looking for custom. Beauregard hailed it.

Trelawny was in shock at the loss of the Seven Stars. His room was turned upside-down, and the corridor outside blackened by the blast. Beauregard had the impression Mountmain had overdone the dynamite. Lestrade's men were still pottering around.

'Ever since the Valley of the Sorcerer, it's been like this,' Trelawny said. 'Blood and shot and death. In Egypt, you expect that sort of thing. But not here, in London, in the British Museum.'

233

'Do you know a man named Mountmain?'

'Declan Mountmain? The worst sort of occult busybody. Half-baked theories and disgusting personal habits.'

'Were you not close to him at Oxford? In the Order of the Ram?'

Trelawny was surprised to have that brought up.

'I wouldn't say "close". I took a passing interest in such concerns. It's impossible to get far in Egyptology without trying to understand occult practices. Mountmain and I quarrelled without relief and I broke with him long ago. To him, it's all about *power*, not knowledge.'

'I believe that last night Mountmain stole the Seven Stars.'

Trelawny sat down, astonished.

'He has many low associations. He would know the cutters and fences who could deal with such booty.'

Trelawny shook his head.

'If it's Mountmain, it's not for the money. I believe I mentioned that the Seven Stars was as hard as diamond. Actually, it is far harder. I doubt if it could be broken into smaller stones for disposal. It would probably be a blessing if that were possible, though the process might well merely disperse the ill fortune throughout the world.'

'If not the money . . . ?'

'The magic, Beauregard. Mountmain believes in such things. For him, they seem to work. At Oxford, he had a fearful row with one of the professors and cast an enchantment on the fellow. It was a terrible thing to see.'

'He sickened and died?'

'Eventually. First, he lost his position, his standing, his reputation. He was found guilty of unholy acts, and claimed that voices compelled him.'

'The Seven Stars?'

'. . . would be of incalculable use to Mountmain. There are references in certain books, the sort we keep under lock and key and don't allow in the index. Though lost since the time of Meneptah, there are references to the Jewel of Seven Stars. It has a shadowy reputation.'

'Mountmain would know this?'

'Of course.'

'He would wish to employ the stone in some species of ritual?'

'Indubitably.'

'To what end?'

Trelawny shook his head.

'Something on a cyclopean scale, Beauregard. According to the *Al Azif* of the mad Arab Al-Hazred, the last time the jewel was the focus of occult power was in the thick of the Plagues of Egypt.'

Beauregard took out his cigar case.

'What do you make of this?'

Trelawny looked at the scrap of cloth.

'Is this part of the debris?'

Beauregard said nothing.

'I'd heard one of the mummies upstairs was damaged. This looks like a funerary binding. It's certainly ancient. I say, you shouldn't just have picked it up as a souvenir.'

Beauregard took the rag back and folded it again.

'I think I'll hang on to it for the moment.'

Kate hadn't got all of the story out of him, but he had doled her out a few of the less arcane facts.

They were in Covent Garden, at a café. The awning was draped with flags. A portrait of the Queen hung proudly in prime position.

'You believe Mountmain has this gem? In his town house? And he has a dead man on the premises?'

Beauregard sipped his tea and nodded.

'If Ireland and dynamite are involved, such niceties as due process and search warrants usually go out the window. So why hasn't Lestrade descended on the scene with a dozen flat-feet and torn the house apart?'

'It's not quite that simple.'

'Yes it is, Charles. And you know it.'

'I don't mind telling you, I didn't much care for your countryman.'

Kate almost laughed.

'"My countryman". I suppose you wouldn't mind at all if I habitually referred to Blackbeard, Charley Peace, Jonathan Wild and Burke and Hare as "your countrymen".'

'I'm sorry. And Burke and Hare were Irish.'

'I believe in Home Rule for the people of Ireland, and Egypt and India come to that. Mountmain's interest in the country of his birth involves replacing the muddled and unjust rule of England with the monstrous and tyrannical rule of Declan Mountmain. Have you read any of his pamphlets? He claims descent from the Mage-Kings of Erin, whosoever they might be. If he ever has a Diamond Jubilee, it will be celebrated by ripping out the beating hearts of Wicklow virgins. Distasteful as all this Union Jackery may be, Vicky doesn't insist her ministers cut throats at the Palace. At least, not since Palmerston.'

'You wouldn't happen to have been passing Mountmain's town house this morning, in the borrowed clothes of a tramp?'

Kate's eyes went wide.

'Wherever did you get that idea?'

'Something glimpsed out of the corner of my eye.'

'What are you going to do about your blessed jewel?'

Beauregard considered the matter.

'I rather thought I might try to steal it back.'

Kate smiled, eyes crinkling behind spectacles. She was much more appealing than generally reckoned, he thought. A face made beautiful by character (and wit) wore far better than one made beautiful by nature (and paint).

'Now that's a lovely notion. Charles, I always admire you most in your all-too-infrequent excursions into larceny. Do not even consider embarking on such a venture without me.'

'Kate, you know that's absolutely impossible.'

'Then why did you mention it? You know me too well to

think I'd just flutter my handkerchief and let you bravely go about your business while I fret the night away in fear of your life. Make no mistake, Charles, that young fellow you saw wasn't the first corpse to be found in the immediate vicinity of Declan Mountmain.'

He could give in now, or he could argue the afternoon away and give in around tea-time. Or he could give in now, and tell Kate that the burglary was set for tomorrow night then make the attempt this evening.

'By the way,' she said, 'if you're thinking of telling me you don't intend to do your house-breaking later than this very night, I shan't believe you.'

'Very well, Kate. You may come with me. But you will not come into the house itself. You shall wait outside, to alert me to any danger. By whistling.'

'We'll discuss the specifics when we come to them.'

'No, now. Kate, promise.'

Her nose twitched and she looked everywhere but at him.

'I promise,' Kate said. 'I'll be the whistler.'

He raised his cup and she clinked hers against it.

'To larceny,' she said, 'and the ruin of rogues of all nations.'

After arranging with Kate to meet later, Beauregard took a cab back to Chelsea. He wished to call on one of his near neighbours in Cheyne Walk. The occult wasn't his field of expertise, and he wanted a little more knowledge before venturing into Mountmain's lair.

Mr Thomas Carnacki, the celebrated 'ghost-finder', admitted Beauregard to his comfortable sitting room.

'I'm sorry to interrupt.'

Carnacki had been entertaining an actorly-looking man. He waved aside the apology.

'Machen and I were just yarning. You know his work, of course.'

Beauregard was unfamiliar with the author.

'I am pleased to meet you, Mr Beauregard,' said Machen,

offering a bony hand. There was a little Welsh in his accent, thinned by London.

'I've come to make inquiries on a matter relating to your speciality.'

'Machen might help, as well,' Carnacki said.

The dapper little man offered Beauregard brandy, which he declined. He wanted to keep his head clear for the rest of the night's business.

'Have you heard of the Jewel of Seven Stars?'

Carnacki and Machen said nothing, in the distinctive manner of people reluctant to venture on to shivering sands.

'I see that you have. I assume you know of its recent discovery, inside a mummy.'

'I doubted its authenticity,' Machen said. 'It's a fabled object.'

'Professor Trelawny is convinced that it is the genuine gem,' Beauregard said to Machen. 'It is certainly as old as the mummy. Three thousand years.'

'That merely means that it's an old fake. Made in imitation of an item that probably never existed.'

'There's a curse, of course,' said Carnacki.

'Of course,' Beauregard agreed.

'One might say, the curse of curses.'

'Trelawny mentioned the Plagues of Egypt.'

'Frogs, locusts, boils, blood, gnats, and so forth,' Machen chanted.

'There's been blood.'

'I hardly think we need to fear the plagues of Egypt. Pharaoh, after all, held the Israelites in bondage. All are free in our Empire.'

Carnacki swilled his brandy, beaming. To him, this was a parlour game. He prided himself on never being rattled.

'It is a mistake to take Exodus, as it were, as gospel,' Machen commented. 'Egyptian records make little of the tribes of Israel. And the plagues are almost totally expunged. Of course, the Egyptians believed that to forget a thing or a person was to

238

revoke their very existence. To blot the plagues from the histories would mean they could be averted in retrospect.'

Beauregard wondered if Mountmain might not see himself as Ireland's Moses. He decided to drop the name.

'Do you know Declan Mountmain?'

As vehement as Kate's reaction to the name had been, Carnacki's and Machen's were more extreme. The ghost-finder spat a mouthful of brandy back into his glass, and Machen's thin lips pressed together in disgust and rage.

'He's one of your occult fellows, isn't he?' Beauregard prompted, disingenuously.

'Mountmain wants to bring things back,' Machen said. 'Old things. Things best left in the beyond.'

'Is he after the Seven Stars?' Carnacki asked. Beauregard had forgotten the little man had the instincts of a detective. 'They'd make a deuced combination.'

He distracted himself during the cab journey by running through the plagues of Egypt, in order. First, the waters of the Nile turned to blood. Second, hordes of frogs. Third, the dust became swarms of gnats. Fourth, an infestation of flies. Fifth, the cattle struck dead. Sixth, an epidemic of boils. Seventh, lightning and hail struck the crops and livestock. Eighth, locusts. Ninth, darkness covered the land for three days. And tenth, the death of all the first-born throughout the country.

In Exodus, the story reads strangely. It's all down to the Lord and Pharaoh. The suggestion seems to be that the Lord visits the plagues on Egypt but influences Pharaoh to ignore them, 'hardening his heart' against letting the tribes of Israel go free. Beauregard remembered officers in India who were like that, alternately inflicting hideous punishments and encouraging the offenders to defy them, as an excuse for continuing with the punishment.

On the whole, it wasn't the sort of behaviour one expected from a proper God. One of Mountmain's eldritch and arcane Old Ones, perhaps.

Carnacki seemed to suggest that the Israelites didn't really come into it. The point was the plagues.

The effect of all ten must have been devastation on a vast scale. In the aftermath, with no crops or cattle, and most people maddened by disease or bereavement, the chaos would take generations to pass away.

If he had been Pharaoh, Beauregard would have felt he had a legitimate complaint that disproportionate sentence had been inflicted.

He had the cab drop him off in Cavendish Square.

Kate turned up on a bicycle. She wore breeches and a tweed cap. He thought better of asking her if she were disguised as a youth.

They walked up Wimpole Street.

'Where do you think Mountmain has the jewel?' she asked.

'I don't expect to find it. I just want to get the lie of the land. Consider this an exploratory expedition. Later, Lestrade and his stout fellows can go through the place and recover the swag.'

'You make a poor cracksman.'

'I should hope so, Kate.'

'Is that the address? It doesn't look all that foreboding.'

Mountmain's house was dark. Beauregard did not make the mistake of assuming it therefore empty or the household abed. He had the impression that the Irish Mage conducted much of his business away from the windows. The room in which Bacon had died was windowless.

'Do you favour the first or the second storey for your illicit entry, Charles?'

'Neither. I hope to go in through the basement.'

Spear-topped iron railings stood in front of the house. The steps to the front door rose above a row of windows at ground level. He assumed these led to the kitchens or the wine cellars.

'Have you noticed the device on the arch-stone above the door?'

Beauregard looked up. Inset into the stone were what looked

like polished nail-heads.

'Ursa Major,' he said.

The glints were in the form of the constellation. He looked up at the cloudless sky. Despite the warm glow of gaslight, the stars in the heavens shone.

'This all leads back to the Great Bear,' Kate said. 'To the stars.'

'I'm going. Remember, if there's trouble, whistle. If I don't come out, alert Lestrade.'

'And the Diogenes Club?'

He was uncomfortable hearing the name on her tongue.

'Them too.'

'One more thing,' she insisted.

He looked at her. She kissed him, standing on tip-toe to peck at his lips.

'For luck,' she said.

He felt a great warmth for Kate Reed. She was a kindly soul. He squeezed her shoulder and scooted across the street, deftly vaulting the railings.

The first window he tried was fastened. He took out his penknife and scraped away old putty. A pane came away entire, and he set it to one side. The black curtain wafted inwards with the rush of night air.

He slid through the curtain, setting his rubber soles down on a flagstone floor about six feet below the level of the window. Glass crunched beneath his boots.

The room was dark. He stood still as a statue, still hearing the crunch as if it were a volley of shots. His breath was even and his heartbeat regular. He was used to this sort of night-creeping, but it did not do to get too cocky.

Had someone dropped something?

He chanced a match and found himself in a store-room. It was as cold as a larder, but the jars and phials on the shelves lining the walls did not suggest domestic arts. Free-floating eyeballs peered at him.

241

If he had tried the next window along, he would have found it broken. Some mischance, or a less professional cracksman, had smashed it in.

A tiny scrap hung from a spar of glass still in the frame. It was a fragment of cloth, similar to the stuff in his cigar case. He thought of a man-shaped huddle, and shuddered. The match burned his fingers. He shook it out and dropped it.

The after-trail of flame wiggled on the surface of his eyes. He located the door, and took a grip of the handle. He had a lockpick in case he found himself shut in. He pulled, and the door moved more easily than he expected. He felt the jamb and realized the door had been locked, but forced. The lock itself was torn out of the wood, but the metal tongue was still out, fixed.

He stepped into a passageway. His eyes were used to the dark. He proceeded down the passage, trying doors. All were broken in, locks smashed.

He took out his revolver.

Someone had invaded this house before him.

The rooms were all like the one he had been in, stores for arcane items. He recognized certain occult implements. One room, a windowless hole, was given over to ancient books, and had been torn apart. Priceless volumes were strewn on the floor, leaking pages like flesh from a wound.

Upstairs, there was a thunderous knocking at the door.

It couldn't be Kate. She would have whistled.

Light leaked down. The gas in the hallway had been turned up. There were footsteps, and offensive shouts.

Mountmain answered his own door. He had probably discharged the butler.

Beauregard couldn't resist a smile.

The light showed a set of double doors, of some metal, at the end of the passageway. They had been abused and wrenched around the locks.

'What the Devil do you want?' Mountmain roared.

'The Seven Stars,' boomed a familiar voice.

242

'What are they? And who are you?'

'You know that as well as I do, Declan. I haven't changed so much since Oxford.'

It was Trelawny.

'Get out of the house, or I shall summon the police.'

'Very well,' Trelawny called Mountmain's bluff.

'Seven Stars, you say?'

'And the mummy! Where's Pai-net'em?'

A tiny hand took Beauregard's sleeve and tugged.

His heart spasmed and he turned, raising his revolver and aiming directly at a startled face.

Kate whistled, almost soundlessly.

He did not waste words in protest. She had disobeyed him and come into the house. She must have seen Trelawny barge in.

Mountmain and Trelawny continued their argument. It sounded as if blows would soon be exchanged. Mountmain was unlikely to hear them moving about beneath his feet.

He nodded to Kate, and proceeded to the double doors.

After a breath, he pushed the doors open.

The room was large, and dimly lit by Aladdin-style lamps. Kate was shocked by the obscenity of the bas-reliefs that covered the walls and the altar. Fishy chimerae and alarmed nymphs coupled with joyless frenzy.

Beauregard was surprised to see the Jewel of Seven Stars lying in the open, on the altar. It held the lamp-lights, and its stars burned.

Kate gasped at her first sight of the jewel.

Another item of stolen property lay on the floor, stretched out face-down before the altar. Its bandages were unravelled round its ankles and arms, and it was broken into a scarecrow pose, crucified rather than curled up at rest.

The mummy of Pai-net'em.

Kate stepped over the mummy and looked at the Seven Stars. Her fingers fluttered near it, tips reddened by the stone's inner glow.

'It's a beauty,' she said.

Beauregard had not bargained for something as easy as this.

'Should we just take it and leave?' Kate asked.

Beauregard hesitated.

'Come on, it's one in the eye for Mountmain.'

She took a hold of the jewel, and screamed.

A spindly arm had shot out, and a sinewy hand grabbed her leg, pulling her down.

It couldn't be the mummy. It was someone wrapped in mouldering bandages, a grotesque guardian for the jewel.

At the scream, Mountmain and Trelawny stopped arguing.

The mummy man rose up, loose-limbed and faceless, and threw Kate away. Her cap fell on the floor, and her hair tumbled loose. The jewel cast a bloody light across his sunken chest.

Living eyes looked out of the dead mask.

Beauregard caught Kate and hugged her. He kept the mummy man covered with his revolver.

Mountmain charged into the room and was struck dumb by what he saw.

'What in the name of Glaaki!'

Underneath ancient linen, a lipless mouth smiled.

Trelawny was at Mountmain's shoulder. He barged past the Irishman and towered over the mummy man.

'Stay back, Professor,' Beauregard warned.

Trelawny reached for the Seven Stars. The mummy launched a claw-fingered hand at the professor's throat, and ripped it away. A rain of gore fell on to the jewel and seemed to be absorbed.

Trelawny fell to his knees, still trying to draw air into his lungs through his ruptured throat. He pitched forward, dead. The mummy hung his head, almost in tribute.

Beauregard put three shots into the monster's chest, about where his heart should have been. He saw dusty divots raised in the cloth-wrapped flesh. It staggered but did not fall.

Mountmain was backing away from the altar.

'Interfering fool,' he snarled at Beauregard. 'Are you content now?'

'What is that?' Beauregard indicated the mummy.

'What do you think? It's Pai-net'em, wanting his jewel back. It's all he's ever wanted.'

The mummy stood over the altar.

Beauregard saw he had been wrong. It couldn't be a man dressed up. The legs were too thin, like shrouded bones. This was an ancient, dried thing, somehow animate, still imbued with soul.

'He's the saving of your rotten world,' Mountmain said. 'But he'll rip you apart. My design may not be accomplished, but you'll get no joy from my thwarting. Mr Beauregard, and whoever you might be, young sir, I bid you good-bye.'

The Irish Mage stepped back through the doors and slammed them shut.

They were trapped with Pai-net'em.

'Young sir!' Kate sneered. 'The cheek of the man.'

The mummy had killed Whemple, Jenks, Bacon and Trelawny. And others. All who stood between it and the Jewel of Seven Stars. Now, Mountmain thought, it would kill Beauregard and Kate.

The mummy bobbed a little, like a limber puppet. Flesh gobbets still clung to its claw-hand. It hovered by the altar, where the jewel was fixed.

Beauregard was prepared to throw himself to Pai-net'em, to protect Kate. He did not think he could come out best in a wrestling match. And clearly his revolver was useless against this dead-alive thing from an ancient grave. Had he lain for three thousand years, seven sparks inside the jewel to keep him warm?

Through the thin bandage, Beauregard saw Pai-net'em's snarl.

'Take it,' Beauregard said, indicating the jewel. 'It was stolen from you. On behalf of my Queen, I return it to you, with honour.'

Did Pai-net'em listen? Could he understand?

The mummy snatched up the jewel and held it to his breast. The Seven Stars sank in and the hole closed over. A red glow throbbed in Pai-net'em's chest. He slumped, dormant.

Kate let out a breath, and clung to Beauregard.

He kissed her hair.

By dawn, Declan Mountmain was in custody, apprehended at Victoria Station attempting to board the boat train. With two corpses (three, counting the mummy) in his house, he would be detained for some time. The Seven Stars, Beauregard had decided, should remain where it was. It did not strike him as a fitting addition to Her Majesty's collection and he had taken it upon himself to relinquish it for the nation. He had an idea Victoria would approve.

Kate, who had to keep out of the way while Lestrade was poking around, sat on the front steps, waiting for him.

'The house is full of stolen property,' he told her. 'Manuscripts from university libraries, artefacts from museums. There are even body parts, too repulsive to mention, which seem not to be of ancient origin.'

'I told you Declan Mountmain was a bad 'un.'

'He'll trouble us no longer.'

Kate looked at him oddly.

'I wouldn't be so sure of that, Charles. We can't exactly stand up in court and honestly tell the tale, can we?'

Kate scratched her ankle, where the mummy had grasped.

'I'd love to write it up, just to see Stead's face as he spiked the story.'

She stood up. They linked arms and walked away from Mountmain's house. It was the Day of the Jubilee. Flags were unfurled and streets were filling, as London began its great celebration.

'I shan't get to go to the Tower,' Kate said. 'And I had a dress picked out.'

'It's always possible you'll end up in the Tower.'

She punched his arm.

'Get away with you, Charles.'

'I'm afraid the best I can offer is a trip to the British Museum, to see Pai-net'em returned to his sarcophagus. I doubt he'll go on exhibition. My recommendation is that he be misfiled and lost in the depths of the collection.'

Kate was thoughtful.

'Nothing's solved, Charles. The Seven Stars remains a mystery. We're not closing the book, but leaving the story to be taken up by the as-yet-unborn. Is that not always how it is?'

Episode 2: The Magician and the Matinée Idol   1922

The February chill made Catriona Kaye wish hemlines weren't being worn above the knee this season. Her bobbed hair, tucked under a cloche hat, left her slender neck bare, prompting her to wrap her fur collar tight around her throat.

Born with the century, now just twenty-two, she sometimes felt her obligation to follow the fashions of the times was a curse. Her father, a West Country parson, was always on at her about the scandalous way she dressed, not to mention her cacophonous American tastes in music. Edwin never chided, sometimes claiming in his lofty manner that she was a useful barometer: when she was up, so was the world; when she was down, calamity was in the offing.

At present, she had much in common with the Grand Old Duke of York's ten thousand men: she was neither up nor down. The wind blowing down Baker Street was winter, but the clarity of the air – no fog, no rain – was spring.

Things were about to change.

Two elderly matrons nearby had noticed the celebrity. They were frankly goggling, like children at the circus. Catriona thought them rather sweet about it.

The celebrity had just stepped out of a door which bore a

famous, and famously hard-to-locate, address: 221B. He wore a fore-and-aft cap, and a checked ulster of Victorian cut. He turned to cast a hawklike gaze at the distance, sharp profile distinct and distinctive, and raised a magnifying glass to his eye.

'Isn't that . . .?' began one of the matrons.

The object of their amazement was accompanied by a shorter, plumper, huffier man, in a bowler hat and moustache. He held a revolver.

'I do believe it is,' the other matron agreed. '*John Barrymore*!'

The Great Profile turned full-face to the admiring dears, one eye hugely magnified by his glass, flashed a thin grin, and gallantly doffed his deerstalker. One matron swooned in the other's arms.

Catriona couldn't help but giggle.

A short man with a megaphone began shouting, chiding the matinée idol for 'playing to the rear stalls'.

'I'm afraid I shall never get the hang of this film business,' Barrymore lamented.

Catriona understood the actor was mostly concerned with his impending *Hamlet*, and had little concentration left over for this photoplay of Mr Conan Doyle's *Sherlock Holmes*, or rather Mr William Gillette's celebrated stage drama. From what she'd seen of the 'shooting', Barrymore's sleuth had quite a bit of the gloomy Dane about him and spent a great deal more time making goo-goo eyes at the heroine than plodding over the scene of the crime with Good Old Watson. Mycroft Holmes would be revolving – very slowly, and with great gravity – in his grave.

Edwin, her 'whatever', affected to be interested in the intricacies of the camera, and spent his time interrogating the crew on tiny technical points. She knew that trick of his, to pretend one overwhelming enthusiasm in order to winkle out all manner of other unconnected information from those he was politely and unnoticeably interrogating.

Not for the first time, she felt a lot like Good Old Watson. She and Edwin were a partnership, but too many people – though not Edwin himself – thought of her as a decorative adjunct to the genius of a Great Man.

Admittedly, she wasn't expected to pen adulatory accounts of the exploits she shared with Edwin Winthrop. In most cases, the principals would certainly not care to find their confidential affairs written up in the popular press. The bally Baskervilles can hardly have been delighted to have the whole nation privy to their nasty squabbles, come to that. There were also, in some instances connected with Edwin's shadowy employers in the late War, questions of state secrecy to be considered.

Barrymore was annoying the director, a man named Parker, with his diffidence. When uninterested in his work, he tended to ignore his Prince's sound advice against 'sawing the air'. She noticed Roland Young, the cove playing Good Old Watson, was managing with extremely British tact not to be annoyed, in such a manner that his actual feelings were plain. Now that was real acting.

After two days of hanging about as the American film crew took location 'shots', she was used to being mistaken for an actress or even one of the Great Profile's surplus mistresses. Remembering Edwin's advice, she took pains never to contradict or confirm assumptions.

As their occasional government commissions went, this was hardly momentous. Their business was usually with the living who were being bothered by the dead; in this case, they were here to protect the interests of the dead against slander. Edwin was doing an unofficial favour for the Diogenes Club, the institution which had found him official employment during the Great War and which still had occasional occasion to call on his services. Mycroft Holmes, the consulting detective's less famous but more perspicacious brother, had once sat on the Ruling Cabal of the Diogenes Club, in the seat now occupied by the somewhat slimmer-hipped Mr Charles Beauregard, to whom Edwin reported.

Last year, Edwin and Catriona had been involved by the Diogenes Club in a row involving a phantasmal samurai who wielded a very substantial sword in the Japanese Embassy, lopping off the heads of several uncomplaining staff members. The bloody business was eventually brought to a satisfactory conclusion, with human devilry exposed and psychic shenanigans explained away. She was now the only girl she knew with a personal scroll of commendation from the Emperor of Japan in her dresser drawer.

This was far more routine. It came down to reputation. Though never under the command of the Diogenes Club, the Great Detective had once or twice assisted his brother with problems, much as Edwin and Catriona now assisted Beauregard. It had been the cause of something of a rift between the Holmes Boyos that Good Old Watson and Mr Doyle had written up a few of these bits of business, going so far as to mention the institution in print and giving some hint as to Mycroft Holmes's actual position in the British government.

That had all blown over now. But Beauregard, out of respect for the memory of his old chief, wanted the cloak of obscurity habitually worn by the Diogenes Club and all its operatives to fall heavy again.

'It will almost be a holiday,' Beauregard had said. 'Mingling with show-folk. Just make sure they stay away from the facts.'

Parker was nagging Barrymore again about his famous moustache. It was still not shaven off. Apparently, it would not show in 'long shots', but would have to go for the 'close-ups'.

Catriona wondered whether Edwin's moustache was only coincidentally identical to the actor's. He professed to disdain fashion when he was making fun of her kimonos or shaven neck, but he could be a touch dandyish in his own appearance.

'You'd be fastidious too,' he would say, 'if you'd spent four years in a uniform stiff with mud.'

The War excused a lot.

Parker stormed away from the actors. Barrymore, treating

the wide step of 221B as a stage, made a bow for the gallery. The onlooking crowds applauded mightily. The director glared in frustration and muttered about cracking the whip when the company got back to the States.

'You, technical adviser,' Parker addressed her. 'What's wrong with that scene?'

'I don't like to mention it, really,' she said.

'It's what you're here for, isn't it? It's that blasted lip-fungus of John's.'

'He could be in disguise,' she said, trying to be generous. Parker laughed bitterly.

'It's the address,' she piped. 'The front door would just have 221 on it. A and B and, for all we know C, would have doors on the landings.'

Parker shook his head and stalked off.

'I am right,' she told his back.

Though they lived – together! in sin! scandalously! – in the Somerset house Edwin had inherited from his disreputable father, they were more often found these modern days in their London *pied-à-terre*, a nice little flat in Bloomsbury which Catriona officially kept as a residence to allow her father to avoid a heart attack by believing she lived apart from Edwin. This evening, with Paul Whiteman's 'Whispering' on the gramophone, they discussed the day's work as they danced, occasionally dropping the odd inconvenient item of clothing.

'Old Beauregard has nothing to worry about, Cat,' said Edwin, directly into her ear. 'Along the chain that leads from Holmes to Watson to Doyle to Gillette to Barrymore, anything that might be taken as real or referring to reality has been stripped away.'

'The Diogenes doesn't figure in the film scenario?'

One hand firmly in the small of her back, Edwin dipped her over, supporting her weight. She often felt on the point of losing her balance, but Edwin would pull her back just in time.

'No.'

They kissed. The song ended. They occupied themselves upon the divan.

Afterwards, propped up among Turkish cushions, drawing on a cigarette through a long holder, kimono loose about her shoulders, she thought again about the errand.

'Surely, after all these years, no one actually cares about the dratted Bruce-Partington Plans any more.'

Edwin laughed lazily. He was drifting towards a doze as she was becoming more awake. He claimed to be catching up on all the sleep missed through four years of shelling day and night.

'It's the principle, poppet. Secrecy. If everybody knew everything, there'd be mass panic.'

She wondered about that.

'Darkness has become a habit for too many, Edwin.'

'You shall cast light, Cat. You are a beacon.'

He stroked her leg. She considered stabbing him with her lit cigarette.

'Rotter,' she snorted.

Edwin sat up, unconsciously passed his fingers over his (John Barrymore) moustache, and paid attention.

'Old secrets, dear,' she said. 'There are too many of them. And new ones piled on top.'

'We only need dawdle about the kinema wallahs for a few more days,' he said, taking her hand. 'Then, I promise, we can find a nice ghost story, a bleeding nun with ghastly groans or a castle spectre with clanking chains. We shall explain it away with the shining light of science and rationality. Bit by bit, we shall banish the darkness from these isles.'

She biffed him with a cushion.

Mostly, the darkness was subject to banishment when they applied themselves. But sometimes . . .

'What more do we need to know about this silly film?'

'Nothing, really. I telephoned Beauregard and passed on all that we've ferreted out. He particularly asked that we be

252

present at the next "location", to represent the nation's interests.'

'The *nation*'s interests?'

'Indeed. The Goldwyn Company has secured permission to take film in the private recesses of the national collection, in the basements of the British Museum – some confrontation between Holmesy and that mathematics professor of sorry memory – and we're to be there to see they don't break anything. They will be "shooting" at night, after everyone has gone home.'

She shook her head.

'I'm a serious person,' she announced. 'A scientific inquirer. My field, in which I am widely published and hailed even at my tender age, is psychical research. I do not mind, under certain circumstances, serving my country as a more-or-less secret agent. However, I draw the line at working as an unsalaried night watchman!'

He embraced her, and she knew she'd give in eventually.

'Haven't you ever wanted to find out what's *really* kept in all those vaults? We shall get to root about among artefacts and manuscripts inaccessible to the public.'

That was not fair. He knew she couldn't resist that temptation.

She kissed him, hungry again.

'You shall shine in the dark,' he said.

The cellar was vast, a vaulted ceiling above a crate-filled trench. Though the tiled walls were cold to the touch, the cellar was remarkably free of damp. At one end, an uncrated Easter Island head, crown scraping the ceiling, surveyed the scene. The statue was as long-faced and beaky as the unprepossessing original currently impersonated by the classically handsome actor grappling centre stage with an ersatz Napoleon of Crime.

'This looks like an underground railway station,' she commented.

'Exactly, Clever Cat,' Edwin agreed. 'Built as a stop for the

British Museum, but never finished. The company was bankrupted. Most of the line caved in, but the Museum has kept this as its deepest store-room. Some things are too huge to stack in an ordinary basement.'

'How silly,' she said. 'Plainly, the underground railway should be operated by a single company for the benefit of the nation, not by competing and inept rival factions who'll honeycomb under London until the whole city falls in.'

He did not give her an argument.

Parker called 'cut!', his megaphone-amplified voice booming through the cellar.

Barrymore – lip shorn at last, not entirely to the detriment of his looks – stood up, and a girl dashed in to reapply grease-paint to his cheeks. The site of his battle with Moriarty was now swarming with 'crew', all intent on tiny tasks.

A youth in knickerbockers assisted 'Moriarty' to his feet. The Prof was impersonated by an authentically frightening-looking fellow with ragged hair, eyes like corpse-candle flames, and a thin-lipped sneer. An assistant director who, she realized, was slightly sweet on her, said Moriarty's im-personator was an Austrian by the aptly villainous name of Gustav von Seyffertitz. He had signed himself with the absurdly Yankee alias of 'G. Butler Clonblough' during the late unpleasantness.

Barrymore could switch his Sherlock off and on like an electric lamp, melodramatic when the camera was cranking but larking outrageously between 'takes'. Von Seyffertitz, whom Barrymore liked because he made him look even more handsome by contrast, seemed always to be 'on', and occupied himself by skulking villainously while the director shouted at Barrymore.

She nudged Edwin, and nodded at 'Moriarty'.

The actor was drifting out of the circle of artificial light, towards the pile of crates, as if drawn to worship at the chin of the Easter Island head.

'That's odd,' Edwin commented.

'You're just jealous.'

So far, they hadn't been able to take advantage of this opportunity to root about among forbidden treasures. The priceless and ancient artefacts were just backdrop, and heaven help anyone who strayed accidentally into the camera's line of fire. The director might well have the powers of instant trial and execution granted to battlefield commanders.

Von Seyffertitz was definitely looking for something. Through pince-nez, he peered at runic marks chalked on the crates, tutting to himself.

'Old Beauregard told us to be on our guard down here,' Edwin said. 'There was some bad business to do with the Museum in his day, round about the Jubilee. He's a bit cranky about it, if you ask me. Long and distinguished service and all that.'

Ever since descending from street level, Catriona had felt a chill that was more than the cold. Beyond the fragile light, the shadows were deeper than they had any business being.

'Mr Beauregard is rarely mistaken,' she reminded Edwin.

It was time for the antagonists to tussle again. Parker called the 'crew' clear, and pulled Barrymore and von Seyffertitz together as if refereeing a boxing match. The Austrian seemed reluctant to leave off his poking-around for something as insignificant as doing his job.

'I'll bet that fellow gets fed up with being defeated,' Edwin said. 'I've seen him as the villain in half-a-dozen flickers.'

Like her, Edwin was secretly devoted to the newest art. They attended the kinema far more than the theatre, and had an especial fondness for the serials made in Paris, *Fantomas* and *Judex*. When she had occasion to use an alias herself, Catriona often picked 'Irma Vep', after the ambiguous villainess of *Les vampires*.

'I wonder if he is ever tempted to fight back properly, and best the hero. Just once.'

She saw what Edwin meant. Moriarty was giving a strong account of himself for an elderly mathematics professor – in actuality, exactly the sort of person it is supremely easy to toss off a waterfall – and Sherlock was taking all the knocks.

Von Seyffertitz wove and punched like a far younger man, landing a few potential bruises on the famous face. Barrymore was in a bit of a sweat. Had the Professor forgotten the scenario? He *was* supposed to lose.

Von Seyffertitz got a wrestling hold on Barrymore and threw him to the floor. The director called 'cut!' Concerned people descended in a swarm. The star was bleeding. Moriarty mouthed an insincere apology.

'My face, my face,' wailed Barrymore, theatrical voice filling the cellar.

Edwin nodded that she should take a look.

She ventured near the actor, handkerchief out.

Blood trickled from both nostrils, replacing the shaven moustache with a red imitation.

'Is my dose broken?'

She staunched the flow of blood, and felt for give in Barrymore's nasal cartilage. She thought his valuable fizzog was not seriously damaged and told him so.

'Thank heavens,' he declared, kissing her forehead, fulfilling the dreams of a million matinée-goers. She felt a sticky, unromantic discharge in her hair and discreetly scraped it off and on to a wall.

'I must save myself,' the actor muttered. 'This doesn't matter.'

Barrymore was relieved beyond proportion. She realized he had been afraid for his long-awaited *Hamlet*.

'Bless you, child,' he said. 'For the merciful news. One cannot play the Prince with a patch of plaster in the middle of one's face. To have lost that for this penny dreadful would have been too much to bear.'

Actors were a rum lot.

Parker called an end to the night's 'shoot'. Until Barrymore's nose recovered, there was no point in going on. An assistant gleefully totted up how much this delay would cost.

'Tomorrow night, I want you to thrash that blasted Austrian

within an inch of his ugly life!' demanded Parker.

'You have my word,' Barrymore said, sounding better already.

The equipment was dismantled, and the company began to withdraw on the double.

Edwin touched her elbow and stepped into shadow, encouraging her to join him.

'Something's wrong,' he said, trench-nerves a-tingle.

She nodded. He was right. She felt it too.

The film lights were turned off, leaving deep darks and illusory afterimages. But there was another light, a reddish glow, almost infernal.

Was there a whiff of brimstone?

Equipment and persons were being crammed into a cage lift which gave the easiest access to the surface.

The glow came from behind the Easter Island head. A shadow, like a man-sized stick insect, moved on the face of the head, clinging to the hatchet-nose.

'Look, Cat. You can see that the tunnel extends beyond that statue. It must be shored up and used as extra storage space.'

The shadow detached itself from the nose and slipped around the head, briefly blotting the crimson glow, and disappeared into the tunnel.

'That was a man,' Edwin said.

'Was it?' she ventured, unsure. There was something in the way the shadow moved.

'Come on, Cat.'

Edwin was after the shadow. She hesitated only a moment and followed him. He had produced a revolver from under his coat. This was no longer a holiday.

She wished she had dressed for this.

The film folk were busy leaving. Only a few remained, and they were intent on their business, noticing nothing.

Edwin paused at the end of the platform and looked at the Easter Island head. 'I wonder how they got it down here?' he mused.

The face seemed to snarl at them.

Edwin led the way, climbing round the head by using the pendulous earlobe as a grip, and dropping to the cinder-strewn bed of the tunnel. She followed, fearing for the state of her silk stockings and white pumps.

In the tunnel, the glow was stronger. Definitely a red lamp somewhere, beyond the array of dilapidated crates. It was also much colder here. She shivered.

The crates were stacked more haphazardly. Some were broken, spilling straw on to the tunnel-bed. Some of the damage looked recent.

Edwin was attracted to a crate that lay open. Straw and African masks were strewn nearby, as if thrown out to make way for new treasure. He lit a match and tutted. She stepped over to look in.

An elderly man, dressed only in his unmentionables, was crammed into the crate, unconscious. She checked his breathing and pulse. Edwin lowered the match, to cast light on the man's face. It was von Seyffertitz, a chloroform burn round his mouth and nose.

'He's been here for a while,' she said.

'Then who was playing the Prof?'

She shivered, not with the cold.

'I say,' boomed a familiar voice, 'who's there? What's going on?'

It was, of all people, John Barrymore.

'It's Miss Kaye, isn't it? The angel of nasal mercy. And you're the lucky fellow who knocks around with her.'

'Edwin Winthrop,' Edwin introduced himself.

'Are you sneaking off to, um, spoon?'

Edwin shook out the match too late. Barrymore had seen von Seyffertitz in the crate.

'Good God, a body!'

Edwin glumly lit another match.

'It's Gustav the Ghastly,' Barrymore said.

'Someone has been impersonating him,' Edwin admitted.

258

'I shouldn't wonder,' Barrymore said. 'He's easy to "do". I can look like him myself. A grotesque face is far easier to hide behind than a handsome one. When I played the uncanny Mr Hyde . . .'

Edwin waved the actor quiet.

Barrymore became aware of the ruby light. He caught on at once that there was something strange about here.

Among the African masks was a shock of white hair. The wig 'Moriarty' had worn. His pince-nez and a false nose were in with the mess.

Their quarry was so intent on his business that he didn't mind leaving a trail. That suggested an arrogance or confidence that was not comforting.

'Come on,' said the matinée idol, striding forward like a proper hero, 'let's get to the bottom of this.'

Edwin took her arm, smoothing her gooseflesh, and held up the match as they walked towards the glow. When the match went out, there was enough light to see by. Somehow, that was more frightening than the dark.

A large brass-bound trunk almost blocked the tunnel. But red light outlined it, revealing that there was a space beyond.

They crept up and pressed themselves to the wall, to look past the trunk.

It was hard to make sense of what they saw. An area had been cleared and a design marked on the cinder-floor in white powder or paint. At various points of the design stood Arabian Nights lamps, burning redly. Catriona did not at first recognize the shape made by the lines and the lights. It was not the familiar magic circle, or a pentagram.

There were seven lamps, spread not quite in a line. She moved her head a little, and saw it.

'The plough,' she whispered.

Edwin's grip on her arm momentarily strengthened.

'Clever Cat,' he said, proud.

The lamps made up the Seven Stars. The constellation of Ursa Major.

An open case – not a wooden crate but a coffin-shaped metal container – lay in the middle of the design. A point of red glinted within the case. She fancied she could see it even through the metal side.

And a thin figure stood over the case, arms spread wide, muttering in an unfamiliar language. The frock coat of Moriarty still hung from his shoulders, lifted by an otherwise-unfelt wind.

A ritual was in progress. With every atom of sense in her body, Catriona felt this was Evil. She knew Edwin and Barrymore were as aware as she of this and were struck quiet.

The man who had been Moriarty took a dagger from his inside pocket, and addressed the points of the constellation, tapping the tip of the dagger to his forehead and then pointing it at the individual star-fires. Then he let his loose sleeve fall back and swiftly carved a series of symbols into his left arm, raising lines of blood that dripped into the crate. Switching hands, he as deftly repeated the carvings on his right arm, allowing a red rain to fall.

Barrymore squeezed into the space between the crate and the wall, drawn into the drama like a star pulled from the wings. Edwin let her go and took hold of the actor's shoulder, holding him back. All three were now jammed into the small space.

She saw that a body lay in the case, a light burning in its chest. Blood sprinkled a papery face and arms.

The ritual-maker was not a young man. His face was as sunken as that of the actor he had impersonated, if not as that of the mummy he was incanting over. He was almost completely bald, and stringy in the arms and throat.

Barrymore got free of Edwin and stepped into the makeshift temple. The ritual-maker saw him and halted, dagger pointed now as a weapon rather than a magic tool.

'Back, play-actor,' he said. 'I've waited too many years to be interrupted now. This has to be done precisely, as I once learned to my cost. It's not easy to separate Pai-net'em from his treasure.'

The ritual-maker spoke with an Irish accent.

Edwin and Catriona stood either side of Barrymore.

'Three interlopers,' the ritual-maker sneered. A drop of his own blood sparked at the tip of his dagger. 'You'll stay well back if you know what's good for you.'

The light in the mummy's chest was pulsing.

'Twenty-five years a convict,' the ritual-maker declared, 'and months of waiting for a chance to come down here. This new wonder of the age, the cinematograph, was just stirring when I went into Princetown Jail. Now, it has opened doors, just as I am opening a door now, a door that will mean the ruination at last of England and all it stands for.'

He was more than a madman.

'I know who you are,' Edwin said, quietly. 'Declan Mountmain.'

The ritual-maker was shocked.

'So I'm not forgotten after all. I had thought all the others long dead. Evidently, England remembers its foes. Who set you upon me?'

Edwin gave no answer, but Catriona thought that this was no accident. Charles Beauregard and the Diogenes Club had foreseen something like this.

She had heard of Declan Mountmain. Some sort of magician from the last century. His reputation was not of the best.

'Your prison didn't kill me,' Mountmain said. 'And now, at last, I shall have my prize. The magicking is complete. Painet'em is bound. I may take the jewel. I'm glad of an audience, as a matter of fact. I might even let you live through the deluge to come, to tell the tale.'

He knelt over the mummy and plunged the dagger into its chest. The corpse's eyes flew open and glared redly. But only the eyes moved, blazing with ancient frustration.

'Tied you proper, you Egyptian fool,' Mountmain chuckled. 'You'll walk no more.'

The magician sawed at the mummy's chest, cutting around the glow like a butcher. He thrust his hand into the hole he had made and pulled out the source of the light.

261

Catriona could only gasp. She felt dizzy.

It was a huge jewel, burning with an inner light.

'With this, I shall bring down a cataclysm whose memory will last when the sun has turned cold.'

Edwin raised his revolver and shot Mountmain.

The magician laughed. She *saw* the bullet strike him in the face, make a ripple as if in the reflection of a face on the surface of a pond, and disappear. The shot embedded itself in the brickwork of a wall a dozen feet behind Mountmain.

'The Jewel of Seven Stars has accepted me,' the magician announced. 'As it once accepted this dead thing.'

Mountmain brought his boot-heel down on the mummy's head, crushing it in its bandages. The eyes no longer moved.

'I am become the Destroyer of Empire!'

Mountmain's laughter filled the tunnel. His eyes shone, each reflecting the Seven Stars.

Whatever else the jewel had done for him, it had transformed him into the incarnation of the melodrama villain he had been impersonating. Mountmain was acting exactly like a Drury Lane dastard, threatening to evict the heroine's mother into the cold, cold snow unless she bent to his wicked will.

The jewel reached out to them.

Catriona felt its pull. She resisted the impulse to faint. She was not the feeble girl who would be tied to the railway tracks.

' "O villainy!" ' Barrymore thundered. ' "Ho! Let the door be locked! Treachery, seek it out!" '

Edwin fired another useless shot, this time at the jewel itself.

John Barrymore leaped upon Declan Mountmain.

The indecision of Hamlet was thrown aside, and he was Sherlock incarnate, incisive brain directing instant action.

She saw how surprised Mountmain was at this attack, how almost amused . . .

Barrymore's hands went to Mountmain's throat.

They grappled, as if tottering on the brink of the Reichenbach Falls. Mountmain fought back fiercely, as he had done when the camera was turning. He clubbed Barrymore's

SEVEN STARS

head with the mighty jewel, making flashes of bloody light flood the tunnel.

Barrymore had Mountmain's dagger, and was gouging at the magician's wavering chest.

' "The point envenom'd too",' Barrymore quoted. ' "Then, venom, to thy work." '

The dagger seemed to affect Mountmain more than the bullet had.

Edwin was calculating the odds.

'The Seven Stars isn't for the taking,' he said. 'It has to be fought for. It has to be earned.'

Catriona was annoyed that, as usual, things were being kept from her. But she got the drift of the situation.

Barrymore and Mountmain fought like tigers. A lamp was knocked over, fire spreading along the white lines of the constellation. Shadows danced on the walls, and writhed on the contorted faces of the magician and the matinée idol.

' "Here, thou incestuous, murd'rous, damnèd Dane, drink off this potion . . ." '

'Pull down the stars,' Catriona said.

Edwin understood at once.

Mountmain had drawn power from his design. It was a condition of the ritual. She kicked one of the lamps out of place, and it shattered against a far wall in a splash of burning oil. She did the same for another.

Edwin stamped on the burning lines, kicking the diagram to pieces.

Barrymore had Mountmain bent backwards over the case, pushing him down on to the mummy's bones. The jewel was trapped between them. There was blood on both men's faces.

Catriona kicked aside the last of the lamps.

Fire spread, but the constellation was gone.

Barrymore and Mountmain cried out together. It was as if needle-fingers scraped Catriona's bones. There was something inhuman in the shared scream.

Edwin held her.

Mountmain lay broken across the coffin-case, one of the mummy's arms round his chest. A last sigh escaped from him, with a wisp of smoke from his mouth.

Barrymore staggered to his feet, slowly. His shirt was torn open, and a great red wound showed on his chest.

' "I am dead, Horatio",' he declaimed.

' "You that look pale and tremble at this chance,
That are but mutes or audience to this act,
Had I but time – as this fell sergeant Death
Is strict in his arrest – O, I could tell you –
But let it be. Horatio, I am dead,
Thou liv'st. Report me and my cause aright
To the unsatisfied." '

As he spoke, Barrymore's voice grew in strength. His wound pulsed, not with flowing red blood but with flowing red light.

'It's *inside* him,' Edwin breathed.

The flesh closed over the light, and the red was in the actor's eyes.

' "O God, Horatio, what a wounded name,
Things standing thus unknown, shall live behind me!" '

Then Barrymore stopped doing Hamlet, stopped doing Holmes. He stood still. His skin was smooth where his wound had been. She thought she saw a faint light inside, as if his heart glowed. The jewel was gone.

Edwin picked up the dagger and looked at the stricken man.

Was he going to cut it out? As Mountmain had from the mummy. If so, would the jewel be his – with whatever that entailed – as it had been the mummy's?

Edwin thought it through and dropped the dagger.

Barrymore shook his head, as if he had just walked on stage without knowing his lines or his role.

The fires were burning out. Edwin arranged Mountmain in the coffin, tucking in his arms and legs, and put the lid on it, fitting it firmly in place.

Barrymore looked around with a 'Where am I?' expression.

'Let's get him out of this place,' she said.

Edwin agreed with her.

John Barrymore looked at the spectre, eyes bright with fear and love.

' "Angels and ministers of grace defend us!
Be thou a spirit of health or goblin damned,
Bring with thee airs from heaven or blasts from hell,
Be thy intents wicked or charitable,
Thou com'st in such a questionable shape
That I will speak to thee . . ." '

Catriona's hand closed on Edwin's. From their box, they could see the spots of sweat on the star's face. This was the opening night of Barrymore's greatest triumph. He seemed fairly to glow.

At last, she understood what the fuss was about. This was how her father must have felt when Irving gave his Dane. How the first audiences at the Globe Theatre must have felt.

The business under the British Museum was months gone, and they were an ocean away, in New York at the invitation of the star, his debt to them repaid with tickets to the opening of the century.

As the play went on, she wondered about the light in the actor's eyes, and thought about the jewel in his chest. He had been good before, but he was great now. Had the jewel anything to do with that? And was there a price to pay?

Then she was caught up in the drama, swept from her box back to Elsinore, when ghosts walked and vengeance warped the heart and soul.

Episode 3: The Trouble With Barrymore 1942

'You are a private detective?' asked the little pop-eyed man with the Peter Lorre voice. 'Yes?'

'That's what the sign says,' I quipped.

My caller stepped nervously around the office door, and giggled the way he did in the movies. He *was* Peter Lorre.

'Can you be trusted with a confidential matter?'

'If I couldn't, I might be tempted to fib about it.'

His giggle became a laugh. The laugh you usually heard when he was torturing someone. It made a person nervous.

'I should have thought of that. You are an astute fellow.'

'In my business, it sometimes helps to be honest. If I weren't, would my office look like this?'

Lorre looked at my filing cabinet, and took in the fizzing neon sign out in the street too close to my window. The sun was just down, and night people were rising from their murphy beds and coming out of their holes. My place of business did not look much like the elegant suite Bogart has in *The Maltese Falcon*. Then again, Sam Spade was a San Francisco dick.

'You were recommended to me by Janey Wilde.'

That figured. They had been in a Mr Moto movie together, two years ago when Hollywood could make films with Japanese good guys. I hadn't seen Janey since I handed back her missing child three months ago. She had called me in on a case I didn't like to think about, a case that didn't jibe with the way I had always assumed the world went.

If she had sent the talking screen's premier sadist to my office, I had a suspicion that the world was about to take another kink. I'd crossed that line once, from the place where mysteries can be wrapped up and the bodies stayed buried, into *Weird Tales* country.

'She impressed upon me your abilities at locating and returning missing persons.'

Besides everything else, I had got her back her baby. That made me a hero, I guess. She'd given me a big bonus but, what with the war and everything, the town had forgotten to throw a parade and give me the key to the girls' locker-room.

'Who's walked away?' I asked, hoping to jog Lorre out of his circumlocutory flirtation.

'"Walked" is not such an apt expression. You have heard, of course, of the Great Profile, John Barrymore.'

He pronounced it 'pro-feel', which – judging by what I had heard of Prince Jack – was not inappropriate.

'He died last week,' I said.

I was sorry as hell about it. I'd never met the man, but he had great talent and had drunk it away. It was hard not to feel something about that.

'I hope you don't want me to investigate a murder. That's the cops' business and they'd rather I left them to it. Besides, I understand Mr Barrymore succumbed to what might best be called "natural causes".'

Lorre shrugged.

'John Barrymore is dead. There is no doubt about that. As dead as Sessue Hayakawa's career prospects. But he is also a missing person. I want you to find him, and bring him back to the Pierce Brothers Mortuary on Sunset Boulevard. For this, I will pay one hundred dollars.'

'For this, you will pay twenty-five dollars a day. Plus expenses. My fees are not on a sliding scale.'

Lorre spread his hands and hunched his shoulders, accepting my terms.

'Someone has snatched Barrymore's body?'

'Regrettably, that is so. I am ashamed to confess that I am that someone. Do not think me callous. I am a European as yet unused to the brutalities of this frontier culture. I was suborned into the act by a well-respected father-figure, the director Raoul Walsh. As an amateur of psychology, I have been conducting extensive self-analysis for years. I recognize in myself a lamentable need to accept the authority of a patriarch. It is a common European failing, most tragically represented by the general adulation of Hitler. He offered me a high position in the Reich film industry, despite my "mongrel" Hungarian background. I wired him that Germany had room for only one mass murderer of his talents and mine. I digress. I'm sorry. It is through embarrassment. Mr Walsh, a forceful individual who is in a position to advance my career should he so choose, suggested I join him in a cruel practical joke at the expense of his friend Mr Errol Flynn.'

Lorre wandered around my tiny office as he spoke, picking up and putting things down, as if given bits of business by the director. I wondered if, after years of self-analysis, he realized he was repeating his act from *The Maltese Falcon*.

'Mr Flynn was greatly upset by the passing of Mr Barrymore. He also has a tendency to idolize father-figures, and saw in Barrymore perhaps the end result of his own dissolution. He organized a wake at the Cock and Bull, a bar catering to the more theatrical type of alcoholic. John Carradine recited speeches from *Hamlet*. David Niven recounted anecdotes of dubious provenance. A great deal of liquor was consumed. Flynn himself told stories of Barrymore's genius and tragedy. He became extremely intoxicated and was struck with a fit of melancholy. At that point, Mr Walsh suggested a somewhat macabre practical joke, which we hurried to put into action.'

Lorre paused. I was following the story. Working in Hollywood, you get used to the name-dropping.

'At the end of the evening, Flynn was incapable of returning to his home unassisted. A taxi-cab was arranged. With drunken difficulty, he opened the front door of his house and switched on the lights, to be confronted with John Barrymore, unembalmed, sprawled in a chair in his hallway. The effect must have been considerable. You see, while Flynn was drinking, Walsh and myself surreptitiously left the Cock and Bull and made our way to the mortuary, where we bribed an attendant. We borrowed the body and transported it across town in Walsh's car, broke into Flynn's house, and propped up the corpse where he would find it. Imagine the ghastly sight it presented. Corpses have an unhealthy, pale glow in the moonlight. And Barrymore's face, empty of life, was a puffy mask of his former self. A truly grotesque thing.'

This sort of thing happens more than you'd think. As Lorre said, Hollywood is a frontier town. Nobodies are elevated to positions of wealth and power in a few short months and then transformed back into nobodies again. Every prince has his court of hangers-on, jesters, assassins, freaks, witch doctors and courtesans.

'So Barrymore is at Flynn's house?' I deduced. 'Why don't you just go over there and snatch him back. Flynn must be out cold by now.'

Lorre smiled again. His teeth were not good.

'Naturally, that was our plan. But when we returned at dawn this morning, we found Flynn's front door hanging open, the chair knocked over, and no sign of either Flynn or the *corpus*. Various of our party have been searching the predictable sinkholes of vice and depravity all day, but we have reached the end of our resources. It has been decided that you are to be commissioned to bring this regrettable matter to a swift, happy and most of all unpublicized conclusion.'

I sensed that under all the irony and his *mysterioso* screen image, Lorre was pretty much disgusted at what he had done. Then again, ninety-nine out of a hundred actors in this town would french-kiss a leper if a bigshot director like Walsh suggested it. Father-figures and idolatry aside, it made sense to keep happy someone who could turn you from a drunken Tasmanian pretty boy into Errol Flynn.

'You think Flynn still has the corpse?'

Lorre shrugged again. 'It is most likely. Unless both have been kidnapped by another party.'

'You've left someone at Flynn's house? In case he comes back?'

Lorre nodded. 'Of course. Mr Walsh took charge, and made sensible arrangements. He is a man of action.'

Lorre gave me a hundred dollars as a retainer. It came in

269

whisky-circled five- and ten-spots, with a few crumpled singles, probably from a bar-room whip-round. I imagined Walsh not having small enough bills on him to contribute.

We shook hands on it. I had a client. I had a case. I had a headache.

'Hold, sirrah!'

A long-legged figure, cloaked in darkness (and a cloak), stood tall in Errol Flynn's hallway, an accusing foil pointed at my breast-pocket. He had shoulder-length hair and a Buffalo Bill beard. His eyes were watery with a whiskyish tinge. I recognized John Carradine.

'I'm the detective,' I said. 'Peter Lorre sent me.'

He stepped back, and saluted, slapping his long nose with the edge of his foil.

'Enter freely, friend. Thou most worthy servant of the higher law.'

Flynn lived in a big house up on Mulholland Drive. I'd heard the stories and expected *boudoir* décor, complete with velvet curtains and pictures of fat little naked people on fat little naked cushions. In fact, the place was in disappointingly good taste.

He even had books. Not sawn-off spines glued together to make a novelty door for a hidden cocktail bar. Not privately published, gorgeously illustrated pornography. Proper books, by fellows such as Shakespeare, Scott, Stevenson and Conrad.

On its side in the hallway was a comfortable armchair. I imagined it stood up, with a dead actor sprawled in it. Not a lovely image.

Carradine bobbed around like a scarecrow on strings as I inspected the scene of the crime. Like Lorre, he knew how to cast himself. In his life, he was a courtier. Others might be Hamlet or Claudius, but he was down for Horatio or Osric. He knew when to put in a 'Fie on it' or a 'Message, sire!' and could swish his sword with the best of them. At this moment, he was getting in my way more than was advisable.

There were two possibilities. Flynn had taken the body and run off, either in a fit of insanity or as a joke to get back at Walsh. Or someone had intervened and snatched the both of them.

Actually, there was a third possibility. Three months ago, I'd have ruled it out altogether. But on a derelict gambling ship out in the Bay my opinion of the world had taken a tumble. Barrymore could have got up, and taken Flynn with him to the world of the dead.

To Flynn, Barrymore might be Jacob Marley. His fate was a hideously plausible prediction of the destination at the end of the road the younger man was taking. Was Flynn even now being shown the drunken ruination he could expect if he didn't reform?

No. That sort of thing didn't happen.

In books and movies, the supernatural has a point. The ghosts teach Scrooge a lesson. My experience is that nothing can be learned from the inexplicable. Like in the cartoons, pianos sometimes fall from the sky and squash random people into pancakes.

There was no point in trying to make sense of this. If Barrymore were dragging a dead leg around the Hollywood hills like Tom Tyler in *The Mummy's Hand*, was that any more insane than the idea of propping up a dead matinée idol in a movie star's hallway just for laughs?

I looked around, for clues. The door-lock was smashed in, showing raw wood where the mechanism had been wrenched away. That didn't square with what Lorre had told me.

'When they planted the body, how did they get in?'

Carradine hung his head to one side in a posture classically intended to display thought to the gallery.

'French windows at the back,' he said.

Lorre had told me Flynn came home and, with drunken difficulty, unlocked his front door. But Lorre hadn't been there. He was imagining the plan as Walsh intended it. Had Flynn been so drunk that he decided not to bother with keys and smashed down his own front door?

It depended on what kind of drunk he was. If he were so soused he couldn't use a key, he would most likely be incapable of the physical task of kicking in a door – not an easy thing off the screen, even if you are Captain Blood and Robin Hood in one. In any case, it was more probable that Flynn would go round the back and get in easily through the french windows (as demonstrated by Walsh's body-snatching party) or take the easy option of sleeping it off in the garden.

I examined the lock. It had been professionally broken. A hefty shoulder had been applied. And a tell-tale black gouge suggested the involvement of a crowbar.

So someone else had broken in after Walsh. Someone better at smashing down doors but not as familiar with the property.

I reconstructed the crime, crossing the Flynn threshold and imagining myself as the wobbly movie star.

Dropped off in his drive-way, he weaves his way up to his front door and finds it broken in. Lorre, in his reconstruction, imagined Flynn coming face to face with the dead Barrymore. That was possible. But he must be alerted by the broken lock to the fact that something is wrong. That percolates through even the most drunken brain. He steps warily into the hallway, imagining himself the hero of his movie, too drunk to be as cautious and cowardly as anyone who didn't think he was Errol Flynn would be.

Standing in his doorway, in a vestibule between the door and the hall, I thought it through. There was a table by the door. In a bowl on the table were a bunch of keys, a money-clip well-filled with bills and a five-hundred-dollar watch. Flynn goes through the ritual of divesting himself of these items after stepping into his house, all the while trying fuzzily to think about the broken door. Is there danger inside?

I stepped out of the vestibule and reached out. I touched the light-switch he must have flicked. I turned the lights off and then on again.

Flynn's eyes would be dazzled.

And he sees?

Barrymore, certainly. Maybe Walsh's joke goes as planned, and Flynn is terror-stricken by the apparition. A puffy-faced, bloodless corpse.

But someone else – most likely, several someones – is there too, about their own business. Probably ill-doing of some sort. This place stank of it.

'Something is rotten in the state of Denmark,' I opined.

'You can say that again, buddy.' Carradine nodded sagely.

As I drove to the Pierce Brothers Mortuary, I thought about the case. The most likely and comforting solution, ridiculous as it sounds, was that Walsh chose to play his prank by coincidence on the night some entirely unconnected thieves chose to break into the Flynn mansion. The thieves get a surprise when they find Barrymore and are themselves surprised by a returning Flynn, and flee the scene, kidnapping the living and the dead.

It didn't play in Peoria. No matter how spooked they were by the body-snatching business, I couldn't imagine thieves who specialized in homes of the rich and famous but left behind several thousand dollars in untraceable notes and an expensive watch. Not the sort of oversight you expect of the larcenous professional.

That meant the two break-ins at the Flynn place were connected. The second was a consequence of the first. The unknown persons were after Barrymore's body.

I wondered about the more fanatical fans. All the women who supposedly committed suicide when God took Valentino away. With a queasy stomach turn-over, I remembered whispers about corrupt morgue attendants who took back-handers to let ghoulish busybodies peer and pry and poke at celebrity corpses. There were stories about Jean Harlow you don't want to hear.

This was California, central clearing-house for cults. Mostly harmless kook groups, but there were others – I had shivery memories of the Esoteric Order of Dagon in Bay City – who were deeply dangerous.

Did some crazed John Barrymore worshipper out there have enough *tana* leaves to bring him back for one last private performance?

It was a fine spring night. With the windows of the Chrysler rolled down, I could smell orange blossom and gasoline on the Los Angeles breeze. There was a war on, of course. But there were always wars on.

The Mortuary was a single-storey structure with a lot of stucco, and a couple of palm trees in the sidewalk outside. They had a marquee, presumably to announce their big funerals. Barrymore, lucky to get work in Bulldog Drummond B pictures these last few years, was back on top again, name in big black letters. This was the last place a star wanted to get billing. Though when Carradine went, he'd be lucky to rate a mention on the 'Also Dead' roster posted outside.

There's a guy who always plays mortuary attendants in movies. A little, skinny, bald, pockmarked character with a voice that reminds you of Karloff and eyes that light up when he thinks of a nice, cold grave. His name is Milton Parsons.

I could swear he moonlights at Pierce Brothers. He was behind the desk, a bellhop in a mausoleum, reading a funeral directors' trade magazine. The cover story was about a shortage of coffin materials, what with the war effort claiming most of the nation's lumber and brass. Wasn't that just like the government, making the undertaker's job difficult at the same time it was supplying him with more corpses?

I showed him my badge. It's very impressive.

'I've come about Barrymore,' I said.

I didn't have to ask if he were the attendant Walsh had bribed. He gulped, Adam's apple bobbing over his wing-collar. He looked sallow and guilty.

'I was assured by Mr Walsh . . .' he began.

'That's okay, fella. There's a war on. Rules don't necessarily apply.'

He smiled, displaying a creepy slice of dentition that made

his face even more skull-like. I wondered how much he'd have charged for a feel of Jean Harlow. I tried to keep my stomach down.

'Have there been any other unusual inquiries concerning Mr Barrymore?'

His eyes glittered. 'A great many have called to pay their respects. Several studio heads . . .'

None of whom would have given him work last week.

'. . . and a remarkable number of ladies.'

Barrymore had been famously profligate in that department since the turn of the century.

'If I might say so, it is becoming an embarrassment that the star is not, as it were, appearing on stage. An understudy will not suffice.'

'I'm doing my best to get him back.'

'I should hope so.'

I imagined Barrymore laughing. Wherever he was.

'Since Walsh took him away, have there been any other *insistent* inquiries?'

'Oh, all of them.'

'Unusually insistent. Groups of people, not single mourners. With perhaps a hefty member of the party, a chauffeur or bodyguard.' I was thinking of the type of muscle used to smash in doors. 'Maybe of an occult bent. You know, creepy types?'

He thought about it. He shuddered.

'Yes, sir. Indeed. Groups of that description have called. Two of them.'

I closed my mouth. 'Two.'

'Shortly after Mr Walsh and Mr Lorre departed, an Irish fellow demanded to be allowed to see the corpse. He offered quite a considerable emolument.'

The attendant must have been sick to have gone with the first offer.

'He became quite abusive when we were unable to strike an agreement. He was accompanied by two unusual individuals. I didn't get much of a look at them, but they struck me as *wrong*

275

somehow. I had the impression that they wore rather too much scent. To cover another smell, perhaps.'

'This Irishman. I don't suppose you got his name?'

The attendant shook his head. He did not enjoy remembering the encounter. I had hit upon something that spooked him.

Imagine how that made me feel.

'Didn't he give you some way to get in touch with him, when the corpse was returned, so you could do business?'

The attendant froze, and clammed up. I filled it in for him.

'You told him about Walsh. You told him who had the body. He paid you.'

He didn't contradict me.

'You said Barrymore was at Errol Flynn's house.'

'No,' he admitted. 'Is that true?'

'Did Walsh have much of a start on the Mystery Man?'

'An hour or so.'

It was impossible that the Irishman had tailed Walsh. Somehow, he had homed in on Barrymore. Did the dead actor come equipped with a beacon?

My head was hurting more.

'And the second group?' I asked. 'You said two suspicious groups made inquiries.'

'I told them nothing.'

'So they weren't paying. Who were they?'

'An Englishman, a French-accented woman and an American who claimed to be a federal agent. The Englishman did most of the talking. He left his card.'

He left that up in the air. I didn't reach into my pocket. There was no need to put a bribe down to expenses yet.

'Do the Pierce Brothers still own the mortuary?' I asked. 'And are they aware of your sideline?'

The attendant scowled and pulled the card out of thin air like a conjurer. He handed it over.

I knew the name before I saw it.

EDWIN WINTHROP. THE DIOGENES CLUB. LONDON.

He had been around the Janey Wilde business also, along with a French woman named Geneviève Dieudonné and a fed called Finlay. I had the impression that Winthrop's special field of interest was *Weird Tales* country.

There was a telephone number on the back of the card.

'Because no money was involved, you didn't tell Winthrop about the Irishman, did you?'

The attendant looked down at his shoes. I shook my head, almost in admiration.

If Edwin Winthrop was surprised to hear from me, he didn't betray it in his even, chatty tones. I mentioned that I was looking for an actor, a recently deceased one, and that his name had come up in the investigation.

'In that case, you better pop out here for a chat. We're holed up in Coldwater Canyon. Just a couple of houses down from Boris Karloff.'

He laughed that off. If Bela Lugosi was involved in this, then all the screen's bogeymen would be represented. That wasn't my kind of movie.

I took the address, which was on Bowmont Drive.

'Careful how you go,' Winthrop advised me. 'The turns get a bit sticky. And a lot of the signs have been taken down, to fool Japanese invaders.'

I knew that.

I drove out to Coldwater Canyon. This was going to be an all-night case. It seemed to me that everyone involved slept only in the day, like Dracula. Except Barrymore, and he was supposed to be sleeping all the time.

I knew next to nothing about Winthrop. He had some official position, but wasn't keen on giving out specifics. There were worse things waiting man than death, Hamlet had said – and John Carradine would agree with him – and that was something princes and governments had always known, and always done their best to conceal from the rabble. I knew that

277

all governments must have people like Winthrop – or our own Special Agent Finlay – to take care of those things, discreetly and without public honour. I didn't like to think how busy they might be.

I couldn't spot Karloff's house, and it took me a while to find Winthrop's hide-out. The whole street was ordinary. It was an ordinary house. A Filipino houseboy led me out on to the patio, where a group of people sat by the swimming pool. The moon was bright, and the only artificial light came from the glow-worm ends of cigars and cigarettes.

Winthrop wore a white dinner jacket and was smoking a foot-long Cuban cigar. A black cat was nestled in his arms, blinking contentedly. Winthrop grinned to see me.

Geneviève Dieudonné, who wore something silvery and clinging that suggested a resistance to the quiet cool of the night air, arose elegantly from a recliner and gave me a dazzling smile. She said she was pleased to see me again.

A grunt from the other man I knew, Special Agent Finlay, suggested he disagreed with his French associate. He waved a paw at me, sucked his cigarette dead, then lit another.

There were other people by the pool. I would have thought them a party, but the only drink in sight was tea, served in mugs, not the best china. This was a meeting and, from the slightly electric air, I guessed an urgent one.

Winthrop introduced me.

A behemoth of a man whose weight was barely supported by a reinforced deck-chair was Judge Keith Pursuivant, a jurist I had never heard of but who greeted me in oratorical Southern style. He wore a voluminous cloak and a wide hat, and might have been Carradine inflated to the size of a dirigible. Also present were a fellow called Thunstone, an academic named Leffing, a little Frenchman whose name I missed, a physician named Silence, and an American with too many Gs in his name to be credible.

'Have you heard of the Jewel of Seven Stars?' Winthrop asked.

'A racehorse?'

Winthrop laughed, and chucked the cat under the chin. 'No. A gemstone. One of the treasures of Ancient Egypt. An item of immense occult significance.'

'*Nom d'un nom*,' cursed the Frenchman. 'A psychic *bombe*, of incalculable magnitude.'

'Let me guess, someone else has it, and you want it?'

'You see through us entirely.'

'It's for the war effort,' Finlay said dourly.

'We're throwing stones at Japan now?'

Strangely, nobody laughed at that. Which gave me a chill. This group might have its comical aspects, but they were deadly serious about their fabulous jewel.

'If it comes to that,' Geneviève said, 'the war might be well lost.'

'Set against us in this business are a crew of very dangerous characters,' Winthrop explained.

'An Irishman?' I ventured.

'You are up on this. Yes, Bennett Mountmain is the man to watch. A worse dastard than his uncle, if that's possible.'

Bennett Mountmain. I had a name.

'He was kicked out of Ireland by the priests. He still claims to be the rightful king or some such rot. We know he's been knocking about in bad places. Haiti, Transylvania, Berlin. Like that swine Crowley in the last show, he's been working for the Huns. He's in close with Hitler's crackpot mages. And he's after the jewel. We think the Nazis have the spear of Longinus. Combine that with the Jewel of Seven Stars, and they might trump our Ark of the Covenant. We'd need Excalibur *and* the Holy Grail to beat that.'

'And the Maltese Falcon?' I asked.

'Oh, that's real too. The Knights Templar still have it. By now, it may be charged with some minor power. We don't need to bother with that. Do we, Gees?'

The fellow with all the Gs nodded. These people had a complex private history I didn't want to go into.

279

You might not think it to look at me, but I do know what the spear of Longinus is. Also known as *die heilige Lanze*. And everybody's heard of Excalibur and the Holy Grail. From that, I could deduce the sort of item this Jewel of Seven Stars was supposed to be.

'Mountmain has the jewel,' Judge Pursuivant boomed. His tones were impressive enough to disturb coyotes out in the canyon. 'All is lost.'

'He may have the jewel,' Winthrop said. 'But that's not the half of it. Getting it out of its vessel is notoriously a sticky business. We know that it is to be done at dawn, and in this mysterious White House of the prophecy. Mountmain's uncle couldn't manage it, which is why we're here all these years later. And the last twenty years will have shaped its aura in all manner of configurations. When you think of the life John Barrymore has lived. The heights, the depths, the triumphs, the humiliations, the genius, the despair. How much was Barrymore and how much the jewel? And how has all this *experience* affected the stone?'

Winthrop was excited, whereas the rest of his company were scared. Maybe he was a man of greater vision than they. Or maybe he was mad.

'We should be in Washington,' Finlay said gloomily. 'We've missed the thing here. We should be there at dawn. The President himself might be in danger.'

Winthrop wasn't convinced.

'We have Washington covered. And North Africa. And *Maison Blanche* in New Orleans.'

Finlay killed another cigarette.

'This jewel,' I asked. 'You say it's in a vessel?'

Winthrop nodded, happily.

'What kind of vessel?'

'Why, John Barrymore's body, of course.'

About midnight I was back in my office in the Cahuenga Building, telephoning hospitals and morgues, asking if a surplus stiff might have washed their way, one that looked oddly familiar if looked at from the side. It was proper detective work, and as tedious and pointless as hell.

Someone – most likely this Bennett Mountmain bird – had John Barrymore, and inside the Great Profile was a rare and fabulously valuable jewel. Of course, if Mountmain hacked out the Seven Stars and dumped the body somewhere I could find it, then I'd still be living up to the letter of my mission. Lorre wanted the body back, not some priceless Macguffin hidden inside it.

I was not yet suspicious enough to wonder whether Lorre had known about the Jewel of Seven Stars. He was only a sinister conspirator in the movies.

After the call-round was finished, I hit a few bars where newsmen hang out and invested some of Lorre's money in buying drinks and pumping for information. You can imagine the sort of newsman who has to stay behind in Los Angeles while all the decent writers head off to become war correspondents, and who also happens to be an after-midnight boozer.

I know a lot of fellows like that.

Having struck Milton Parsons, I wondered if I'd come across a convenient squealer who was the spitting image of Elisha Cook Jr, a shifty, sad-eyed little man who had the secret of the plot and was willing to swap it for a pathetic sliver of conversation. Of course, if I found an Elisha it was most likely he would wind up horribly dead by dawn, as an example.

Sometimes, it doesn't work out like that.

Nobody had even heard of Bennett Mountmain.

I got back to my office at about three, and found men waiting for me. I walked right into trouble. A fist sank into my gut before I could get my hat off. Someone tried to take my coat off without unbuttoning it, yanking it from my shoulders to improvise a strait-jacket. I heard my spiffy coat rip as I was trussed.

The manhandlers were a couple of blank-faced goons in shabby overcoats. They smelled like Tijuana whores, but I didn't get fairy vibrations off them. They wore the scent to cover another smell. That was a familiar note.

In my chair sat a man with a gun. It was a very nice gun, an automatic. He showed it to me without actually pointing it anywhere, twirling it by the trigger guard. I happened to notice that the safety catch wasn't on. My visitor was a locked-room murder mystery waiting to happen.

'Twenty years I've waited,' my visitor said.

He had an Irish accent, soft but sinister. I knew who this was, but didn't say so.

'And before that, my uncle wasted a lifetime. To be so close to the achievement of such a purpose and have it snatched away. Do you have any idea, you foolish little detective, what that kind of frustration can make you do?'

I was just deducing something when the gun went off. A bullet spanged off my filing cabinet, putting a dent in it and ringing the thing like a coffin-shaped bell. The bullet ricocheted my way, and thunked into the meaty shoulder of one of the men holding me.

He didn't say a thing. He barely even moved. I saw a slow trickle of dark blood seep into his sleeve. The man's lack of complaint frightened me.

Mountmain was pointing the gun now. At me.

'Where is it?' he asked.

'This is where I say "I don't know what you're talking about," and you sneer "But of course you do, foolish little detective"' – I liked the phrase – 'and try to beat it out of me for an hour or two. The flaw in your plan is that I really don't know what you're talking about.'

There was no harm trying it on.

'You are working for the Diogenes Club,' he sneered. His favoured mode of expression was the sneer.

'I am working for Mr Moto.'

With deliberation, he shot the man he had wounded. This

time, he put a bullet in the man's forehead. His hat blew off in a red cloud. No matter how John Barrymore looked, this fellow looked worse. The trickling hole between his eyebrows didn't help.

'That's someone I rely on and, in a strange sort of way, am fond of,' Mountmain said. 'Now imagine what I'll do to you, whom I've never met before and to whom I've taken an intense dislike.'

'This would have something to do with a recently deceased Sweet Prince?'

'Give the man a goldfish.'

'And a rock?'

Mountmain's sneer verged on a snarl.

'A rock? You could call it that. If you were a very stupid person indeed.'

I did my best to shrug. Not easy.

Until five minutes ago, I'd assumed Mountmain had Barrymore. Certainly that was what Winthrop thought. And he had read the programme, which gave away all the story I had missed.

Not so.

'Your response time is excellent,' I said. 'I only started asking about you two hours ago.'

Mountmain sneered away the compliment.

'Ten thousand dollars,' he said, 'if you lead me to the jewel. If not, you'll be tortured until you tell what you know. In unspeakable ways.'

'I've never been tortured in a speakable way.'

'Americans are such children. You always "crack wise". But you don't know what "wise" means in Europe.'

He took my letter-opener from my desk. He flicked his cigarette lighter, raising a flame. He held the flame under the blade, looking from it to me.

'I'd have taken the ten thousand dollars,' he said.

'You've waited twenty years for something. If you wouldn't put up with torture after that, you're not the man I think you are.'

283

He almost smiled. 'Very cleverly put. Indeed, I'd endure anything. But that's because I know what's at stake.'

The blade was red.

'You, *macushla*, know nothing.'

I tried to wrestle free, but the two goons – if that was all they were – held me fast. Mountmain stood up. He put his lighter away and spat on the red-hot blade. There was a hiss.

My office is on the sixth floor. Behind Mountmain was the window, and beyond that the irritating neon light. A face hung upside-down at the top of my window, a fall of blonde hair wavering.

I was impressed. Geneviève had climbed either up from the street or down from the roof.

She clambered like a lizard, her arms and torso visible through the window, and lunged forwards, breaking through the glass.

Mountmain turned as her arms went around his waist. He stabbed with my letter-opener, and she grabbed it with her bare hand. I smelled burning flesh and heard the sizzle. She bared sharp – unnaturally sharp – teeth and hissed, but did not scream. Mountmain bent backwards.

He shouted words in a language I didn't know.

I was let go and the goons rounded on Geneviève.

The office was too small for much of a fight. Geneviève took hold of the first goon, the one with the holes in him, and stuffed him out of the window. He fell like a stone. I felt the building shake as he smacked against the sidewalk.

The other goon hung back.

Mountmain scrambled to the doorway and tipped an invisible hat, sneering another command in old Irish or whatever. Then he left us with the goon.

This was a bigger specimen. It had an acre of chest, and eyes like white marbles. Geneviève made a face at it.

'It's been around too long,' she said. 'The binding is coming loose.'

I had no idea what she was talking about.

284

Come to that, I was only just taking in the subtle changes in her. She still wore the evening gown, and had even scaled the building in heels, but her face was a different shape, sharper somehow. She had pointed teeth and diamond-shaped claw-nails.

We were in the world of the weird.

Geneviève held out her wounded hand. I saw the weal shrivel and disappear, leaving her white palm unmarred. The goon lurched towards her.

She knelt down, scooped up the letter-opener, and stuck it into his head. He halted, like a statue, but his eyes still rolled. He fell over, rattling the floorboards, and lay on his back.

'Do you keep food-stuffs here?' she asked.

'Is this the time to eat?'

'Table salt. I need salt.'

She was on the mark. I've had too many meals in the office, while working odd hours. I have a stash of basic groceries in the bottom drawer of the filing cabinet, below the liquor. Without questioning her, I found a half-full bag of salt. It must have been there for years.

She smiled tightly as she took it, never looking away from the goon. With a pointed finger, she yanked his jaw open. Then she poured salt into his mouth, filling it entirely until trails spilled out.

'Needle and thread would be too much to ask. Do you have an office stapler? A first-aid kit?'

There was a small box of pills and salves. She took a roll of bandage and wound it around the lower half of the goon's head, mummifying the salt inside his mouth. Then, she stood up.

The goon shook, and came apart. He dissolved into what Mr Edgar Allan Poe once described as a 'loathsome mass of putrescence'.

'Zombies,' she spat. 'Hateful things.'

I drove, with Geneviève beside me, legs up on the seat like a child. She chattered and I interjected, and we tried to figure it out.

'Mountmain must have had Barrymore, but lost him,' I said.

'He'll have him again soon. More importantly, he'll have the jewel. I'm surprised he bothered to call on you. It shows an impatience that is not good for him.'

'How did he find Barrymore in the first place? The mortuary attendant couldn't have known where Lorre and Walsh took him.'

'That's a nasty business. Scrying. It involves disembowelling a cat. Twice in one night would be pushing it, but my guess is that having failed to get what he wanted from you, he'll be here – kitty-kittying in some alleyway.'

'He can find Barrymore by gutting a cat?'

'Magic. Hocus pocus. It works, you know.'

'With so much at stake, couldn't you find a cat willing to give its life for the war effort?'

'It's not as easy as that. You have to be steeped in black magic for it to work. And that's not a good thing to be. It has long-term implications.'

'But Mountmain doesn't care?'

'I should think not. That's why black magic is a temptation. You get ahead easily, delaying the pay-off until it's too late.'

'What are you, a white witch?'

She laughed, musically. 'Don't be silly. I'm a vampire.'

'Blood-sucking fiend, creature of the night, accursed *nosferatu*, coffin-dwelling undead . . .'

'That sort of thing.'

I let her go with it. Obviously, it wasn't worth arguing.

'Where are the rest of you? Winthrop and the others?'

'I'm afraid we have certain differences among ourselves. The war makes for odd alliances. I have a distaste for government work, which has been set aside for the moment. I've been keeping track of the Jewel of Seven Stars since its rediscovery. Edwin is a servant of the Crown. The Diogenes Club, and its equivalents in the allied nations, wants to get hold of the Seven Stars to use as a weapon of war.'

'How can a jewel win the war?'

'Think of it as a lens. It can focus intense destructive power. It seems to have a specific purpose. It is a device for destroying empires.'

'Like Germany and Japan? Sounds good.'

'You don't mean that. You haven't thought through what it means. It's not enough to win. You have to win without tainting yourself, or you're just piling up debts future generations will have to pay. Edwin can rationalize that; I can't. Of course, it's likely I'll be around to go through whatever future generations have to put up with.'

'Mountmain wants the jewel to help Hitler?'

'And himself. His family believes in a destiny. He is the head of something called the Order of the Ram. It is foretold that the Ram will reign over the last days of the world. You know who Nostradamus was?'

'Fortune-teller?'

'That's the bimbo. In his suppressed quatrains, he was surprisingly specific about the Mont-Mains. An expression disturbingly equivalent to "thousand-year Reich" crops up quite a lot.'

'Errol Flynn has the body,' I said.

She was quiet, and thoughtful.

'He's the only player left in the game. Mountmain wouldn't have taken him seriously, a drunken hero. He got hold of the body and escaped. Then Mountmain must have revised his first impression and assumed Flynn was acting to a deliberate plan rather than careering about at random. He'd start looking around for confederates, and that would lead to the person rattling his cage, to wit: me.'

'I loved him in *The Adventures of Robin Hood*,' she said. '"It's injustice I hate, not Normandy!"'

'But where is Flynn? It's a shame your prophet didn't say where we could find him.'

'Michel de Notre-Dame wasn't always accurate. Sometimes he didn't understand what he saw. Sometimes he filled in with nonsense. He does describe a crisis, but his suggestion is absurd. He says that the jewel is to be found at the White House. Edwin has someone in Washington. And Finlay is on a plane, racing the sun. Just in case the jewel is spirited across country by dawn.'

'*Dawn?*'

'Two hours away. That's where the quatrain is highly specific. Even allowing for changes in the calendar since 1558.'

I shook my head. 'There are white houses in California.'

'To be frank, it could mean anything. The expression Nostradamus uses is *Maison Blanche*.'

I stopped the car. We were outside the Warner Brothers lot. Lorre's home base. And Errol Flynn's. The pre-dawn light was already turning the water tower into a Martian War Machine.

I laughed out loud.

This was what it was like. When you saw it, and nobody else did. This was what made a detective.

'It's here,' I said.

'How can you know that?'

'*Variety*. The trade paper. Most of my work is related to the studios. I keep up with the industry. Peter Lorre's shooting a film at Warners at the moment. With Humphrey Bogart and Ingrid Bergman.'

Geneviève was prettily puzzled. Her face had settled down to her ingénue look again.

'I don't see . . .'

'It's called *Casablanca*, Geneviève. *Casa Blanca. Maison Blanche*. White House.'

She looked across the lot, to the sound stages.

'Not the White House in Washington, not the city in North Africa. Here, *Casablanca*, Hollywood.'

I drove on to the lot.

There were night-watchmen around, and a few early-arriving or late-staying technicians. I asked a uniformed guard if he'd seen Flynn. The man didn't want to say anything.

'I know he's on a bender,' I said.

Finally, he nodded to a stage. 'He'll be sleeping it off now,' he said. 'He's a good lad, and we don't mind covering for him. The stories you hear don't mean anything.'

I thanked him.

I could not resist a little triumph when I told Geneviève I was right.

We walked rapidly to the stage and found an unlocked door.

Inside was an Alice world. Half the stage was converted into a nightclub, with ceiling fans, a beat-up piano, twenty-five yards of bar, a back-room full of gambling equipment and row upon row of bottles of cold tea. Glasses and guns and hats were strewn around, each precisely in the spot it would need to be for shooting to resume. There were black cameras, like huge upright insects, halted where the club carpets gave way to bare concrete. Unlit lights hung from frames above.

In the centre of the set were two men, slumped over a bottle.

Flynn was so drunk and scared that he was drinking cold tea as if it were best bourbon. Barrymore was dead, but moving. The supposedly dark set was lit by a ruby glow from inside the dead man's chest.

Flynn raised a glass to his idol.

'What's it all for, Jack?' he asked. 'All this mess, this nightmare, this fantasy, this horror? Is it just for play, just a game? To be packed up and put away by some snot-nosed kid who's lost interest?'

He slammed his glass down.

'I don't want it like that. I want Hamlet and Sherlock Holmes and Don Juan and Robin Hood and Custer. I want us to be heroes, to save something worth saving, to respect maidenly virtues and reflect manly ones. We shouldn't just be pathetic, whoremongering drunks, Jack.'

Barrymore was nodding.

There was no life in him. At least, none of his own. It was the Jewel of Seven Stars, animate. Geneviève took my arm, and gripped like a vice.

'To the glorious damnèd,' Flynn toasted, tossing his glass away, playing hell with the continuity.

Barrymore's starched shirt was open and his chest was bulging. A cinder glowed inside his translucent flesh, outlining the black bars of his ribs.

'If Flynn takes the jewel, he'll be John Barrymore all over again,' Geneviève said. 'Personal triumph and degradation. But only personal. It will be shielded from the world. Rather, the world will be shielded from it.'

'But it'll kill him,' I suggested.

Geneviève nodded. 'Everybody dies,' she said.

'Except you.'

In a tiny, long-ago frightened little girl's voice, she repeated, 'Except me.'

Streaks of sunlight were filtering through the unshuttered glass roof of the stage. I wondered if Geneviève Dieudonné would shrivel at dawn, like the salt-stuffed zombie in my office.

A shot sounded.

Geneviève yelped. She looked down at a scarlet patch on her silver chest. Blood spread and her eyes were wide with surprise.

'Except me,' she said, crumpling.

I turned, my gun out.

Bennett Mountmain strolled on to the stage.

He wore a stinking cat's skin on his forehead and upper face, like a caul, eyeholes ripped in the blood-matted fur.

'Silver bullet,' he explained.

Geneviève moaned and held her wound. She seemed for the first time helpless. She was muttering in French.

Mountmain walked past me, with contempt.

Flynn stood up and barred his way, shielding Barrymore.

'You again,' he snarled. 'The treasure-hunter. You'll have to fight your way past my cold steel to snatch Cap'n Blood's doubloons for your coffers.'

Wearily, Mountmain held up his gun.

'Go ahead, varlet, and shoot,' said Flynn. His face was red and sunken, but he was twice the hero he seemed on the screen.

He appeared to grow, to have some of the ruby glow, and he threw open his mouth and laughed at Mountmain.

The Black Magician fired, and his gun exploded in his hand.

Flynn's laughter grew, filling the stage, setting ceiling fans whirling. There was a demonic overtone to it. He stood with his legs apart, hands on hips, eyes shining.

Barrymore tipped forward, and a large stone fell out of his chest on to the prop table.

The light of Seven Stars lit up the *Casablanca* set.

Mountmain was on the floor, rolling in agony, weeping tears of bloody frustration. Geneviève was trying to sit up and say something. I knelt by her, to see what could be done.

There was blood on her back too. The bullet had shot right through her. The holes in her were mending over and opening again as I looked. Her blonde hair was white. Her face was a paper mask.

'Take the jewel,' she said. 'Save Flynn.'

I crossed the room.

Flynn looked at me. He was unsure. He had recognized Mountmain for what he was. But not me.

'Pure and parfait knight,' he said.

That was just embarrassing.

He stepped aside. I picked up the Jewel of Seven Stars. Tiny points shone inside it. I expected it to be warm and yielding, but it was cold and hard. I wanted to throw it into the sea.

'You've found it,' a British voice said. 'Good man.'

Winthrop had left his scrying caul outside, but his forehead was still smeared. As he wiped the last of the blood away, I remembered the cat he had been cradling in Coldwater Canyon.

'Edwin,' Geneviève said, weakly, shocked. 'You haven't . . .'

'Can't make an omelette without breaking eggs,' he said, unapologetically. 'You don't approve, of course. Catriona wouldn't either. But you'll thank me for it in the long run. May I?'

He held out his hand. I looked at the jewel. I wanted to be

rid of it. Flynn was still there. I sensed an attraction from the gem to the star. The sun was not yet up. I could plunge the stone into Flynn's chest and hide it for another generation. At the cost of a man's life.

Who's to say Errol Flynn wouldn't ruin himself without supernatural intervention? Plenty have.

Mountmain yelled hatred and defiance and frustration. He was bleeding to death.

Winthrop's hand was still extended. It was my decision.

People were pouring on to the stage. Winthrop's colleagues, cops, studio guards, Warners staff, uniformed soldiers, uniformed Nazis. I saw Peter Lorre, and other famous faces. Everybody was in this movie.

'Catch,' I said, tossing the jewel up like a bridal bouquet.

Mountmain stood up, extending his ruined hand. Judge Pursuivant landed on him, crushing him to the floor.

Winthrop made a cricketer's catch.

''Owzat,' he said.

Geneviève sighed through pain. I think she had stopped bleeding.

Someone asked in a loud Hungarian voice what the dead body of John Barrymore was doing on his set. Lorre breathed soothing sentiments, and a couple of grips removed the untenanted vessel from the site. Flynn, now merely drunk, further infuriated the director with cheery idiocies. That part of the story was swept aside. Hollywood hi-jinks. They happen all the time.

It came down to Winthrop, Geneviève and the jewel.

And me.

'We must be wise, Edwin,' Geneviève said.

The Britisher nodded. 'We have a great responsibility. I swear we shall not misuse it.'

'We may not have the chance to decide. You can feel it, can't you? As if it were alive.'

'Yes, Gené.'

Mountmain was dead, his spine snapped by Pursuivant. It had all come back on him, the black magic. Just as Geneviève had said it would.

Winthrop seemed sobered, shaken even. He couldn't get the last of the cat-blood off his face. He had done his duty, but now he was asking himself questions.

I hated that. I knew I'd be doing the same thing.

A soldier was beside Winthrop, with a lead box.

'Sir,' he prompted.

Winthrop dropped the Jewel of Seven Stars into the box, and the soldier hesitated, eyes held by the red light, before clamping shut the lid. He marched off, other soldiers trotting at his heels, drawing Pursuivant and the others.

Winthrop helped Geneviève on to a stretcher. She was fading, bare arms wrinkling like a mummy's, face sinking greyly on to her skull.

'What wash that?' someone asked me. 'The red shtone in the boxsh?'

I turned to the star of *Casablanca*, a man satisfyingly shorter and older than me.

'That,' I said, 'was the stuff that dreams are made of.'

Episode 4: The Biafran Bank Manager   1971

On the road to Somerset, Richard Jeperson drove into an anomaly. It was after midnight, a clear night in May. Behind the leather-covered wheel of his Rolls-Royce ShadowShark, he mulled over the urgent message that had brought him from Chelsea to Somerset.

Then the quality of the dark changed.

He faded the dashboard-mounted eight-track, cutting the cool jazz theme that had underscored his drive. He braked, bringing the wonderful machine to a dead halt within three yards.

He heard no night-birds.

'Weirdsville,' he mused.

After slipping his flared orange frock-coat over a purple silk shirt, he got out of the car.

He was parked on a straight road that cut across the levels. The stars and the sliver of moon were bright enough to highlight the flat fields of the wetlands, the maze of water-filled rhynes that made a patchwork of the working landscape.

Nothing wrong there, on the dull earth.

But in Heaven?

Tossing his tightly curled shoulder-length hair out of his eyes, he looked up.

An unaccustomed spasm of fear gripped him.

He saw at once what was anomalous.

He skimmed the constellations again, making sure he had his bearings. The North Star. Cassiopeia, the seated woman. Orion, the hunter.

Ursa Major, the Plough, was gone.

A black stretch of emptiness in the universe.

He had chanced on wrongnesses before, but nothing on such a cosmic scale. This could not be a localized phenomenon. If the seven stars were really gone, the whole universe had been altered.

He found himself shivering.

The moment passed. He looked up, and the constellations were aright again. The Plough twinkled on, seven diamond-chips in the Heavens. Richard was cold, with a heart-chill that was more than the night. The world was not aright just yet.

He got back into the ShadowShark and drove on.

Two hours earlier, he'd been in the basement of his home in Chelsea, meditating. He was half-way through a ritual of purification involving a week of fasting. He had gone beyond the hunger that had chewed his stomach for the first three days. He had shifted up a plane of perception. Strength was pouring into him, and his mind was forming pearls of understanding around grits of mystery.

Against his express orders, Fred – one of his assistants – had interrupted his meditation, calling him to the telephone. He didn't waste time in protest. Fred had been selected for his reliability. He'd not have broken in unless it was something of supreme importance.

After exchanging a few words with Catriona Kaye, Richard had ordered Fred to get the Rolls out of the garage and despatched Vanessa, his other associate, to pick up three portions of cod and chips wrapped. Throughout the drive, he had been working the wheel and gear-shifts one-handed, while feeding himself with the other. He could not afford the physical weakness of fasting. His stomach knotted as he stuffed himself. He overcame the side-effects of such a sudden imposition on his body by mental force alone. By breaking off the ritual, he lost much. Wisdom leaked from his mind as fish and chips filled his belly.

It was a haunting. Normally, he'd have taken Fred or Vanessa with him. But this was not one of his usual exploits on behalf of the Diogenes Club, the venerable institution that referred many problems to him. This went to the heart of his whole life. The Diogenes itself, or rather, its most respected elder statesman, Edwin Winthrop, was under siege from forces unknown.

He drove with both hands now. He had a sense of the enormous scale of the interests at stake.

Jeffrey Jeperson, the man who adopted him – a boy with no memories – from the rubble of war, had served on the Ruling Cabal of the Diogenes Club with Winthrop. Richard had been brought up with stories of Edwin Winthrop's secret services to his country. He had taken his first tentative steps into the arcane as Winthrop's most junior assistant. With old Mr Jeperson dead and Brigadier-General Sir Giles Gallant retired, Winthrop was the last serving member of the Cabal that had seen the Diogenes through the tricky post-war years, when its many enemies had worked to see its ancient charter revoked and its resources dissipated.

Winthrop, nearly eighty, took little active part in the working of the club that was more than a club. He knew well enough to withdraw and let younger men have the reins, just as he had taken over from his own mentor.

Richard wondered if Winthrop entirely liked or trusted the people who now belonged to the club. The likes of Cornelius and King, who puffed *kif* in the smoking room, and toted transistor radios, where an inadvertent cough was once grounds for instant expulsion, to keep up with the cricket. The new generation, among whom Richard counted himself, seemed to dabble in the occult like dilettantes, rather than marching into the darkness like Victorian explorers or mapping plans for the conquest of the unknown like imperial generals.

But Winthrop had been a firebrand before he was a blimp. He still had his secrets.

Now those secrets were crawling into the open.

The anomaly convinced Richard the haunting was even worse than Catriona, Winthrop's lifelong companion, had indicated.

The ShadowShark cruised into the village of Alder. All the farmhouses were dark. The Manor House was a little way out of the village, in its own grounds. Richard drove past the small church and the Valiant Soldier pub, then took the almost-hidden road out to Winthrop's family house.

The car tripped an electric eye and the wrought-iron gates swayed open automatically. Lights burned in the house, which seemed bigger after dark than Richard remembered it.

Catriona was waiting for him on the porch. A small, pretty woman, as old as the century, she seemed fragile, but Richard knew her to have a rugged constitution. Now she seemed her age, nervous and worried.

'Richard, thank God you've come.'

'Peace, Cat,' he said, hugging her.

'It's worse than you think.'

'I think it's pretty much as bad as it can get. Sometimes stars are missing.'

'You've noticed?'

They looked up, reassuring themselves. The Plough was there.

'How often?' he asked her.

'More and more.'

'Let's go indoors.'

The panelled hallway was empty. Richard noticed at once that the Turkish carpet had been taken up and rolled into a giant sausage against one wall, like a record-breaking draught-excluder. The floor was polished wood tiles, in a herringbone pattern, discreet charms of protection carved in corners.

Catriona gasped in horror.

'It was here,' she said. 'Moments ago.'

She scanned the floor, dropping down on her knees and feeling the wood with gloved hands.

'Just here,' she said, almost at the foot of the main staircase. It was still carpeted, a claret weave held down by brass rails.

Catriona began tugging at the stair carpet, wrenching tacks loose. Richard went to her and helped her stand. Her knees popped as he got her upright. She was alarmingly light, as if she might drift away.

'Lift the carpet,' she said.

He took out his Swiss army knife and used the screwdriver to extract the bottom five rails. Like a conjuror whipping a table-cloth out from under a complete dinner service, he pulled the carpet loose, popping tacks, and tossed it back in a great flap on to the upper stairs.

Catriona gasped again. Richard knew how she felt.

Burned into the bare wood of the stairs was the black shape of a man, like a shadow torn free and thrown away. It seemed to be crawling up to the landing, one hand reaching up, fingers outstretched, the other poised to overreach its fellow, pulling the bulk of the shadow upwards.

'It was on the ground floor just now,' Catriona said. 'Before that, outside, a burnt patch on the lawns, the drive-way – on *gravel*! – the front steps. It lay under the mats on the doorstep.'

'You've seen it moving?'

'Watched kettles, Richard. I've sat and stared for hours, keeping it still, keeping it at bay. But look away for a moment, and it shifts.'

He sat on the stairs, just below the man-shape. The outline was distinct. The light wood round the outline was unaffected, a little dusty, but the shape was matt black. It seemed like a stain rather than a brand. He touched it with his fingertips, then laid his flat palm where the small of the man's back would have been.

'It's warm,' he said. 'Body temperature.'

It was as if someone with a high fever had lain there. He looked at his fingers. No black had come off on them. He flipped the longest blade out of his knife and scored across the ankle. The black went into the wood.

'There are others, out on the moor, gathering.'

He turned to look at Catriona. The woman was strung taut, and he knew better than to try to soothe her. She'd been around the weird long enough to know how serious this was.

'It's an attack,' he said, standing up, brushing dust from the knees of his salmon-coloured flared trousers. 'But from what quarter?'

'Edwin won't talk. But it's to do with the War, I'm sure.'

When people said 'the War', depending on their age, they meant the First or Second World War. But Catriona meant a greater conflict that included both World Wars. It had started a great deal earlier, in the mid-nineteenth century – nobody could agree quite when – but finished in 1945, with the defeat not only of Germany and Japan but of an older, not entirely human, faction that had used the Axis powers as cat's-paws.

Outside the Diogenes Club, almost no one understood that War. Richard, who had no memory of his childhood, had lived through the aftermath. He'd heard Edwin's account of the War, had examined many of the documents kept in the secret library of the club, and saw all the time the lingering effects, written into the ways of the world in manners untraceable to most of humankind but as glaring as neon to the initiate.

'He says it's not over. That we made a great mistake.'

Richard looked into Catriona's pale blue eyes, struck breathless by their lasting loveliness, and sensed her controlled terror. He embraced her and heard her squeal of shock.

'We looked away,' she said.

He turned back, still holding Catriona by her shoulders.

An orange score-mark, where he had scratched the wood, shone in the stairs. The shape's feet were on the next step up, its head and arms were under the still-attached carpet.

'If it gets completely under the carpet, it'll be able to move like lightning. Once it's out of sight, it's free.'

He left Catriona and started working on the stair-rails. In minutes, he'd exposed the shadow's head and skinned the carpet up to the first-floor landing.

'I'll stay here and watch,' she said. 'You should go and see Edwin. He's in the *camera obscura*.'

Two staircases led up from the first-floor landing. One was the ingress to an attic apartment mysteriously occupied by an ancient female dependant Edwin in happier times referred to as 'Mrs Rochester'. The other led to the *camera obscura*, a large space in which an image of the house and its surroundings was projected by an apparatus of reflectors installed around the turn of the century by Edwin's father.

Richard paused on the landing. It was carpeted by a linked series of Indian rugs, which could be easily pulled up. The far staircase, to Mrs Rochester's rooms, was in shadow. He thought he could hear her breathing, as he had often done twenty years ago. Most boys would have had nightmares about the asthmatic invalid, but Richard had no dreams at all, no memories to prod his night-thoughts to fancy.

He climbed up to the *camera obscura* and stepped into the dark room.

Edwin stood, leaning under a giant circular mirror, looking down at the mostly shadowed table. The distinct shapes of the house, the grounds, the village and the moor were outlined. By moving the mirror, Edwin could spy further afield.

Nothing was moving.

'Shadows,' Edwin said, his voice still strong. 'Reflections and shadows.'

He dipped his hand into the image, waving through the church, scaling his skin with old stone.

'Richard, I'm glad you're here.'

'It's not a happy place, Edwin.'

Edwin's dark face twisted in a smile. 'How would you put it: "A bad vibes zone"?'

'Something like that.'

'It's a Hiroshima shadow.'

'Yes.'

At the sites of the atom bomb detonations, vaporized people left such shapes on the walls and streets, permanent shadows.

'I'm to pay for what I did.'

'You weren't the only one, Edwin. You're not even the only one left.'

'But I'm special. You see, I played it both ways. I had two chances. The first time, I was wise or cowardly and let it go. The second time, I was foolish or brave and took hold of it.'

'There was a war on.'

'There was always a war on.'

'Not now.'

'You think so?'

'Come on, Edwin. This is the Age of Aquarius. You more than anyone should know that. You helped throw the foe back into the outer darkness.'

'You've grown up being told that, boy.'

'I've grown up knowing that.'

The darkness that lay like a veil in his mind, blacking out the first years of his memory, throbbed. Things were shifting there, trying to break the surface.

'Do you want to see something pretty?'

Edwin Winthrop did not ramble. Even at his age, he was sharp. This was not a casual question, addressed to a child who had long grown up.

'I love beauty,' Richard said.

Edwin nodded and touched a lever. The table parted, with a slight creak.

Red light filled the room.

'It's the Jewel of Seven Stars,' Richard said.

'That's right.'

The gem lay on black velvet, its trapped light-points shining.

'The Seven Stars. They weren't there earlier. In the sky. That's not supposed to happen.'

'It's a sign, boy.'

'What isn't?'

'Very good. Everything is a sign. We won the War, you know. With this, essentially. People cleverer than I looked into it and saw a little of how the universe worked.'

Richard looked behind him. In the darkened room, shadows could glide like serpents.

'And I gave this to them. Not the Diogenes Club, me. Just as twenty years earlier, I let the jewel go. The club has always been people like you and me, Richard. We like to pretend we're servants of Queen or country. But when it comes to this bauble, we're on our own. So far as it belongs to anyone, it's mine now. Can you imagine Truman letting Oppenheimer *keep* his bomb? Yet the club let me take this souvenir when it was all over.'

'Men can be trusted, Edwin. Institutions change. Even the Diogenes Club.'

'Do you want this?' Edwin indicated the jewel.

It seemed to pull in Richard's gaze, sucking him into red depths. A moment's contact made him squirm inside. He broke the spell, and looked away.

301

'Very sensible. It can bring great gifts, but there are prices to be paid. A talented man was once elevated to genius by it, but his life dribbled away in waste and pathetic tragedy. We won a War, but we changed so much in the winning that I'm not sure we even came through it. I don't just mean Britain lost an Empire. It's more than that. Mrs Rochester told me I took too many short-cuts. So I must pay. You've always seen the dark in me, Richard. Because, through no fault of your own, there's a dark in you.'

Richard shook his head, vigorously. He could not let this pass.

'I'd have died in a concentration camp if it hadn't been for the Diogenes Club, if not for men like my father and for *you*, Edwin. I was a boy with no memory. You've given me more than life. There's been a purpose.'

'I've a terrible feeling we've just left a mess for you to clean up. All these, what do you call them, "anomalies", all these wrongnesses in the world. Think of them as fall-out. And the other horrors, the ones everyone notices, the famines, the brushfire wars, the deaths of notable men. When I laid my hand on this' – he grasped the jewel, his hand a black spider over the red glow, flesh-clad bones outlined by the gem's inner light – 'I took the worst short-cut, and I made it acceptable. There used to be, in Beauregard's time, an absolute standard. I destroyed that.'

Richard did not want to believe his old friend. If there was chaos where once there had been order, he was a child of that chaos. Where Edwin had gone by intellect, he ventured with instinct.

'Now I must pay. I've always known.'

'We'll see about that,' Richard said, determined.

A flash of light filled the room. Not from the jewel. It was lightning, drawn into the *camera obscura* from outside. Violent rain drummed on the roof. A storm had appeared out of cloudless night sky.

Down below, in the hallway, there was a hammering.

As they emerged on to the landing, light fell on Edwin's head.

302

Richard had no time to be shocked by the new lines etched into his friend's face.

They made their way to the main staircase.

Catriona lay in a huddle on the stairs. The shadowman was gone. The front doors stood open, and someone stood on the mat, looking down.

The polished floor of the hallway was crowded. A dozen shadowmen, overlapping, reaching out, were frozen, swimming towards the foot of the stairs.

The house was invaded.

'Ho there above,' shouted the newcomer, a woman.

Lights flickered as thunder crashed. Rain blew into the hall, whipping the woman's long coat round her long legs.

Richard was by Catriona, checking her strong pulse. She was just asleep. He looked at the woman in the doorway. The door slammed shut behind her, nudging her into the hall. She stepped gingerly on to the tangle of shadows.

She had a cloud of white hair, Medusa-tangled by the storm, with a seam of natural scarlet running through it. Despite the white, her face was unlined. The flicker of the lights made her freckles stand out.

The woman was of Amazon height and figure, well over six feet, extra inches added by her hair and stacked heels. Under a deep-green, ankle-length velvet trenchcoat, she wore a violet blouse, no bra, frayed denim hotpants, fishnet tights and calf-length soft leather pirate boots. She had a considerable weight of jade round her neck and wrists and pendant gold disc earrings the size of beermats.

Richard, though immediately impressed, had no idea who this woman was.

'All in this house are in grave danger,' she intoned.

'Tell us something we don't know, love,' he replied.

She strode across the chaos of shadowmen, slipping off and shaking out her wet coat. Her arms were bare. High up on her right arm was an intricate tattoo of a growling bear, with the stars of the constellation picked out in inset sequins.

'I'm Maureen Mountmain,' she announced, 'High Priestess of the Order of the Ram.'

'Richard Jeperson, at your service,' he snapped. 'I assume you know this is Miss Catriona Kaye and the gent whose house you are invading is Mr Edwin Winthrop.'

'There's someone else here,' she said, looking up at the ceiling. 'I sense great age, and a strong light.'

'That'd be Mrs Rochester. She's sick.'

Maureen laughed open-mouthed. She was close enough for Richard to catch her scent, which was entirely natural, earthy and appealing. Maureen Mountmain was extremely attractive, not just physically. She had a fraction of the magnetism he'd felt from the Jewel of Seven Stars.

'I don't know her real name,' he admitted.

'It's God-Given,' Maureen said. 'Jennifer God-Given.'

'If you say so, love.'

'I told you my name was Maureen, Richard. Not "love", "darling", "honey" or "pussycat".'

'I stand corrected, Maureen.'

'Do people call you Dick?'

'Never.'

'There's always a first time, Dick.'

There was a tigerish quality about Maureen Mountmain. The claws were never quite sheathed.

'Mountmain,' said Edwin, shakily. 'I know that name.'

'Do not confuse me with any of my family, Mr Winthrop. My Uncle Bennett and my Great-Uncle Declan, for instance. I believe you were present at their happy deaths. Mountmain men have always been overreaching fools. The womenfolk are wiser. If you heed me, you might live out the night.'

Richard wasn't sure whether he wanted to trust Maureen. He knew about the relatives she'd mentioned, from Edwin and from a comprehensive study of dangerous crackpots. If she was as well up on the War as he thought she was, she might fancy herself the Witch Queen of the Western Isles.

Come to that, she might earn the title.

'Don't just stand there gaping, eejits,' she said. She indicated the shadowmen at her feet. 'You have other visitors. This is serious.'

Catriona stirred. Richard helped her sit up.

'Very well, Miss Mountmain,' Edwin said, a little of his old iron back. 'Welcome to the Manor House. I am pleased to meet you.'

Edwin slowly made his way down the stairs, past Richard and Catriona. He stood at the foot of the stairs and held out his hand to Maureen.

'There's been bad blood between the Diogenes Club and your family,' he said. 'Let it be at an end.'

Maureen looked at Edwin's hand. It occurred to Richard that she could snap Edwin's neck with a single blow. Instead, she embraced him fiercely, lifting him a little off his feet.

'Blessed be,' she announced.

Richard felt Catriona's fur rising. A feud might be over, but enmities lingered.

'I remember Declan Mountmain,' Catriona said. 'An utter bastard.'

'Quite right,' Maureen said, releasing Edwin. 'And Bennett was worse. If either of them had been able to make use of the weirdstone, there'd be precious little of the world left by now.'

Catriona stood, daintily, and nodded a curt acceptance of Maureen Mountmain.

'What Declan and Bennett wished for may still come about,' Maureen said urgently. 'They were bested, and the greater forces who used them checked, by the rituals your Diogenes Club used in the War. But you woke up the Seven Stars, bought a short-term victory at the cost of long-term trouble.'

Edwin nodded. 'I admit as much,' he said.

'Do not bother justifying your actions. All men and most women would have done the same.'

Most women?

'And you could have done it earlier, when victory would have seemed even cheaper and been far more costly. For that, the world owes you, Miss Kaye, a debt that'll never be understood. Your influence, a sensible woman's, tempered this man's instincts. Like my uncles, Edwin and, I intuit with certainty, Dick here, are fascinated by the weirdstone. To them it is like a well-made gun that should be fired or a show-off's automobile that must be driven. Men never think that guns have to be fired *at* something or cars driven *to* somewhere.'

Richard bristled. This bedraggled demi-goddess had the nerve to barge into someone else's home and deliver a lecture in occult feminism.

'Women have faults too,' she said, in his direction. 'Men like guns and cars, women like men who like guns and cars. Who is to say which is the more foolish?'

'What's happening here?' Richard asked.

Edwin looked down.

Maureen stepped in. 'A crisis, of course.'

'It's coming for the Seven Stars,' Edwin said, 'swirling about the house, converging on the gem.'

'What is coming?'

'The Biafran Bank Manager,' Edwin chuckled blackly.

'*What?*'

It was a strange thing to say. But Edwin was no longer the firm-minded man Richard remembered.

'A joke in poor taste,' Maureen explained. 'He means the Skeleton in the Closet.'

Richard had heard it before, a reference to a television advert. It was one of a wave of desperate jokes made in response to the heart-breaking photographs of starved men, women and children that came out of Biafra during the famine. Any disaster that couldn't be contained by the human mind spilled over in sick humour, graveyard comedy.

'Why now?' Richard asked.

'It's been coming a long way, my boy,' Edwin said, 'for a long time.'

'He's been building you up for this,' Maureen said. 'Your life has been a series of initiations.'

Edwin looked at her sharply, with new respect.

'I've had to teach myself, old man. But I've been coming along too.'

'It's true,' Edwin said. 'Richard, I knew I wouldn't be capable of facing what is coming. I thought, almost hoped, I'd be dead by the time the changes really got under way, and you were the one we chose to take over. You're stronger now than I ever was. You have talents. We had to work for things which are easy for you. I know that's no comfort.'

Richard felt a deep resentment. Not at the way his life had been shaped, but that the great purpose he had always sensed had been imperfectly revealed to him while an outsider, the daughter of old enemies, had understood.

Thunder crashed again, and the lights went out. They came on again and the shadowmen on the floor were crowded round the foot of the stairs, black fingers reaching upwards. The quality of the light was different, wavering. Filaments fizzed at the end of their tether.

It was the anomaly again, and they were inside it.

The lights strobed, leaving photo-flash impressions on his eyes. The periods of darkness between the periods of light lengthened. The shadowmen were in motion, revealed by a pixillation of still images. They crowded together as they swarmed up the stairs, passing under Richard and Catriona. A fresh wave spread out from under the closed front doors, scrambling round Maureen's boots. Richard held Catriona and tried to gather his spiritual strength, controlling his breathing, feeling the focus gather in the centre of his chest, preparing for an assault.

The shadowmen flowed up on to the landing, gathering around Edwin, arms seeming to lift from the floor, as insubstantial yet sinewy as steel cobwebs.

From inside his jacket, Edwin took the Jewel of Seven Stars.

The lightbulbs all exploded at once. Glass tinkled on to polished wood.

The shadowmen were frozen.

Red light filled the hall, spilling down from the landing. Edwin held the jewel up. The Seven Stars shone, like the ones no longer in the Heavens. The constant light held the shadowmen back.

'So that's it,' Maureen said, awed. 'I never dreamed.'

'You feel it, like everyone,' Edwin said. 'The *temptation*.'

'I can't blame you,' she admitted.

Edwin set the jewel on the floor. Once out of his hand, the jewel changed. Its light, which had been fuelled by the wielder, dimmed. The shadows round Edwin grew. A thin arm, like a black stocking on a wind-whipped washing line, wrapped around his leg. He sank to one knee, pulled down. Another shadow latched on to his arm.

Catriona broke free, suddenly strong, and ran up the stairs, Richard and Maureen at her heels. They hesitated at the landing.

Edwin lay on the floor, twisted. Shadowmen twined round him, pinning him down, growing tight. The lightpoints of the jewel, lying nearby, glowed like drops of radioactive blood.

Catriona released a single sob, and clung to the banister. Richard felt Maureen's strong hand on his arm, sensed her body close to him. This was entirely the wrong time to be aroused, but he had no control over his surging blood.

The shadowmen wrapped Edwin like a mummy's windings. He disappeared under black, elongated forms. The shadowmen coalesced into one man and flattened, leaving a final Hiroshima shadow.

'It took him,' Maureen said.

The anomaly hadn't passed. It wasn't over.

Maureen stepped past him and reached down for the jewel. Richard took her arm, holding her back, feeling the warmth of her bare skin, fighting the fog of desire in his mind, torn by a deep need to throw her aside and take the jewel for himself. With Edwin gone, it was up for grabs.

'No,' he said, finding his strength.

Maureen's outstretched fingers curled into a fist.

'No,' she agreed.

They separated and stood either side of the jewel. It was changed. Edwin had passed into it or beyond it.

'It'd make a novel doorstop,' he suggested.

She laughed, with an appealing edge of hysteria.

Catriona still stood, clinging to the banister, eyes sparkling with unshed tears, the life she had shared with Edwin torn away and crumpled up.

'This is like a blasted relay race,' Richard said. 'Do we pick up the baton?'

'We have to do something with it.'

'Take it upstairs,' Catriona said. 'She'll know what must be done.'

'She?' Richard and Maureen asked.

'Mrs Rochester. Geneviève, her name is. She'll be waiting. I'll be up myself, when I've composed myself. I'd like to be alone now, anyway. Alone with . . .'

She indicated the last shadowman. This one would stay put.

'Together,' Maureen said.

They lifted the jewel between their right hands. Richard felt Maureen's cheek against his, and the side of her body as they slipped arms about each other. She had a few inches on him. Between their palms, the Seven Stars glowed.

They made their way to the far staircase.

Mrs Rochester – Jennifer God-Given – Geneviève Dieudonné – lay on a narrow, coffin-shaped pallet. A tie-dyed blanket was gathered over her legs. She looked a thousand years old, and was plugged into a standing dripfeed. A bandage was fixed to her side, stained with greenish seepage.

Her million wrinkles arranged themselves into a smile.

'I apologize for my appearance. Your uncle shot me, dear. With silver. If he'd had better aim, I'd not be here.'

'You know who I am?' Maureen said.

'Madame Sosostris knows all,' Geneviève intoned.

309

Another name? No, a joke.

They set the jewel down at the old woman's feet. It nestled in the folds of her blanket, like a hot-water bottle.

'Edwin's gone,' Richard said.

'I know. He stepped into the shadows. Against my advice, but it's too late to bother with all that. He was, at heart, a good man. Despite everything.'

Maureen was clinging closer to Richard. For the first time, he had a sense she too was afraid. Her obvious courage was in need of the occasional injection of bravado.

'Will you die?' Maureen asked the ancient woman.

'No, no, no,' Geneviève chuckled. 'At least, not just yet. You might not think it to look at me, but I'm getting better. The tide of years caught up with me, but it's drawing away from the shore now.'

'Do you need our blood?'

Richard noticed only now the sharp little teeth in the old woman's shrunken mouth.

'Not yet,' Geneviève said. 'You mustn't think of me until you've bound the jewel. We've a chance to damp down the ill effects of its use, just briefly. There's a ritual which will truly end yesterday's War, which will pack back into the stone all the nastiness that has trickled out since we opened it up back in '44.'

'Will everything be . . . better?' Richard asked.

'Not really,' Geneviève admitted. 'Nuclear reactions will still be part of physics, and you all have to live with the consequences. All the rest of it, you must take responsibility for. The Jewel of Seven Stars didn't make men stupid or venal or mad. It just fed on those things and spewed them out a thousandfold. But with the stone wrapped, the old world will have a chance.'

'Why didn't Edwin perform this ritual?' Maureen asked.

'He'd spoiled himself for it. Something sad about a cat. And Catriona couldn't stand in for you. The participants have to be from both factions. You're a Mountmain, dear. And Richard

310

is the creature of the Diogenes Club. Adversaries whose allegiances run counter to the official history. Churchill and Hitler were equally opposed to Diogenes and aligned with your uncles. There were great villains on Edwin's side and saints tied up with the Mountmains. It's too late to blame anyone. You just have to end the cycle, to make way for that Aquarian nonsense.'

As Geneviève spoke, Maureen took his hand in a tigerish grip.

'This ritual,' he began, 'what exactly . . .?'

'What do you think?' Geneviève laughed.

Richard looked up into Maureen's eyes, and saw understanding in them.

Magical sex always struck Richard as contrived, requiring the consideration of mathematics in a process that worked best when run on sheer instinct. You had to keep your head full of angles of the compass and meaningless rituals, locked up within your own skull when your body wanted to flow mindlessly into another. And magick rituals tended to be performed on cold stone floors hardly suited to comfort or arousal.

This was not like that at all.

They were together on cushions spread over the *camera obscura* table, the jewel between them. In their own anomaly, they ebbed and flowed like the tides, bloodstreams and bodies pushed and pulled by primal forces. Daybreak brought fields and woods and buildings into the room, patterning their bodies. At the centre of a harmonious universe, energies poured in through their open minds, bound up and redirected by their coupling. Mirrors shone warm sunlight down on them.

Tantric sex, the most common form of sex magic, was all about building up spiritual energy by making love at length but never reaching the dissipation of climax.

This was not like that at all.

They peaked three times apiece.

'The seventh,' she whispered.

They passed the jewel between them, running it over their bodies. Richard looked through the stone, past the stars, seeing Maureen's face rubied with joy. They kissed the Jewel of Seven Stars, and Maureen took it, pressing it to her yoni.

He entered her again, pushing the weirdstone into her womb.

Joined by the jewel, they came again, finally, together, completing the pattern of seven stars.

Then they slept.

Richard awoke, all sense of time lost. His coat had been arranged around him.

Maureen was gone.

He still felt her, tasted her, scented her.

The Jewel of Seven Stars was gone too.

Dressed, clothes abrading the tender spots of his body, he explored the house.

The Hiroshima Shadow marked Edwin's passing.

Catriona was in Mrs Rochester's room. Geneviève was sitting up, hidden behind a veil of mosquito netting.

'She took the stone,' he said weakly.

'Her family have been after it for years,' said a voice from behind the netting.

'She visited,' Catriona said. 'After she left you, she came here. She was glowing, Richard.'

'Like a ripe orange,' the voice – so unlike Mrs Rochester's frail whisper – said, 'so full of *life* that she had some to share. Edwin made up for what he did with the stone, and she made up for what her uncle did to me.'

The veil fell.

The woman on the bed was not Mrs Rochester. She was lithe, red-lipped and unhurt. But it was Geneviève, young again.

SEVEN STARS

'Now,' she said, 'the old War is over.'

The anomaly was gone. The War was finished. A great purpose of his life, undefined in his mind until last night, was concluded. But he still had his darkness, the shadowed part of his mind and memory. Because a part of his life was gone, he clung tenaciously to what he could remember, fixing memories like butterflies pinned to a card. Edwin Winthrop was a memory now, and Mrs Rochester. And Maureen.

Their coming together ended something, cleared the stage for many beginnings. But that was it. Her taste would fade. But the memory would stay.

Geneviève got out of bed for the first time in thirty years. Her old woman's nightgown hung strangely on a body barely grown. Underneath her years, she was impossibly young. She hugged Catriona, and Richard. She danced on the points of her toes. The jewel-light shone in eyes reddened by Maureen's blood.

Catriona was bereft, Geneviève reborn.

What of Richard Jeperson? What of the Diogenes Club?

A fresh cycle would begin.

Episode 5: Mimsy   *1999*

One day in Spring, the Devil called her.

'Sally Rhodes Investigations,' she said brightly into the phone, trying to sound like a receptionist.

'Miss Rhodes,' he said, voice distorted a little, perhaps addressed to a speaker phone, 'this is Derek Leech.'

She hung up.

The voice had scraped her bones.

She looked from the office half of her front room to the living room half. Jerome, her son, was building a Lego robot, notionally supervised by Neil, her boyfriend, who was curled on the ancient sofa, making notes on a scribble-pad. Neil was still assembling an argument for the book he'd been thinking of starting for three years. Lego structures spread about the floor, weaving round the cat-basket and several of Neil's abandoned coffee mugs.

Normality, she thought.

Kid. Man. Pet. Toys. A mess, but a mess she could cope with, a mess she loved.

The phone rang again. She let it.

The office half of the room was ordered, different. A computer, a fax, files, a desk. This was where she thought. Over there, on the sofa, amid the lovable mess, was where she felt.

She was breaking her own rules.

The ringing phone jarred on her emotions.

At her desk, she was in business. She had to be harder, stronger.

She picked up the phone, but didn't announce herself.

'Miss Rhodes, for every second you don't hang up, I shall donate one hundred pounds to your favoured charity, which is, I believe, Shelter.'

It did not surprise her that Leech knew she supported Help for the Homeless. The multi-media magnate knew everything about everyone. Atop his Pyramid in London Docklands, he had all the knowledge of the world at his disposal.

'Go ahead,' she said.

'Regardless of our past differences, I admire your independence of spirit.'

'Thank you. Now what is this about?'

'A friend of mine needs your services.'

'You have friends?'

She imagined Leech had only acolytes, employees and possessions.

'The finest friends money can buy, my dear. That was a joke. You may laugh.'

'Ha ha ha.'

'My friend's name is Maureen Mountmain. She has a daughter, Mimsy, who has gone missing. Maureen would like to retain you to find her.'

'You must have people who could do that. If this Maureen Mountmain is really your friend, why don't you turn the dogs loose?'

'You have resources no one I employ could have.'

That was the most frightening thing anyone had ever said to her. Leech let it hang in the air.

'Sally, you've inconvenienced me. Twice. Your life would be much easier if you had chosen not to stand in my way. You have something of the purity of a saint. No one in my organization can say as much. Only someone of your virtues could handle this job. I appeal to you, as a secular saint, to help my friend.'

She let seconds tick by.

'Do you accept?'

She counted slowly up to ten in her mind, making a thousand pounds for the homeless.

'I'll take the job,' she said, 'on condition that I'm retained by this Mrs Mountmain . . .'

'Miss.'

'. . . Miss Mountmain, and not by you personally or any sneaky subsidiary company.'

'You'll not take the King's shilling.'

'Cursed gold?'

Leech laughed, like ice-cubes cracking in a bowl of warm blood.

'Once this call is completed, your business is with the Mountmains. I act, in this instance, only as intermediary.'

She knew there was a hidden clause somewhere. With Leech, nothing was straightforward. His way was to rely on the fallibility of those he dealt with. Despite his stated opinion of her, she knew she was as likely to be gulled into a moral trap as anyone else.

Jerome pestered Neil for his expert opinion on the robot spider scuttling around the floor.

'My associate, Ms Wilding, will give details of the

315

appointment she has arranged for you with Miss Mountmain. I have enjoyed this conversation. Goodbye.'

The phone clicked, and a woman came on. Sally took down an address and a time.

When she hung up, she realized her heart was racing. It had been a while.

She'd been working on everyday stuff these last few years. As it happened, she'd done a lot of work with runaway children. Though sometimes she walked away well-paid and satisfied from a tearful reunion, she more often traced some kid caught between a horrific home life and an ordeal on the streets, then wound up sucked into an emotional, legal and ethical Gordian knot.

The weird stuff was in her past.

Even with Jerome and Neil, physical left-overs from that period of her life, in the flat, she'd almost convinced herself she didn't live in that world any more. She had kept up with the inescapable growth of Derek Leech's earthly dominion, but tried to forget the strange devices at its heart.

Perhaps she was wrong. Perhaps he wasn't the Devil, but just an ambitious businessman. He had used magic in the past, but that was only trickery. Conjuring, not sorcery.

She tried and failed to convince herself.

'Mummy, look, I've made a monster.'

'Lovely,' she said. 'Neil, you're on kid-watch and the phone. I'm out on business.'

Neil looked up at her and waved a cheery paw.

'I accept the mission,' he said.

She kissed them both and left the flat.

The address she had been given turned out to be a Georgian mansion in Wimpole Street. It stood out among perfectly preserved neighbours, showing signs of dilapidation and abuse. By contrast with polished brass door-trimmings and blue plaques announcing the former residence of the great and good, the Mountmain house looked like a squat. Over the lintel was spray-painted 'Declan Mountmain, Terrorist and Devil-Worshipper, Lived Here 1888-1897'.

Maureen Mountmain, who answered the door herself, was tall and thin, with a strange red streak through snow-white hair. She wore long black velvet skirts and a tatted shawl over a leather waistcoat. Her neck and wrists were ringed with jade and pearls. Her face was stretched tight, but Sally didn't see tell-tale face-lift scars. Tiny blue tattoos were picked out under her chin. There was a great strength in her but she lacked substance, as if every surplus atom had been sucked away over the years.

Sally wanted to ask how well Maureen knew Derek Leech, and what their connection was, but that wasn't the point.

She was hurried into the hallway, which stank of patchouli. The original wooden panels had been painted over with dull purple. Childish patterns, like the crescent moons and stars on a cartoon wizard's conical cap, were scattered across the walls and ceiling. On a second look, Sally saw the painting-over extended to framed pictures which still hung, chameleoned, up the staircase.

'When she was little, Mimsy only liked purple,' Maureen said, proudly. 'She can be very insistent.'

'Do you have any pictures of her?'

'At an early age, she heard about the aboriginal belief that photographs could capture souls. She smashed any cameras she saw. With a hammer.'

Sally thought about that for a moment. She wondered if Mimsy took her hammer with her.

'Any drawings or portraits?' she asked.

Maureen shuddered. 'Even worse. Mimsy believes art not only captures the soul but distorts and malforms it.'

'She's very concerned with her soul.'

'Mimsy is extremely religious.'

'Did she attend any particular church? That might be a good place to start looking for her.'

Maureen shrugged. As Sally's eyes got used to the gloom of

the hall, she noticed just how distracted Maureen Mountmain was. Her pupils were shrunk to black pin-holes.

'Mimsy rejects organized religion. She has declared herself the Avatar of the Ram. She hopes to revive the Society of the Ram, an occult congregation my family has often been involved with.'

'Devil-Worshipper and Terrorist?'

'Mimsy put that up there. She was proud of her heritage.'

'Are you?'

Maureen was unwilling to say.

Sally knew something had happened to this woman. Deep down inside her, there was extraordinary resilience, but it had been besieged and eroded. Maureen Mountmain was a walking remnant. It was too early to be sure, but Sally had an idea how Miss Mountmain had been broken and who had done the deed.

'Might Mimsy be with her father? You live apart?'

Again, Maureen was unwilling, but this time she put an answer together.

'Mimsy doesn't know her father. He is . . . unavailable to her.'

'If it's not a rude question, do *you* know Mimsy's father?'

For the first time, Maureen smiled. In her wistfulness, she was beautiful. Sally knew from the flicker of wattage that this woman had once shone like a lantern.

'I know who Mimsy's father is.'

She didn't volunteer any more.

'May I see Mimsy's room?'

Maureen led her upstairs. The whole first floor of the house was a ruin. Several fires had started but failed to take. A medieval tapestry, of knights hunting something in green woods, was half scorched away, leaving the men in armour surrounding a suggestive brown shape. There were broken items of furniture, statuary and ceramic piled in a corner.

Maureen indicated a door smashed on its hinges.

'You say Mimsy left,' Sally said. 'You don't think she was abducted?'

'She walked out of this house on her own. But she might not have been herself.'

'I don't understand.'

'She took with her a precious item. A keepsake, if you will. Something that was important once. It was her belief that this item communicated with her, issued orders. A large red stone.'

'A ruby?'

'Not exactly. The weirdstone is known as the Seven Stars, because of a formation of light-catching flaws which look like the constellation.'

Maureen angled up her chin to show her tattoos. Sally realized they were seven blue eyes, also configured like the Great Bear.

'Is this jewel valuable?'

'Many would pay dearly for it. I certainly did, though not in money. But it's not a thing which can be owned. It is a thing which owns.'

'Mimsy thought this jewel talked to her?'

Maureen nodded.

Sally looked around the room. After the build-up, it was a surprisingly ordinary teenager's bedroom. A single bed with a frilly duvet, matched by all the lampshades. Posters of David Duchovny, Brad Pitt and a pretty boy pop singer she was too out-of-date to recognize. A shelf of books: thick occult-themed paperback nonsense – *Flying Saucers From Ancient Atlantis* – mixed with black-spined, obviously old hardbacks. Outgrown toys were placed like trophies on a mantelpiece: Turtles, Muppets, a withered rag doll.

She tried to imagine Mimsy. Long ago, before all the weirdness, Sally had taken a degree in child psychology. It was just about her only real qualification.

'Imaginary friends are projections,' she suggested. 'Mimsy might have displaced on to the jewel, using its "voice" to escape responsibility. It's more sophisticated than "I didn't break the vase, the pixies did", it's "I broke the vase, but I was obeying orders".'

'Mimsy is twenty-seven,' Maureen said. 'In her life, she has never made an excuse or obeyed orders. It is her belief that the jewel talks. I don't doubt this is true.'

'A subjective truth, maybe.'

'You don't believe that, Miss Rhodes. You know Derek Leech. You know better. There's such a thing as Magic. And such a thing as Evil.'

Sally was off balance. She had thought this was about a teenage runaway.

'Does she have a job? A boyfriend?'

'She can always get money from people. And she has lovers. None of them means anything. Mimsy has only one emotional tie.'

'To you?'

'No. To the weirdstone.'

'Neil, pick up,' she told her own answerphone.

She was calling from her mobile, out in the open in Soho Square. Merciless sun shone down, but the dry air was cold.

Neil came on, grumbling.

'I thought you were answering the phone,' she said.

'Jermo and I were watching *Thunderbirds*.'

She let that pass.

'I need you to do some research, historical stuff.'

One of Neil's uses was trawling the Internet for ostensibly useless information. He had even been known on occasion to go physically to a library and open a book.

'Write these keywords down. The Jewel of Seven Stars, the Society of the Ram.'

'Dennis Wheatley novels?'

'One's an object, the other's a cult. And see what you can find out about the Mountmain family. Specifically, a fellow named Declan Mountmain from the late nineteenth century, and a couple of contemporary women, Maureen – must be in her late forties though she doesn't look it – and Mimsy, twenty-seven.'

320

'As in borogoves.'

'Mimsy. No, it's not short for anything.'

'No wonder she ran away from home. Calling a kid Mimsy is semiotic child abuse.'

'There are worse kinds.'

She folded up the phone and thought. Mimsy's father – whoever he might be – was out of the picture, supposedly. She'd accept that for now.

Unconsciously, she had come to the square to make her call. It was where she had met Jerome's father. Connor had been lolling on the benches with the other bike messengers, waiting for jobs to come in. He had been killed in a street accident, also near here.

She was reminded not to trust Derek Leech.

Mimsy, obviously, was a horror. But how much of one? Spoiled brat or Antichrist? She found herself aching for Mimsy's Mumsy. Despite purple panels and hippie scent, and the timid worrying at the memory of her daughter, Maureen was a survivor. She wondered if she was looking at her own future in Maureen Mountmain.

Sally had a tattoo. A porpoise on her ankle. That didn't make her strange. She had worked on a case once with Harry D'Amour, an American private detective who was covered in tattoos which he claimed worked as a psychic armour. You needed armour for what was most vulnerable, and you couldn't tattoo your heart.

'What's up, Sal?'

Her ex-boyfriend sat down next to her. He wore Lycra cycling shorts and a joke T-shirt with a thick tyre-track across the chest.

'Hello, Connor,' she said, unfazed.

'I've never thanked you for avenging my death,' he said.

He looked impossibly young in the bright sunshine. He had been nearly two-thirds her age. Now he was just over half her age.

'You look good,' he said.

321

'I dye my hair.'

'But just a little.'

'Just. You have a son. He's a good kid. Jerome.'

'I didn't know.'

'I thought you might not.'

'She's a strange one, Sal. That's why I'm here. Why I've been allowed to talk to you.'

'This is about Mimsy Mountmain?'

Connor looked sheepish. They hadn't been together long and, baby or not, it wouldn't have lasted. He had always been looking for an angle, less interested in a leg over than a leg up. But she was sorry he had been killed.

Jerome loved Neil – that was one reason Neil had lasted – but had grown up, like Mimsy, without a Dad.

'It's not so much Mimsy, it's this rock thing. The jewel. You're to mind out for it. It can cause a lot of trouble. Not just for you there, but for me here. For us here.'

'Where is here?'

'Somewhere else. You'd be able to explain it. I can't. Sorry, Sal. Gotta rush.'

He stood up and looked around. She wondered if he'd come on his bike.

'Did I ever tell you I loved you?'

'No.'

'Funny that.'

He left. Sally wondered why she was crying.

When she got back to Muswell Hill, she heard the retch of the printer as she climbed the steps to her flat. After her ghostly encounter, she had spent an afternoon getting in touch with old contacts who knew something about what is euphemistically known as 'alternative religion'. Though a few of them had heard of Declan Mountmain as a historical fruitcake, no one could tell her anything about his present-day descendants.

She let herself in, and found Neil and Jerome busy downloading and printing out. In the last few months, Jerome had gone from helping Neil with the computer to being impatient with the grown-up's inability to get on as well with the machine as he did.

'There's a lot of dirt, Sal-love,' Neil announced, proudly.

Sally hugged Jerome, surprising him.

'Gerroff,' he said, wriggling.

She laughed. She had needed contact with Connor's flesh-and-bone offspring. It grounded her, dispersed some of the weirdness build-up.

'It wasn't Dennis Wheatley,' Neil said. 'It was Bram Stoker. He wrote a novel called *The Jewel of Seven Stars*. It was made into a Hammer Film with Valerie Leon.'

Like a great many men his age, Neil had encyclopedic recall of the bosomy starlets who appeared in the Bond films, Hammer Horrors, Carry Ons and *Two Ronnies* sketches of the early 1970s.

'You know Stoker based Dracula on Vlad the Impaler. He also based this *Seven Stars* effort on scraps of truth. It's about an Ancient Egyptian witch who possesses a modern lass. There was, apparently, a real Jewel of Seven Stars, found in a proper mummy's tomb. It disappeared after a break-in at the British Museum in 1897. Guess who was the number-one suspect?'

'Is this like Jack the Ripper? Pick an eminent Victorian?'

'No. It's highly guessable. I'm talking Declan Mountmain, who was sort of a cross between Aleister Crowley and Patrick Bergin in *Patriot Games*. Half mad warlock, half psycho Irish separatist. He tried to blow up Lord's, during a Gentlemen *v.* Players match. He had a nephew, Bennett, who was by all accounts even worse. He was in with the Nazis in World War Two and was killed in Los Angeles while spying for Hitler.'

'No wonder Maureen's off her head.'

'I've got some great shots from a Hippie History website, of Maureen at Glastonbury in 1968. She's got up as a fertility priestess, body-painted green all over and extremely topless. I

323

had to send Jermo into the other room while I downloaded them.'

'I saw the rude lady,' Jerome piped up.

'Well, I tried to send him. Anyway, Maureen was not only the Wiccan babe of the Summer of Love but an early *Comet* Knock-Out, one of Derek Leech's first Page Three girls. Those shots will be on the Net somewhere, but you have to pay a fee to get them. Do you think Leech is this Mimsy's father?'

She thought about it. It fitted together, perhaps a bit too neatly.

'There are other players in this. And the jewel comes into it somehow.'

'I've got a big cast for you, going back a hundred years, snatched from a lot of occult and paranoid conspiracy sites, the type you have to play sword-and-sorcery games to get on to. Some famous names. But there are interesting gaps. Names rubbed out of the record, like those pharaohs who were so disgraceful that they were removed from history. I keep coming across these references to "the War" in contexts that make me wonder which one is being fought.'

She looked at the sheaf of printed-out articles for a while, trying to piece it all together.

'It's this bloody stone,' she said, at last. 'That's what's wrong. In 1897, it supposedly disappears. Then it turns up in a treasure chest in Wimpole Street and waltzes off with Mimsy. But there's this one tiny mention of it in the reports of Bennett Mountmain's death in Los Angeles.'

'So he took it on holiday? Maybe it was a talisman of his devotion to the Führer.'

'But how does it come to Maureen, and Mimsy? In 1942, this Captain "W" of the deleted name seems to have snatched it back for England. Or Egypt. Or Science. I think the jewel has been stolen back and forth between two krewes down the years. The Mountmains and some other shower, the mystery "W"'s bunch. The others mentioned only by initials. Mr "B" from 1897, even this "R.J." from the seventies. We need more about the Initials. Could you spend tomorrow on it? You might have to stir yourself to the British Museum and the Newspaper Library.'

'I'll take Jermo to see the mummies.'

Jerome stuck his arms out and limped across the room.

'How does he know what the Mummy walks like, Neil?' she asked. 'Have you been showing him your Hammer videos?'

'He gets it from *Scooby-Doo*.'

She playfully strangled him.

'So perish all unbelievers who defile the innocent minds of young children,' she intoned, solemnly.

They kissed and cuddled, and Jerome told them not to be soppy.

If a grown-up woman of twenty-seven wants to go missing and not be found, the legal position is that it's very much her business. Here, the abandoned mother might be able to lay a charge of theft against the absconded daughter, but Sally now knew enough about the Seven Stars to realize accusing anyone of stealing it would result in a potentially endless series of criss-cross counter-charges.

Mimsy had walked out of her mother's house a week ago.

Maureen had at last coughed up an address book, with Mimsy's friends marked by pink felt-tip-pen asterisks.

Sally spent two days making telephone calls.

None of Mimsy's 'friends' – current worshippers, cast-off lovers, bedazzled sidekicks, bitter rivals – admitted any knowledge of her.

But the drudgery was useful.

Everyone she talked with revealed, by their attitude, a bit more about the quarry. The impression Sally had already gained from Maureen was strengthening by the minute.

Mimsy Mountmain was quite a package. In her early teens, she'd made a million pounds as a songwriter. Sally remembered the titles of a few pop hits whose tunes and lyrics had vanished from her mind. She hadn't needed to work since but had published a series of slim volumes of poetry in an invented language.

At sixteen, she put a young man into a coma by battering him with a half-brick. The court returned a verdict of self-defence and she was written up, in the *Comet* among other papers, as a have-a-go heroine. Then, under less clear-cut circumstances, she did it again. This time, the cracked skull belonged to a married bank manager rather than an unemployed football fan. She did three years in Holloway, and came out as the undisputed princess of the prison.

Her ex-lovers were all stand-outs. Politicians, celebs, serious wealth, famous criminals, beauties and monsters. Some of them hadn't come through the Mimsy Mountmain Experience without sustaining severe damage.

It might be that Mimsy was more than just missing.

She tried to read one of Mimsy's poems. Without being in the least comprehensible, it gave her the shudders. She had an idea Mimsy was up to something.

'It's not a family,' Neil said, without taking off his coat, 'it's a club.'

Sally looked up. Neil brought Jerome into the flat.

'We saw mummies!' her son said.

Neil flopped open a notebook. 'Ever heard of a journo named Katharine Reed? Irish, turn of the century, bit of a firebrand?'

Sally hadn't.

'She left a memoir, and in that memoir she alludes in an offhand way to a Charles Beauregard who is almost certainly your Mr "B". The *DNB* has pages on him. Reading between the lines, he was something between a spy and a spy-catcher.'

'I know the feeling.'

'He became something high up in the Secret Service, and his protégé was a Captain Edwin Winthrop.'

'Him I've heard of. He co-wrote a book about authentic hauntings in the West Country. Sometime in the Twenties.'

'That's the one. And he is your Captain "W", to be found in Hollywood in 1942.'

Sally considered hugging Neil.

But the mention of the Secret Service was unsettling.

'These initials. Our mystery men. You're saying they're spooks?'

'Yes. Authentic hauntings.'

'Have you a name for the last one, "R.J."?'

'Sadly, 1972 wasn't long enough ago for any of the secret stuff to have been disclosed yet. And a lot of the files on the others, even Beauregard, are sealed until well into Jerome's adult life. He'll have to finish the puzzle.'

'I'm going to be a spy when I grow up,' Jerome announced.

'That'll be useful,' she said. 'What did you mean about a club?'

Neil grinned. 'You'll love this. Remember Mycroft Holmes?'

'Who?'

'Brother of the more famous . . .?'

'Sherlock?'

'Give the girl a kiss,' he said, and did. 'Yep, Mycroft, who Conan Doyle informs us "sometimes *was* the British Government", was, as it turns out, a real person. His private fiefdom was a gentlemen's club in Pall Mall, the Diogenes. It was a cover for a special section of British Intelligence. When Mycroft retired or died, this Beauregard took over and played the hush-hush game even more seriously. For the best part of this century, the Diogenes Club was Britain's own Department of Weird Shit. You know what I mean.'

'Only too well.'

'Aside from the wonderful Kate Reed, none of the people mixed up in this thought to write memoirs – though I've found references to a suppressed issue of *Black Mask* which supposedly ran a story that gave away too much – which means it's all locked up in Whitehall somewhere. When you sort this out . . .'

'When!'

'When. I have confidence in you. Anyway, when you sort this out, there might be a book in the Diogenes Club. Britain's *X-Files*. There's a hook. And at this late date, the secrecy issue is long dead.'

'I'm not so sure about that.'

'Come on, Sal-love. It's great stuff. Look, mummy's curses, Sherlock Holmes, Hooray for Hollywood, spies and ghosts, a fabulous lost treasure, Nazi Irishmen, hippie chicks with extremely large breasts, politics and black magic, terrorism, old dark houses, the plague.'

'Think it through, Neil. You say it's all still secret.'

'Just bureaucracy. We can get in there.'

'When the War is over, the secrets come out. We know about that Scottish island Churchill dosed with anthrax? The Eastern Bloc refugees we handed over to Stalin for genocide? All that came out. Why not this stuff about the jewel?'

'Too trivial to be taken seriously. I mean, it's absurd, right? Spooks.'

'When the War is over, the secrets come out. These secrets aren't out. Because the War isn't over.'

'You're being a wet blanket, love.'

She backed off from an argument. Neil didn't like being a dependant, but none of his outside projects ever quite came together. And he resisted being brought into the firm as a partner.

'I'm sorry,' she said.

While she was on the bus, her mobile bleeped. It was Maureen. Sally ran down the list of the people she'd talked with, and floated out some of the material Neil had gathered on the Diogenes Club. Surprisingly, a door opened. Then closed again.

'They're out of business,' Maureen said. 'Have been for a long time. Winthrop I knew. At the end. That was the last War. This is something new.'

'Is it about Mimsy or the Seven Stars?'

Maureen hesitated.

The bus was stuck in Camden High Street.

'Sally, when you find Mimsy ... you won't hurt her, will you?'

She thought of the two coma men. Only one had got better.

'If she doesn't want to come home, that's fine by me,' said Maureen. 'I just want to know if she's all right.'

She had heard that on every missing child case. If Jerome wandered off, she wouldn't be convinced he was all right until he was back home. But Jerome wasn't twenty-seven.

'I think Mimsy can take care of herself,' she said, trying to reassure Maureen.

'The Jewel of Seven Stars isn't important to me.'

After Maureen had rung off and the traffic started moving again, Sally thought to ask herself the question.

So, who is the jewel important to?

A morphing billboard outside the bus shifted from an ad for the new *Dr Shade* movie to one for the *Daily Comet* to one for Cloud 9 satellite TV. All Derek Leech products.

The traffic thickened again, and Sally felt trapped.

Despite what she had told Neil and Maureen had told her, she had to go to Pall Mall. It wasn't that she thought this Diogenes Club was germane to the investigation, but she wanted to look at it, to block off that avenue before it took up too much time. Besides, she was curious.

It took several wanders up and down the Mall before she found the tiny brass plate on the big oak doors. All it said was Members Only. The building was shuttered and out of use. She hammered on the doors, to see if she could raise some member from a decades-long sleep. No one came.

She stood away from the building.

The Mall was busy, with Easter Holiday tourists enjoying the country's new climate in short-sleeved shirts and pastel dresses. There might be a drought on, but she could get used to this Californian London. Doom-merchants, however, said it was a sign of the end of the world.

A slim blonde girl in white wafted across very green grass, towards her. She wore a wide-brimmed straw hat and dark glasses with lenses the size and colour of apples.

For a moment, she thought this was another ghost. It was something about the way the light hit her hair. She reminded Sally of Connor.

'Nobody home,' the girl said.

She was too young to be Mimsy, not yet out of her teens. She had the trace of an accent.

Sally shrugged.

'You're looking for the jewel,' the girl said.

Through the green lenses, tiny red points shone. This pretty waif had enormously hungry eyes.

'I'm looking for the woman who has the jewel,' Sally said.

'Mimsy,' the girl said, head cocked. 'Poor dear.'

'I'm Sally Rhodes. Who are you?'

'Geneviève Dieudonné. Call me Gené.'

'Are you Mimsy's friend?'

Gené smiled, dazzling. Sally realized this girl had an archness and composure that didn't fit with her initial estimate of her age.

'I've never met her. But I *feel* her. I share blood with her mother. That was a great sacrifice for Maureen. She was just pregnant. There's a sliver of me in Maureen, left behind like a sting in a wound. And a tinier sliver in Mimsy. Along with all the other stuff. She was conceived around the Jewel of Seven Stars. That's why it speaks to her.'

Gené wasn't insane. But she was talking about things beyond Sally's experience.

'The bauble that causes the trouble, Sally,' Gené said. 'I've danced with the stone, like the gentlemen who used to doze beyond those doors, like the Mountmain Line. Down the years we all revolve around the Seven Stars. Sometimes, years and years slip by and I don't think of the thing, but always it's there, the knowledge that I share the planet with the Jewel of Seven Stars, that it'll be back.'

'That's an odd way of putting it.'

'I'm an odd sort of person.'

'Are you one of Leech's?'

'Good Heavens, no. I've been called a leech, though.'

When Gené smiled, she showed sharp little teeth, like hooks carved of white ice.

'What do you want from me?'

'A partnership. I help you find the girl, and you let me have the jewel.'

'What do you want with it?'

'What do people want with jewels? I wish I knew. Since you ask, I'll tell you. If possible, I'll get rid of it. It was buried for thousands of years without causing too much trouble. If I could securely bury it again, or stow it away on a deep-space probe, I'd do it. It fell out of the sky once. For years, I wondered about those seven flaws, the seven stars. Then, when we launched *Voyager*, I understood. On our rocket we engraved a star map, to show where it came from. The jewel is dangerous, and I want to damp the fire. Satisfied?'

'Not really.'

'I wouldn't be either. You remind me of myself at your age. Seriously, Mimsy – whether she knows it or not, and I think she does and welcomes it – is in danger as long as she has that stone with her. Your job, I understand, is to find Mimsy and make sure she's safe . . .'

How had she known that?

'. . . and I can help you.'

'If you can find Mimsy, why don't you? Why do you need me?'

'I'm not a solo sort of person. Difficult in my position, but there you are. I work best with a stout-hearted comrade. Someone to keep me down to earth.'

'I like you, Gené. Why is that?'

'Good taste.'

Gené kissed Sally on the cheek, with an electric touch.

'Come on, Sal. Let's get a cab. I think I know where to start.'

331

Sally was usually sparing with taxi travel. It was still most practical to get around London on the bus and tube, and she had to account for her expenses. But Gené had a handbag full of money, in several different currencies. She got them into a black cab and told the driver to take them to Docklands.

'You rattled a lot of webs when you went through Maureen Mountmain's address book,' Gené explained. 'Bells rang, and I hopped on a plane from Palermo. I've read up on you. You're good. They'd have liked you at the Diogenes Club, though they were funny about women.'

It was evening now. Not dark yet, but the light was thin and cold. They were venturing into Docklands just as most people were leaving. The Eighties modern office buildings were unnaturally clean in their emptiness: life-sized toys fresh from their boxes.

The black glass pyramid caught the last of the sun.

'It's coming back to Leech,' Sally said.

'Not really. But I think you'd have come here yourself soon.'

'If I can help it, I stay away.'

'Understood. But you've covered Mimsy's human connections with no luck. You're drawing back and looking at the whole picture. That's what made you go to the Mall. What you have to do is think of yourself as part of the pattern, to see how you fit in, where you can be triangulated.'

Sally saw what she meant.

'I'm in the pattern because of Leech. He doesn't do anything for no reason. This isn't a favour to a friend. This is part of a plan.'

Gené clapped.

'I'm the last person Leech loves. He said – and he's always annoyingly truthful – that only I could do this job. He wants me to find Mimsy.'

'And the Seven Stars,' prompted Gené.

'There's a link between Leech and Mimsy. It's broken, or at least played out to its full length. Is he after the jewel?'

'Leech's dominion is of this world,' Gené said. 'He only wants what I want, to keep the Seven Stars out of circulation. I'm not happy to make common cause with him, but there you are. This business scrambles all your allegiances.'

'I thought Leech might be Mimsy's father.'

'Good guess, but no. That was Richard Jeperson, one of the Diogenes fellows. Mimsy is unpredictable precisely because she is the fruit of an opposition, the Mountmain Line and the Diogenes Club. And whatever I threw in didn't help. Whatever havoc she wreaks, we can all take the blame.'

Gené had the cab stop a few streets away from the Pyramid.

When it had driven off, the road was empty. The last of the light was going. It was a cloudless night, but the blanket of sodium orange street-lighting kept the stars at bay.

'One of the reasons I like you, Sal, is that you believe me. Over the years, almost no one has. Not at first. But you've stepped into the dark enough times to know the truth when you hear it.'

They looked up at the Pyramid.

'The Jewel of Seven Stars is a tool for ending empires,' Gené said. 'It ended the rule of a pharaoh. Declan Mountmain wanted to use it on Britain. Bennett Mountmain thought he could win the War for Hitler. Edwin Winthrop turned it on Germany and Japan. It could be used on that Pyramid.'

Sally imagined Leech's empire in ruins.

'But there's a cost. The world is still living with the consequences of the way Edwin and the Diogenes Club wound up the last War. I think Leech is one of those consequences. If the times weren't out of joint, he wouldn't have taken hold and grown like a cancer.'

'Leech thinks Mimsy is a *threat*?' She couldn't believe it. But it made sense. 'A mad woman from a long line of mad people? Armed with a chunk of dubious crystal? Do you have any idea of just who Derek Leech is? Of how far beyond human reckoning he is?'

'Why you, Sal? Why did he pick you?'

'He said I was a saint.'

Gené spread her arms and opened her hands.

'I'm not a saint. I'm a single mum. I'm kissing forty. My life and business lurch from crisis to crisis.'

'*Twice* you've stopped him, Sal. You've saved people from him.'

'In the end, that meant nothing. He had other plans.'

'No one else has ever stopped him. Not once.'

Sally saw what Gené meant. 'So I'm the only person he can think of who could stand between him and Mimsy.'

'Not just Mimsy.'

The night was all around. Gené took off her dark glasses. Her eyes were alive and ancient, points of red burning in their depths.

They had spent the night by the Pyramid. Nothing had happened. Her instinctive faith in Gené's inside knowledge was fraying. It would have been much more convenient if Mimsy had turned up in Derek Leech's lobby, brandishing the Jewel of Seven Stars like a *Star Trek* phaser.

Red light came up in the east, and Sally phoned for a minicab. She didn't think the night wasted.

She and Gené – Geneviève – had talked.

Without saying what she was, Gené had revealed a lot. She filled in, apparently from personal knowledge, a lot of the gaps. If Neil ever wrote his book, she'd be a prime source. But she wasn't scary, like Leech. She was proof that you could live with the weirdness and not be swallowed up by it. She had a real personality.

Gené had made mistakes. She said what she thought, without filtering it through a brain that framed everything as a series of crossword clues with hidden killer clauses.

In the cab, Gené was jittery.

'I'm sorry,' she said. 'I led you down the wrong path. Something happened last night. And we missed it. My fault. I thought the Seven Stars would revolve round Leech. Maybe

334

they will, but not yet. Maybe there's too much Mimsy in the brew . . .'

Her mobile jarred her out of the half-sleep she had fallen into. The minicab was caught in the morning influx of commuters into Docklands.

It was Neil.

'The police have been round,' he said. 'It's to do with your client. She's been killed, Sal-love.'

She was shocked awake.

'Maureen?'

'Yes. You'll have to check in and give a statement. The pigs know you were working for her.'

Cold inside, she asked the question.

'Was it Mimsy?'

'She wasn't killed with a hammer. From what they let slip, I don't think it could have been murder. She had an allergic reaction to insect bites.'

Sally hung up and redirected the cab driver to Wimpole Street. She told Gené what had happened.

'Bitten to death?' Gené mused.

There was a policeman at the door, but Sally got through by saying she had been asked to give a statement. Gené looked at the man over her sunglasses and was waved in without comment.

'Neat trick.'

'You wouldn't want to learn it.'

The hallway was changed. All the purple paint was gone and there was a thick, crunchy carpet. Sally realized she was standing on a layer of bloated, dead flies. The purple paint had been stripped by a million tiny mouths, which had etched into the surfaces of everything. A cloud must have filled the house. The curtains were eaten away completely; dried white smears scabbed the window-glass.

'She's trying to use it,' Gené said.

'I have to see,' Sally said.

'I know.'

They went upstairs. Policemen stood around the landing, and a couple of forensic people were expressing appalled puzzlement. Photographs were being taken.

A detective inspector issued orders that none of this was to be released to the press. He looked a hundred years old, and was too tired to shout at anyone for letting Sally and Gené into the house.

Sally explained who she was and that the dead woman had hired her to find her missing daughter. She admitted she hadn't managed to do so.

'If she's missing the way her Mum is, you might as well give the money back.'

'To whom?' she asked.

Actually, she hadn't been paid in advance. Leech would certainly cover it, but Sally didn't want to take his tainted money.

'It's not an allergic reaction,' Gené said. 'Flies don't sting.'

'No,' the inspector agreed. 'They chew.'

Sally looked into Mimsy's room. Maureen Mountmain lay on the bed. She was only recognizable by her distinctive hair, white with a red streak. Her naked bones lay in a nest of dead flies.

'It's started,' Gené said.

She had tried to call Neil but couldn't get through. Gené was silent in the cab, seeming far older after the long night and the horrors of Wimpole Street. There was a long-shot suggestion that it was all down to the new climate, hatching flies early and driving them mad.

Sally tried not to be anxious. There was no home to bring Mimsy back to. She was off the case. In Muswell Hill, Gené dropped her off.

'Don't worry, Sal. It'll take years. I'm sorry to lose you, but you can get on with your life. It comes down to those of us who

336

live outside human time, Leech and me and the Seven Stars. Give my love to your son. I'd like to meet him one day.'

Sally watched the cab go. She wondered where Gené was headed. She had said something about needing to get in out of the sun. And getting something to drink.

If she was going to fail anyone, she was glad it was Leech – she thought now that he had wanted her to check Mimsy, somehow – though she was ripped open and bled empty about Maureen.

She went upstairs.

She had not been able to get a call through because Neil was using the modem, digging up material on the Fourth Plague of Egypt. He thought it was germane to the investigation.

'There is no investigation, dear,' she said. 'No client.'

Jerome wandered in, dressed in his too-small pyjamas.

'Who was the pretty lady?' he asked.

'Were you peeking out your window?'

He didn't answer.

'Okay,' she said. 'I give up. What was the Fourth Plague of Egypt?'

'You should know that,' Neil said. 'It's in *The Abominable Dr Phibes*. Flies.'

'You won't be out of pocket,' Leech said. 'I've authorized a payment. You may forward it to Shelter, if you wish.'

'I don't deserve to get paid. I did nothing. I found out nothing. Mimsy is still missing. And the Jewel of Seven Stars.'

The phone was cool in her hand.

'You *have* found something out, then.'

Leech sounded different. Tired? Maybe it was the connection?

'A little. Nothing relevant.'

'I had hoped you might influence Mimsy, by your example. I see now that was overly ambitious of me.'

Had he set Sally Rhodes, with her sword of righteousness,

337

against Mimsy Mountmain, with her weirdstone, hoping they would cancel each other out?

'Can she hurt you, Derek?' she asked.

'This call is over. Good-bye, Sally.'

She listened to the dead line. It was now a question of living with the fear, of getting through the plague years. Derek Leech had an empire, and she had a computer-crazed kid and a boyfriend who'd never grow up. She knew, at last, that she was fitter to survive.

Episode 6: The Dog Story   2025

The client had fixed the meetsite, Pall Mall. Neutral ground, equidistant from his Islington monad and her Brixton piedater. He was used to getting-about. Types who needed an Information Analyst didn't want the need known. It usually meant they were in a reverse, and even a rumour could key terminal panic. Vastcorps were conservative, prone to dump at the first smokesign, trailing a plankton-field of small investors who'd unload at decreasingly sensible prices. A whisper could drag down an empire toot sweet.

Though he spoke with what he knew from old teevee to be an English accent, Jerome thought of Pall Mall, like all else, as Paul Maul.

The London Board of Directors had got so weary of Former Americans visiting the Mall and asking where the stores were that the strip had been rezoned for commercial development. Preservation-ordered buildings, no longer needed after the out-shifting of admin to Bletchley, were sub-divided into franchise premises: Leechmart, Banana Democracy, Guns'n'Ammo, Killergrams. Some stores here were so chic they had actual goods in stock, for real-life inspection.

The client had called the place Pal Mal, like an elderly person would. Her face ident, however, scanned as girlish. For an inst, he'd optioned asking her if her parents knew she was accessing their comm hook.

She had a name, not a corporate ident. Geneviève Dieudonné. He'd worked for private citizens before, though he was usually indentured to corps or gunmints. He did not come low-budget. She'd have to meet his price, either in currency or access.

She had specified an old address, between fast outlets, clothes shops and the dream parlours. A prime site neglected in the redevelopment. He was to wait outside for her.

It was a cool day at street level. The cloud-kites were over the East End, which let unfiltered sunlight pour down here, bleaching everything pastel. A few other get-abouts strolled in the chill light, toting parasols. The odd unperson nipped out, though they were supposed to stay behind the scenes, darting across the open to shade, covering their eyes against the burning glare.

He sat on a pink play-bench and turned down his earpiece, lulling the info-flow. If the client had a problem, he needed to clear his mind.

He was distracted anyway, by a barking dog. A couple of gay get-abouts were shamed by their unruly Alsatian. The hom tried to calm the dog, adjusting the collar with the handset; the fem apologized to passers-by, explaining there must be a glitch in the mood-collar.

A micro-event, but it rang a bell.

On the people-mover, there'd been another dog, a miniature yapping in an old woman's grip. Get-abouts had got about, shifting to another a carriage.

Two geek dogs. Not info on which to build a case.

'Jerome Rhodes?'

She wore a thick wraparound eye-shade, a heavy sun-cloak and a wide-brimmed black straw hat with a scarlet silk band. She must have skin cancer in her genetic background, or be extra-cautious, or need the disguise. She was a pretty lady: he intuited he might have seen her before, once, long ago.

He stood and offered his hand, making a fist so the bar-code on the back was smooth. She did not produce a reader to confirm his ident. She also did not offer her hand.

'You conch that without ident exchange, no contract is legally enforceable?'

It was surprising how many of his clients were ignorant of the regs of Information Analysis.

She shrugged, cloak lifted a little by the air-flow.

'I should terminate this meet,' he said.

She took off her eyeshade and looked at him.

'But you won't,' she whispered.

It was as if she saw through his eyeshade, accessing his brain.

'I want you to locate a ghost,' she said.

That wasn't an unusual request. Ghosts were rogue idents, projected into the Info-World, often leashed to their physical persons by a monofilament of ectoplasm. Some spook-makers cultivated a swarm of ghosts. You had to mind it was a baseline form of Multiple Personality Disorder, that ghosts sprang from meat-minds.

Something about the way she had put it didn't quite scan. He was acute to precise meanings, even when words offered multiple readings.

She'd meant 'ghost' the way he took it. But she had a B story minded, another meaning.

'A ghost, as in . . .?'

She smiled at his prompt.

'As in Jacob Marley? As in Henrik Ibsen? Perhaps. But, primarily, the breed of ghost you know about.'

He had a reputation as a ghost-buster. Two years ago, Walt McDisney hired him to bust a cadre of disgruntled ex-employees who assumed the idents of wholly-owned cartoon characters and harassed accessors of Virtual McDisneyland. That was a big case for Rhodes Information, involving Info-World banditry, pop culture terrorism, copyright violation and several different layers of obscenity law. The culprits were under Household Arrest for the rest of their lives, shut out of the Info-World forever.

The barking Alsatian had set off another animal, a snapping terrier. They were noise-making in disharmony, not competition. Jerome heard a third canine whine, joining in from backstage. A lot of unpersons kept dogs on traditional strings.

The client was distracted, too. She slipped her eyeshade back on, but he'd caught the narrowing of her eyes. It was if she had suffered a sudden brainpain.

'What's the ghost's tag?'

'Seven Stars.'

Jerome pulled out his earpiece, shutting off info-flow, suddenly concentrating on only the A story.

'Seven Stars?'

He needed a confirm. She gave it.

'Seven Stars isn't a ghost,' he said. 'Seven Stars is a terroristcorp. Gunmints have gone after them. And vastcorps. What info do you have that puts us in a better start position than the heavy hitters?'

'Seven Stars is one person, physically. Of course, she might be considered a Legion.'

He tagged the reference.

'Mark. Chapter five. Verses eight and nine. "For he said unto him, Come out of the man, thou unclean spirit. And he asked him, What is thy name? And he answered, saying, My name is Legion: for we are many."'

'King James Version, Jerome. Very impressive. I thought Post-Christians used the Jeffrey Archer translation.'

'I'm not a P-C,' Jerome said. 'The Bible is of cultural importance beyond religious significance.'

'How are you on the Old Testament?'

He didn't want to get into a Trivial Pursuit session, so he shrugged modestly.

'Look up Exodus, chapters seven to twelve.'

'The Plagues of Egypt?'

'Very good. To answer your original question, I have the ident of Seven Stars. The meat-name.'

He winced. He had not expected vulgarity from her.

341

'It's Mimsy Mountmain.'
She spelled it for him.

He still didn't quite believe Seven Stars was one person. Most theorists put them down as an Info-Army, covertly funded by a consortium to disrupt the Info-World. The vastcorps all had their private security people out looking for them, not to mention various Global Information Police forces.

Over the last year, Seven Stars had been busy.

At first, the Scramble Bombs seemed random, disruptions of the info-flows. Vastcorps and gunmints set aside their info wars to post rewards for the expulsion of Seven Stars. Derek Leech himself, the visionary of the Information World, the ultimate stay-at-home, stepped out of his Pyramid for the first time in a dozen years to appear on a realwelt platform with the Managing Director of London, the CEO of McDisney-Europa and the Moderator of the Eunion.

Then came serious pranks, calculated to undermine client confidence. Jerome had been amused, with the cynicism about stay-at-homes endemic among get-abouts like him, when 100 million people were convinced by a phreak edition of *On-Line Vogue* that the latest fashion was for rouged and exposed anuses. When a hundredth of the subscribers lipsticked their recta, it counted as a genuine fashion trend and the real *Vogue*, a Leech publication, was obliged by law to report it. The fact that the fashion-followers' registration fees went to an untraceable account in Virtual Switzerland was an extra giggle.

The pranks became murderous, and Seven Stars seemed scarier. A few high-profile ident assassinations were costly embarrassments for heads of state and CEOs, deleted from the Info-World or metamorphosed so their access signatures made all users read them as unpersons. After an ident assassination, you could always get another life, even if it meant going back twenty years and starting all over. When a random percentage of Leech-Drug prescriptions was tainted, a substantial death-toll of meat-lives – realfolk – mounted. Stay-at-homes struck dead in their monads were reclassified by their Households from home-user to waste material.

If the long-foretold Collapse were to come, Seven Stars might look good for the role of Antichrist. Empires were shaking, and a lot of independents were going psycho 'in the tradition of' Seven Stars.

One person. One ident. Mimsy Mountmain.

Jerome had asked the client for back-up confirmations. She just knew. That was scary in itself.

He was as good at reading people as at conning info-mass. People had read-outs and flagged items too. He believed the client. Though there was something about her that didn't scan.

Back at the monad, he jacked his earpiece into the Household and pulled in a few info-blips. He often started with a random trawl, seeing if connections could be made.

The dog story was an epidemic. The first theory was that a sound pitched only to sensitive canine ears was causing all dogs – including the few wolves left in realwelt zoos – low-level irritation. However, no such ultra-sound could be detected by instruments other than dog-brains.

Even through his monad-block's sound-proofing, Jerome heard distinct animal noises. He was grateful that he didn't have a companion or minion dog. There were reports of minion dogs – gene-designed for guard and attack duties – savaging stay-at-home masters. It couldn't be an Info-Prank. Dogs weren't generally jacked into anything but the Actual.

He set searchers on Mimsy Mountmain, cloaking himself for caution. For added coverage, he put a search out on Geneviève Dieudonné. It was always a smart keystroke to learn as much about the client as the quarry. Often, something the client didn't know about themself was the breakthrough clue.

He subscribed to the usual police sites, from which he downloaded the surface material on Seven Stars. He didn't want to chance a full-on search yet. The last thing he wanted was to flag his own name. Seven Stars could have him wiped. Or killed.

Should he make a comm link with Sister Chantal and initiate discussion on the Plagues of Egypt? Since the Fall of the Vatican, she was freelancing out of Prague but would still be up on Biblical scholarship. He skinned his thought package. He had a perfectly good reason to call Chan, but was reluctant so to do. He had an emotional case-file on her, and knew she'd interpret a call as personal rather than professional. Then they'd have to go forward or back. And he wanted to stay where they were.

He left it as it was.

The dog story was a mushrooming news-bomb, eclipsing other developing stories. Most channels offered feeble alternates – something about an astronomical anomaly, a human interest orphan massacre, a new development in endocrinology – but the dog story was global, a stone mystery, affording a full response spectrum from farce to horror. He couldn't afford to get caught up in the mediamass of speculative coverage.

On Cloud 9, the premier Leech newsline, extreme theorists were getting the coverage: a canine groupmind, begging for a cosmic bone; a conceptual breakthrough, representing the sudden attainment of sentience in a competitor species; a literal curse of God, a rebuke for the collapse of most organized churches in the Religious Wars of '20.

Jerome forced himself to tune out on the dog story.

His search results were downloading. The first thing he learned was that Mimsy Mountmain was a real person, born 1973 – which made her fifty-three now. Her mother was listed as Maureen Mountmain (d. 1999), her father was not known. There were sealed police records from the 1990s, which he'd take the trouble to gut later. Nothing much after the turn of the century. Hot links fed off to biographies of several family members, stretching back to the 1800s. They would be a distraction just now, but he made a mental flag to find out why they were supposed to be so interesting.

The real woman of mystery was Geneviève Dieudonné.

A person of that name had been born in France in 1416. She apparently died – there was some doubt about exact circumstances and date – in 1432. At sixteen.

A person of that name had been born in Canada in 1893 and died under her married name of Thompson in 1962. A life's worth of data on her scrolled past swiftly.

A person of that name was mentioned in the acknowledgements of *Some Thoughts on the Bondage of Womanhood*, by Katharine Reed. Published 1902.

And a person of that name was on the payroll of the Free French for several months in 1942. She worked in Los Angeles, presumably for the War Effort, though the nature of her service was not listed.

There was no record of the woman he had met this afternoon.

Geneviève 1893-1962 had left a portfolio of photographs, from childhood through to old age. Geneviève 1902 and Geneviève 1942 – definitely different from the 1893-1962 woman and probably from each other – left no pics.

It seemed likely his client had used an off-the-peg ident to contract with him – she had not offered him her hand for reading, he minded – but must also have gone to some trouble to find a name that would not yield miles of scroll on many different people down through the centuries. Over a thousand people on record were called Jerome Rhodes.

An afterthought downloaded. A search gave you public-record info first, then revisited any sealed files you'd previously accessed. This blip came from his own master contacts file. A Geneviève Dieudonné was listed as a contact of the Sally Rhodes Agency in 1999. Unless on some major rejuvenative surgery kick, this could not be the same woman.

His mother had, as usual, not kept a proper record. From the notation, it was ambiguous as to whether this Geneviève was a client or an informant. She did not seem to have paid anything, which was just like Mum. Too many deadbeats rooked her out of a fee for services rendered.

He would have been five or six. He minded the times. Neil, Mum's boyfriend, was teaching him how to find things out. They had even gone to paper-and-dust libraries to look things up. It was the start of his induction into the Info-World.

Had he seen Miss Dieudonné then? At first sight, the client had seemed to ring a distant alarm. But this couldn't be the same woman.

Was his client trying to tell him something by using a name that would be in his mother's records?

Logically, he could comm-link with his Mum, retired and living in Cornwall. But he didn't like to bother her yet. He could access info on his own, and didn't need to crawl to her when problems got thorny. She had taught him to be self-reliant. Maybe neurotically so. If that was the case, he'd get it seen to eventually.

As things were, he was employed, but not contracted, to find a ghost whose name he knew on behalf of a meat-woman who was anonymous. Nice irony. He appreciated it.

He had several favoured ports into the Info-World. He usually sidestepped the dreamwelt sites that impressed the neos and plugged straight into streams of pure data, not even bothering with a customized simile. Most of the ghosts he had busted revealed too much about their meat-selves in their self-designed wish-fulfilment avatars. They all had an unhealthy preoccupation with self.

It always amazed him that the geek gunslingers were so locked into games-playing they never took in the view. It was like ignoring the stars. To him, the thrill was in the info landscape, the waves and currents and trends and collapses. He could endlessly access, anchored on a loose chain, becoming one with the world, letting it flow around and through him.

But this time, he wanted to seem like a neo.

He customized a ShadowShark and swam into dreamwelt

through a Multi-User Carnival. It was a mixture of market-place and playground, where the hustlers peddled surprise packages, containing either valuable gen or worthless tosh at the purchaser's risk, and the zap-heads conducted endless duels or orgies, getting in and out of the way.

Basically, it was a Dress-Up-and-Play Area.

To operate here, he needed not only to project a poseur's ident but also to intimate that there was a neo tosser at home, jacked into his parents' ports, belly bloated and limbs atrophied as he let the dreamwelt be more his home than the plush monad where he was meat-locked.

He morphed the ShadowShark from fishform to carform, and got out, wearing the distinctive cloak, mask, goggles and boots of Dr Shade, the wholly-owned Leech International superhero. He had been fond of the *Dr Shade* films as a kid, despite (or maybe because of) Mum's unaccountable loathing of them (and all other Leech efforts).

The Dr Shade image was kiddie-cool enough to pass here. He had most of the heroes and heroines and gods and monsters who mingled in the carnival pegged as neo tossers. All womenshapes were Amazons with unfeasible breasts, and faces iconic of cool rebellion wandered by. Outlaws who coughed up registration fees and site subs. The Info-World welcomed phreaks and madpersons, but if you didn't pay your phone bill you were shut out, marooned for ever in realwelt.

He was clever enough even to maintain a flimsy intermediate persona as 'Jonathan Chambers', Dr Shade's secret ident. If probed deeply, he'd pull out, leaving behind traces typical of a neo tosser.

As Dr Shade, he slipped through the carnival.

The dreamwelt darkened. A pack of feral kids on armoured bikes wove in and out of the crowds, blasting each other – and bystanders – to fast-re-forming pixel-clouds.

Fantasy figures exposed their assets in neon-lit windows, offering eighteen varieties of non-copyright sexual access. A lot of neos bankrupted their parents by letting their bar codes be read by the info-whores and compounding the fees to infinity.

As usual, this all seemed silly. But, as usual, it was a place to start.

He passed up all the offers of sex and slid into the darker streets where the snitches lurked. Info was air and water here, but could be bought and sold like anything else.

A news-blurt cut through the scene, shaking the overhanging eaves and the artfully strewn shadows. The dog story had escalated. Gunmints issued instructions for humane disposal of soon-to-be-dangerous companions or minions. Dreamwelt denizens were warned that if they were in a realwelt monad with a dog, they should jack out immediately and disable it. Horrorshow pics flashed: users yanked out of info jaunts by ripped-open throats.

The blurt finished. The alley scene settled.

There was a scuttle of snitches. Extending his shadowcloak, he netted the one he was after. She made a fluttering attempt to break free, then graciously gave in, landing delicately on his palm.

'Hello, Tink,' he said.

The cartoon fairy twinkled a greet.

Because J.M. Barrie had left the royalties on *Peter Pan* to Great Ormond Street Children's Hospital, and an Act of the Old Parliament had extended that income in perpetuity, there was a copyright glitch. After the Mouse Wars, unlicensed McDisney avatars were purged from the Info-World, but the *Peter Pan* crew, with a few tiny alterations (the loss of the WMcD logo), were able to survive.

He had seen the loophole at the time and left it open. So Tinkerbell owed him her dreamlife.

'What can you tell me about Seven Stars?'

The fairy buzzed and glowed like a tiny phosphor grenade and tried to get away.

'That tells me something,' he said, in Dr Shade's scary voice. 'It is foretold that the coming of the Seven Stars will bring about the Collapse,' Tinkerbell shrilled.

It was the Info-World's version of Armageddon. One big plug-pulling, and global shrinkage to a dying white dot. Despite a million fail-safes, superstitions abounded, especially in the wake of the Vatican's Fall. There were always intimations of Collapse.

'Where can I find Seven Stars?'

'You can't,' the fairy shrilled. 'They find you. Then no one else does. Ever.'

Tinkerbelle turned to a blip of light and vanished.

'But I believe in fairies,' he declared.

Even here, removed from the actual, he heard the cacophony of dogs. The constant barking, breaking through all the mutes and muffles and sound-proof shields, scraped his nerves.

'Mum,' he said, 'two names. Geneviève Dieudonné. Mimsy Mountmain.'

She looked distracted.

A lot of dog noise came over the comm-link. His mother lived in a country retirement site, where animals were a special feature.

But the names clicked.

Sally Rhodes stopped moving about the room and stood so the reader could fix her image. He adjusted the projection, so her three-dimensional bust – solid and flesh-tone, though with the tell-tale hologram sparkle – sat on his desk.

She had cut her hair and let it go grey. Her face was unlined, without the benefit of a skin-stretch.

She made a kiss-mouth and he touched his lips to the tridvid image. They both laughed.

Then his mother nodded him to sit back.

'I tried to find Mimsy Mountmain once, for her mother. And for someone else. Her mother was killed before I could get anywhere. I was paid off. Case closed. As far as I know, the blasted girl never did show up.'

'And Geneviève?'

'She was part of it. She was also looking for Mimsy.'

'She still is. At least, someone with her name. Actually, it can't be the same woman.'

'Blonde, looks about sixteen, slightly French accent, stays out of the sun, old-fashioned-girl outfits?'

'Sounds like her.'

'If it is, give her my love. It's unfinished business. I'm sorry I'm out of it.'

'So am I.'

'Nonsense. You need to be on your own.'

'How did you meet Geneviève?'

'She accosted me. In Pall Mall.' Mum pronounced it the old way.

'Snap,' he said.

'I was looking for something called the Diogenes Club. They were out of business, but involved with whatever Mimsy Mountmain was up to. It went back years.'

'The Diogenes Club?'

'That's right. Neil dug up some stuff on them. Nothing useful, as usual.'

Jerome wondered about it. He said goodbye.

'Give yourself my love too,' said Mum.

'I will. And mine to you.'

They 'kissed' again, and cut the link.

There was shooting outside. Not a running battle, as there had been briefly three years ago in the last of the Religious Wars. This time, it was a succession of single shots.

Jerome turned the window on and scanned Upper Street. Men in armour dealt with dogs. They used jolt-guns, one charge to the back of the skull. A clean-up krewe followed, collecting the corpses. A lot of the dogs trailed leashes, and all had collar-controls. Some unpersons harassed the pest officers. The dog story was stepping up, as if the unheard sound had become shriller, more maddening. Other species with near-canine levels of pitch were getting agitated.

Warnings were posted against approaching or sheltering affected animals. A raft of human interest stories offered cautionary tales of children savaged by loved family companions. Clinically blind people mind-linked to seeing-eye dogs reported that their skulls were ringing with sound, and censor blotches on the reports suggested not a few of them had become dangerous and were being treated like the street packs.

Over and over, news-streams emphasized that this was a global phenomenon. Global.

How many dogs were there in the world? Including wolves.

His teeth were on edge. He imagined he could sense the unheard sound. His eyeballs sang silently.

Did everybody feel this?

He didn't feel like comm-linking around his associates, and asking. There were thousands of mushroom sites on the dog story. Mediamass obscured any useful gen. It would take a while to purge the extremists and for a sensible centre position to coalesce. In the meantime, stay-at-homes were staying put, and get-abouts were accepting restrictions. Suggested codes of practice for travel in cities and designated country sites.

An across-bands newsblurt cut in. A major announcement was imminent on the dog story. He knew that meant a thirty-second deep-core ad probe was coming. He tore out his earpiece and hummed the 'Anvil Chorus' with fingers stuck in both ears. He did not need to be infected with psycho-dependency on some new flavour of echt-burger.

Then he tuned in again. Seven Stars was claiming responsibility. The ghost's message concluded with: 'For the dogs, it will end soon.'

A scramble of experts got on-stream and began pouring opinion and speculation on to the maelstrom. He jacked out of all access and tried to think.

When one of his deep-level search engines paid off, Jerome thought somebody must be extracting the urine.

He had an address for Mimsy Mountmain. She was

supposed to be a terminal stay-at-home, a shut-in on life support. She was maintained in the Mall. His client had met him outside the building in which his quarry lived.

The dog story was a constant distraction. It was hard to hack through to info that concerned him. The dog story criss-crossed and trailed over every other pathway. It had been the same during the Religious Wars.

Emergency legislation was being passed, globally. Dog ownership was now illegal. There were painless extermination programmes. Some of the more liberal sub-gunmints were merely interning the animals and working on a 'cure'.

Not having a dog, Jerome didn't care. The dog story just got in the way.

He was increasingly spooked.

He tried to get back in touch with Geneviève, but there was no back-up listing for the Brixton address she had given him as her piedater. The node they had used as a comm-link had been discontinued and the charges for its creation and dissolution all laid to his account.

He had let her see his bar-code. She must have a hidden reader, maybe an Eyeball.

It turned out that his client was the ghost.

He had seen her in the meat. She was real, not a projection of some unknown veg like Tinkerbell.

And now she was gone.

As Dr Shade, he was back in the carnival. The party seemed to be slowing down. The dog story was throwing the Info-World in turmoil. It happened like that. Mammoth realwelt events made users jack out for once, depopulated the dataways. Fine. That made it easier.

Now, he was looking for Geneviève Dieudonné.

1893-1962 wasn't her. 1416-1432, though. There was something in that equation. That Geneviève didn't get to be older than his seemed to be.

What about 1902 and 1942?

He glided through archive sites, shadowcloak passing over icons and portals. Few but academic researchers came here. The neos were only interested in the now, the crashing wave of the present. And vastcorps employed balanced factions of muck-raking exposé merchants and raking-over cover-up krewes.

He moved into the past, down an almost-empty conduit. Similes of buildings lined the way, in regressing architectural styles, each with a foundation stone giving away the year in question. The buildings housed the records.

Geneviève had yielded too few mentions. So he had to trawl wider. He had set up search engines to look for the Diogenes Club. Most of them crashed against security barriers, alerting all kinds of official warnings. He had received desist notices, but no enforcement operatives were coming at him, from inside or outside the Info-World. Regulation boards were too busy with the dog story.

During a crisis, there was a window of opportunity.

He fought against déjà vu, as he stood outside the simile of the building he had seen in realwelt yesterday morning. Then, he had just wondered why it hadn't been gutted for stores. Now, he knew it had significance.

There was even a simile of the bench where he had met his client. An information package lay on it, tied up with a big blue bow.

He looked at the gift. It could easily be a trap. He opened it. Inside was a key-string. He ran the string through the swipe-slot, and the front door of the Diogenes Club opened.

Inside, the quality of the mimesis upgraded. As Dr Shade, he entered a gentlemen's club. He heard a rustle of newspapers, the discreet footsteps of servants. He smelled various types of tobacco smoke and the old leather of the club-room chairs.

An attendant ushered him upstairs.

The Chambers of the Ruling Cabal were derelict. Cobwebs wound over everything, spun between chairs and tables and desks and map-stands. He walked through the web without breaking strands. Everything sparkled slightly.

The darkness was dispelled as someone turned up a gas lamp. It was a well-wrapped mummy, androgynous in form, adept in movement. The mummy's eyes flickered. They were tiny screens. Red figures scrolled down.

There were others. A dog-headed man, in a broad Ancient Egyptian collar. The actor, John Barrymore. A swaddled invalid in a cocoon-like wheelchair, her head supported by a leather brace. And a red entity, a gem-stone which shone with the light of stars.

Seven Stars.

Of course, all these were avatars of one person. One intelligence.

He took off his goggles, and let his simile resemble himself.

'We understand you're out of pocket,' Barrymore said. 'You've been the victim of a prank.'

'I was sent to find someone who seems not to be lost.'

All the faces of Seven Stars smiled at once. Even the jewel.

'We're in a position to compensate you, and to prosecute your interests. To turn your commission round, we'd be willing to pay you well to find out the whereabouts of your former employer, the undead Mademoiselle Dieudonné.'

'Interesting,' he said.

He had a realwelt address. His mother's paper records were still in the firm's vault, and it had taken only an hour or so to find the notes Neil had deposited after the abandonment of the 1999 investigation. There, on headed notepaper, in a fine hand, was a personal thank-you note, signed 'Gené'. Without accessing the Info-World, he had confirmed that the address – a suite at a private hotel in Kensington – was still occupied. It was a throwback to his mother's type of detective work. He didn't allow himself to make comm-links, for they contrailed through the Info-World, flagging themselves. He used printed-out directories and even walked across the city, avoiding dogs and euthanasia krewes, to ask questions of a human desk clerk.

The hotel was off-record. Jerome worked out it had been bought – for cash – around the turn of the century. A phantom access signature implied it to be the property of a deceased lady named Catriona Kaye, run by a permanent trust administered by a firm of lawyers, kept open in accordance with Miss Kaye's will.

Actually, it was a hidey-hole.

Invisible to the Info-World, it was a vampire's coffin.

He couldn't claim credit for brilliant analysis. Geneviève had given him her address – the note, dated 1999, even mentioned him – and all he had done was confirm it.

'For Mam'selle Dieudonné's location, we will pay a sum equivalent to your aggregate earnings over the last five years.'

This came from the mummy.

That flagged it. He was almost but not quite annoyed enough at Geneviève to turn her over.

But the comm-link gave it away.

'I'll think about it,' he told the Seven Stars. 'It'll take time to get and confirm the info you want.'

'Very well. You have one hour.'

Jerome jacked out and cut access.

The realwelt rang with the sounds of dying dogs.

He was shocked. The sudden withdrawal from the dreamwelt was a heart-kicker, advised against by all help programmes. But the realization had been jolt enough.

He had nearly been gulled.

Now, he had to get across realwelt London. There was a severe curfew in force. All people-transport services, above and below ground, were suspended. Groups of dog-lovers had banded together to resist the extermination krewes, augmented by unpersons ready to riot for any cause, and there were outbreaks of fighting in St James's Park and Oxford Street. He would have to get round that.

He could not drive, because he'd have to log a route plan in his auto's master programme, and that would register in the

Info-World. In the basement, he still had the last of the bikes
he had pedalled through childhood. His Dad, dead before he
was born, had been a cycle messenger, and he'd felt that in
pumping along tracks or out on the road he was sending out
an I Am Here notice to the beyond, paying tribute in his own
way to the man he had never known.

In his mind, he mapped a route, zig-zagging round trouble
spots, with a few tricky double-backs to throw off anyone who
might be following.

Before he stepped out on to Upper Street, he took out his
earpiece and left it on the table beside the door. He checked
himself for any other devices with Info-World signatures.

This was like being forced to walk after learning to fly. But
doing without the wings made sense.

He cycled down the street. All the surviving dogs of London
were howling. He recalled an early-century saying, one Neil
had been fond of: Real is real.

She was waiting for him outside the hotel, hair shining with
sun, unafraid of the rays. His heart sank and he searched
himself.

'Real is real,' she said, almost apologizing.

She wasn't wearing the hat, cloak and eyeshade today. That
had almost been a Dr Shade outfit, he realized.

'We had real people following you, not just search
engines.'

'Then you knew, when you asked for the address . . .'

'We just wanted to see if you fit the pattern. We've met a
series of people like you. Almost a family tree. We've learned
to appreciate you. You've fed into us.'

'You're not Geneviève?'

She shook her head.

'No. Of course not. Though I do look like her. She wasn't
my father or my mother, but she left something of herself in my
mother, something that shaped me.'

'You're talking in the singular.'

'About Mimsy, yes. I am Mimsy.'

He had been right. Too late.

'But *we* are Seven Stars.'

'Is there a Geneviève?'

'Yes. She's inside. Upstairs.'

He turned to go into the hotel.

'By the way,' Mimsy said, 'beware of the dogs.'

The howling of all the dogs in London came from inside the hotel. A helmeted body lay jammed half-way out of the revolving door, protective clothing shredded.

Using a side-door, he got into the lobby and found the rest of a euthanasia krewe along with dogs alive and dead. He snatched up a jolt-gun and found it uncharged. Mimsy followed him. Indoors, she still shone. A red light, centred in her chest, radiated through transparent flesh and thin fabric. Star-points glinted, hard chips in the softer light. She was difficult to look at directly.

The dogs ignored her, but came for him.

They were too caught up in their own pain to concentrate on savaging him, but he still took too many nips and bites as he waded up the main stairs.

He threw dogs away.

On the first-floor landing, a giant rottweiler, augmented as a guard minion, snarled at him. Its teeth were steel, probably envenomed. Veins stood out on its bulbous forehead. Its eyes were maddened red jelly.

He tensed, expecting a final attack.

Something burst inside the dog's skull. Grey gruel squeezed out of its eyesockets. It fell like an unstrung puppet.

He could almost hear the killing sound. His regrown front tooth ached. The plates of his skull ground against each other. Pressure built up inside his ears, producing pain in the drums and all the spaces of his head, throbbing under his cheekbones, around his eyes, at the base of his brain.

Dogs pawed towards him and fell. Skulls detonated like

bombs, spraying blood and brain matter across faded floral wallpaper.

He took hold of the banister and hauled himself up to the next landing. Mimsy skipped up beside him, unaffected. She had the mummy's red eyescreens. That avatar had been closest to her.

'This is just the first of them,' she told him. 'The new plagues. This is the curse of dogs.'

The main door of the suite was open. A man lay dead in it. He wore a black single-piece suit and had the sign of the Seven Stars on his forehead. His throat had been torn out by some animal a little daintier than a dog. Neat slices opened his veins.

'One of mine,' Mimsy admitted. 'The old girl still has some bite.'

He tried to equalize the pressure in his head, opening his mouth and forcing a desperate yawn. It helped momentarily.

'Don't worry,' Mimsy said. 'The plague will soon be over.'

She picked up a frothing Pekinese and chucked its chin. The little dog's skull pulsed like a hatching egg. She pointed it away from her, and the dog's eyes shot out on geysers of liquid brain.

'Ugh,' she said, dropping the dead thing.

He stepped over the dead man.

On a curtained four-poster bed was Mimsy's transformed twin. This was the real Geneviève, arced like a bow, clawed fingers and toes hooked into torn bedclothes. She lashed from side to side, whipping long hair. Her bloody mouth was full of swollen fang-teeth. Her eyes were red but not with an LED light.

Veins in her temples were swelling.

'She's not human, poor love,' Mimsy said. 'She can hear things dogs can.'

Jerome wanted to go over to the bed but Geneviève snarled at him to stay away. He minded she didn't trust herself not to strike out at him.

'If she isn't human, what are you?'

358

'Oh, I'm completely human,' Mimsy said.

'You singular. What about you plural.'

'Seven Stars,' she said, pulling down her neckline to show the red light burning under her ribs. It grew in intensity, as the unheard noise grew.

The cries of the dogs were cutting off, one by one.

Small objects on a bedside table rattled. Vibrations throbbed through Jerome, through the hotel, the city, the world.

Mimsy's flesh parted as the jewel rose to the surface. It climbed up into the base of her throat. It seemed to be talking.

'We are come from afar,' it said. 'We are the Plague-Bringer.'

For the last time, Mimsy spoke. 'Just think,' she said, 'within a minute, dogs will be an extinct species. And vampires.'

The howling had all but stopped.

The dogs were all dead. All over the world, dogs' brains burst in their heads.

Jerome ran to the bed and took Geneviève's hand. He was not surprised at the ferocity of her grip. He looked into her red eyes, hoping for an answer.

The thing that walked around in Mimsy Mountmain's body filled the room with red light.

Geneviève's eyes started from their sockets.

He *could* hear the maddening sub-audible whine now.

Cracks in Geneviève's forehead spread away from her temples, leaking thin blood, snaking up into her hair. Her mouth was open in a tooth-ringed circle.

'You're Jerome,' she said, through agony. 'You are all that's left.'

Bloody tears the size of beetles crawled from her eyes, ears and nose.

1416-2025?

She sat up in bed. A final jolt of killing current shot through her. Her head came apart with a crack. Bloody hair whipped him across the face and she was a limp doll.

The whine cut off, leaving a gaping silence.

In that silence, a world was left mad.
He turned, seeing red. Seven Stars walked out of the room.

Episode 7: The Duel of Seven Stars

The shock of death. Is it greater for her, after so long? Despite what the records say, she didn't quite die in her sixteenth year. She just stopped being human.

The young man holds her. She wants his blood.

The noise in her skull cuts off. A red fringe flops over her eyes. The pain ends.

Nothing.

A frozen moment. In a museum. Looking at a man looking at a mummy. His face reflected in the glass of the display case. Hers not. But he senses her, turns. Thinks about her. For a moment.

In another life . . .

Geneviève Sandrine Ysolde Dieudonné. Geneviève the Undying, daughter of the physician Benoit Dieudonné, daughter-in-darkness of Chandagnac, of the bloodline of Melissa d'Acques.

For her, it is over.

She is in darkness, unfeeling. She might be in woman-shape. Or something immobile, a sarsen stone, a tree. She sees nothing, but she senses.

There are others. Not waiting for her, but accepting her, recognizing her.

Five others.

She knows they were once living too. And in that moment of knowing, she accepts her final death. The five are now six. They reach for her, not physically. She knows them, but their names do not come to mind.

360

Neither does her own.

Together, the six shine. At last, she knows perfect love.

Not yet complete, though. The Six must become Seven. Lucky Number Seven.

Then . . .

Red light.

Consciousness resumes, continues. She can think, remember, picture herself, imagine a world beyond. She has a sense of her body. There is still pain, and warmth.

She is not dead. Not any more.

She is alone. Her five companions are gone. Bereft, her heart aches. A tear gathers in her eye.

Blood trickles into her mouth. Young blood, rich, peppery. It flows through her, bringing a jolt of wakefulness. Her teeth sharpen against her tongue. More blood is spilled on to her lips. She licks, red thirst alive, and feels strength growing.

Her night-senses come alive. She is acutely aware of the roughness of the cotton shift she is wearing, and of the scents that cling to it.

Hospital smells sting her.

She cannot sit. Her head is fixed in place by a contraption of steel clamps and plastic tubes. She swivels her eyes, and sees fluid flowing through the tubes, into her.

There is an alien object inside. Where the last pain was, she senses an inorganic plate, patching over the ruin of her burst skull.

She tries to raise a hand to her head. She is restrained, by a durable plastic cuff. She tries harder, and the plastic snaps.

Someone takes her hand.

'Getting your strength back, I see.'

Alarms sound.

'You're in the Pyramid,' the young man tells her. He is not a doctor. His face is familiar. 'In London Docklands, what's left of it. The Derek Leech International Building. Some of the staff call it the Last Redoubt.'

The young man is Jerome, Sally Rhodes's son.

He was there when she died.

Judging by the changes in his face, that must have been years ago.

'How long . . .?'

'Seven months.'

She sits up in bed.

'You've missed a ton,' he says. 'The Plagues. The Wars. The Collapse.'

She holds her head.

Her hair is close-cropped, for the first time in centuries.

'I think it's snazz,' Jerome says. 'You look like Joan of Arc.'

'Good God, I hope not.'

She remembers Jeanne d'Arc. It was during her war that Geneviève received the Dark Kiss, became a vampire. There was blood all around.

She feels the back of her skull, fingertips pressing the skin over the plate.

'I don't understand what Leech's doctors did,' Jerome says. 'I've still not really scanned the info that there are such things as vampires.'

'Sorry,' she shrugs.

'Not your fault. Any rate, you're back from the dead. Leech says it's magic and medicine. You weren't properly alive, so it was easier to bring you back than it'd have been if you were . . . um?'

'A real live girl?'

'Yes, well, exactly. You were put back together months ago, but the hardest part was what Leech calls "summoning you up". Getting you to move back in, as it were. He's had a team of spooks – mediums, mages, nutters – working on it. In the end, I think he did it himself, reached out into the wherever and dragged you back. All this is new ground to me.'

'Me too,' she admits, again fingering her skull, gliding

362

fingertips over her fur.

'Do you want a mirror? The scars on your head are healing. And you have none on your face.'

'A mirror would be no good to me. They don't take.'

Jerome goggles. She catches a little of his amazement, and sees herself through his eyes, alarmingly tiny in a big bed, face small and pretty on an egg of a head.

'I gave blood,' he confesses shyly.

'I know,' she replies, taking his hand.

Things have changed while she was away. The boiling point of water is now 78°. That was the effect popularly known as the Plague of Fire. Around the world, spontaneous combustion is a general hazard, and this past summer has seen the uncontrolled burning of much surviving forested land and not a few townships and cities.

Monsters have come out of the sea, just as in the films of the 1950s, and devastated conurbations. That was the Plague of Dragons, though most called it the Plague of Godzillas. There are other natural catastrophes: insects have predictably run rampant again. Of course, with the interconnectedness of everything, it is hard to distinguish a genuine plague from a side-effect like war, famine, mass psychosis and post-millennial panic.

The Plague of Babel ended electronic communications. The Information World did not shut down, as the Collapse Theorists prophesied, but it now habitually scrambles three out of every four transactions, providing convincing but fabricated images as well as texts and sound effects. Many of the scrambles are garbage, but some are malicious. Economic and military wars have been triggered by caprice.

An Empire is falling. And the Emperor has busied himself not with shoring up the barricades but with engineering her resurrection.

She wonders why Derek Leech cares so much about her.

'You are familiar with the suppressed quatrains of Nostradamus?'

'Of course.'

'In 1942, one of them led you to the Seven Stars.'

'I didn't see it. The gumshoe did.'

'Michel was sadly given to obscurity.'

'I often wondered why he never predicted anything happy. Or world-changing in a trivial sense. Elvis's appearance on the Ed Sullivan Show. The discovery of penicillin.'

Leech does not smile.

He is seeing her in his office at the apex of the Pyramid. Through the tinted screen-windows, the fires ravaging the city are crimson carpet patches. Black gargantuoids, lizard-tails whipping, sumo-wrestle in the burning ruins.

Banks of screens are grey and dead. This is the central node of a global net of information-flow, the heart of an electronic Yggdrasil that has bound together humanity and subjugated them to a man-shaped creature. It is a room full of obsolete junk.

A few – Jerome's mother, for one – had protested that Leech's increasing dominion of the world reduced people to components in a global device, locked into cell-like monads, consuming garbage info, indentured spectators and consumers.

Under Derek Leech, history became soap.

When Edwin Winthrop allowed the Jewel of Seven Stars to be focused against the Axis Powers and their Ancient Masters, he smashed Empires but dipped his hands in blood. The trust handed down to him was subtly betrayed, a chink was opened in the world, and through that chink had squeezed Derek Leech.

Now the Seven Stars rain plague on Leech.

She should be happier.

The plagues come too late, when Leech's Pyramid is at the top of the world. They flow down the black glass sides of this building and spread out to the corners of the map.

This is the end, she thinks.

Leech takes a book from his desk. It is the only book she has seen in the Pyramid. Though access to electronic information is compromised, there is not a general falling-back to print or scribbled memos. Paper, its combustion point lowered from Bradbury's 451, is a hazard.

'During the late War, you were allowed access to only the quatrains relevant to the short term. Edwin Winthrop kept a lot from you, but a lot was kept from him. His ultimate part in all this, for instance. And yours.'

He has her attention.

At a touch, he untints the glass. The fires leap up in vividity. Even the eyes of the battling beasts now burn like unhealthy neons.

In the sky, the moon is blood-red. And Ursa Major is missing.

'This is *wrong*,' Leech said. 'Whatever you think of the world you left, this is not an acceptable alternate.'

She has to agree.

'The old world, things as they were before, can be bought back.'

'Brought back?'

'No, *bought*. Everything is economics. Things can be as they were, according to Nostradamus, with seven lives twice-lost. Seven dead will return to the Earth, and die again. You are the first, and through you the other six will be gathered. There is a death beyond death.'

'I don't fear it.'

Everyone asks her what it was like. She hasn't been able to explain.

'I envy you, Geneviève. You know things I will never access. I must content myself with everything else.'

'So, when it's over, you'll rule in Hell?'

'That, sadly, Nostradamus is silent on.'

'Ain't it just the way?'

'Indeed.'

In the heart of the Pyramid, she is ushered into an orrery, one of Leech's famous magical devices. A globe of interlocking brass and copper and steel partial spheres, gimballed like a giant gyroscope, it is a schematic of the solar system. It is an impressive bit of clockwork, but here is just a focus.

Leech has offered to dress the process up with ritual and chanting. Blood sacrifices, if necessary. But it is down to her to reach out, to travel back to the sphere from which he summoned her, to reach her companions. If they are brought to this world, they will be the Seven, who alone – according to Mad Michel – can check the unleashed plagues of the Seven Stars.

She has not told Leech that there are, by her reckoning, only Six Samurai. After all, de Notre-Dame – whom she now regrets not visiting personally when she was a vigorous 150 and giving his throat a good wringing – is often only ball-park accurate.

One thing in the cards is that she alone will survive the coming Duel of the Seven Stars. She has already died twice – her change from human to vampire counts – and so she alone of the Merry Band has already paid her due and will live on, to see what Leech makes of the world and, unless she misses her guess, to do her best to see it isn't as dire as it might be.

The Seventh of her Circle bothers her. Does his or her absence invalidate the whole quatrain?

Damn all cloudy prophets and smug seers. Cassandra didn't get half the kicking she deserved.

She becomes the Sun, taking her seat in the centre of the orrery.

'I shall try to shine,' she announces.

Leech isn't here, though she knows he is watching over her from somewhere. He is a creature of the eaves, peering out of the darkness, a cosmic couch potato. Technicians of enchantment, plastic young women she thinks of as attendant demons, work the levers. And Jerome, another loose component in this clanking magical machine. If this is for anyone, it is for him. In honour of his mother.

She shuts herself down.
The orrery revolves.

Her five companions expect her. They have been incomplete. She is the pathway. Through her, they channel themselves. She senses more. Scraps of lives lost. Some familiar to her, some strange. As one, they dwindle into reality.

The orrery concludes its cycle.

She pulls herself out of the contraption, brain a-swarm with trace memories. The phenomenon is more acute than the mostly random mind-link she has with those living whose blood she has taken. It's like sharing skull-space with strangers.

'She's alone,' a woman says. 'It's over. We've failed.'

'No,' says Jerome. 'Not yet.'

Jerome helps her stand. He looks into her eyes.

Now, at last, the Circle is complete.

The red thirst comes upon her like a raging wave. Her fang-teeth sprout like bone-knives. The strangers in her skull add to her need.

'Leech said a blood sacrifice would complete the forging of the circle,' Jerome whispers, popping his collar-seam. 'Take mine.'

Her predator's lizard-like brainstem overrides all civilized restraint. In this state, she has no conscience, no personality, no qualms. She has only red thirst. She is a blood junkie, the worst sort of vampire bitch.

Her mouth fastens on Jerome's throat in urgent rape. She bites into his jugular vein, tearing through the skin and meat, and sucks in the great gouts of blood.

She feels his heartbeat under her hand.

His blood pours into her, along with much else. His mind is sucked entirely into hers, jostling with the other strangers. Chunks of stringy meat-stuff cram into her throat. She swallows and expands.

This is Geneviève, the Monster.

She sucks desperately until his heart is still and her body is bloated with blood.

She can not absorb all she has taken. Her mouth is full, her cheeks swollen.

This has happened before, three times in six hundred years. These are her most shameful secrets, the unwilling sacrifices she has taken to ensure her continuance. She tells herself the red thirst is irresistible, like a possessing spirit, but that is a rationalization. At bottom, she is convinced that she can will herself not to kill. She does not do so, through choice. She lets the lizard-stem take over.

Whether Jerome is a willing sacrifice or not, she has sinned again. She has lost something of herself. It is too late to give him the Dark Kiss, to bring him back as a vampire. He is dead, drained meat.

The attendant demons are appalled, and stay back, afraid she will turn on them. The strangers in her skull, blooded, are growing. They speak to her, like the voices that bothered Jeanne d'Arc.

'Soon, soon, soon,' they whisper.

Four men, one woman.

No. Five men, one woman.

They are Seven. As predicted.

She is heavy, full to bursting, belly bloated, throat stretched like a snake's.

The taste of blood is ecstasy on her tongue.

At her feet lie Jerome's clothes. He is gone from them. Without his blood and his ghost, the meat has dissolved completely. His whole substance is in her.

'*Now*,' they cry, with one voice.

She opens her mouth, and a cloud of red matter explodes from her, pouring into the air.

Six shapes resolve in the cloud of bloody ectoplasm. The first is a thin brown man with an open wound in his chest. He wears a classical garment and Ancient Egyptian court head-dress. This, Geneviève knows, is Pai-net'em, who kept the Jewel of Seven Stars to himself for three thousand years.

Then comes a handsome man all in black. His clothes are Elizabethan in cut, but his sharp moustache is 1920s style. He carries a plaster skull in one hand and a duelling sword in the other.

'Time is out of joint,' John Barrymore announces. 'O cursèd spite, that e'er I was born to set it right.'

Next is Edwin.

He comes together as he was long before she knew him, in a muddy officer's uniform, young and haunted, ears ringing from bombardments.

'I died,' he says. 'In the trenches. The rest was just in my mind. No. Geneviève. You were part of it. The world after the War.'

She takes his hand, feels him calm down.

'There were shadows like men,' he says.

Now, a woman joins them. Maureen Mountmain, as full of life as when Geneviève fed off her. She is less bewildered than the others.

'It's the end of it,' she says. 'Mimsy must be stopped.'

A young man Geneviève does not know has appeared. He wears cycling shorts and a baggy T-shirt. Very 1990s. His temples are shaved.

'Who are you?' she asks.

'Despatch, love.'

He opens a shoulder-bag, and looks for a parcel.

The last of the seven is Dr Shade, the comic-strip avenger. He emerges from the last of the red mist, cloak trailing. His face is covered by a surgical mask and goggles.

A fictional character?

'That was a rush,' says Dr Shade. 'Gené, you bit me. You really bit me.'

It is Jerome. He pulls down his mask, and presses his tongue to his teeth.

'But I'm not a vampire,' he says. 'What am I?'

'You look like Dr Shade,' she says.

'That makes sense.'

'I'm glad it does to someone.'

Death has made Jerome jauntier. He isn't the serious Information Analyst she remembers. He has inwardly taken on some of the aspects of the pulp hero whose uniform he wears.

'We're the old world's last hope,' Pai-net'em says, not out loud but in their minds. 'We are to check the plagues, and destroy the jewel.'

The bike messenger, in particular, looks appalled.

Jerome's mind still races, dragging Geneviève – who is still aware of the ties of blood between them – along behind him.

'I know who you are,' Jerome says to the messenger.

'I'm Connor,' the cyclist says.

'You're my Dad,' Jerome says. 'You died.'

'We all died,' Edwin says.

'And we will all die again,' says Pai-net'em. 'Our sacrifice will heal the world. Pharaoh can rule again, justly.'

Pai-net'em had a lot to learn about Derek Leech.

'Why us?' Jerome asks. 'Why us seven?'

'Because we're all responsible for it,' Maureen says. 'We touched it and it touched us. We died so that the Seven Stars might rise, in the body of my daughter. Some of us were destroyed long before our bodies were broken.'

Barrymore nods, understanding.

'And now we're going to die again?' says Connor. 'No, thank you very much. I didn't lay down my life to redeem the world. I was knocked over by a fucking van.'

'Dad,' Jerome says, shocked. He is older than his father got to be.

'You lived on in him,' she says.

'Big deal. He's dead too, right? What a mess. I wasn't going to ride a bike all my life. I was young. I could have made it. I had projects.'

'Excuse me, Connor,' begins Edwin. 'Few of us are here by

choice. We all resisted being part of this circle. We didn't volunteer. Except for the first of us.'

He looks at Pai-net'em, the Pharaoh's minister.

'And the last,' she adds, remembering Jerome baring his throat.

'And who are you all?' Connor asks.

'We're the psychic detectives, Dad,' Jerome says, sounding more like Dr Shade than ever. 'We're the Three Musketeers and the Four Just Men, the Seven Samurai and the Seven Sinners. We are the masked avengers and the spirits of justice, protectors of the innocent and defenders of the defenceless. We are the last hope of humankind. There are mysteries to be solved, wrongs to be righted, monsters to be vanquished. Now, are you with us? To death and glory, for love and life?'

Barrymore looks as if he wished he'd made that speech.

Maureen wants to make love with this masked man, *now*!

Edwin is quietly proud. Jerome Rhodes would have been Diogenes Club material.

'If you put it like that, *son*,' Connor says. 'Include me in.'

The Seven are whole.

Complete.

She feels their strength growing.

They stand together, in a circle. They link hands, and their strengths flow into each other.

'Pardon me for intruding in this inspirational moment,' Leech says, through a loud-speaker, 'but we are on a time-table.'

Leech has made available to them a customized short-hop skimmer. Jerome recognizes the lines, and realizes it is a Rolls-Royce ShadowShark, melded with an assault helicopter and a space shuttle. It is sleek, black and radar-invisible. She imagines Leech must be a little sad at parting with it. It is a wonderful toy.

Jerome, of course, knows how to fly the ShadowShark.

The flight is already keyed into the vehicle's manifest. She

371

could have guessed where it is supposed to end. It is where it all started.

Egypt.

She is the last to board.

Leech is there to see them off. She knows that he wishes he were part of it.

Some would have traded with him if they could. From her, they knew what Notre-Dame foresaw for them. To succeed in this, they would have to die. Again.

'I will see you when this is over,' Leech says.

'If Michel wasn't playing a joke.'

She climbs into the ShadowShark.

Continental Europe is mottled with fires. Rockets streak in from the Urals. Jerome easily bests the missiles. There are flying creatures, nesting among the cloud-shields. The skimmer takes evasive action.

The Seven no longer need to talk.

Geneviève, used to touching the minds of those she feeds on, is knotted emotionally by how much more complex, more vital this is.

For the first time, she is alive and aware. Going on alone afterwards will be a tragedy. She will be haunted for ever by the loss of this companionship, this clarity, this love.

She senses the bindings growing. Between Connor and Jerome is a rope of blood kinship. She is strung between Maureen and Jerome, both of whom have given life to her. Pai-net'em and Barrymore and Winthrop fit into the circle, perfectly. Their similarities are ties. Their differences are complements.

They drink of her memories, the many lives she has sampled. She lets Pai-net'em's ancient history and Barrymore's blazing talent flow into her. She knows their loves: Edwin's lifelong irritated devotion to Catriona, Maureen's hot burst of generous desire with Jeperson, Connor's calculated but real attachment to Sally.

Throughout their times, the Seven have revolved around the Jewel of Seven Stars, closing in on a tiny constellation. Between them, they understand the bauble, a lump of red malice tossed at the Earth, and know its limitations.

As they close on the Nile, they become more aware of the pulsing thing at the end of their flightpath. They are hooked, and being reeled in.

If she could stop time, this was the moment she would pick. Before the holocaust.

By the bubbling waters of the Nile squats a clear ruby pyramid, in which burn the seven stars.

At first, Geneviève thinks the jewel has grown to giant size, dwarfing the sphinx and the old pyramids, but it is a solid projection.

The jewel is inside.

Multitudes gather on the shores of the great river. In the past months, cults have sprung up for the worship of the Seven Stars, or emerged from historic secrecy to declare themselves the Acolytes of the Plagues. Oblations are offered up to the Red Pyramid.

Occasionally, swathes of death are cut through the crowds. That merely encourages more to gather, pressing closer, praying and starving and burning and rotting. Robed priests ritually cast themselves into the boiling river.

Having been dead, twice, and begun to form a sense of what comes after, Geneviève at last knows the Jewel of Seven Stars is not a magical object. It offers only random cessation, cruel and needless.

It cannot create.

Pai-net'em, who lay with the jewel in him, listening through the years to its insectile whisper, thinks it is a machine. Barrymore, who tore genius from himself as he was driven on by the jewel, feels it to be a malign imp. Maureen still believes it the cat's-paw of the Elder Gods for whom her uncles devoted their lives to blaspheming. To Edwin, it is a puzzle to be solved

373

and put away. To Connor, it is unjust death, robbing him of the future. To Jerome, it is all misinformation, all garbage, all lies, all negatives, all deadtech.

And to her?

It is her enemy. And her salvation.

She knows now why the first curse – the Plague of Dogs – was aimed at her. Mimsy must have accessed the suppressed quatrains, probably when she took over the premises and archives of the Diogenes Club. Mimsy Mountmain had enough of a human mind to know that the vampire who had left traces of herself in her veins was the focus of the Circle of Seven, the only force that could break the weirdstone.

She's still my daughter, thinks Maureen.

Geneviève is infected with love for the girl in the Red Pyramid. The girl who looks so like her, as she was before the Dark Kiss, who has also been robbed of a life, of love and a world, by the Jewel of Seven Stars.

Mimsy is going to die, too.

The ShadowShark settles by the Red Pyramid, on a stretch of sand blasted into glass. There are corpses set in the glass, staring up at the red sky.

They get out of the skimmer, and look at the Red Pyramid. The Seven Stars shine, trapped inside.

Geneviève feels assaulted in her mind, as when the whine that maddened dogs was killing her. The steel plate in her skull grows hot.

Pai-net'em wipes the sound from her mind.

She stands, propped up by Maureen. Her mind feels clean, invigorated.

Together, they are strong.

Barrymore and Pai-net'em open a portal in the side of the Pyramid, extending their hands and willing a door to appear. On the lintel, Barrymore creates masks of Tragedy and Comedy, which Pai-net'em equips with sphinx bodies.

Barrymore gives a theatrical bow.

A whip-like tendril shoots out of the portal and lashes the actor. His flesh explodes, bursting his doublet and hose. His skull, still moustached, looks surprised. He collapses. His voice dies in their mind.

It is a sword of pain. The loss is a devastation.

Pai-net'em grasps the tendril with both hands, and yanks hard, wrenching it loose. As he pulls, a grey wrinkling runs up his arms. His face withers to mummy-shape, and he crumbles again, coming apart as dust and dirt.

Coming hard on the first loss, this knocks the Circle back. Only Jerome is strong enough in himself to support the others.

They are all going to die. She knew that. But these first deaths are still deadly blows.

Her heart is stone.

Edwin takes the lead, and steps over the still-twitching tendril. She follows, and the others come after her.

Connor, she knows, wants to turn and flee, to go far from the Pyramid, to make a life here, in this world, to have all the things he missed. Only his tie to Jerome, which he doesn't understand, keeps him on course. To him, it is possible that this is some dying fantasy, as Edwin had thought his whole post-1917 life was, and that it doesn't matter.

A tunnel leads straight to the heart of the Red Pyramid.

Statues look down at them. Faces that mean something. Voices plead and threaten.

To Edwin, it is Catriona above all. Also Declan and Bennett Mountmain, Charles Beauregard and Mycroft Holmes.

To Maureen, it is Mimsy, Richard, Leech.

To Connor, it is the agents and producers who could have opened a life for him. Contracts are offered, cheques processed, projects greenlighted.

To Jerome, it is Mum, Neil, Sister Chantal, Roger Duroc.

To her, it is the Three.

Forgotten lives, taken in red fugues. Dafydd le Gallois, Sergei Bukharin, Annie Marriner.

375

And Jerome. Not Three any more, Four.

Her dead call to her, cajole, promise, abuse, fret.

There are others, a myriad bled and sampled and absorbed. They bother her like gnats. She is torn into by Chandagnac, the minstrel who had turned her and been destroyed when she might have saved him. And all those she had known and let die by not passing on the Dark Kiss, all she had let grow old and die by not succouring them with her blood.

She is a selfish parasite. She should not continue this charade of heroism.

The world is well lost, and her with it.

Jerome saves her, this time. The most recently dead, he has had less time to brood, to adjust, less sense of business left unfinished. Bolstered by those aspects of Dr Shade he had taken into himself, he fought off his temptations first, and is available to help her through.

He doesn't blame her. He is grateful to her.

In this adventure, he has finally come to know his father, to understand his mother, to get out of his monad and become a part of something greater than himself. At last, he has found a realwelt as vital to him as the Info-World.

She climbs along the thread of his love. She leaves her dead behind.

The silencing of the voices comes at a cost. Connor is empty and dry and old. Edwin riddled with bullet-wounds, choking on poison gas, caked with the filth of Flanders. They are not destroyed, but they can go no further.

'Go, for us, as for yourselves,' Edwin says.

Jerome stands between Maureen and her. He takes their hands, and leads them into the centre of the Red Pyramid.

A final door opens.

The Jewel of Seven Stars is wearing Mimsy Mountmain. Geneviève feels, after six hundred years, that she is looking into a broken mirror. Mimsy's hair is still long, and her face is a perfect thing of tiny jewel facets of red fire.

This is where the plagues came from.

'Mimsy,' Maureen appeals.

The Jewel Woman turns, red-screen eyes noting their presence.

Jerome raises Dr Shade's gas-gun and fires at the Jewel Woman. His pellet shatters against the gem-shields over her face.

Once, there was a girl. Her tiny wishes and frustrations, nurtured by the jewel, powered the thing, pouring energy into it like a battery, subtly shaping the forms of the plagues it wreaks. Now, that girl is gone, a footnote. This is an alien. Geneviève isn't sure whether it is a creature or a machine, a God or a demon. If it has thoughts, they are beyond her understanding. If it has feelings, they are unearthly.

Maureen tries to love the jewel, to venerate it, to wake her daughter.

If it had fallen on another world, among other beings, would it have been different? Was it humanity that used this gift to unleash plagues? The first time, when Pharaoh gazed into its depths and wished to extend his rule beyond the known world, it was an accident, but man's character let loose something that was deserved.

Could Mimsy really be responsible? She was shaped and robbed of choice as much as anyone else. Nostradamus saw her fixed course too. The shadowmen that took Edwin were accumulating, in other forms, in this Red Pyramid. Mimsy was already wrapped in darkness.

Maureen touches Mimsy. The Jewel Woman thins.

'It's all right, love,' Maureen says. 'Let it end.'

Mimsy's face, soft and bewildered, is clear. The jewel carapace is gone. Jerome shoots her in the head.

Geneviève feels the pellet passing into her own brain.

Eyes alive with betrayal, Mimsy falls, the Jewel of Seven Stars rolling from her chest. The years, held back by the spell, surge like a tide as Mimsy grows old and dies within seconds. She is a corpse before the discharge from Dr Shade's gas-gun dissipates.

Maureen sobs. Geneviève hugs her, pulled close by their blood-bond. They are both ripped open by the death of the girl who had come from both of them.

The jewel is still active. It had been inside Maureen when Mimsy was conceived, when Geneviève tasted her blood. It is the dead girl's heart. The seven stars throb inside it, like drops of glowing blood.

The Red Pyramid is collapsing around them. Scarlet dust cascades.

Jerome picks up the Jewel of Seven Stars. Its lights reflect in his goggles. Through him, Geneviève feels its tug. It opens up possibilities. It is a source of great power. If they keep it, maybe it can be focused. For good. The world need not be left for Leech.

Jerome might *become* Dr Shade, not just dress as him.

No, says Pai-net'em. He is still part of them, freed if anything by his second death. Not yet. Perhaps never. The stone is at its weakest, emptied of plague, its host torn away, its influence overextended. It can be ended. Now.

Maureen is dead in Geneviève's embrace. She lays the woman down, brushing white hair away from her beautiful face. She has tried to do her best, to escape her family's past, to find something of worth in her inheritance. Of them all, she has loved the most.

There is night all around. The pyramid is thinned to a structure of fading light-lines. The jewel-worshippers wail at a sensed loss.

Jerome makes a fist round the jewel and squeezes. The red glow is wrapped in his black leather gauntlet.

She hears the first crack. Jerome squeezes harder.

'Get out of range, Gené,' he says. 'When this goes, I go with it. I have to die again, mind. You get to live for ever. Tell Mum Connor was one of the good guys . . .'

The others are growing thin in her mind. Loneliness is gathering like a shadow.

Without the Seven Stars, how will humankind fare?

What is left for her?

378

'Go on, Gené. Run.'

'No,' she says. 'It's not fair.'

She takes the jewel from him. She is far stronger than he is. Vampires have the grip of iron.

'You died for me last time,' she says, kissing him. 'Now, it's my turn. Give Sally your own message. And watch out for the world. Try not to let Derek Leech get back too much of what he had. And play outside sometimes.'

She leaves him, faster than he can register, darting with vampire swiftness through the transparent ruins. She runs out into the desert, fleet enough to skim over the soft sands. The Jewel of Seven Stars screams in her mind as she squeezes it. The faults grind against each other, the starfires boil.

It is not too late to give in.

She could *use* the weirdstone.

Other voices give her strength.

There is a loophole in Notre-Dame, as usual. If she dies a third time, the obligation is lifted from Jerome.

She is far from the Nile, far from water, lost in unchanging sandscape. This country has not changed since she was born. Not since the settling of the continents.

She falls to her knees and looks up at the sky. Twinkling in the night, she sees Ursa Major. It is back again. The plagues are over. The world is set to rights.

And is on its own.

Dafydd, Sergei, Annie, Jerome.

She deserves this.

But at last she accepts forgiveness.

She crushes the jewel to red grit. Seven flames burst into fireballs, and she burns with love.

All find their moments.

Pai-net'em is honoured by Old Pharaoh, the great and wise king.

Edwin sees Catriona's smile for the first time.

John Barrymore is assaulted by applause.

Maureen Mountmain cradles Mimsy to her breast, and shares perfect love.

Connor gets the green-light on a life.

She is in the British Museum, snatching a glimpse of the reflection of a man's face, thinking of possibilities.

Jerome is free of them, journeying into the unknowable future. The thread that connects them to him stretches, and then breaks.

The sand drifts over her bones, burying them with a red scatter of jewel fragments. The Seven Stars pass from the skies, and the sun rises on the desert.

CHARLES BEAUREGARD. Beauregard appears in the first three novels in the *Anno Dracula* cycle, *Anno Dracula*, *The Bloody Red Baron: Anno Dracula 1918* and *Dracula Cha Cha Cha* (aka *Judgment of Tears: Anno Dracula 1959*). In the timeline of those novels, as in the stories here, Beauregard is a stalwart adventurer, something between a spy and a detective, who serves the interests of the Diogenes Club (q.v) and the British Empire in the late Victorian era and rises to a high position in British Intelligence during World War One. Like Richard Jeperson, Beauregard is one of the first characters I created. I wrote stories about him, or featuring him, when I was a teenager, and even began a novel – *Beauregard in the Fog* – that would have prefigured some of the game-playing of *Anno Dracula* by pitting him against Fu Manchu, with other Victorian heroes and villains (Alan Moore, please note) in the background.

THE DIOGENES CLUB. Sir Arthur Conan Doyle created the Diogenes Club, and introduced it in 'The Greek Interpreter', the story which also brings on stage Sherlock Holmes's brother, Mycroft. Later, in 'The Bruce-Partington Plans', we learn that not only does brother Mycroft work for the British government but, under certain circumstances, he *is* the British government. The extrapolation that the Diogenes Club, where

Mycroft is to be found, is the ancestor of Ian Fleming's Universal Export as a covert front for British Intelligence is not original to me, since I copped it from Billy Wilder and I.A.L. Diamond's script for *The Private Life of Sherlock Holmes*. My version of the Diogenes Club, central to the stories collected in *Seven Stars*, also appears, albeit on that alternate timeline, in the *Anno Dracula* cycle.

GENEVIEVE DIEUDONNÉ. The Geneviève of this collection is the third alternate I've presented for this French-born vampire. The first – with no accent in her forename – appears in the books I wrote as Jack Yeovil for Games Workshop: *Drachenfels*, *Beasts in Velvet* (a cameo), *Genevieve Undead* and the novella 'Red Reign'. The second, probably primary, Geneviève is the heroine of *Anno Dracula*, a background presence in *The Bloody Red Baron: Anno Dracula 1918* and returns in *Dracula Cha Cha Cha*. She'll probably show up in the next volume, *Johnny Alucard*. The Geneviève of *Seven Stars* has only previously been glimpsed in the novella 'The Big Fish' (cf: The Gumshoe). The three can be told apart because their middle names vary, but they are at heart the same girl.

MORAG DUFF. Scots politician and future Prime Minister Morag Duff appears in my story 'SQPR' (see: *The Original Dr Shade & Other Stories*), and also turns up as a satellite of Derek Leech (q.v.) in my novel *The Quorum*. In my notes on 'SQPR' in the *Dr Shade* collection, I confessed my shortcomings as a prophet since the premise was that John Major lost the election he won the week the story was published. However, I spoke too soon since every policy and attitude I ascribed to Morag Duff seems now to be a plank of Tony Blair's New Labour government.

ROGER DUROC. Religious fanatic, mercenary of the future and general trouble-maker, Duroc is a major villain in the *Dark Future* cycle I wrote as Jack Yeovil for Games

Workshop: *Route 666, Demon Download, Krokodil Tears* and *Comeback Tour*. He was co-created by Eugene Byrne – there was going to be a Eugene solo novel (*The Violent Tendency*) in the sequence, and we would have collaborated on the big finish *United States Calvary* – and we took the name from the little boy in the Longman's Audio-Visual French course we were both taught in the early 1970s.

THE GUMSHOE. My story 'The Big Fish', available in *Shadows Over Innsmouth* (edited by Stephen Jones), *Cthulhu 2000* (edited by Jim Turner) and my collection *Famous Monsters*, is a conflation of the styles and characters of H.P. Lovecraft and Raymond Chandler. The first-person PI narrator of 'The Big Fish' isn't quite Chandler's Philip Marlowe, since his mean streets have even darker corners, but he tries hard; 'The Trouble With Barrymore' is a direct sequel to 'The Big Fish'.

ROB HACKWILL. Rob Hackwill, the monster hero of the *Where the Bodies Are Buried* films, débuts in my story 'Where the Bodies Are Buried' (see: *Famous Monsters*, or the collection *Where the Bodies Are Buried*) to haunt Robert Hackwill, the small-town politician whose bullying inspired writer Allan Keyes to name the character after him, and reappeared in 'Where the Bodies Are Buried II: Sequel Hook' (in the same places) to haunt Keyes himself. The two stories here complete the cycle. Hackwill, the bully-turned-councillor, appears also in my novel *Life's Lottery*, while the monster (and Keyes) rate a few mentions in *The Quorum* and the novella 'Out of the Night, When the Full Moon is Bright' (in *The Mammoth Book of Werewolves*, or *Famous Monsters*). The real Robert Hackwill, whose name I stole, is an announcer for Euronews, one of those cable channels.

RICHARD JEPERSON. My first efforts at fiction, which date back to the early 1970s when I was learning to type, featured this character (I even completed a Jeperson novel when I was 16, a vampire story). It was appropriate to resurrect him when I decided to do a series set in that period and paying homage to the likes of *The Avengers* and the Jon Pertwee vintage *Dr Who* and the 120-page paperbacks I used to buy (Peter Saxon's The Guardians series, Frank G. Lauria's Dr Orient books). I also brought back his sidekicks Vanessa and Fred. I see Richard as a cross between Dr Strange and Jason King, and hope he'll be back.

CHANTAL JUILLERAT. Like Roger Duroc, Chantal – ninja nun, computer exorcist – was created for the Dark Future series; she is the heroine of *Demon Download*, and I have a terrific picture of her by Martin McKenna (the face of Audrey Hepburn, the body of Diana Rigg) framed above my desk. The Chantal of 'Where the Bodies Are Buried 2020' lives in a different timeline and decade, and isn't used up yet.

CATRIONA KAYE. Like Edwin Winthrop, Catriona was created for my play *My One Little Murder Can't Do Any Harm* (1981). She pops up all over my work, in the novels *Jago, An English Ghost Story* and *The Bloody Red Baron: Anno Dracula 1918* and the story 'The Pierce-Arrow Stalled, and . . .' (*Famous Monsters*).

ALLAN KEYES. Brit-born, Los Angeles-based horror writer-director Keyes (think Clive, think Wes, think John) is the creator of Rob Hackwill, the monster. Besides the 'Where the Bodies Are Buried' stories, he shows up briefly in *The Quorum*.

DEREK LEECH. My collection *The Original Dr Shade & Other Stories* features three stories revolving about possibly demonic, certainly malign, yet refreshingly honest multi-media tycoon Derek Leech: 'The Original Dr Shade', 'SQPR' and 'Organ Donors'. The last is a curtain-raiser for *The Quorum*, and establishes the adversarial relationship between Leech and single mother/private detective Sally Rhodes. Leech is often a background presence in my stories (cf: the 'Where the Bodies Are Buried' series, 'Out of the Night, When the Full Moon is Bright'). At his most diabolical, he is the narrator of *Life's Lottery*.

KATE REED. Katharine Reed was originally going to be a character in *Dracula*, but Bram Stoker never managed to include her. To make up for that, she has increasingly become central to my *Anno Dracula* cycle, showing up in all the novels and the novella 'Coppola's Dracula' (first part of the forthcoming *Johnny Alucard*). Since Mina Harker in *Dracula* has one friend (Lucy) who is beautiful and flighty, it struck me that her other friend should be gawky and sensible, which is how we arrive at Kate. I also gave her some of Stoker's own Dublin Protestant background.

JEROME RHODES. The son of Sally Rhodes (q.v.), Jerome is conceived in 'Organ Donors', a toddler in *The Quorum* and a grown-up investigator in 'Where the Bodies Are Buried 2020'. I named him after my nephew, who is about the same age.

SALLY RHODES. Private eye Sally Rhodes appears in a clutch of stories collected in *The Original Dr Shade & Other Stories*: 'Mother Hen', 'The Man Who Collected Barker', 'Twitch Technicolor', 'Gargantuabots vs the Nice Mice' and 'Organ Donors', but gets her largest canvas in *The Quorum*, which explains how she picks up the boyfriend she has in 'Mimsy' and further explores her relationship with Derek Leech (q.v.). She also turns up in *Life's Lottery*, to set a good example.

IAIN SCOBIE. Besides his appearance here, he gets a mention in *Life's Lottery* for the benefit of those who are paying attention.

DR SHADE. A scientific vigilante from British pulp magazines, who makes a sinister venture into the real world, Dr Shade was created for 'The Original Dr Shade', which was first published in *Interzone* and has been often reprinted. As an aspect of Derek Leech, he also lurks about in *The Quorum*. A movie script, *The Original Dr Shade*, co-developed with Adam Simon, is sitting on a shelf somewhere.

EDWIN WINTHROP. WWI veteran-cum-manipulative-psychic investigator Edwin Winthrop first appeared, with his girlfriend Catriona Kaye (*q.v.*), in the play *My One Little Murder Can't Do Any Harm* (1981), in which he was played by me and exposed a villain by feigning his own death during a séance. He is a leading character in *The Bloody Red Baron: Anno Dracula 1918*, and shows up also in *Jago*, *Demon Download* and 'The Big Fish'.

ELIZABETH YATMAN. She was in the crowd in *Jago*, and her sister Mary is a major character in *Life's Lottery*. I've never quite figured out just what made Elizabeth such an extreme character, but she strikes me as the most appalling of the many monsters I've made.